BloodWalk

by

Lee Killough

BLOODWALK

A MM Publishing Book
Published by Meisha Merlin Publishing, Inc.
PO Box 7
Decatur, GA 30031

Editing & interior layout by Stephen Pagel
Proofreading by Laura Perkinson
Cover art by Kevin Murphy
Cover design by Larry S. Friedman

http://www.angelfire.com/biz/MeishaMerlin

ISBN: 0-9658345-0-6

First MM Publishing edition: June 1997

Printed in the United States of America
0 9 8 7 6 5 4 3 2 1

Table of Contents

Dedicated to the memory of Pat Killough, my toughest critic but also my leading cheerleader, and a man with a keen editorial ear that I miss very much.

Lee Killough

Foreword

When Stephen Pagel approached me about MM Publishing reprinting some of my books, I accepted with delight. Not only have I known Stephe since his fandom days in Wichita and want to support his publishing enterprise, but I could not refuse the chance to see the Garreth Mikaelian books back in print. *Blood Hunt* faced a hard road to publication in the first place, returned to me twenty-three times, usually with a rejection that read, "This is a delightful book. We passed it around the office and everyone loved it. But…it is a vampire novel that isn't a horror story. That makes marketing it an impossible problem. So with regret we return the manuscript to you."

Tor books solved that problem by marketing it as horror anyway. Readers have had no problem with the fact that the books are not horror and Mikaelian is—or was back then—a different kind of vampire. Readers love him, in fact. Their only problem has been finding copies of *Blood Hunt* and its sequel, *Bloodlinks*. Paperback books are truely ephemera these days, hardly on the shelf before they vanish to make way for even newer books. At conventions fans approach me wanting to know where they can buy copies of the books. At home I receive letters asking me if I have copies to sell. Unfortunately I do not. Until now I could only suggest haunting used book stores in the hope that a copy might turn up there. I will never forget the phone call that woke me at midnight one night. A fan called from California to tell me, triumphantly, that after combing every bookstore and used bookstore in Berkeley he had finally found a copy of *Blood Hunt*.

So nothing makes me happier than making the two Mikaelian books available again. For all you readers, then, who tried and failed to find copies the first time around, here he is; come and get him. Enjoy.

Lee Killough

BLOOD HUNT

The Body
in the Bay

1

Where do they begin, the roads that lead a man to hell?

. . . With a ritual . . .

Lien Takananda sits at the kitchen table wearing her bathrobe, her short helmet of gray-touched black hair still rumpled from sleep. She holds three Chinese coins in her hand and concentrates, only subconsciously aware of her husband, Harry, in the bathroom, singing a lascivious parody of a saccharine popular song as he shaves. Almond eyes on the copy of *I Ching* before her, she asks the same question of the sage that she has asked every morning for over fifteen years, since Harry joined the San Francisco police: "Will my husband be safe today?" And she throws the coins.

The hexagram produced by the six throws is number 10, *Treading. Treading upon the tail of the tiger* the text reads. *It does not bite the man. Success.*

She sighs in relief, then smiles, listening to Harry sing. After a minute, she gathers the coins again, and as she has done for most of the past year, asks on behalf of Harry's partner, "Will Garreth Mikaelian be safe today?"

This time the coins produce hexagram number 36, *Darkening of the Light*, with two moving lines. She bites her lip. The text of both the hexagram and the individual lines is cautionary. However, the moving lines produce a second hexagram, 46, *Pushing Upward*, which reads: *Pushing upward has supreme success. One must see the great man. Fear not.*

She reads the interpretation of the text just to be certain of its meaning. Reassured, Lien Takananda rewraps the coins and book in black silk and returns them to their shelf, then begins preparing Harry's breakfast.

. . . with nagging grief . . .

Garreth Mikaelian still feels the void in his life and in the apartment around him. Through the open bathroom door he can see the most visible evidence: the bed, empty, slightly depressed on one side but otherwise neat. Marti's sprawling, twisting sleep used to turn their nights into a wrestle for blankets that left the bed in a tangled knot every morning.

He looks away quickly and concentrates on his reflection in the mirror. A square face with sandy hair and smoky gray eyes looks back at him. Burly, he fills the mirror... a bit more so than he would like, admittedly, but the width does give the illusion of a big man, larger than his actual five foot eight.

And makes you look like a cop even stark naked, my man, he silently tells the reflection.

He leans closer to the mirror, frowning as he works the humming razor across his upper lip. He looks older than he would like, too. Barely twenty-eight and already he can see lines etching down his forehead between his eyes and around the corners of his mouth... lines not visible six months ago.

Don't I ever stop missing her? He had not cared this way when Judith walked out. There had been more relief than anything, in fact, though he had missed his son. But, then, Marti was different from Judith. He could talk to her. After what she saw as a nurse in the trauma unit at San Francisco General every day, he had not been afraid of shocking or frightening her by talking about what happened to him at work, or of the examples he witnessed of man's unrelenting and fiendishly imaginative inhumanity to man. He could even cry in front of her and still feel like a man. They were two halves of the same soul.

His fingers tighten around the razor, dragging it under his chin. His vision blurs. *Fate is a bitch!* Why else give him such a woman and then put her in an intersection when an impatient driver tried to beat the light...

When does the pain stop? When does the emptiness fill?

At least he has the department. He can bridge the void with his work.

. . . With a corpse . . .

The body floats facedown in the bay, held on the surface by air trapped under its shirt and red suit coat. Carried on the tide, supported by its chance water wings, it drifts into the watery span between Fisherman's Wharf and the forbidding silhouette of Alcatraz Island. Bobbing, it awaits discovery.

2

"Lien says you need to be careful today, Mik-san." From where he stood pouring himself a cup of coffee, Harry Takananda's voice carried to Garreth above the homicide squad room's background noise of murmuring voices, ringing telephones, and tapping typewriters.

Squatted on his heels pawing through the bottom drawer of a filing cabinet, Garreth nodded. "Right," he said around the pencil in his mouth.

Harry added two lumps of sugar to the coffee. "But she says there is good-fortune in acting according to duty."

"Devoted to duty, that's me, Harry-san." Now, where the hell was that damned file?

Harry stared into the coffee, then added two more lumps of sugar before carrying the cup back to his desk. He sat down at the typewriter. The chair grunted in protest, bearing witness to how many times Harry had added those extra lumps over the years.

Rob Cohen, whose desk sat just around a pillar from Harry's, asked, "Do you really believe in that stuff?"

"My wife does." Harry sipped his coffee, then hunched over the typewriter. "I went through the book once and found that of the sixty-four hexagrams, only half a dozen are outright downers. The odds are she'll throw a positive hexagram most mornings, so, Inspector-san"—he steepled his fingers and bowed toward Cohen, voice rising into a sing-song—"if it give honorable wife peace of mind, this superior man should not object, you agree?"

Cohen pursed his lips thoughtfully. "Maybe I should introduce *my* wife to *I Ching*, too."

At the filing cabinet, Garreth grinned.

The door of the lieutenant's office opened. Lucas Serruto stepped out waving a memo-pad sheet. His dark, dapper good looks always made Garreth think of an actor cast to play the detective lieutenant in a movie where the cop was the hero. Garreth envied the way Serruto could make anything he wore appear expensive and custom-tailored. "Any volunteers to go look at a floater?"

Around the squad room, heads bent industriously over papers and typewriters.

Serruto surveyed the room for a minute, then shrugged. "Eenie, meenie, minie—Sergeant Takananda, the Cicione killing is in the hands of the D.A., isn't it? That leaves you with just the Mission Street liquor store shooting."

Harry looked up. "Yes, but that's so—"

"Good. You and Mikaelian take the floater." He handed Harry the memo sheet. "The Coast Guard is waiting for you bayside."

With a sigh, Harry gulped his coffee. Garreth shoved the file drawer closed and stood up. They left, pulling on coats.

Driving out of the parking lot, Harry headed toward the Embarcadero. The city flowed past the car, muted by fog, swathed in it. The radio crackled and murmured, dispatching officers across the city. Foghorns hooted.

"Let's try to get out before midnight tonight, shall we?" Harry suggested. "Lien wants to feed us supper before it mummifies keeping warm."

"*Us*? You're asking me over again?" Garreth shook his head. "Harry, I can't keep eating your groceries. If nothing else, Lien's cooking is changing my name to Girth Mikaelian." He ruefully ran a thumb inside his snug belt.

"She'll have my hide if I *don't* bring you. Lacking a houseful of kids"—Harry's smile did not hide an old regret in his voice—"she has only you and her art class kids to mother. Don't fight it."

There had been several weeks after Marti's death when Lien's mothering was all that saved him from becoming a basket case. Garreth owed her a great deal. "I'll come."

The car swung onto the Embarcadero. Harry hugged the wheel, as though leaning forward would help him see through the fog better. "Sometimes I wonder what it would be like living somewhere that has a real summer, and maybe even sunshine in August."

"Come along the next time I go to Davis to visit my kid and find out."

They turned in at the pier number on the memo sheet and drove down to a barrier of vehicles. There they climbed out. Fog enveloped them, cold and damp. Garreth shoved his hands in his trench coat pockets and huddled deeper into the collar as he and Harry walked the rest of the way.

Out near the end of the pier the usual post-violent-death circus had set up: uniformed officers, Crime Lab, Photo Lab, an ambulance crew from the medical examiner's office along with an assistant M.E., and this time, Coast Guard, too.

"Hi, Jim," Harry said to one of the Coast Guard officers.

Jim Birkinshaw smiled. "Hell of a way to start a morning, Harry."

Garreth moved as close to the body as possible without interfering with the photographer. The victim had been stretched out on his back, but he still looked less than funeral-parlor neat. His rumpled coat had twisted up around his neck, and a spreading stain of salt water surrounded him.

Strange how you could always tell the dead ones, Garreth reflected. They looked different from living people, even different from someone unconscious. They lay awkwardly, slack, collapsed into postures no vital body would assume.

He pulled out his notebook and began taking down a description of the corpse. White male, brown hair of medium length, 160 to 180 pounds. Five ten? Garreth found estimation difficult in a horizontal position. Red suit coat with black velvet collar and lapels, black trousers, black boots with inseam zippers. Evening wear. Garreth moved around the outside of the group at work to look at the face for an age determination.

Birkinshaw said, "I don't think he'd been in the water long. The pilot of the Alcatraz excursion boat spotted the coat on his first run out this morning."

"A wonderful treat for the tourists," Harry said, sighing.

Garreth jotted down the discovery details, then wrote a dollar sign. Even wet, the clothes retained a quiet elegance. That kind of understatement came with a high price tag. The carefully manicured nails on the outflung gray hands matched the clothing.

The photographer stepped back and was replaced by the assistant M.E., a wiry Oriental woman. In the course of examining the dead man, she pulled loose the twisted coat. Garreth caught his breath, a gasp echoed by others around him. The action rolled the dead man's head into an unnatural position and exposed a gaping wound in the throat, a slash stretching from ear to ear and so deep that spine showed.

Deadpan, Birkinshaw said, "Almost took his head clear off. Looks like his neck's broken, too."

Garreth grimaced. Birkinshaw had known ... had been waiting gleefully for the moment when the rest of them discovered it. Garreth knelt down beside the corpse and studied the face with its half-open eyes. *Age, midthirties,* he wrote. *Eyes, blue.* The face showed care, too ... closely shaven, sideburns and mustache trimmed.

He stopped writing, staring at the dead man's neck ... not at the puckered gray edges of the wound, but at a mark below it to one side of the Adam's apple, almost black on the pale skin and about the size of a half dollar. A feeling of déjà vu touched him.

The mark caught the attention of others, too. Birkinshaw nudged Harry. "Maybe he was on his way home from a heavy date when he was attacked. That's the biggest hickey I've ever seen."

Garreth did not think it could be a hickey. He had made a few as an adolescent and they never looked like this. It reminded him more of the marks he had seen on people's arms from hemorrhage into the soft tissues from a poor lab tech's venous stick. "What can you tell us?" he asked the assistant M.E.

She stood up. "I'd say he died between six and nine hours ago. Cause of death seems obvious. It probably happened without warning. The wound is a single continuous incision with no accompanying nicks to indicate that the killer started to cut and was knocked away. No defense wounds on the hands or arms. From the depth of the wound, someone of considerable strength inflicted it. Do you want us to call you when we're ready to start the autopsy?"

"Please," Harry said. "All right, Mik-san, let's see what he can tell us about himself."

Kneeling beside the body, Harry and Garreth searched it. The hands were bare, but pale skin on the left third finger and right wrist indicated the removal of a ring and watch. Probably married, Garreth thought. Left-handed.

In the coat they found a handkerchief, not monogrammed, and a half-empty pack of sodden cigarettes along with a disposable butane lighter. Nothing helpful, like matchbooks that might tell them where he had been.

The items went into a property envelope.

No billfold in the trousers. Nothing in the left front pocket, either.

"Looks like robbery," Birkinshaw said. "Dressed like he is, he'd be a good target. Junkies, maybe?"

"Why break his neck on top of cutting his throat?" Garreth dug into the last trouser pocket. His fingers touched something. "Cross your fingers and hope we're lucky, Harry."

He turned the pocket inside out to remove the object without touching it, on the off chance that the killer might have touched it, too, and left a fingerprint. A key with a plastic tag attached fell into the clear plastic envelope a Crime Lab man held out.

Harry took the envelope. "Jack Tar Hotel. Overlooked by our killer, do you think?"

"Maybe he was interrupted before he could finish searching the pockets," Garreth said.

Harry murmured noncommittally then looked up at the Coast Guard officer. "Jim, will you check the bay charts and see if you can give us an idea where our boy here went into the water?"

"Right. We'll call you on it."

The ambulance attendants zipped the dead man into a plastic bag and loaded him on a stretcher. Thinking about the bruise, Garreth watched them lift the stretcher into the ambulance. Where had he seen a mark like that before?

He asked Harry about it on the way back to the car.

Harry frowned. "I don't remember a case of ours like that."

"It wasn't our case, I'm sure." But he had still seen that mark, and heard someone else making a snide remark about a super-hickey. He wished he could remember more.

3

The signboard in the lobby of the hotel read: "Welcome, American Home Builders Association."

Harry showed his badge to the desk clerk and held up the envelope with the key. "Who has this room?"

The clerk looked up the registration card and handed it to Harry. "Mr. Gerald Mossman."

Copying down the information on the card, Garreth saw a Denver address and a company name: Kitco, Inc. "Is Mossman a member of the convention here?"

The desk clerk said, "Yes. That's the convention rate for the room."

"Do you know where we can find Mr. Mossman?"

"The convention people might. Their registration table and function rooms are up the stairs there."

They climbed the stairs and showed their badges again, this time to the people at the registration table. "I'm Sergeant Takananda. This is Inspector Mikaelian. Do you have a Gerald Mossman registered with the convention?"

"He's an exhibitor," came the reply. "The exhibition hall is down where you see the open doors."

At the doorway, however, a young man stepped in front of them, barring their way. "No admittance without a badge."

With a quick, wicked grin at each other, Garreth and Harry produced their badge cases and dangled them before the young man.

He looked down his nose at them. "Those are the wrong—" He broke off, coloring, and stammered, "Excuse me ... I meant—I'm supposed—may I help you? Do you have business here?"

"Yes," Harry said. "Where is the Kitco display?"

"There's a floor diagram just inside." He hastily stepped aside for them.

The diagram located Kitco at the far end of the hall. There they found a woman and two men, smartly dressed and flawlessly groomed, working before a photographic montage of kitchen cabinets. Leaflets and catalogs lay on tables at the front of the booth.

The woman turned a brilliant, professional smile on them. "Good morning. I'm Susan Pegans. Kitco manufactures cabinets in a wide variety of styles and woods to fit any decor. May I show you our brochure?"

Harry said, "I'm looking for Gerald Mossman. He's with this exhibit, isn't he?"

"Mr. Mossman is our sales manager, but he's not here at the moment."

"Can you tell me where he is?"

"I'm afraid not. Is there anything I can do for you?"

Garreth opened his notebook. "Does he fit this description?" He read off that of the dead man.

Her smile faltered. "Yes. Steve ..."

The taller of the two men left the people he was talking to and came over. "I'm Steven Verneau. Is there a problem?"

Harry showed his identification. "When did you last see Gerald Mossman?"

The blusher on the woman's face became garish paint over a bloodless face. "What's happened to him?"

Harry eyed her. "Could we talk somewhere away from this crowd, Mr. Verneau?"

"Sure."

"Steve," the woman began.

Verneau patted her arm. "I'm sure it's nothing. This way, Sergeant."

He led them to a lounge area off the exhibition hall and moved into a corner away from the few people there. "Now, what's this about?"

There never seemed to be any easy way of saying it. Harry made it quick. "We've found a man in the bay with Mossman's hotel key in his pocket."

Verneau stared, shocked. "In the bay? He fell in and drowned?"

Garreth said carefully, "We think he was dead before he went in. He appears to have been robbed."

"Someone killed him?" Other people in the lounge looked around. Verneau lowered his voice. "Are you sure it's Gary?"

Garreth gave him the description.

Verneau paled. "Oh, no!"

"We need to have someone come down to the morgue and identify him," Harry said. "Can you do it?"

Verneau went whiter yet, but nodded. "Just let me give Alex and Susan some excuse for being gone."

4

Garreth had never liked the morgue, not so much because death filled it as because it felt inhospitable to life. From the first required visits during training at the Police Academy, he had seen it as a place of harsh light and hard surfaces, where sound echoed coldly and people reflected distortedly in the glazed brick, stainless steel, and tiled floors. It reeked of death, an odor that pervaded everything, hitting him as he came in the door and lingering tenaciously in his nostrils for hours after he left. This year he had come to despise the place, particularly the storage room with its banks of refrigerated steel cabinets. No matter that he intellectually recognized the necessity of the morgue, and that the dead here served the living ... every time he heard the click of the cabinet latch opening, the rolling bearings as the drawer slid out, he relived the nightmare when the face under the sheet was Marti's and half his soul had been torn away.

He stood with face set, ready to catch Verneau if need be, but although the salesman went deathly gray, he remained on his feet. "Oh, my God!"

The attendant lowered the sheet and they left the locker area.

"When was the last time you saw him?" Harry asked.

Verneau swallowed. "Last night. The exhibition hall closes at seven and we walked out together."

"Do you know what his plans for the evening were?"

"Eating out with conventioneers, I suppose. He did Monday night, and that was his usual practice … to make personal contacts, you know."

"Did he happen to mention any names, or where he was going?"

"I don't think so."

"A watch and ring were taken from him. Can you describe them?"

Verneau shook his head. "Maybe his wife can. She's in Denver." He ran his hands through his hair. "Oh, God; I can't believe it. This was his first trip to San Francisco."

As though that should be some charm against harm. Garreth said, "He had a large bruise on his neck. Do you remember seeing it last night?"

"Bruise?" Verneau blinked distractedly. "I—no, I don't remember. Who would do something like that? Why?"

Harry caught Garreth's eye. "Why don't I take Mr. Verneau back to the hotel and start talking to people there? You get on the horn to Denver P.D. and have them contact the wife. See if she knows his enemies. Tell them we need a description of his jewelry ASAP to put out to the pawnshops. Come on back to the hotel when you can."

5

Garreth hung up the phone. Denver was sending someone to break the news to Mossman's wife. They promised to get back about the jewelry. A message from the Coast Guard lay on Harry's desk. According to their charts, the body had most likely gone in somewhere along the southern end of the Embarcadero and the China Basin, although probably not as far south as Potrero's Point. Garreth noted the information in his notebook while he munched on pink wintergreen candy from the sack in his desk. They would need to start talking to people in that area, too. Perhaps someone had seen something.

Serruto came out of his office to sit on a corner of Garreth's desk. "What's the story on the floater?"

Garreth told him what they had so far.

Serruto frowned. "Robbery? Odd that the thief wouldn't take the hotel key, too, so he could rifle the room."

"Unless it's only supposed to look like a robbery."

The lieutenant tugged at an ear. "You have other thoughts?"

Garreth ate another piece of candy. "There's a bruise on his neck." He held a circle of his thumb and first finger against his own neck to indicate the size and location. "I remember another case with the same kind of mark, also with a broken neck. It's been within the last couple of years."

Serruto pursed his lips for a minute, then shook his head. "I'm afraid I don't remember anything like that. Keep thinking. Maybe you'll remember more." He went back into his office.

Garreth looked around the room. Evelyn Kolb and Art Schneider worked at their desks. He asked them if they remembered the case.

Kolb pumped the top of the thermos she brought to work every day, filling her cup with steaming tea. "Not me. Art?"

He shook his head. "Doesn't ring any bells."

Nor did it for anyone else in the squad room. Garreth sighed. *Damn.* If only he could remember something more. If only he could remember who worked the case.

Loud footsteps brought his attention around to the door. Earl Faye and Dean Centrello stormed in. He raised his brows. "You two didn't wreck another car, did you?"

Faye flung himself into his chair. Centrello snarled, "You know the Isenmeier thing? Turkey tried to cut up his girlfriend? Well, we have everything set to arrest the dude, statements from the neighbors and a warrant in the works. Then the lady says it's off. She refuses to press charges. Seems he asked her to many her."

"Save the warrant," Schneider said. "You can use it next time."

"Lord, I'd hate to see this fox chopped up," Faye said. He rolled his eyes. "Everything she wears is either transparent or painted on. The first time we went to see her—"

Kolb cocked a brow at Garreth. "Comes a pause in the day's occupation that is known as the fairy-tale hour."

Faye frowned but continued talking. Garreth listened with amusement. Faye was walking proof that the art of storytelling had survived the age of electronic entertainment. If short on anecdotes, he waxed eloquent on women or sports, or described crime scenes in graphic detail.

That thought nudged something in Garreth's head. He suspended all other thought, hunting for the source of the nudge. But the telephone shattered his concentration. The feeling of being close to something faded.

With a sigh, Garreth reached for the receiver. "Homicide, Mikaelian."

"This is the coroner's office, Inspector. We're starting the autopsy on your floater."

Garreth gathered a handful of wintergreen candy to eat on the way over to the wing where the coroner's office was located. He knew he would not feel like eating later.

6

Not every room in the morgue echoed, Garreth reflected. The autopsy room with its row of troughlike steel tables did not. It always sounded horribly quiet ... no footsteps or casual chatter, only the droning voices of the pathologists dictating their findings into the microphones dangling from the ceiling and the whisper of running water washing down the tables, carrying away the blood.

The Oriental doctor had already opened the abdominal cavity and removed the viscera when Garreth came in and stood at the head of the table, hands buried in his suit coat pockets. She nodded a greeting at him, never breaking her monologue.

The water ran clear this time, Garreth noticed. Even that in the sink at the foot of the table, usually rosy from the organs floating in it awaiting sectioning, sat colorless. The doctor examined the organs one at a time, slicing them like loaves of bread with quick, sure strokes of her knife and peering at each section ... and tossing some slices into specimen containers. She opened the trachea its full length and snipped apart the heart to check each of its chambers and valves. As Garreth watched, a crease appeared between her eyes. She moved back to the empty gray shell that had been a man and went over the skin surface carefully, even rolling the body on its side to peer at the back. She explored the edges of the neck wound.

The neck had another mark, too, Garreth noticed, one that had been hidden before by the dead man's shirt. A thin red line ran around, biting deep on the sides. A mark from a chain ripped off?

"Trouble?" he asked.

She looked up. "Exsanguination—blood loss—is indeed the cause of death. However ..."

Garreth waited expectantly.

"It did not result from the throat wound. That was inflicted *after* death. So was the broken neck. The cord is completely severed but there's no hemorrhage into it."

Déjà vu struck again. Death by bleeding, wounds and a broken neck inflicted after death. Now he *knew* he had knowledge of a previous crime with similar circumstances. Garreth bit his lip, straining to remember the previous case.

"He didn't bleed to death internally and I can't find any exterior wound to account for—"

There had been something else strange about that bruise on the other man. Now, what had it been? "What about the bruise?" he interrupted.

"... for a blood loss of that magnitude," the doctor went on with a frown at Garreth, "unless we assume that the punctures in the jugular vein were made by needles and the blood drained that way."

That was the other thing about the bruise!

"Two punctures, right? An inch or so apart, in the middle of the bruise?"

She regarded him gravely. "I could have used your crystal ball before I began, Inspector. It would have saved me a great deal of work."

Garreth smiled. Inside, however, he swore. He remembered that much, those facts, but still nothing that could help him locate the case in the files, not a victim or detective's name.

The remainder of the autopsy proceeded uneventfully. Lack of water in the lungs established that the victim had been dead before entering the water. The skull and brain showed no signs of bruises or hemorrhage to indicate that he might have been struck and knocked unconscious. The stomach contained no food, only liquid.

"Looks like he died some time after his last meal. We'll analyze the liquid," the doctor said.

Garreth bet it would prove alcoholic.

When the body was on its way back to its locker, Garreth prepared to leave. He had missed lunch but had no appetite. Perhaps he should just go on to the hotel. At least the fog had burned off, leaving a bright, clear day.

Before leaving the morgue, he called up to the office. Kolb answered. "Is there a message from the Denver P.D. with descriptions of some men's jewelry?" he asked her.

She went to look and came back on the line in a minute. "No, but there's a message to call—damn, I wish Faye would learn to write legibly. I think the name is Ellen or Elvis Hague or Hugie. I can't read the number at all."

"Never mind. I think I know." Mrs. Elvira Hogue was one of the witnesses to the Mission Street liquor store shooting. He looked up the number in his notebook and dialed it. "Mrs. Hogue? This is Inspector Mikaelian. You wanted to talk to me?"

"Yes." Her thin, old-woman's voice came back over the wire. "I saw the boy who did it, and I learned his name."

Garreth whooped silently. Once in a while the breaks came their way! "What is it?"

"You remember I told you I've seen him in the neighborhood before? Well, he was here this morning again, bold as brass, talking to that Hambright girl up the street. I walked very close to them and I heard her call him Wink."

"Mrs. Hogue, you're a wonderful lady. Thank you very much."

"You just catch that shtunk. Mr. Chmelka was a nice gentleman."

Garreth headed for R and I—records and identification—to check the name Wink through the moniker file. They came up with a make, one Leroy Martin Luther O'Hare, called Wink, as in "quick as a," for the way he snatched purses in his juvenile delinquency days by sweeping past victims on a skateboard. Purse snatching had been only one of his offenses. Wink added burglary and auto theft to his yellow sheet as he approached legal adulthood, though he had not been convicted of either charge.

With Wink's photograph tucked among half a dozen others of young black males, he drove to Mrs. Hogue's house.

She quickly picked out Wink. "That's him; that's the one I saw this morning and the one I saw coming out of the liquor store after I heard the shooting."

Garreth called Serruto.

"We'll get a warrant for him," the lieutenant said.

Garreth visited Wink's mother and the Hambright girl, first name Rosella. He also talked to the neighbors of both. No one, of course, offered any help. Garreth gained the impression that even Wink's mother hardly knew the person Garreth asked about. The neighbors denied any knowledge of comings and goings from Mrs. O'Hare's or Miss Hambright's apartment.

"Hey, man, I gots enough to do chasin' rats over here without wachin' someone else over there," they said, or else: "You wrong about Wink. He no good, but he no holdup man. He never owned no gun."

Garreth dropped word of wanting Wink into a few receptive ears whose owners knew he could promise some reward for turning the fugitive, then he headed for the Jack Tar. He would see Serruto about staking out the mother's and girlfriend's apartments. For now, he had better check in with Harry before his partner put out an APB on him.

7

"So we both came up empty today," Harry said, hanging up his coat in the squad room.

"Except for identifying our liquor store gunman and the odd results of the autopsy."

"I'd just as soon do without the autopsy." Harry grimaced. "Who needs a bled-out corpse who died before his throat was cut?"

Garreth had arrived at the hotel just in time to follow Harry back to Bryant Street.

"The meetings are breaking up for the day," Harry had said. "Everyone will be going out to play. We'll start in on them again tomorrow, and this time you can join the fun."

In the squad room Garreth rolled a report form into his typewriter. "Did I miss anything interesting at the hotel?"

"Just Susan Pegans fainting dead away when we told her about Mossman. No one I talked to, conventioneers or other exhibitors around Kitco's booth, saw him last night or knew where he was going."

Garreth began his report. "Did you go through Mossman's room?"

"Right away. There was about what you'd expect ... a couple of changes of clothes and a briefcase full of company propaganda. A return plane ticket to Denver. He traveled light in the city; there's a false bottom in his shaving kit where I found his credit cards, extra cash and traveler's checks, and personal keys. No billfold, so he must have had that on him when he was killed. He made two calls, one Monday and one last night, both a little after seven in the evening and both to his home phone in Denver."

"Tomorrow why don't I check with the cab companies to see if one of them took a fare of Mossman's description anywhere last night?"

"Do that."

Garreth remembered then that he needed to talk to the lieutenant.

He knocked on Serruto's door. "May I see you?"

"If it's about the warrant on O'Hare, we have it. There's an APB out on him, too."

"I'd like to stake out his mother's and girlfriend's apartments. He's bound to get in touch with one or the other."

Serruto leaned back in his chair. "Why don't we see if the APB and your street contacts can turn him first? Two stakeouts use a lot of men." He did not say it, but Garreth heard, nonetheless: *We can't spend that much manpower on one small-time crook.*

Garreth nodded, sighing inwardly. All are not equal in the eyes of the law. "Yes, sir." And he went back to his typewriter.

An hour later he and Harry checked out for the night.

8

Garreth always liked going home with Harry. The house had the same atmosphere Marti had given their apartment, a sense of sanctuary. The job ended at the door. Inside, he and Harry became ordinary men. Where Marti had urged him to talk, however, Lien bled away tensions with diversion and serenity. A judicious scattering of Oriental objects among the house's contemporary furnishings reflected the culture of her Taiwanese childhood and Harry's Japanese grandparents. The paintings on the walls, mostly Lien's and including examples of her commercial artwork, reflected Oriental tradition and moods.

Lien stared at them in disbelief. "Home before dark? How did you do it?"

Harry lowered his voice to a conspiratorial tone. "We went over the wall. If someone calls, you haven't seen us." He kissed her with a great show of passion. "What's for supper? I'm starved."

"Not lately." She patted his stomach fondly. "Both of you sit down; I'll bring tea."

Strong and well laced with rum ... an example of what Garreth considered a happy blend of West and East. Between sips of tea, he pulled off his shoes and tie. One by one his nerves loosened. These days, he reflected, Harry's house felt more like home than his own apartment did.

During dinner Lien monopolized the conversation, heading off any threat of shop talk with anecdotes from her own day. She brushed by the frustrations of finishing drawings for a fashion spread in the Sunday paper to talk about the art appreciation classes she taught at various grade schools in the afternoons. Garreth listened, bemused. Her kids came from a different world than the one he saw everyday. They never took drugs or shoplifted. They were well fed and well dressed, bright-eyed with promise. Sometimes he wondered if she deliberately told only cheerful stories, but he never objected; he liked hearing about a pleasant world populated by happy, friendly people.

Not that he regretted becoming a cop, but sometimes he wondered what he would be doing now, what kind of world he would live in, if he had finished college ... if he had been good enough to win a football scholarship like his older brother Shane, if he and Judith had not married so young, if she had not gotten pregnant his sophomore year and had to stop working, leaving them with no money to continue school.

Or would things have been any different? He had always worshipped his father and wanted to be just like him. He loved going down to the station and watching the parade of people and officers. While Shane had been starring in backyard scrimmages and Little League football, Garreth played cops and robbers. Police work had seemed a natural choice when he had to go to work.

After dinner, helping Lien with the dishes, he asked, "Do you believe people really have free choice, or are they pushed in inevitable directions by social conditioning?"

She smiled at him. "Of course they have choices. Background may limit or influence, but the choices are still there."

He considered that. "Consulting *I Ching* isn't a contradiction of that?"

"Certainly not. If anything, the sage supports the idea that people have control over their futures. He merely advises of the possibilities." She looked up in concern. "What's the matter? Are the dreadful broody *what-if's* chewing at you?"

He smiled at her understanding. "Sort of."

Or maybe what really chewed was the thought that tonight one man no longer had any choices at all. Someone else had taken them away from him.

The body in the bay with its peculiar bruise haunted him, lurking in the back of his mind the rest of the evening, even through the excitement of watching the Giants win a 1-0 squeaker. He stared at the TV screen with Harry and asked himself who would stick two needles into someone's jugular and drain out all his blood. Why? It seemed too bizarre to be real. And why did his memory refuse to give up the information he wanted on that other case like it?

Garreth had no particular desire to go home to his empty apartment, so after leaving Harry and Lien, he headed his car—a bright Prussian red Datsun ZX he and Marti had given each other on their last anniversary—back to Bryant Street. He sat in the near-empty squad room doodling on a blank sheet of paper and letting his mind wander. Bruise … punctures … blood loss. He recalled a photograph of a man in a bathtub, arm trailing down over the side to the floor. A voice said, "Homicide isn't like Burglary, Mikaelian. This is the kind of thing you'll be dealing with now."

He sat bolt upright. Earl Faye's voice! It had been Faye and Centrello's case. Faye had told Garreth—new to the section, unpartnered as yet, and stuck with paperwork—all about it in elaborate, gory detail.

Garreth scrambled for the file drawers. Everything came back to him now. The date was late October last year, just about Halloween, one of the factors which had fascinated Faye, he remembered.

"Maybe it was a cult of some kind. They needed the blood for their rituals."

Methodically, Garreth searched. The file should still be here. The case remained open, unsolved. And there it was … in a bottom drawer, of course, clear at the back.

Seated cross-legged on the floor, Garreth opened the file. Cleveland Morris Adair, an Atlanta businessman, had been found dead, wrists slashed, in the bathtub of his suite at the Mark Hopkins on October 29, 1982. The death seemed like suicide until the autopsy revealed two puncture wounds in the middle of a bruise on the neck, and although Adair had bled to death, his wrists had been slashed postmortem by someone applying a great deal of pressure. That someone had also broken Adair's neck. Stomach contents showed a high concentration of alcohol. The red coloring of the bathwater proved to be nothing more than grenadine from the bar in his suite.

Statements from cabdrivers and hotel personnel established that Adair had left the hotel alone on the evening of October 28 and gone to North Beach. He had returned at 2:15 A.M., again alone. A maid coming in to clean Sunday morning found his body.

Hotel staff in the lobby remembered most of the people entering the hotel around the time Adair had. By the time registered and known persons were sorted out, only three possible suspects remained, and two of them were eventually traced and ruled out. That left the third, who came through the lobby just five minutes after Adair. A bellboy described her in detail: about twenty, five ten, good figure, dark red hair, green eyes, wearing a green dress plunging to the waistline in front and slit to the hip on the side, carrying a large shoulder bag. The bellboy had seen her on occasion before, but never alone. She usually came in with a man ... not hooking, the bellboy thought, just a very easy lady. He did not know her name.

What interested Faye and Centrello about her was that no one saw her leave. Their efforts to locate her failed, however.

Nor did they find any wild-eyed crazies who might have made Adair their sacrifice in some kinky ritual.

The Crime Lab turned up no useful physical evidence, and robbery was apparently no motive; Adair's valuables had not been touched.

Garreth reread the autopsy report several times. Wounds inflicted by someone applying a great deal of pressure. Someone stronger than usual? The deaths had striking similarities and differences, but a crawling down his spine told him that his gut reaction believed more in the similarities than in the differences. Two out-of-towners staying at nice hotels whose blood had been drained through needles in their jugulars, then the bodies doctored to make it seem that they had bled other ways. It had a ritual sound about it. No wonder Faye and Centrello had hunted cultists.

After a jaw-cracking yawn, Garreth glanced down at his watch and was shocked to find it almost three o'clock. At least he would not notice the emptiness of the apartment now. He would be lucky to reach the bedroom before he collapsed.

9

Every eye in the squad room turned on Garreth as he tried to sneak in. From the middle of the meeting, Serruto said, "Nice of you to join us this morning, Inspector."

Garreth tossed his trench coat onto his chair. "Sorry I'm late. A potential witness wouldn't stop talking. Have I missed much?"

"The overnight action. Takananda can fill you in later. Now we're up to daily reports. Let's start with your cases. You've identified the Mission Street holdup man. Any word on him yet?"

"On my way in this morning I rattled some cages close to him," Garreth said. "We'll see what that produces."

"So we're just waiting to collar him, right? How about the floater?"

Garreth let Harry answer while he tried not to yawn. Despite the hour he had fallen into bed, sunrise woke him as usual.

"I've been awake since six," he complained to Harry after the meeting broke up. "So I went to work. After I rattled cages, I went by China Basin and talked to people there. So far no one seems to have seen a body being dumped in the bay." He poured himself a cup of coffee. *Do your stuff, caffeine.* "Where are the lab and autopsy reports you said we have back?"

Harry picked them up from his desk and tossed them at Garreth. In return, Garreth handed Harry the Adair file. "I finally remembered where I saw a bruise like Mossman's before. Take a look at this."

The lab and autopsy reports told Garreth nothing new. No bloodstains on the clothes, confirming that Mossman could not have had his throat cut on the street. However, there had been soiling which analyzed as a mixture of dirt, residue of asphalt and vulcanized rubber, and motor oil. It would seem Mossman had gone to the bay in the trunk of a car. No surprise there.

The autopsy report merely made official what Garreth had seen yesterday. Analysis of the stomach contents found a high percentage of alcohol, as he had thought there would be.

He glanced at Harry, who sat staring at the Adair reports. "What do you think?"

Harry looked up. "I think we'd better get with Faye and Centrello on this."

They made it a five-man meeting in Serruto's office.

With both files in front of him, Serruto said, "I can see definite similarities." He looked over at Harry and Garreth. "Do you want to pool resources with Faye and Centrello on this?"

Harry said, "What I want to do is give Earl and Dean a chance to take over this case if they want it. After all, the Adair thing was theirs."

Centrello grimaced. "I don't want it. You two play with the cult crazies for a while. I'll be glad to give you anything I know that isn't in the reports, but if you solve it, the glory is all yours."

Faye looked less certain, but he did not contradict his partner.

Serruto frowned at the Adair file. "Are you thinking cults on the Mossman thing, too, Harry?"

"I'm certainly going to check out the possibility."

"Don't get too tied into it; it didn't solve the Adair killing."

"Words of wisdom," Harry said as they left for the hotel.

"You know, both men had alcohol in their stomachs, so they were drinking not long before they died." Garreth pursed his lips. "I wonder if they drank in the same place?"

Harry punched for the elevator. "Adair went to North Beach. When you visit the cab companies, check for North Beach destinations on those trip logs."

Garreth sighed. "You know every jack man of those conventioneers went to either North Beach or Chinatown that night."

Harry grinned and slapped Garreth's shoulder. "You'll sort them out. That's detective work, Mik-san. Think about me, trying to find someone who knows where Mossman went. I can't believe he didn't mention something to someone."

A thought struck Garreth. He frowned at Harry. "You talked to quite a few people?"

"It seemed like hundreds."

"And no one knew a thing. Maybe he didn't want people to know. He's a married man and if he had something hot going ..."

Harry pursed his lips. "Verneau said this was Mossman's first trip to San Francisco and he didn't make any local calls from his room. If he had a lady, she would have to be either a member of the convention or someone he met Monday. Susan Pegans fainted when we told her Mossman was dead, and that wasn't even telling her *how*. Skip the cab companies for a bit and help me at the hotel. We'll start with our saleswoman."

10

Susan Pegans stared at the detectives with eyes flashing in outrage. "No! Absolutely not! I didn't go anywhere with Gary. He's a very happily married man. He calls his wife every evening when he's away from home."

But Garreth heard the note of regret in her voice as she said it. He was willing to bet she would have gone with Mossman in a moment, given an invitation.

"Alex Long and I had dinner in Chinatown with a couple of Iowa contractors and their wives. Ask Alex."

They would, but for the moment, Garreth continued to press her. "Had you seen him spending an unusual amount of time with any single person here?"

"He spent time with everyone. What does it take to make you understand that Gary doesn't—" She broke off, eyes filling with tears. She wiped at them with the handkerchief Garreth handed her. "Gary didn't play at conventions, not ever. He worked. Why do you think he was sales manager?"

"But you knew where he was going Monday night. Verneau said he told all three of you," Harry said.

"Yes, so we would know who had been contacted and not duplicate efforts."

"Yet you didn't think it strange when he said nothing to you about Tuesday night?"

She shrugged, sighing. "I wondered, yes, but ... I thought he'd tell us Wednesday. I—" She broke off again, shaking her head.

"Pity unrequited love," Harry murmured as they left her. "Well, do we take her at her word or start questioning some of the other ladies? You'll have noticed how many really beautiful ones there are here."

"Maybe we ought to think about guys, too," Garreth said. "That would be a better reason for keeping it quiet."

"You talk to beautiful young men, then; I'll stick to the ladies. Just find *someone* who went out with him,"

Garreth found no one. He worked his way straight down the section of the membership list Harry gave him and heard negative answers in every interview. As far as Garreth could determine, Mossman had said to hell with the convention on Tuesday. Checking with Harry later, he found his partner having no better luck.

"Maybe you ought to start on the cab companies," Harry said. "I'll keep working here."

"Let me bounce one more idea off you. You mentioned that he may have met someone Monday evening. So let's talk to the people he was with on Monday. Do you have their names?"

"Verneau gave them to me." Harry checked off two names on the membership list. "You take this half of the group."

Garreth made it easy on himself. He rounded up both and talked to them at the same time, hoping one might stimulate memory in the other. "Where did you go?" he asked them.

Misters Upton and Suarez grinned at each other. "North Beach. That's some entertainment up there"

"It offers a little of something for everyone. Do you remember the names of the clubs you visited?"

"Why do you want to know about Monday?" Suarez asked. "Wasn't Gary Mossman robbed and killed on Tuesday night? That's what's going around."

"We need to know about people he met on Monday. Please, try to think. I need the club names."

They looked at each other. "Big Al's," Suarez said.

Between them, Suarez and Upton named half a dozen of the better known clubs. Garreth jotted the names down. "Any others?"

"Oh, yeah. We must have hit a dozen or more. We'd just walk down the street and drop in, see a girl or two dance, and go on."

"Did you talk to anyone?"

Their eyes narrowed. "What do you mean?"

Garreth gave them a man-to-man smirk. "You were five guys out on the town alone. Didn't you buy drinks for any girls?"

The contractors grinned. "Well, sure. We kind of collected four and took them along with us."

Four. Garreth raised an eyebrow. Who had not had one? "Did Mossman pay special attention to any of them? Did he ask any of them back to the hotel?"

"No."

"Are you thinking he met someone Monday he might have seen again Tuesday, and that's who killed him?" Suarez asked.

"We're checking all the possibilities. Can you give me the names of the girls? I also need to know if he met anyone outside your group."

"The girls only told us their first names, and Mossman didn't talk to anyone except us and the girls," Upton said.

"Give me the girls' names then and their descriptions." Inwardly, Garreth groaned. Track down four girls in North Beach by first name and description. Shit.

"Except the singer," Suarez said.

Garreth blinked, feeling he had missed a connection somewhere. "Except what singer, Mr. Suarez?"

The contractor shrugged. "We were in this club—I don't remember the name—and Mossman couldn't do anything except stare at the singer. She kept looking at him, too, giving him the eye. I remember he hung back a bit as we left, and when I looked around, he was talking to her. It was just for a minute, though."

"What did this singer look like?"

Suarez grinned. "Spectacular. Tall, and I mean *really* tall, man. Her legs went on forever. She was built, too."

Something like an electric shock trailed up Garreth's spine, raising every hair on his body. He stared at Suarez, hardly breathing. "Do you think she was five ten?"

"Or taller. She had on these boots, see, and—"

"What color was her hair?"

"Red. Not that bright color but darker, like mahogany."

Red-haired Woman

1

Harry was dubious. "He had a few words with a red-haired singer Monday night. What makes you think he went back to do more on Tuesday?"

"A hunch."

Certainly he could think of no other reason. No real evidence connected Mossman to this woman any more than evidence connected Adair to that other redhead. Only the similarity in height and coloring suggested that the two women might be the same. Still ... two mysterious deaths and two memorable redheads. He had a feeling about it.

"My Grandma Doyle gets what she calls Feelings ... that's with a capital F. She's Auld Sod stock, full of blarney and superstition, but—well, that Green Bay–LA game that wiped out my brother's knee, we were all watching the TV and at half-time she went to her room. She said she didn't want to watch Shane get zapped. And sure enough, in the middle of the third quarter ... scratch one knee and one Rams end."

"Coincidence?" Harry suggested.

"Except that's just one instance. My grandmother's Feelings are famous in our family. On the other hand, maybe my hunch is nonsense, but crazies come in all shapes and sizes so we'd better check the redhead out."

Harry nodded. "That reason I'll go along with. But let's eat first; I'm starved."

So was Garreth. Lunchtime had long passed. "How about Huong's?"

Huong's, though a hole-in-the-wall greasy chopsticks eatery up a side street off Grant Avenue, served some of the best fried rice and egg rolls in San Francisco. For love of them, Garreth had learned to ignore the greasy smoke that seeped out of the kitchen and covered the walls and Chinese signs on them with a uniform coat of dingy gray, and to beg silverware from waitresses who understood little English and barely more of Harry's and his fractured Chinese.

Harry considered. "It'd be too much trouble to drive over there when we have to come back here again. How about settling for less this time?"

With stomach longing for fried rice, Garreth settled for a club sandwich in the hotel coffee shop.

"One thing," Harry said while they ate. "Whether the redhead is in it or not, we need to know where Mossman went."

"I'll get on the cab companies."

He called them from the assistant manager's office. To be on the safe side, he expanded the time limit and asked for single fares picked up at the hotel between 7:00 and 8:30 P.M. Garreth expected to develop writer's cramp, but while it appeared that fleets of cabs had picked up passengers Tuesday evening, most trips carried groups. Less than a dozen cabs made single-fare trips in that time period.

He wrote down the cab number, destination and cabdriver's name for each trip. Then it became a matter of having drivers on duty stop by the hotel to look at a picture of Mossman that the Kitco booth supplied him or calling on them at home. "Was this man a passenger in your cab Tuesday night?" He particularly pressed the five whose destinations had been in North Beach. However, none could identify Mossman.

"That doesn't mean I couldn't have taken him," one female cabbie said. "I just don't remember him, you know?"

Garreth met Harry back at the hotel. "Zero. Zip."

Harry looked at his watch. "Well, let's call it quits here, then."

Garreth seconded the motion and they headed back to Bryant Street.

While they typed up reports at the office, Harry said, "What do you say to taking Lien out for a change? I'll call her, and you make reservations for three somewhere."

Garreth shook his head. "Tonight you have her to yourself. I'm going to eat at Huong's and fall into bed early."

"You sure?" Harry whipped his report out of the typewriter and signed it after a fast proofreading.

"Go home to your wife."

Harry waved on his way out.

Garreth kept typing. Some time later Evelyn Kolb came through. She said, "There's a telex for you from Denver. I think Art put it under something on your desk."

"Under?" He dug through the pile of papers on the desk, frowning. Under, for God's sake. It could have gone unseen for days.

The telex, when he found it, had the descriptions of the jewelry. He read quickly. A man's gold Seiko digital watch with expansion band and enough functions to do everything but answer the telephone; a plain gold man's wedding band, size 8, inscribed: *B.A. to G.M. 8-31-73.*

"Oh, God," he sighed, feeling his chest tighten. "Today was their wedding anniversary. What a hell of a present."

Kolb grimaced in sympathy.

Garreth made himself go on. A sterling silver pendant two inches long, shaped in the outline of a fish with the Greek word for fish inside the outline. "Is that enough silver to bother stealing?" he asked.

Kolb pumped tea out of her thermos. "If some kind of cult killed your man, they might not like Christian symbols."

Garreth toyed with the telex. "It's almost too bizarre." He wondered if it was possible that instead of a cult, they were dealing with someone who wanted Mossman dead, but made it as weird as possible to confuse everyone. The telex also said the wife knew of no serious enemies her husband had, but of course that would have to be checked out. For now, he typed up the jewelry descriptions for a flier to distribute to the pawnshops, then finished his reports.

2

"No more. *Bu yao*," Garreth said to the waitress who extended the coffeepot toward his half-empty cup.

He could not be sure he had the Chinese pronunciation right, but it came close enough to convey his meaning. With a nod and a smile, the girl turned away.

He drained the cup and stood, reaching for the check with one hand and into his pocket for the tip with the other. He left the girl a generous one; she had struggled hard to overcome the language barrier between them. At the cash register he paid the withered little old woman almost hidden from sight by the machine. "Delicious, as always, Mrs. Huong."

She smiled in return, bobbing her head. "Come back again, Inspector."

"Count on it."

Outside, he walked down the steep half block to Grant Avenue and stood on the sidewalk there, surrounded by passing evening throngs of tourists and the bright kaleidoscope of shop windows and neon signs with their Chinese pictographs, contemplating alternatives to going home. Perhaps he should turn over a few rocks in Wink O'Hare's neighborhood. This was about the time of day the little vermin was most likely to stick his head out of his hole. On the other hand, just a few blocks up the hill, Grant Avenue intersected with Columbus Avenue and Broadway in the beginning of North Beach's bright-lights section, and somewhere among the bars and clubs sang a tall red-haired woman who might or might not be involved in murder.

He stared up the hill, weighing the choices. Finding Wink should have priority—he still had the gun he had presumably used to shoot the liquor store clerk—but evening in North Beach frankly appealed to Garreth far more than the despairing poverty of Wink's turf. He had his sources keeping eyes and ears open, and as long as he was on his own time anyway ...

He turned uphill.

Chinatown gave way to blocks of glittering, garish signs proclaiming the presence of countless clubs. Barkers paced the sidewalks, calling to passersby in a raucous chorus ... beckoning, wheedling, leering, each promising the ultimate in exotic entertainment inside his club. Garreth absorbed it all, color and noise, as he threaded his way through the crowd, but also kept alert for unnecessary bumps against him and fingers in his pockets. He spotted some familiar faces ... about the time they recognized him, too, and swiftly faded into the crowd.

He hailed a barker he had met on previous occasions. "How's business, Sammy?"

"All over legal age, Inspector," Sammy replied quickly. "Come on in and see the show, folks! All live action with the most gorgeous girls in San Francisco!"

"Any redheads, Sammy?"

Sammy eyed him. "Sure. Anything you want."

"Maybe a very tall redhead, say five ten, with green eyes?"

The barker's eyes narrowed. "This redhead got a name? Hey, mister!" he called to a passing couple. "Your timing is perfect. The show is about to start. Bring the little lady in and warm up together. What do you want her for, Mikaelian?"

"A date, Sammy. What else? Who do you know with that description? She sings in the area."

Sammy laughed. "Are you kidding? We've got more showgirl redheads than the stores have Barbie dolls. Come on in and see the show, folks! Real adult entertainment, live on our stage! Our girls have curves in places most girls don't have places, and they'll show you every one!"

"I need names, Sammy," Garreth said patiently.

Sammy sighed, not patiently. "Names. Who knows names?

Try the Cul-de-Sac across the street. There's a red-haired singer I seen there. And maybe in the Pussywillow, too. Now, will you move on, man? You're spoiling my rhythm."

Grinning, Garreth moved across the street into the Cul-de-Sac. Yes, a barmaid said when he ordered a rum and Coke, they had a red-haired singer. She came on after the dancer.

He sat down at the bar, which ran around the edge of the stage. A blonde dragged an enormous cushion out onto the stage and proceeded to writhe nearly naked on it in simulated ecstasy. In the midst of her throes, she rolled over, saw Garreth watching her with amusement, and said in a bored monotone, "Hi, honey. And what's your day been like?"

"About like yours, unfortunately, hours wasted grinding away at thin air," he replied.

A fleeting grin crossed the blonde's face.

The singer appeared presently. Garreth left. The redhead's hair color was bottle-bred brass and she looked old enough to have sung on the Barbary Coast itself.

He talked to barkers on down the street, collecting a notebook full of possibilities, but in checking them out, he found women with the wrong color of red, wrong height, and wrong age. In two hours he checked over a dozen clubs with no success and stood on the sidewalk outside of the last with an ache working its way up from his feet. He looked around, seeking inspiration.

"Hi, baby. All alone?" a husky voice asked behind him.

Garreth turned. A woman in her thirties with elaborately curled dark hair arched a plucked, painted eyebrow at him. "Hi, Velvet," he said. Her real name, he knew from busting her when he worked Vice, was Catherine Bukato, but on the street and with the johns, she always went by Velvet. "How's your daughter?"

Velvet smiled. "Almost twelve and more beautiful every day. My mother sends me pictures of her regularly. I may even go home to see her this winter. You up here working or playing tonight?"

"I'm looking for a woman."

Velvet hitched the shoulder strap of her handbag higher. "You're playing my song, baby."

"The woman I want is red-haired, young, and very tall. Taller than I am. She sings somewhere around here. Would you happen to know anyone like that?"

Velvet's eyes narrowed shrewdly. "I tell you what. My feet are killing me. Why don't you play like a john who has to work up his courage?

Buy me a drink where I can sit down for a while and I'll think on it."

Garreth smiled. "Pick somewhere."

She chose the nearest bar and they found seats in a rear booth. She ordered, then kicked off her shoes and stretched her legs out, propping her feet up on the seat on the far side of the booth. She closed her eyes. "That's what I needed. You know, for a cop, you're almost human, Mikaelian."

"Every Thursday night." In the right quarters, inexpensive kindness could reap valuable benefits. Velvet's sharp eyes and ears missed little on the street.

A fact she knew he knew. Opening her eyes, she said, "So let me pay for the drink. Who's this woman you're looking for?"

Garreth gave her a detailed description.

Velvet's drink came. She sipped it slowly. "Tall? A singer? Yeah, I've seen someone like that. I can't remember where, though. What did she rip off?"

"I'm in Homicide now, not Burglary. I just want to talk to her."

Velvet's drawn brows rose again, skeptical. "Oh, sure."

"If you have a chance, will you ask around? Its important that I find her."

Velvet eyed him a moment, but then nodded. "How can I refuse someone who always asks about my kid? You have a kid, Mikaelian?"

"An eight-year-old boy named Brian."

For the remainder of the time it took her to finish her drink, they talked children and exchanged the pictures they carried. As Garreth handed back Velvet's snapshot of her daughter, the prostitute started to laugh.

"What's funny?" Garreth asked.

Her teeth gleamed in the dimness of the bar. "What a pair we are, a cop and a hooker, sitting in a bar talking about our kids." She drained her glass, sighed, and fished around under the table for her shoes. "Well, time to go back to work. Thanks for the coffee break."

They headed for the door.

"I hope this won't make trouble for you with Richie, getting nothing for the time," Garreth said.

She looked up at him. "Look, if it isn't too much trouble, maybe you could give me a little something, a kind of advance on information I'm going to give you? It'll help with Richie."

He dug into his pocket for his billfold and came up with two tens. "One for Richie Soliere and one for you to buy something for your daughter, all right?"

She folded away the bills with a smile. "Thanks a lot." Then she tossed her head and dropped back into her husky "professional" voice. "Good night, baby."

He watched her walk off into the crowd, then counted what remained in his billfold. The impulsive generosity had nearly cleaned him out. It would make the rest of the swing through North Beach a dry trip. He hoped Velvet gave him a good return on his investment.

3

Rob Cohen raised a brow at Garreth. "That's the third time you've yawned in the last five minutes. You single guys sure lead a fast life."

Harry regarded Garreth sharply, however. "You worked all night after all?"

Garreth shrugged. "I couldn't sleep." He gave Harry a recap of the North Beach canvas. "It was a waste of good shoe leather, though; I didn't find her."

"Maybe you're lucky. Your hexagram this morning was number forty-four, *Coming to Meet*. 'The maiden is powerful. One should not marry such a maiden.'"

A sudden chill raised the hair down Garreth's spine. He wondered at it. *I Ching's* prophecies usually neither disturbed nor encouraged him. He thought of Grandma Doyle's Feelings. However, he made himself slap Harry's shoulder. "Don't worry, Taka-san. I have no intention of marrying *any* maiden in the near future."

Too late he realized that the flip response had been wrong. Harry's almond eyes went grave. "You know the text isn't to be taken literally. What's the matter?"

The chill bit deep into Garreth's gut. "Nothing." A lie? He could not be sure. His chest felt so tight he had trouble breathing. "Guess I'm just superstitious enough not to like having that caution turn up when I'm hunting a woman." He hurriedly changed the subject. "Here's the flier on Mossman's watch, ring, and pendant that's going out to the pawnshops."

Harry read it over. "Good."

The tightness and chill eased in Garreth. "What do you want to do this morning?"

"I think one of us ought to get started checking out cults and the other take China Basin. Shall we flip for it? Loser takes the cults."

Garreth chose tails. The quarter came up heads. Harry grinned as he left for China Basin.

Garreth sat down with the Adair file and read through the reports to see which groups Faye and Centrello had investigated. On the half dozen he found reports on, only one had a formal name, Holy Church of Asmodeus. The others were listed by leaders' names. The groups varied in size, organization, and object of worship. Some seemed to be satanists or devil worshipers. Others appeared to be variations of witchcraft and voodoo. One group claimed to be neo-druids. All, however, had been rumored to use blood in their ceremonies. A few admitted it, but insisted it was either animal blood or small amounts from members, voluntarily given. Analysis of blood samples on altars and instruments confirmed that most was animal blood. One of the few human samples proved to be A positive like Adair's, but investigation of the group failed to establish opportunity for any of the members and, further, more detailed analysis of the blood sample found enough differences in minor factors to rule out the possibility of the blood being Adair's.

Nevertheless, Garreth turned all the names in to R and I for a check of current activities, then called Sergeant Dennis Kovar in Fraud.

"Denny, what complaints have you had in the past year about oddball church and cult groups?"

Kovar laughed. "How much time do you have to listen? I don't need to lift weights after picking up the current file a few times a day. Parents and neighbors are all out for the blood of these groups."

"What about the groups? Do you have any word that any of *them* are using blood?"

Silence came over the line for a moment before Kovar answered. "What are you looking for?" He listened silently to Garreth's reply, then said, "I don't have many complaints about those groups. They aren't asking for monetary donations. They keep a low profile so they won't be noticed. But you might talk to Angelo Chiarelli. He's undercover full-time and officially attached to Narco, but he's fed information to me on some of these fraudulent church groups and contacted a few kids in the cults for Missing Persons. Maybe he can help you."

A call to Narcotics produced a promise to pass on Garreth's request. "You understand we can't just go calling on him every day, and he's too busy doing his own job to run errands for other sections."

Garreth sighed. "He doesn't have to work on my case. I just want any possible information on blood-using cults that he may know about."

"We'll get back to you."

He even called the Humane Society about complaints of people killing and mutilating animals and went out to buy underground papers. When Harry came back to the office around two, they exchanged notes over coffee and doughnuts.

Harry's interviews in China Basin produced nothing for them. The underground classifieds had some cult ads, but no direct route of contacting the groups.

"We'll have to get some scrawny kid straight out of the Academy, who can get past their security," Garreth said. "The ASPCA has some complaints of animal mutilation we might follow up on, too."

"What about Chiarelli?"

"Still no word back from Narco yet. Here's everything R and I has currently on the cults Faye and Centrello investigated."

And what, Garreth wondered, leaning back in his chair with a sigh, did it mean until they knew where Mossman had been? Until they knew, they had no way of establishing opportunity for the cults. Checking movements was treadmill work.

Still, it needed to be done, and over the next four days they visited the cult groups Faye and Centrello listed, then those with ads that their rookie contacted for them. They visited people who had reported animal mutilations to the Humane Society. Garreth did not like most of the cultists he met—some he detested on sight—but he found them very educational: women who simultaneously attracted and chilled him, people who he would have taken for dull businessmen on the street, and some, too, who looked like escapees from Hollywood horror movies. No group, though, had a very tall red-haired female member.

None of Mossman's jewelry appeared in the pawnshops.

At the same time, they hunted up the four girls who had joined Mossman's group on that Monday night—and cleared all four of any Tuesday night involvement with Mossman—and kept prodding their contacts for Wink O'Hare's hiding place. Garreth spent his evenings in North Beach on a systematic search for the singer. On Tuesday, September 6, one week after Gerald Mossman died, Garreth found her.

4

Calling the singer tall seemed an understatement. In boots with four-inch heels, to go with the satin jeans, shirt, and Stetson of her urban cowgirl outfit, the redhead towered over the patrons of the Barbary Now as she walked between the tables singing a sentimental Kenny Rogers song. The red hair, black in shadow, burning with dark fire where the light struck it, hung down her back to her waist and framed a striking, square-jawed face. Watching the long legs carry her between the tables, Garreth remembered the description the bellboy had given of the woman in the Mark Hopkins lobby. She had to be the same woman. Surely there could not be two like this in San Francisco. He would slip something extra to Velvet, above the usual, to thank her for finding this woman.

The hooker had called the office that afternoon. He and Harry had been out, but she left a message: *If you're still looking for that redhead, try the Barbary Now after 8:00 tonight.*

So here he and Harry were, and here was a redhead.

"Nice," Harry said.

Garreth agreed. *Very* nice. He beckoned to a barmaid. "Rum and Coke for me, a vodka collins for my friend, and what's the name of the singer?"

"Lane Barber."

Garreth watched her. He did not blame Mossman for having stared at her. Most of the present male eyes in the room remained riveted on her throughout the song. Garreth managed to take his own off just long enough to see that.

The barmaid brought their drinks. Garreth tore a page out of his notebook and wrote on it. "When the set finishes, will you give this to Miss Barber? I'd like to buy her a drink."

"I'll give it to her, but I'd better warn you, she has a long line waiting for the same honor."

"In that case"—Harry took out one of his cards—"give her this instead."

The girl held the card down where the light of the candle on the table fell on it. "Cops! If you're on duty, what are you doing drinking?"

"We're blending with the scenery. Give her the card, please."

Three songs later, the set ended. Lane Barber disappeared through the curtains behind the Piano. She reappeared five minutes later in a strapless, slit-skirted dress that wrapped around her and stayed on by the grace of God and two buttons. She made her way through the tables, smiling but shaking her head at various men, until she reached Garreth and Harry.

She held out the card. "Is this official or an attention-getting device?"

"Official, I'm afraid," Harry said.

"In that case, I'll sit down." Garreth felt her legs rub against his under the small table as she pulled up a chair. She smiled at Harry. "*Konnichi wa*, Sergeant Takananda. I've always enjoyed my visits to Japan. It's a beautiful country."

"So I hear. I've never been there."

"That's a pity." She turned toward Garreth. "And you are—?"

"Inspector Garreth Mikaelian."

She laughed. "A genuine Irish policeman. How delightful."

She was not really beautiful, Garreth realized with surprise, studying her as well as he could in the flickering candlelight, but she moved and talked and dressed to seem that way, and something radiated from her, something almost irresistible in its magnetism. She looked no more than twenty or twenty-one.

"Now, what is this unfortunately official visit about?" she asked. "It can't be a traffic ticket; I haven't driven anywhere in weeks."

"Were you working last week?" Harry asked.

She nodded. Oddly, the flame of the candle reflected red in her eyes. Garreth had never seen that in humans before. He watched her, fascinated.

"Do you remember speaking to a man on Monday who was in his thirties, your height when you're barefoot, and wearing a red coat with black velvet lapels and collar? He was with four other men, all older than him."

She shook her head ruefully. "I must have talked to over a dozen different men that night, Sergeant. I do every night. I like men. I'm afraid I can't recall any particular one."

"Maybe this will help." Garreth showed her the picture of Mossman.

She tilted it to the flickering light of the candle and studied it gravely. "Now I remember him. We didn't really talk, though. I flirted with him while I sang because he was nice-looking, and as he left, he came over to say how much he liked my singing." She paused. "You're from Homicide. Is he a suspect or a victim?"

The lady was cool and fast on the uptake, Garreth reflected. "A victim," he said. "Someone cut his throat Tuesday night. Did he come back here at any time on Tuesday?"

"Yes. He asked me out, but I didn't go. I don't date married men."

Harry said, "We need to know exactly what he said and did Tuesday. What time did he come in?"

"I don't really know. He was here when I did my first set at eight. He stayed all evening and we talked off and on, but not too much. I didn't want to encourage him. Finally I told him I wasn't interested in going out with him. The bartender, Chris, can confirm that we sat there at the end of the bar. About twelve-thirty he left."

Garreth made notes by the light of the candle. "Was that the last you saw of him?"

"Yes. Lots of men don't know how to take no for an answer, but he did."

"I suppose you have a fair number of guys try to hustle you. Do you ever take anyone up on the offer?"

She smiled. "Of course, if the man interests me. I don't pretend to be a nun. What business is it of yours?"

"Where do you usually go, your place or his?" Her eyes flared red in the candlelight, but she replied evenly, "Yes."

Garreth dropped the subject, recognizing evaporating cooperation. There would be time enough later to question her about Adair, if need be. "I'm sorry; that was irrelevant. I'll need your name and address, though, in case we want to talk to you again."

"Of course." She gave him the address, an apartment near Telegraph Hill.

"Are you a permanent resident of the city?" Harry asked.

"I travel a good deal, but this is home base, yes."

"Are you a native like Harry there, or an immigrant like me?"

"Yes," she replied, and when their brows rose, she smiled. "Women are more fascinating with a bit of mystique, don't you think? Leave me mine until you absolutely must have the information, can't you?" She glanced at her watch. "It's almost time for the next set. Please excuse me."

She rose and left, walking gracefully toward the piano. Garreth looked after her, sighing. He could not see her as a bloodthirsty cultist.

Harry grinned at him. "Do you still want to involve her in two murders?"

She began a song in sultry tones that jostled Garreth's hormones pleasantly. "I'd rather date than arrest her," he admitted. "She seems cooperative enough and she didn't hesitate to admit she'd seen Mossman Tuesday. Still ..."

"Still," Harry agreed. "You never know, so we'd better check her out."

5

In the darkness of his bedroom, lying awake, Garreth heard the foghorns start. The years living here had taught him to recognize the patterns of a few, like the double hoot of the one on Mile Rocks and the single every-twenty-seconds blast of the one on Point Diablo. *Fog moving in*, he thought.

He stopped consciously listening when the horns and diaphone on the Golden Gate Bridge joined the chorus. The dial of his watch glowed on the bedside table, but he resisted the urge to look at it. Why see how long he had lain awake?

He sat up, hugging his blanketed knees. What was wrong? Why should he be bothered that their interviews with the manager of the Barbary Now and the singer's neighbors last night and today turned up nothing to connect her with the murders?

"I wish everyone I hired were as dependable," the manager had said. "She's always on time, always polite to even the biggest asshole customers, never drunk or strung out. Lane never causes trouble."

Her neighbors echoed the sentiment. One said, "You'd hardly know she's there. She sleeps all day and comes home from work after we've gone to bed. If she brings anyone home, I don't know it because she never makes a sound. She's away on tour sometimes and it may be a week before I realize she's gone."

"Do you ever see any of her friends?" Garreth had asked.

"Once in a while. They're men, mostly, leaving in the morning, but all very well dressed ... none of the dirty, hairy, blue-jean types."

Altogether their questions produced a picture of an ideal neighbor and employee. So what did he find so disturbing about that? Maybe just *that*. He had an innate suspicion of people who kept a profile low to the point of invisibility. Even granting differences between professional images and private lives, he could not quite reconcile such a lifestyle with the sexy, coolly sophisticated young woman from the Barbary Now. *The maiden is powerful, I Ching* said. *One should not marry such a maiden.* Beware of that which seems weak and innocent.

And yet, he could not picture her threading a needle into Mossman's jugular, either ... not with his present knowledge of her.

"I need to know more," he said aloud into the darkness.

The midchannel Golden Gate diaphone sounded out of the fog in its bellow-and-grunt voice, as though replying to his remark.

He would talk to her landlord, he decided, lying back in bed, and then to more of the Barbary Now personnel. He would see if all their opinions matched the ones he had already heard.

That decided, he lay relaxed, listening to the hooting and bellowing of the foghorns reverberate through the night. The rhythmic chorus carried him into sleep.

6

The woman inside the protective grille across the doorway wore a bathrobe and slippers. She blinked through the grille at Garreth's identification. "Police? This early?"

"I'm sorry about the hour, Mrs. Armour, but I need to ask a few questions about a tenant of yours." He himself had been up for hours, finding out who owned the house where Lane Barber lived.

Mrs. Armour opened the grille with a frown and led the way up a steep flight of stairs to a sunny kitchen looking out over the fog that shrouded the lower marina and bay. "Which one, and what have they done?"

"I don't know that Lane Barber has done anything. She merely knows someone involved in a case I'm investigating."

The frown faded. She sat down at the table, returning to the toast and coffee that Garreth's ring had obviously interrupted. "Coffee, Inspector?" When he accepted with a nod, she poured a cup for him. "I'm glad Miss Barber isn't in trouble. Actually, I would have been surprised if you'd said she was."

Mrs. Armour, too? Garreth added cream and sugar. "You know her well?"

"Not personally, but she's one of my best tenants. I have a number of properties in that area and most of them are rented by restless young people who are here this year and gone the next. I wish you could see the state they leave their apartments in. It's appalling. But Miss Barber pays her rent on time every month and when I go in with the painters to repaint her apartment, as I feel ought to be done every few years, her place is always spotless. She takes beautiful care of it."

Garreth stopped stirring his coffee. "Every few years? How long has she been a tenant?"

Mrs. Armour pursed her lips. "Let's see. I think I've had her apartment done three times. She must have been with me about ten years. No ... I've painted four times. She's been there twelve years. She's my oldest tenant."

Twelve years? Garreth blinked. "How old was she when she moved in?"

"Very young, but at least twenty-one. I remember she told me she was singing in a club."

Garreth stared at her. The singer was twenty-one *twelve years* ago? He clearly remembered the face above the candle; it had not belonged to a woman in her thirties, although her level of sophistication certainly seemed more commensurate with that age than with twenty-one. Had she had a face-lift, perhaps?

"What has her friend done?" Mrs. Armour asked.

For a moment, Garreth struggled to think what the woman was talking about. "Oh ... he died. In the time Miss Barber has been your tenant, have you ever had any trouble with her? Has the apartment ... smelled strange, or have neighbors complained of strange people coming and going?" Cult types. It occurred to him that if she lived in the middle of a shifting population, former neighbors may have seen things present ones could not know about.

"Smelled strange? Like marijuana?" Mrs. Armour sat bolt upright in indignation. "Certainly not! I've never had a single word of complaint about her."

Garreth could not believe in this paragon. It was obvious, however, that Mrs. Armour was not going to add any clay to the lady's feet, so he thanked her for her help and headed for Bryant Street.

As he came into the squad room, Harry said, "You're supposed to call Narco."

Garreth peeled out of his trench coat. "I hope it's about Chiarelli."

He called after the squad meeting. It was about Chiarelli. A Sergeant Woodhue said, "It's arranged for you to meet him. Join us in the garage at twelve-thirty."

Garreth hung up. "Let's hope Chiarelli can help us."

"Maybe. But my hexagram this morning said, 'In adversity, it furthers one to be persevering,' and yours read, 'Success in small matters. At the beginning good fortune; at the end, disorder.'"

Garreth grimaced. "Thanks. I really needed to hear that."

He thought about his conversation with the landlady on the Barber girl's age. A strange lady, this redhead. He ran her name through R and I. It came back negative for local and state, even negative NCIC— the FBI had nothing on her. She did not even have a traffic ticket. In fact, he discovered that she had no driver's license. That brought a frown. She had said something about driving when they talked to her. Had she been only joking?

"Do you think she can be thirty-three years old?" he asked Harry. "She looks much younger."

"In the lighting of that bar, Methuselah would look like an adolescent; it's designed that way. How else could some of those hookers snag a john?" Harry raised his brows at Garreth. "Why so concerned about her age? Isn't that part of the mystique?"

"Maybe there's such a thing as too much mystique." The first chance he had, Garreth decided, he would ask the lady a few pointed questions and dispel some of it.

7

A voice over Sergeant Woodhue's walkie-talkie said softly, "It's going down now."

Suddenly the old warehouse filled with narcotics officers. Garreth hung on Woodhue's heels, the sergeant's words at the briefing echoing in his head: *This is the drill. We're busting a buy. Chiarelli, who's going by the name Demesta, will be there. You're a hot-dog cop along for the fun. When Chiarelli bolts, you go after him.*

The men involved in the buy scattered like cockroaches before a light. Garreth searched among them hurriedly, looking for someone who matched the description Woodhue had given him—a lean runt in an over-size old army jacket—but he could not see Chiarelli. In the melee and half dark, he had trouble distinguishing any particular individual.

Then Woodhue pointed and barked, "Get Demesta!"

Garreth saw the army jacket then, faded to pale green, with dark patches where the insignia had been removed. It dwarfed the man inside it, a man who bowled over an officer and was vanishing into the junk littering the building. Garreth took after it.

Chiarelli went out of a broken window in a shower of flying glass from remaining shards in the frame. Trying to avoid cutting his hands as he followed, Garreth swore. *See the stupid cop jump out the window*, he thought sardonically. *See him break his leg.*

But somehow he landed outside without crippling himself and looked up in time to see his quarry scramble across a set of railroad tracks and disappear into a passage between two more warehouses. Garreth pounded after him. At the beginning, good fortune? The hell. It looked more like disorder all day.

A hand reached out of a narrow doorway to grab Garreth's coat and jerk him inside the building. "Let's make this fast, man," Chiarelli said. "You're interested in cults?"

Garreth nodded, panting slightly. "I have two men who've been bled to death through needles stuck in their necks. We think maybe a cult did it."

"Like the Zebra murders? Christ!" Chiarelli shuddered and crossed himself. "So you want the names of people or groups who might use blood in their rituals."

"Right. Can you help me?"

Chiarelli sighed. "I'm not really next to that scene, you know, not unless some group also uses drugs, but ... I guess I've heard a few things. Give me paper and a pen."

Garreth handed him his pen and notebook.

Chiarelli printed with the speed of a teletype and talked almost as fast as he wrote, passing on more information than he had time to write. "Some is just addresses, not names. There have been weird stories about this house on Geary. Screaming and smells like burning meat." He had similar comments on every person or address he wrote down. When finished, he handed the notebook back. "Will that help?"

Garreth glanced over the pages, amazingly legible for the speed at which they had been written. "I hope so. Thanks." He started to turn away.

"Wait a minute," Chiarelli said. "We have to make it look good for me or I'm blown."

"I'll just say you outran me."

He shook his head. "Not good enough. You don't look like you've been chasing me all this time."

"How do you want to handle it, then?" He saw Chiarelli's fist double and stepped back, shaking his head. "Hey, not that—"

But the fist was already in motion. It sank into Garreth's stomach. He went down onto hands and knees in a wheeling galaxy of pain and light. His gut rebelled at the treatment by rejecting what remained of his lunch and he huddled retching on the dusty floor.

A wiry arm slipped under his and helped him to his feet as the paroxysm subsided. Chiarelli's face floated beyond a blue haze. "Take it easy. You'll be all right in a couple of minutes," he said cheerfully.

Garreth would have gone for Chiarelli's throat, but he could only lean against the wall and concentrate on breathing. He could not even swear at Chiarelli, just gasp and groan.

"Sorry, man, but it has to look real."

Chiarelli did not have to worry about that, Garreth reflected bitterly.

"See you around, man." Chiarelli slipped out the door.

Garreth continued to lean against the wall for several more minutes, then made his way slowly back to the site of the bust.

Seeing him coming, Harry exclaimed, "Garreth!" and rushed to catch his arm. "What happened? Are you all right?"

Garreth leaned against a handy car, holding his stomach. "Bastard ambushed me. I thought I was never going to make it up off that damned floor."

"So you let him get away, hot dog?" Woodhue said.

Several prisoners snickered. Garreth glared at them. "Next time I won't bother chasing him. I'll hobble the son of a bitch with a piece of lead ... permanently."

Harry helped him to a car. "Nice acting," he whispered.

Garreth climbed into the car, remembering Chiarelli's smirk. "Who the hell is acting?"

He sat silent all the way back downtown. Not until they had left the Narco officers and returned to Homicide did he give the notebook to Harry. "We'd better run these names through R and I, then find out who owns or lives in these houses."

Harry regarded him with concern. "Are you sure you're all right? Maybe you ought to go home and take it easy the rest of the day."

"I'm fine. We have work to do." He started to take off his coat and winced as the motion stretched bruised muscles.

Harry hustled him toward the door. "Go home. I'll tell Serruto what happened."

"I don't want to go home. I'll be fine," Garreth protested.

"No one who refuses time off can possibly be fine. I'm a sergeant, but you're just an inspector, so I'm pulling rank and ordering you out, hear? Or do I have to have someone take you in handcuffs?"

Garreth sighed. "I'll go quietly, papa-san."

He left Chiarelli's pages of his notebook with Harry and headed for his car. He slipped the key into the ignition but did not start the engine immediately. As much as he hurt, he hated the thought of going home. He ought to give up the apartment with all of its sweet and painful memories and find another. Perhaps one of those places around Telegraph Hill that Mrs. Armour had mentioned.

The thought of them told him what he really wanted to do. He wanted to see Lane Barber again, to talk to her by daylight and find answers for the increasing number of questions she raised about herself. Then he started the engine.

8

She did not come to the door until Garreth had rung the bell five times. He realized that she must be sleeping and would find his visit inconsiderate and inconvenient, but he remained where he stood, leaning on the bell. She finally opened the door, wrapped in a robe, squinting against the light, and he discovered that even by daylight, she looked nothing like a woman in her thirties. If anything, she seemed younger than ever, a sleepy child with the print of a sheet wrinkle across one pale, scrubbed cheek.

She scowled down at him. "You're that mick detective. What—" Then, as though her mind woke belatedly, her face smoothed. He watched her annoyance disappear behind a facade of politeness. "How may I help you, Inspector?"

Why did she bother to swallow justifiable irritation? Did police make her that nervous? Perhaps it was to observe this very reaction, to see what she might tolerate to avoid hassles, that he had persisted on the bell.

"I'm sorry to wake you," he lied. "I have a couple of important questions to ask."

She squinted at him from under the sunshade of her hand, then stepped back. "Come in."

Moving with the heavy slowness of someone fighting a body reluctant to wake up, she led the way to the living room. Heavy drapes shut out the afternoon light, leaving the room in artificial night. She switched on one lamp and waved him into its pool of light. She herself, however, sat in shadow in a suspended basket chair across from the chair by the lamp. A deliberate maneuver on her part?

"This couldn't wait until I got to the club?" Weariness leaked through the careful modulation of her voice.

"I'll be off duty by that time. I try not to work nights if I can help it; the police budget can't stand too much overtime."

"I see. Well, then, ask away, Inspector."

With her face only a pale blur beyond the reach of the light, Garreth found himself listening closely to her voice, to read her through it, and discovered with surprise that she did not sound like he felt she should. Inexplicably, the voice discorded with the rest of her.

"Can you remember what you and Mossman talked about Tuesday night?"

She paused before answering. "Not really. We flirted and made small talk. I'm afraid I paid little attention to most of it even while we were talking. Surely it isn't important."

"We're hoping that something he said can give us a clue to where he went after leaving the Barbary Now. Did he happen to mention any friends in the city?"

"He was far too busy arguing why we should become friends."

Suddenly Garreth realized why her voice seemed at odds with the rest of her. She did not talk like someone in her twenties. Where was the slang everyone else used? Just listening to her, she sounded more like his mother. What was that she had called him at the door? A mick. Who called Irishmen *micks* these days?

Garreth looked around, trying to learn more about her from the apartment, but could see little beyond the circle of lamplight. The illumination reached only to a Danish-style couch which matched his chair and a small desk with a letter lying on it.

He said, "He told you he was married, didn't he?"

"He wore a wedding ring. I could see that even in the Barbary Now's light."

"Of course." Garreth stood up and moved toward the door. "Well, it was a slim chance he'd say anything useful, I suppose. I'm sorry to have bothered you." On the way, he detoured by the desk to read the address on the letter. Knowing someone she wrote to might be useful.

"It's a price I pay for my unusual working hours." She stood and crossed to the lamp. "I'm sorry I couldn't help."

Garreth had just time enough to read the ornately written address before the light went out, leaving the room in darkness.

On the steps outside, after her door closed behind him, he reread the address in memory. The letter had to be incoming; it had this address. However, it had been addressed not to Lane Barber, but to Madelaine Bieber. The similarity of the two names struck him. Lane Barber could well be a stage name, "prettied up" from Madelaine Bieber.

He eyed the garage under the house as he came down the steps to the sidewalk. Did she drive or did she not?

He tried the door. Locked. However, by shining a flashlight from his car through the windows, he made out the shape of a car inside and illuminated the license plate. He wrote down the number.

Motion above him brought his attention up in time to see the drape fall back into place in the window over the garage. Lane, of course, watching him, but ... out of curiosity or fear? Maybe the license number would help provide an answer to that.

Back at Bryant Street, he ran Madelaine Bieber through R and I, and asked for a registration check on the license number.

"The car is registered to a Miss Alexandra Pfeifer," the clerk told him. The address was Lane's.

"Give me a license check on that name."

The picture from DMV in Sacramento looked exactly like Lane Barber. Miss Pfeifer was described as five ten, 135 pounds, red hair, green eyes, born July 10, 1956. Which would now make her twenty-seven.

Then R and I came back with a make on Madelaine Bieber. "One prior, an arrest for assault and battery. No conviction. The charges were dropped. Nothing since. She's probably mellowed with age."

Garreth raised a brow. "Mellowed with age?"

"Yeah," the records clerk said. "The arrest was in 1941."

Garreth had the case file pulled for him.

Madelaine Bieber, he read, had been singing in a club in North Beach called the Red Onion. A fight started with a female patron over a man, and when the woman nearly had her ear bitten off, she preferred charges against the singer. Miss Bieber, aka Mala Babra, was described as five ten, 140 pounds, red hair, green eyes. Birth date July 10, 1916. The picture in the file looked exactly like Lane Barber in a forties hairstyle.

Garreth stared at the file. If Lane were born in 1916, she was now sixty-seven years old. No amount of face-lifting would ever make her look twenty-one. This Bieber must be a relative, perhaps Lane's mother, which would explain the likeness and similar choice in professions. But why was Lane receiving her mother's mail? Perhaps the mother was a patient in a nursing home and the mail went to her daughter. It was something to check out. But another question remained: Why have a false driver's license and a car registered to that false license name?

Mystique? Lane generated nothing but, it seemed. The lady definitely deserved further attention.

9

At eight o'clock, when Lane came out through the curtains for her first song, Garreth sat at a table talking to a barmaid while he ordered a drink. "How long has she been singing here?"

The barmaid, whose name tag read *Nikki*, shrugged. "She was here already when I came last year."

"What do you think of her?"

Nikki sighed. "I wish I had her way with men. They fall all over themselves for her."

Lane worked her way through the club as she sang. On one turn, she saw Garreth. For a moment, her step faltered and a musical note wavered, then she smiled at him and moved on.

After the last song of the set, she came over to his table. "We meet again. I thought you weren't going to work overtime tonight."

He smiled. "I'm not. I'm here for pleasure. I'd also like to apologize again for disturbing you this afternoon."

She smiled back. "That isn't necessary; I realize you were only doing your job."

"Then may I buy you a drink?"

"Later, perhaps. Right now I've already promised to join some other gentlemen."

Nikki, passing the table, said, "Don't waste your time; you're not her type."

Garreth watched Lane sit down with three men in flashy evening jackets. "What *is* her type?"

"Older guys in their thirties and forties. Guys with bread to throw around. And her man of the evening is always a tourist, an out-of-towner. She only likes one-night stands."

Garreth recorded it all in his head. He asked casually, "Man of the evening? She lets herself be picked up often?"

"Almost every night, only *she* does the picking up. The suckers just think they picked her up."

"Really?" *Be an audience. Keep her going, Garreth, my man.*

"Really. She chooses one, see, and tells him to leave but that she'll meet him later. She never goes out the door with one of them."

"Then how do you know that's what happens?" He kept his voice teasing.

"Because," Nikki said, lowering her voice, "I've overheard her giving them instructions. She tells the guy that the boss is her boyfriend, see, and that he's very jealous, but then she tells the sucker he's turned her on so much, she's just *got* to see him. He leaves thinking he's really a superstud. Every night she tells a different guy the same thing."

"Always a different guy? No one ever repeats?"

Nikki shook her head. "Sometimes they try. She's polite, but she never goes with them again." Nikki sighed. "She must do something they really dig. I wonder if I should try the tigress bit, too."

"Tigress bit?" *You're doing great, honey; don't stop.*

"Yeah. If they come back for another try, the guys she's gone with always have this huge hickey on their necks. I've never—"

The whole world screamed to a halt for Garreth. He felt electricity lift the hair all over his body. "Hickey?" he asked breathlessly. "About this size and located here?" He demonstrated with a circle of thumb and finger.

The barmaid nodded.

She's dirty! But for a moment Garreth could not be sure whether he felt satisfaction or disappointment at proof of her involvement. Perhaps both. Wanted or unwanted, this gave him a legitimate excuse to ask all the questions of her he liked.

He gave Nikki a five-dollar bill. "For you, honey. Thanks."

He made his way to the table where Lane sat. Nodding to the three men with her, he said, "Sorry to interrupt, gentlemen, but I need to speak with the lady for a minute."

Lane smiled. "I said, later, perhaps."

"It can't wait."

One of the men frowned. "The lady said later. Bug off."

Ignoring him, Garreth leaned down to Lane's ear. "I can use my badge and make it official."

She glanced up sharply at him. Her eyes flared red in the candlelight again. Why did her eyes reflect when most people's did not? Garreth wondered. Lane stood, smiling at the men, cool and gracious. "He's right; it can't wait. I won't be a minute." As they walked away from the table, though, the tone of her voice became chiding. "So you're on duty after all. You lied, Inspector."

"So did you. You said you didn't see Mossman after he left the club on Tuesday, but we found him with a bruise on his neck just like the ones the girls here tell me you put on all your men."

She glanced around. "May we talk outside?"

They left the club. Outside, the street stretched away from them in both directions, glittering with the lights of signs and car headlights, smelling of exhaust fumes and the warmth of massed humanity. Like accents and grace notes, whiffs of perfume and male cologne reached them, too. Voices and cars blended into a vibrant roar. *My city*, Garreth thought.

Lane breathed deeply. "I do so love the vitality of this place."

Garreth nodded agreement. "Now, about Mossman ..."

"Yes, I saw him. What else could I do? He would have waked all the neighbors, pounding on my door that way. He got the address from the phone book."

"So you invited him in?"

She nodded. She strolled down the street and Garreth followed. "I invited him in," Lane said, "and then ... well, he was a charming man and ... we ended up in bed. He left about three, alive, I swear. But he insisted on walking, even though I warned him not to and offered to call a cab."

Garreth counted two possible flaws in the story. Three o'clock lay on the edge of the limits given by the M.E. for Mossman's time of death. He would have had to die very soon after leaving Lane's apartment. And would a man careful enough to leave his keys and extra money and credit cards hidden in his hotel room ignore the offer of a cab and walk down a street alone in the middle of the night?

They turned the corner. Once around it, the traffic thinned and the noise level dropped dramatically. Garreth asked, "Why didn't you tell me this before?"

She sighed sheepishly. "The usual reason: I didn't want to be involved."

"The autopsy found puncture wounds in the middle of the bruise on Mossman's neck. How did they get there?"

"Punctures?" She stared down at him. "I don't have the slightest idea. They weren't there when he left me."

Garreth said nothing in response to that. Instead, he waited, curious to see what more she might say to fill the conversation gap.

But unlike most people, who felt uncomfortable with silence and would say anything, often incriminating things, to avoid silence, she did not rise to the bait. She walked wordless beside him as they turned another corner.

Now almost no traffic passed. Garreth found himself preternaturally conscious of the near empty street. Here on the back side of the block, they seemed a hundred miles from the crowds and lights.

He asked, "Did you ever meet a man named Cleveland Adair?"

Her stride never faltered. "Who?"

"Cleveland Adair, an Atlanta businessman. We found him dead last year with a bruise and punctures just like Mossman's. A woman matching your description was seen in the lobby of his hotel shortly before his estimated time of death."

He expected denial, either vehement or indignant. He was even prepared for her to try running away. Instead, she stopped and turned to look him directly in the eyes. "How many deaths are you investigating?"

Her eyes looked bottomless and glowed like a cat's. Garreth stared into them, fascinated. "Two. After all, it looks like the same person killed them both."

"I suppose it does. Inspector," she said quietly, "please back up into this alley."

Like hell I will, he thought, but found he could not say it aloud. Nor could he act on the thought. Her eyes held his and his will seemed paralyzed. Step by step, as commanded, he moved backward, until he came up short against a wall.

"You're here alone." Her hands came up to his neck, loosening his tie and unbuttoning the collar of his shirt. Her hands felt cool against his skin. "Have you told anyone where you are or about my little love bites?"

Yes, he thought, but he spoke the truth. "No." Should he have admitted that? He could not find concern in him; all he cared about at the moment was staring into the glowing depths of her eyes and listening to her voice. "I haven't told anyone."

"Good boy," she crooned, and kissed him gently on the mouth. She had to bend down her head to do it. "That's a very good boy." Her voice dropped to a whisper. "I don't think you should ever tell."

He barely heard her. Her voice reached him from a great distance, like all sensation at the moment: the rough brick of the wall at his back, the chill of the evening, the increasing rate of her breathing. Somewhere deep inside, uneasiness stirred, but listening to it seemed too much trouble. He found it easier to just stand passive and let her tip his head back against the wall.

Her lips felt cool on his mouth and cheek, and her fingers on his neck as she probed to one side of his windpipe. His pulse throbbed against the pressure.

"That's a nice vein," she whispered in approval. Her breath tickled as she spoke between kisses. "You're going to like this. You'll feel no pain. You won't mind a bit that you're dying." She kissed him harder and he felt the nip of her teeth. Her mouth moved down over his jaw to his neck. "You're a bit short for me so this will be awkward unless you stand very still. Whatever happens, don't move."

"No." It emerged in a sigh.

"I love you, Inspector. I love all men of power." Her teeth nipped harder, moving toward the spot where his pulse beat against her fingers. "You don't have money or position like the others, but you have knowledge, knowledge I can't afford to have spread around, so that gives you more power than most of my lovers. Still, I have more. I have the power of death, and the power to take your power from you. I love doing that."

She bit harder. A distant sensation told him her teeth had broken his skin, but he felt no pain, only a slight pressure as she sucked.

"What—" he began.

Her finger brushed across his lips, commanding him to silence. He obeyed. All desire to talk had left anyway. A wave of mixed warmth and cold moved outward through his body from where her mouth touched him. He shivered in pleasure and moved just a little, straining toward her mouth. *Yes. Nice. Go on. Don't stop.*

Presently, though, he wondered if maybe she should. He felt very weak. He needed to sit down before he collapsed.

His knees buckled, but her hands caught him under the arms and held him against the wall. She must be very strong, a languid thought came through the tingling of his nerves … certainly stronger than she looked, to be holding up someone of his weight so easily. Dreamily he thought, *The maiden is powerful, just like the sage said.*

But with the thought of *I Ching* lassitude disappeared. Fear rose up through him like a jet of ice water. Two men the singer knew had died of blood loss. Now she kissed his neck in the very spot where the other men had had punctures and bruises and he felt himself weakening, too! With a profound shock of horror and revulsion, he realized why. Lane Barber was sucking his blood!

He shuddered and tried to pull loose, pushing at her shoulders with his hands. His body obeyed only sluggishly, however, and when she noticed his effort, her body pressed harder against his, pinning him to the wall.

Use your gun, you dumb flatfoot.

But her hand easily kept him from reaching it.

Abandoning pride in favor of self-preservation, he opened his mouth to yell for help. Her hand clamped across his mouth, silencing him.

Garreth's breath caught in fear. He did not have the strength to fight her. Only her weight against him held him upright. She was killing him, as she had killed Adair and Mossman—were human teeth really sharp enough to bite through skin into veins? Where had she learned such depravity?—and he could do nothing to stop her. He was dying, helpless to save himself.

In desperation, he bit at her hand to make her let go of his mouth. He sank his teeth in deep, using all his fading strength. Skin gave way. Her blood filled his mouth, burning like fire. Convulsively, he swallowed, and his throat burned, too ... but with the fire came a surge of new strength. Lane jerked the hand to free it, but he hung on, making the most of the opportunity to hurt her. More blood scorched down his throat. He managed to bring both hands up to her shoulders and push her back.

But it was too little effort coming too late. She tore loose from him, her hand from his mouth and her mouth from his throat. He felt her teeth rip through his flesh. As she backed away from him, he fell, collapsing to the ground.

The pain of striking the ground barely reached him. He only saw, not felt, the blood streaming from his torn throat to make a crimson pool around his head. A suffocating fog muffled all sensation ... touch, sound, and smells.

"Good-bye, lover," a distant, mocking voice said. "Rest in peace."

Her footsteps receded into the darkness. Garreth tried to move, to drag himself to the mouth of the alley where he might find help, but a leaden heaviness weighted him down, leaving him helpless. He could not move, only stare into the growing, cooling pool of blood. He cursed his stupidity ... for coming after her alone, for not letting someone know what he had found out, but most of all, as his breathing and heartbeat stumbled, faltered, and faded, he cursed himself for underestimating her ... just what *I Ching* warned against. How could he explain this to Marti when he saw her?

See the idiot cop, he thought bitterly. *See him bleeding to death ... dying alone in a cold and dirty alley.*

Passage

1

Rest in peace. Like hell. Death is not peace. It leads not to Marti, nor to any kind of heaven … not even to oblivion. Death is not that kind. Death is hell.

It is dreams … nightmares of suffocation and pain, of restless discomfort, of aches when one cannot move to ease them, of itches impossible to scratch. It is hallucination invading the void, playing blurrily before half-open eyes that are unable to focus or follow … imaginary hands on him, patting him, then lights, footsteps, sirens, voices. *Oh, God! Call the watch commandeer … I didn't kill him, Officer! I'd never kill no cop, and anyway how could I do that to him? I just took the gun and stuff out of his pockets. Would I show you where the body was if I'd done it? … Garreth? … Easy, Takananda. Garreth! Oh, God, no! … He hasn't been dead long; he's still warm … Are there loose dogs in this area?*

Death is hell, and hell is dreams, but mostly, hell is fear … panic stricken, frantic. Are all the dead aware? Do they remain that way? Is this to be eternity … lying in twilight and nightmares, throat aching with thirst, body crying for a change of position, mind churning endlessly? Does Marti lie like this in her grave, insane with loneliness, begging for peace, for an *end*? *No, not for her … please, no.*

He hates giving up life, but accepts that in the jungle, death is the price of carelessness, of error, and he has errored badly. Surrendering life to rejoin Marti would be welcome. He could even accept oblivion. This, though … this limbo? The thought of having to endure it for eternity terrifies him.

He screams … for himself, for Marti, for all the dead trapped sleepless and peaceless and tormented in their graves. He screams, and because it is without sound, unvoiced, it echoes and reechoes endlessly down the long, dark, lonely corridors of his mind.

2

The horror escalated. A sheet over him blocked the vision of his eyes; temperature had become all one to him, unfelt; and the lack of breath prevented him from smelling anything, but he knew he lay in the morgue. He had heard its cold echoes on arriving, had felt himself slid into a drawer and heard the door close. Now he heard, had lain listening for countless time, the hum of refrigeration units about him while he dreamed nightmares and wished Lane had thrown him in the bay, too. Maybe he would have gone out to sea. Better to be fish food than lie in this hated purgatory of cold and steel. He prayed his parents did not have to see him here.

That was when he thought of the autopsy. One would have to be done. His heart contracted in fear. What would it be like? How would it feel to lie naked in running water on cold steel, sliced open from neck to hips, shelled out like a pea pod ...

Heart!

He could not cease moving or hold his breath, but his mind paused, waiting. Yes, there it was! Like the distant boom of a drum, his heart sounded in his chest. It squeezed. A slow ripple moved outward from it along his arteries. He felt almost every inch of them. A long pause later, the drum beat again, then again.

He listened in wonder. If his heart beat, he could not be dead. His body lay leaden, held unmoving to the surface beneath him, but a silent cry of joy banished the darkness inside him. Alive!

He drew a breath ... slow, painfully slow, but a breath nonetheless.

He could have sworn he was not breathing before, nor his heart beating. He had felt—how he had felt!—the silence of his body. What miracle caused the heart and lungs to resume function? He could not imagine, and at the moment, overjoyed with the sound and feel of them, he did not give a damn about the reason.

But he remained in a morgue locker, naked in a refrigerated cabinet. Unless he found a way out, the cold would kill him again. Could he attract attention by pounding on the locker door?

He tried, but the weakness that had held him motionless the past—how many?—hours persisted. He still could not move.

Could he survive until they came to take him out for the autopsy?

He did not feel the cold of the locker right now. Perhaps if he kept alert, he could fight off hypothermia.

He wished, though, that he could change position. His body consisted of one continuous, unrelenting ache, stiff from neck to toes.

By concentrating and straining, he finally managed to move. Like the first heartbeat and the first breath, it came with agonizing slowness. Still, by persisting, he managed to shift his weight off his buttocks and turn on his side. Not that that helped a great deal; he still felt uncomfortable, but at least the position of the aches changed.

He tried again to knock on the locker door, but he moved in slow motion, and the sound he produced was barely audible even to him. He would just have to wait for them to open the door.

He fought his way onto his stomach to change the pressure points once more.

He did not sleep. Certainly he did not rest, but in spite of himself, he must have dozed because the motion of the drawer sliding out startled him. He had not heard the door open. Light flooded him blindingly as the sheet came off.

"What clown put this stiff in on his belly?" a voice demanded irritably.

If he raised upright, would they faint? Garreth wondered. He wished he could find out, but gravity dragged at him, weighting him. He went without resistance as they rolled him onto the stretcher and rearranged the sheet over him.

"Hurry," another voice said. "This one's a cop and Thurlow wants to get him posted as soon as possible."

Garreth worked his hands to the edges of the stretcher and clamped his fingers around the rubber bumper. Even if he could not move fast enough to attract their attention and they missed the faint motion of his chest, they could hardly overlook this.

The stretcher stopped. An attendant pulled off the sheet. Hands took him by the shoulders and legs and pulled ... but Garreth's grip held him on the stretcher.

"What the hell is going on?" snapped the voice of the medical examiner.

"I don't know, Dr. Thurlow. His hands weren't like that when we put him on the gurney."

Now that he had their attention, Garreth forced open his eyes. Half a dozen gasps sounded around him. He focused on Dr. Edmund Thurlow. "Please." The whisper rasped up out of his throat with a plea from his soul. "Get me out of here."

3

Were the doctors at the far end of the intensivecare unit speaking in unusually loud voices? Garreth wondered. He heard every word clearly.

"I tell you he was dead," Thurlow insisted. "I detected no vital
signs, no heartbeat or respiration, and his pupils were fixed and dilated."

"I think it's obvious he couldn't have been dead," another doctor said. "However, that's beside the point now. The question is, can we
keep him alive? His blood pressure is nonexistent and we have brady-
cardia as well as a reduced temperature and respiration rate."

"Well, he's getting blood just as fast as we can pour it into him.
We'll just keep running bloodwork on him and see how he does."

Garreth looked up at the suspended plastic bag with its contents
the same dark red as Lane Barber's hair. His eyes followed the tubing
down to his arm. The blood made him feel better, but still not good.
Exhaustion dragged at him. He desperately wanted to sleep, but he could
not find a comfortable position, no matter how he shifted and turned.

"What about the throat injury?" a doctor asked.

"I think the skin sutures we put in will be sufficient," came the
reply. "The trauma doesn't appear nearly as severe as what you described, Dr. Thurlow."

"We have photographs of what I saw." Thurlow's voice sounded
defensive. "Both the left jugular and common carotid suffered multiple
lacerations, almost to the point of complete severing. There were also
multiple lacerations of the trachea and left sternocleidomastoid muscles."

"And yet just over twelve hours later the vessels and trachea
appear intact. The muscle is healing, too. I can't believe that this is a
recent injury."

"I don't pretend to understand it; I only know what I found when
I examined him in the alley."

They went on talking, but Garreth tried to ignore them. Careful
not to move the arm with the needle in it, he shifted position again. The
cardiac monitor above his bed registered the effort with an extra bleep.
Moving proved pointless, however. Nothing made him comfortable. His
bed stood near the window, and the glare of sunlight added to his discomfort.

Footsteps approached. If it was the nurse, he decided, he would beg for something to drug him to sleep. Then he smiled weakly as Harry and Lieutenant Serruto appeared around the curtain.

"Hi," he whispered.

"Mik-san," Harry replied in a husky voice. His hand closed hard over Garreth's.

Serruto said, "They're letting us ask you a few questions."

"Yes. What the hell were you doing up there?" Harry demanded. "I'm your partner. Why don't you tell me what you're doing?"

"Easy, Harry," Serruto said.

Garreth did not mind. He heard the frantic worry beneath the anger and knew how he would have felt in Harry's place. "Sorry."

"What happened?" Serruto asked.

Talking hurt. Garreth tried to find a short answer. Reaching up to the heavy collar of bandages around his throat, he managed to whisper, "Lane Barber bit me."

They stared. "*She* bit you! Did she overpower you or what?"

How could he explain the loss of will that allowed her to stand him passively against a wall and tear his throat out? Damn, that light hurt. He shut his eyes.

"Please. Close the curtains. Sun's too bright."

"There's no sun," Harry said in a tone of surprise. "We've been socked in with heavy fog since midnight."

Garreth opened his eyes again in astonishment. Noises that sounded overly loud and light that hurt his eyes ... bleeding to death produced one hell of a hangover. But to his relief, Harry closed the curtains. It helped a little.

"Lane bit Mossman and Adair," he said with an effort. "Drank their blood."

"Christ!" Harry shuddered. "The barmaid thought Barber might be kinky, but she's really bent."

Barmaid? Garreth did not ask the question, but he raised his brows in query.

Serruto explained. "We went around to the Barbary Now. Harry thought that you might have been there. The barmaid told us what you two talked about."

If that was so, Harry must have made the same connections *he* had. He looked questioningly at Harry. Harry sighed, shaking his head, indicating to Garreth that they had not arrested Lane.

"She's skipped," Serruto said. "Caught a plane to be at her mother's bedside, she told the manager."

Harry said, "Something spooked her. When she came to work, she told the manager that she might have to leave suddenly. She'd even arranged for another singer to come in. After her walk with you, she sang a second set, then made a phone call—to her family, she told the manager—and said she had to leave."

Garreth's visit had spooked her. She saw him taking down the license number of the car. "Search her apartment?"

They nodded. "Nothing," Serruto said. "No personal papers in the desk or trash. Some had been burned in the fireplace. The lab is seeing what they can recover from them. Refrigerator and cupboards bare. A closet full of clothes, so she didn't take much with her. The manager has no idea where her mother might live."

A nurse pulled back the bed curtains. "Lieutenant, that's enough for now." When Serruto frowned, she slid between him and the bed and herded both the lieutenant and Harry away.

Harry called back, "Lien sends her love. She'll visit as soon as it's allowed."

When they were gone, the nurse moved around the bed, tucking in sheets. "For someone so weak, you're a restless sleeper."

For the first time in his life. "I'm not comfortable. May I have a sleeping pill?"

"Absolutely not. We can't allow anything that depresses body functions." She leaned across him, pulling up the covers. As she did so, the smell of her filled his nostrils … a pleasant mixture of soap and fabric softener and something with an odd but strangely attractive metallic/salty scent. "A bit later I'll send an aide to give you a back rub. That may help."

The aide, when she came, gave a good back rub, but not even that helped. The sheets felt hot and sticky every place they touched him. He twisted in vain looking for a cool spot.

But though he could not make himself comfortable, he felt better with each unit of blood put into him. The dragging weight of his body lightened and he moved with less effort. A thirst that had persisted all day turned into strident hunger and he looked forward eagerly to supper.

An eagerness which suffered sharp disappointment when he saw the broth, gelatin, and tea they allowed him. "I don't get real food?" He thought longingly of fried rice and Lien's sweet-and-sour pork.

"We don't want to strain your circulation by making it work at digestion."

Maybe *we* did not, but *he* would not have minded. Then again, perhaps he would. After eating, his stomach churned uneasily, as though debating whether to keep the offering or not. Garreth lay quiet, willing the nausea away. Could this be part of last night, or was it an aftermath of Chiarelli's punch?

At length, the nausea subsided ... and Garreth discovered he felt much better. Full of new blood and a symbolic meal, he felt surprisingly normal. Though he still needed sleep, he found some of the aches had subsided. He wished he had a TV to watch.

A doctor appeared later in the evening, introducing himself as Dr. Charles. Garreth recognized one of the voices from the group that morning.

"You're looking much better, Inspector. I'm very pleased with your blood picture. Now, let's check a few things."

He used a stethoscope and rubber hammer and tongue depressor, listening, peering, tapping, probing. While he worked, he hummed. Occasionally the hum changed key, but Garreth could not tell if that had any significance or not. What he did notice was the same metallic/salty odor about the doctor that he had noticed on the nurse, and the aides, too, come to think of it. Did they all wear the same antiperspirant or something?

"Oh, you're doing much better. What you need now is a good night's sleep, and if you're doing this well in the morning, we'll move you out of Intensive Care," the doctor said.

Garreth, however, did not feel the least like sleeping now. He wanted a TV or visitors. Lacking both, he could only lie in bed listening to the heart monitors bleeping in ragged syncopation around the room. He closed his eyes, but opened them again when his mind began replaying the nightmare in the alley. Where had she learned that perversion?

Why did they keep Intensive Care lighted so brightly at night? he also wondered. There was enough light to read by. How could anyone sleep in a glare like this?

He still lay awake when dawn came, and then, astonishingly, for what must be the first time in his life, the first rays of the sun were followed by an intense desire *to* sleep. Only he could not. Just as suddenly, he rediscovered all of yesterday's aches. The sheets heated up and Garreth found himself once more in a ceaseless hunt for a comfortable position. Worse, when breakfast came, his stomach voted against it. It came back up almost as soon as it went down.

On his morning rounds, Dr. Charles frowned gravely about that. Garreth told him about Chiarelli.

"We'll schedule for a barium series tomorrow and see about your stomach."

In the meantime, they fed him intravenously. He lay with clear liquid running into one arm and blood—after the morning bloodwork, they decided he needed still more blood—into the other. He would look like a junkie by the time they dismissed him, he reflected.

The air filled with that metallic/salty scent, stronger than ever. Only this time, none of the staff were around him. Sniffing out the source, Garreth discovered that it came from the tube feeding blood into his arm.

The hair on his neck stirred. *That* was what he was smelling, *blood?* He smelled the blood in people? Why now, when he never had before? He shivered uneasily. Weird. What was happening to him?

Before he had a chance to answer the questions about himself, Serruto arrived with a stenographer to ask official ones. Those seemed to go on forever, though objectively he knew the lieutenant made it a relatively short statement. After Serruto left, Garreth was moved to a private room and then left to sleep. He wished he could. He felt exhausted, and ready to cry in frustration at being unable to sleep.

Garreth did not even attempt to eat lunch. The mere scent of it set his stomach lurching.

Lien came for a short visit in the afternoon. "You look terrible," she said, "but at least you're alive. I had a frantic call from your mother yesterday morning."

Garreth's stomach tightened. "They'd heard about me on the news?"

"No, it hadn't been broadcast yet. She said your grandmother dreamed you'd been killed, that Satan tore out your throat." Lien paused. "It's uncanny, isn't it?"

But typical of Grandma Doyle.

"Unfortunately, at that time we thought you *were* dead. The happiest phone call I've ever made was the one later to let her know you were alive after all. She said to tell you they'll be up in a couple of days to visit."

He would like that. Maybe Judith would let them bring Brian, too.

Lien chattered about her job and art classes, relieving him of the necessity of saying anything. While she talked, she distracted him from his discomfort, but once she had left, he went back to fighting aches and hot sheets. To make matters worse, his upper gums started to hurt for no reason.

He eyed the cushioned chair by the window. That might be a helpful change; it would be a change anyway. So he threw back the covers and eased over the side of the bed.

In two steps he had fallen flat on his face, giving himself a bloody nose and—he discovered with horror—loosening his upper canines. They wiggled when he touched them with his tongue. He was trying to crawl back into bed when an aide found him.

Dr. Charles wasted no time being polite or solicitous. "That was a stupid thing to do. In the first place, you're not ready to get out of bed, and when I decide you are—when *I* decide, Inspector—you will be helped in and out. Under no circumstances are you to do it alone. I presume that as a police officer you know how to take orders. Well, I'm giving you one. *Stay in bed.* Do *nothing* without asking permission first. Is that clear?"

Garreth shrank back meekly into the bed. "Yes, sir."

"Good. We have the barium study scheduled for you tomorrow. A dentist will check your teeth as well." He stalked out.

Toward evening Garreth managed to doze some, but he never really slept, never truly rested. With nightfall, though, he felt better, just like the night before. The desire to sleep vanished, though he remained tired. He turned on the TV.

A nurse, coming in to check his vital signs, turned it off. "Dr. Charles wants you to sleep."

As soon as she left, however, he switched the set back on, keeping the volume as low as he possibly could and still hear. That proved to be very low indeed. It seemed that his sharpened hearing was persisting. He also used that hearing to listen for nurses in the corridor, so that he could shut off the set before they caught him with it on.

After midnight, Channel 9 started its *Friday Fright Night* feature, three horror movies in a row. Garreth settled back to watch, as he often had since Marti died. However melodramatic, the movies diverted him. Tonight's offerings began with *Dracula.* He sighed. How appropriate. His entire life these days seemed to revolve around blood, or the lack of it.

Into the movie, with everyone worrying about Miss Lucy's mysterious wasting disease, Garreth reflected that his one complaint with these shows was the way the characters waded up to their necks in clues and yet never realized they had a werewolf, demon, or vampire loose among them. On the other hand, perhaps that was reasonable. In a real-life reaction to such a situation, no one would guess, either. They would hunt for a rational explanation and refuse to accept anything less. Like with Miss Lucy. They thought the broach on the shawl caused the punctures on her neck. No real-life person would consider a vampire bite as—

The thought ended in a paralysis as though he lay in the morgue again, without heartbeat or breath. He could not move, only stare unseeing at the TV screen with mind churning. No, that was impossible. It was a *crazy* thought! *I'm losing my mind*, he thought. Lane Barber might be psychotic and a killer, but a human one, certainly. Nothing more or less. How could she be anything else?

So she slept all day. She worked nights. If she kept no food in her apartment, perhaps she hated to cook and always ate out. She bit men she made love to and some of them died, but two men with punctures in their bruises did not mean punctures in every bruise.

On the TV, Miss Lucy slathered in bloodlust, turned vampire by Dracula's bite.

Thirst started to burn in Garreth's throat and he reached involuntarily for the bandage around his neck. No. He jerked his hands away. *That really is impossible!* If every vampire bite made a vampire, the world would be hip-deep in the breed. Look at all the men Lane had bitten.

He turned off the TV with a decisive stab of his finger. The blood loss must be affecting his mind. Vampires did *not* exist. He had no insatiable urge to bite the nurses, did he, despite his thirst and their attractive blood sent? He had not developed a desire to don a black opera cape and take the form of a bat. He just happened to feel better at night.

But cold continued to run up and down his spine, and knots worked uneasily along his gut.

Anger flared in him. This was nonsense! He would end it once and for all. Easing out of bed, he groped his way to the bathroom and peered into the mirror. The face he saw every morning while he shaved stared back at him.

There. Satisfied? Everyone knew vampires did not make reflections. Moreover, barring the drawn appearance and pale color, his square face looked exactly as always. His canines, though sore and loose from his fall this afternoon, looked no longer than usual.

Then he realized he had not turned on the light.

He quickly flipped up the switch ... and wished he had not. The eyes in the mirror, perceived before as normal gray, now reflected the light as Lane's had, flaring red ... fire red, blood red, hell red.

Garreth slammed down the switch in a spasm of panic and clutched the edge of the washbowl for support, trembling. No! This was insane. Impossible!

And yet ...

He sat down on the closed lid of the toilet. And yet, how was it that he, who always woke with the sun, now felt better at night? Why could he see in the dark? Why did he smell the blood in people and throw up solid food? On the other hand, if he had become—

He could not finish the thought. It stumbled and died before a new flood of panic. *Run!* a voice screamed inside him. *Run!*

It brought him off the toilet and to the bathroom door, where he clung to the jamb, breathing hard. He had to get out of here. There was a logical explanation for everything but he needed somewhere to think. Somewhere quiet. He could not do it in this place with its reek of blood and voices shouting up and down the halls and interns and nurses coming in all the time to poke and prod him.

How to get out, though? While they could not keep him against his will, demanding to be released in the middle of the night might make them consider him irrational. He could not just walk out without clothes.

But he had to get away somehow!

Shaking, he made his way back to the bed and pulled the call-light cord.

"May I help you?" a female voice asked from the speaker above the call light.

"I need to go to the bathroom. Will you send an orderly to help me, please?"

A female aide appeared a few minutes later, not an orderly. She opened the cabinet beside his bed.

"Please, not the urinal," Garreth said. "I can't use that thing. I feel much better. Can't you let me use the bathroom if someone takes me there?"

"I'll see," the aide replied, and left.

While Garreth waited, crossing mental fingers, he ripped the draw sheet on his bed into several long strips and wrapped them around his waist under his hospital gown. When the door opened again, he smiled in relief at the brawny orderly.

"You're sure you want to try this?" the orderly asked.

Garreth nodded. He had no trouble making the gesture sincere.

"Okay." Putting an arm around Garreth, the orderly supported him getting out of bed and walking across the room.

The orderly's cheerfulness stabbed Garreth with guilt. He consoled himself with the thought that if all went right, no one would be hurt.

The orderly left him in the bathroom. Garreth waited a few minutes, running the water, then sat down on the floor and called for help.

The orderly hurried in. "Did you fall? Are you hurt?"

"Help me up, please."

As the orderly leaned over to do so, Garreth threw an arm around the muscular neck and tightened down. The orderly collapsed flat on the floor in Garreth's neck lock.

"I don't want to hurt you," Garreth said, "but if you don't shuck your shirt and pants in one minute, you're going to have the biggest pain of your life in your neck."

"Mr. Mikaelian, you—" the orderly began in protest.

"Take off the shirt and pants," Garreth said.

It was not easy with both of them lying on the floor, but the orderly managed. Garreth tied his hands with the strips from the draw sheet, gagged him with another strip and a washcloth, and tied him to the pipes of the washbowl, out of reach of the call-light cord beside the toilet. Then Garreth changed into the orderly's clothes, rolling up a cuff to shorten the trousers to his length. He helped himself to the orderly's shoes and socks.

"I'm sorry about this, but I want a quicker discharge than I think the doctor is willing to give me. At least I'm leaving you your skivvies. I'll see the other clothes are sent back."

The orderly sighed in combined disgust, anger, and bewilderment.

Garreth walked out, shutting off the light and closing the bathroom door.

No one looked twice at him in the corridor. He took the elevator down and walked out of the building without once being challenged. On the street he hailed a cab. The resolution that let him walk without staggering ran out. He slumped back in the seat.

"Hey, buddy, you okay?" the cabbie asked

Oh, God. The cabbie smelled of blood, too, though with the reek of sweet and cigar nearly overwhelming it. The combination sent waves of nausea through him. "I'm fine."

The fifteen-minute ride home seemed interminable. Keeping the cab waiting, he unlocked the door with his hidden spare key and went in to change clothes. A sweater with a turtleneck reaching almost to his ears hid the bandage on his throat. He clipped his off-duty Charter Arms Undercover .38 on his belt, then dropped the extra set of car keys and his bank card into the pocket of a sports jacket. He had to endure another ride in the cab to his bank's automatic teller and one last one to the lot where he had parked the ZX.

It was with relief that he paid off the cabbie, adding some extra money along with the orderly clothes. "See that these reach an orderly named Pechanec at General will you?"

Then he was free, on his own. He started the car. But he hesitated before backing out of the parking slot. Where did he go now? "On his own," it occurred to him, this time meant alone ... very, very alone.

4

Garreth drove blindly, not caring where he went. Some place would feel right, and there he would stop, and think. Rational answers he had overlooked before would become apparent. Then perhaps he could make the terrified child within him realize that there was nothing to run from, nothing to be frightened of.

Eventually he found himself in a deserted parking lot, but it was with shock that he looked up and recognized Mount Davidson. The white cross atop the hill loomed above him, his strange new night vision seeing it luminous with icy fire against the night sky.

Relief and triumph followed surprise. This proved his imaginings false. How could he possibly have come to a place like this if he had ... changed.

Climbing out of the car, he made his way up the slope toward the cross. Still no terrible agony engulfed him. If anything, each step made him feel better. Sitting on the ground at the base brought sheer relief, with all the aches of the past several days draining away.

Garreth stretched out full length and buried his face in the grass. The earth felt delicious, so cool, so clean and sweet-smelling. Funny. He had never liked sleeping on the ground as a kid on scouting campouts, but now it felt better than any bed, certainly better than that torture rack at the hospital. What a joy it would be to just to continue lying here, to pull the earth over him and sleep forever.

Pull the earth— He sat bolt upright, shaking, horror and gut-wrenching fear flooding back. *What the hell are you thinking, man!* He really was going wacko. He had better take himself back to the hospital before his delusions had him jumping some unsuspecting jogger.

But Garreth could not make himself move, even though he suddenly felt as though his presence defiled the hill. The earth drew him. It even soothed the thirst growing more ravenous by the hour. The sun, he decided. He would wait for the sun. If nothing happened when it rose, there was nothing wrong with him except that he had gone bananas and needed a room at the funny farm. And if—well, it would be a clean end with no one having to know what a foul thing he had become.

Garreth crossed his legs, folded his hands in his lap, and waited.

Eventually the sky lightened.

His heart pounded. Feeling it, he scolded himself. *Don't be a fool. Nothing's going to happen.* But his heart continued to slam against the wall of his chest while the sky grew brighter. Pulses throbbed in his aching, burning throat, in his arms, legs and temples.

The upper rim of the sun appeared over the horizon. Garreth braced himself. A beam of light lanced westward to the great white cross above him. He fought an urge to bury his face in his hands and made himself lift his chin to meet the sun

There was no agony, no searing dissolution. The light burned through his eyes, however, turning the throb in his temples to a pounding headache. A great weight pressed down on him, draining his strength, dragging at his limbs. The earth beckoned to him, called him to the sweet coolness that would shut out this miserable, blinding, exhausting sun—

"No!" He lurched to his feet. "Damn you!" he shouted at the sun. "Kill me! You're supposed to kill me. Please! I won't be—*that!*" He screamed into the terrible blood-red sky of dawn. "I won't be! No! No! NO!" Screamed in fury and despair, over and over and over.

Garreth could not recall running down Mount Davidson or fishing trooper glasses from the glove compartment of the car and gunning the ZX out of the parking lot, but he found himself driving again, with mirror lenses hiding the eyes of his image in the rearview mirror. Driving where, though? He slowed down, groping for orientation. And slowed still more as a patrol car passed him going the other direction. He carried no driver's license; that sat in the Property Room along with the rest of his billfold contents, state's exhibits.

A street sign finally told him where he was. From that he guessed where his reflexes were taking him: Lien ... who had kept him sane the last time his life came crashing down around him.

Garreth parked the car around the corner at the end of the block Harry did not pass on the way to work and followed the narrow footpath between the backyards to the Takananda gate. Slipping over, he sat down behind the big oak tree shading the flagstoned patio and settled against the trunk to wait.

From inside the house came the sounds of morning: a shrill electronic beeping of the alarm clock, running water, the murmur of voices. The telephone rang. Harry's voice rose. Moments later the front door slammed and the motor of the car roared to life. Tires squealed around the corner at the far end of the block.

Garreth pushed to his feet and came around the tree onto the patio.

Lien saw him from the kitchen. Her almond eyes went wide. "Garreth!" She ran out of the house to him. "What on earth are you doing?"

He managed a wry smile. "Visiting."

Her eyes flashed. "Don't lie to me, Garreth Doyle Mikaelian! Harry just had a call about you. Come in this minute and sit down! You look ready to fall on your face."

He followed her gladly and dropped into the closest chair.

She sat on the hassock in front of him, frowning in exasperation and concern. Her nearness brought a warm wash of bath-talcum scent overlying that of blood. "Why did you run away from the hospital?"

He could give a half-truthful answer. "I couldn't eat their food or sleep in their bed. I wanted out."

She stared. "Have you lost—" She broke off to resume in a patient voice, "Garreth, you almost *died*. You're in no condition to be going anywhere. You need medical care. Come on; I'll drive you back."

She started to rise.

Garreth reached out to catch her wrist. "No! I can't go back. I—I'm—" But the words caught in his throat. He could not tell her about the hateful thing he had become. Hell ... he could not even say the words to himself. Thank God for the glasses so she could not see the animal glow of his eyes. "Lien, I have to sleep and I haven't been able to since I went into that place. Let me stay here today, and promise you won't tell anyone where I am, not even Harry. Please!"

She stared from his face to her wrist and said softly, "Garreth, you're hurting me."

He let go as though stung. *Shit*. "Damn! I'm sorry."

Lien rubbed the marks left on her wrist by his fingers. "I never knew you were so strong. Garreth ...

How could he be so thoughtless? He had seen some of his strength when wrestling the orderly. "I didn't realize—I never meant—I'm sorry," he said miserably.

"Garreth!"

He looked at her.

She patted his arm. "You can stay on one condition. That you do nothing but rest. Do you promise?"

He nodded.

She smiled. "Fortunately it's Saturday and I don't have to work, so you won't be alone. Harry went off without breakfast. Would you like his waffles?"

His throat burned with hunger but the thought of waffles brought a spasm of nausea. He grimaced. "I'm not hungry."

Lien frowned at him "Garreth, you—" Then she sighed. "All right. Now get yourself into bed in the guest room."

A bed. He would never be able to sleep on a bed. "I'd rather sleep out on the patio."

"Patio!" she said in horror. "It's chilly out there."

"Please. I can't breathe in here."

His desperation must have shown in his voice. Her forehead furrowed but she made no further protests even when he passed the lounge chair to lie down on the grass well in the shade of the tree. His last conscious sensation was of Lien covering him with something.

5

He slept, but not in oblivion. Garreth dreamed ... frantic, terrifying dreams ... of the alley and Lane tearing out his throat, of being Gerald Mossman, split open and shelled out on an autopsy table, of chasing joggers through Golden Gale Park and tearing out *their* throats to gulp down the salty fire of their blood. He fled from the murders, running back through the park to the Conservatory. Inside, though, it had become a library. Titles of the books glared from the spines in pulsating red lettering: *Dracula, The Rise and Fall of the Roman Vampire, Foundation and Vampire, The Vampire Strikes Back.*

Spinning away from the stacks in revulsion, he found himself among s group of children sketching bats and wolves under Lien's direction. He started to back away but Lien caught his arm and, pushing him down in a chair, cradled his head against her chest.

"Hush, Garreth, hush." She rocked slightly, stroking his hair as he remembered her doing once after Marti died. "The superior man doesn't panic. Let's try studying this thing calmly. Look." She released him and began two lists on her sketch pad. "It's obvious that everything legends say about vampires isn't true. Yes, you rest best on earth, you smell and crave blood, and something is happening to your teeth. On the other hand, while daylight is uncomfortable and debilitating, it doesn't kill you. There's no nonsense with mirrors, either. That would violate physical laws. The subject needs more research, but perhaps *most* of the legend is false. Maybe you don't have to stop being the person you are, the person Harry and I love. Once your basic needs of rest and food are met, why shouldn't you be able to go on living your life as you always have? Do you understand, Garreth?" Her voice rose, became more insistent. "Garreth?"

That was a real voice, not a dream. He opened his eyes, waking as he had all his life, from sleep to awareness in a breath. That, at least, had not changed. The sky showed crimson through the tree above him and Lien knelt at his side with an expression of relief.

"You're the soundest sleeper I've ever seen," she said. "I don't think you moved all day. I couldn't even see you breathe. I kept coming out to make sure you were still alive." She paused. "Did you know it's almost impossible to feel your pulse? Your skin is cold, too. Garreth, please, *please*, let me take you back to the hospital."

He sat up stiffly, groping for the dream. An exploring tongue found his teeth looser. Had the dream Lien been right? Could he go on being the same person? "Isn't Harry home yet?"

"He called to say he'd be late. They're turning the city upside down looking for you."

Garreth flushed at the reproach in her voice. "Thanks for not giving me away."

"You needed the rest." She stood. "Come inside. It's freezing out here."

It did not seem so to him.

"What do you think you can stomach for supper?"

His throat burned. A cramp contracted his stomach. He let it pass before answering. "Just tea, please."

She turned around sharply. "This is ridiculous. You have to eat! Are you trying to kill yourself?"

Maybe that would be best. Dreams were often just dreams. He did not want to think about eating. "Please, Lien."

She fixed the tea and stood with arms folded, watching him sip it. "If you won't go back to the hospital, at least show up at Bryant Street long enough to let them know you're alive so they can go back to hunting people who deserve it."

He hated lying to her. He did it anyway. "All right. I'll turn myself in to Harry."

She hissed in exasperation. "Don't be childish. It isn't like that and you know it."

"I'm sorry." The tea curbed none of his hunger, none of the thirst, but at least its warmth soothed the cramps. He stood, clipped on his gun, and put on his coat.

Lien followed him to the door. "Please take care of yourself."

He hugged her. "I will. Thanks for everything. You're a super lady."

Picking up the car from around the corner, he drove to the public library in the Civic Center. The subject needed research, his dream Lien had said. From the books containing information on the vampire legend, he chose some half a dozen and after skimming them, copied a number of pages to study over multiple cups of tea in an all-night cafe. It went fine as long as he considered the information just research, as long as he did not think of it as applying to him personally. Once he let awareness seep in, though, all the horror, the dread, returned in an icy flood. His hands shook so much he could not hold either cup or papers.

It all seemed so preposterous, a nightmare. If only he would wake up. Or consider it just a delusion born of the trauma of Lane's attack.

He humored the delusion and resumed reading, still shaking. There appeared to be two kinds of vampires, those like Dracula who walked around talking and reasoning, and the zombies like Miss Lucy, mindless, dripping dirt and graveclothes, driven only by their lust for blood. Lucy had been bitten by Dracula, but he, like Mina Harker, had swallowed some of his attacker's blood in turn. Did that make the difference?

A question none of the reading answered, however, was why Lane let him live. She had broken Adair's and Mossman's necks to destroy their nervous system and prevent them from rising again. Why had she not done the same for him?

"Inspector Mikaelian?"

He started. A uniformed officer smiled down at him. "I saw your car out front. We've been looking for you."

It had been only a matter of time. Moving unhurriedly, Garreth folded the copied pages and slipped them into the inside pocket of his sport coat. "What are you supposed to do when you find me?"

"We've already called Lieutenant Serruto in Homicide."

Garreth stood. "Am I under arrest?"

The officer looked young. His eyes widened in shock. "Oh, no, Inspector. It's just an Attempt to Locate. You need medical treatment, the bulletin said."

"I don't, but doctors have to play God. Let's go."

They waited in the parking lot for Serruto. He arrived with Harry driving. The lieutenant did not bother getting out of the car, just rolled down the window. "Give one of the uniforms your car keys, Mikaelian. Drive the car to the lot at Bryant Street," he told the uniformed officers, "and leave the keys on my desk in Homicide. Get in, Mikaelian."

Garreth debated trying to run. Even fasting, he bet he could still outrun the rest of them. He weighed that against the suspicion bolting might raise.

"Get in," Serruto repeated in a voice with steel beneath it.

Garreth climbed in the back seat, eyes on the nonfunctional handle of the door closing behind him. Trapped!

"Thanks," Serruto told the officer, and then, as the car left the parking lot, "You monopolized a lot of manpower hours, Mikaelian."

Garreth slunk down in the seat, flushing guiltily.

"Mind telling me the meaning of this stunt?"

Wishing he sounded less defensive, Garreth said, "I don't like hospitals. I felt better but didn't think they would believe me."

"Really?" Harry said. "Lien called. She told me you were almost comatose all day."

"I won't go back to the hospital."

Serruto turned around on the seat to face Garreth. "We can raise a charge of assault to confine you if need be."

Garreth dug his nails into the palms of his hands. *Be cool, man. Vampires can hypnotize with a look.* Do it. He looked Serruto straight in the eyes, trying to remember what Lane had done to him. "I don't look sick to you, do I?"

Serruto stared back, eyes widening, then said in a flat voice, "No. What do you want to do, then? You can't come back on duty without an okay from a doctor."

"I know. I just want to rest at home for a few days. Then I'll go back for a checkup and let them run their blood tests or whatever." He continued to hold Serruto's eyes.

"All right. You have sick leave at home."

"Ah ... could you arrange a new ID card and badge for me, and a temporary driver's license until I can replace the one in the evidence locker?"

"See me Tuesday about it."

Garreth bit his lip to keep from grinning. It worked!

"Why don't you stay at our place?" Harry asked. "We have a guest room."

That would not do at all. "I'd rather be home."

But Serruto had turned around again and was out of Garreth's influence. "You go to Takananda's tonight or we charge you with assault and take you to the hospital."

Garreth made himself smile. "Yes, sir."

6

Garreth did not really sleep. He felt anything but sleepy and he wanted to be sure he was awake before Harry and Lien, so that he could sneak back inside. Sleeping outdoors during the day was one thing; discovering that he had slept out in a chilly night, even when he did not feel the cold, would disturb them. He rested, though—reminded of the times he had gone camping as a Boy Scout, except that this time he felt comfortable instead of wanting an air mattress between him and the ground—and while he rested, he considered solutions for the sleeping situation. A coffin was ridiculous, but he did need some kind of container for a layer of earth.

He sat up, thinking again of the Boy Scouts. An air mattress might work. As soon as possible, he would leave here and try it out.

In the morning he played with the eggs and toast Lien fixed for him, managing to look like he was eating without actually doing so. He drank only sugared tea and took the vitamins she forced on him.

"Since Harry is on duty today," she said, "will you come to church with me?"

The knot in his stomach came not from hunger this time—he no longer felt hunger, only lightheaded euphoria, a common feeling brought on by fasting, he remembered Marti telling him once—but from fear. Church! Well, he might as well find out how it affected him.

"Of course I'll go."

Lien drove. Garreth sat with his hands clenched in the pockets of his coat, his eyes hidden from her and the sun by the mirror-lensed trooper glasses. He could not remember the last time he had actually felt religious, though he still went to church with his mother and grandmother when he visited home. He had gone regularly as a child, sandwiched with Shane between his mother and Grandma Doyle, where he could be thumped on the head with a grandmotherly knuckle if he wiggled too much.

Lien's church was Roman Catholic, but it reminded him of the Episcopal one at home. Garreth could not shake the conviction that he should not be here, but sitting beside Lien, he felt no pain other than that of guilt. Lien touched him with holy water coming in and it did not burn. Would it if he had grown up Catholic? If anything, the light coming through the stained-glass windows and the rhythm of the Mass gave him a kind of peace. He had a feeling that if the tall priest had looked more like Father Michaels—a small, round, laughing man who smelled pleasantly of pipe tobacco and was continually relighting that pipe at the coffee period following Morning Prayer, from a seemingly inexhaustible supply of kitchen matches in the pocket of his black coat—Garreth would have been tempted to confess his vampirism and ask for absolution. Or was that cure for his condition pure myth, too?

Leaving, Lien said, "Shall we eat lunch at Fisherman's Wharf?"

His teeth rubbed against the inside of his upper lip, so loose they felt ready to fall out. He had no doubt they would, and that new, sharp ones were even now pushing through his sore gums. A need to be alone overwhelmed him.

"Another time, please? I think I'd like to go home and sleep." If she argued, he was ready to take off his glasses and use his power on her.

Though her forehead creased in concern, she did not fight him. "Call me if you need anything."

He walked her back to her car, then caught a bus for a shopping center, where he bought an air mattress and several bags of earth from the garden section. At home he slit the end of each section of the air mattress and poured in earth a handful at a time until he had a layer of earth an inch or so thick. Mending tape sealed the mattress again.

Garreth lay down experimentally on the resulting pallet. Tension ran out of him like knots untying. The slightly lumpy surface felt as comfortable as the softest of beds. He sighed in satisfaction. It worked.

Before he let himself fall asleep, though, Garreth worried the loose teeth free. Pushing his tongue into the spaces left, he felt sharp points coming through the gums and shivered. Somehow the teeth signaled a watershed, a point of no return at which he could no longer doubt the thing he had become. The chill of that thought followed him into sleep.

7

Hunger woke him, violent, racking cramps that doubled him in bed, ravenous thirst which would no longer be denied. Garreth felt his teeth with his tongue and found them fully grown, sharp as needles, though to his surprise, they were no longer than the teeth they had replaced. His gut knotted with more than cramps. The metamorphosis was complete and he could no longer avoid the one problem he had refused to think about: food. Tonight he had to find a solution.

Garreth staggered out of bed to the bathroom and doubled over the washbowl gulping down water. But neither hot nor cold water slaked the burning thirst; it only eased the cramps enough that he could stand upright.

In the mirror his face loomed gaunt, pale, and unshaven. He was losing weight, he noticed, and grimaced bitterly. *After all the times I've dieted without success, this is a hell of a way to—*

He forgot all about weight and stared at his reflected teeth. With the drawing back of his lips in the grimace, the canines, narrower than his previous ones, had grown, extending nearly half an inch. And as he relaxed, they retracted again. Glancing toward the bed in the other room, he thought of Marti and for the first time, rejoiced in her death. At least she had been saved the agony of seeing him like this!

The length of his beard astonished him, until he thought to switch on the TV and check the programming against the guide—he had better buy another watch to replace the one being kept as evidence. This was *Monday* evening. He had slept nearly thirty hours.

He unwound the bandage from his neck. Without surprise he found the flesh scarred but healed. Count the recuperative powers of the vampire as fact, then. Using a pair of nail scissors, he cut and pulled the sutures. Another turtleneck hid the luminous ivory scars.

Is this proper attire for the hunting vampire? came a bitterly sardonic thought.

He snatched up a coat and headed for the door.

Garreth found he still could not think about what he intended to do, how to do it, or where. He let his body take him, guided by its new instincts. He found himself on a bus headed for North Beach. Of course ... Lane's turf, rich with game.

He sat staring out the bus window, heartsick, hating himself. How could he bring himself to do this to other human beings? What if he refused? What happened to the starving vampire since he had never heard of them dying for lack of food?

Leaving the bus at the corner of Columbus and Broadway, he considered the possibility of suicide. It offered a clean solution ... maybe. If vampires could commit suicide. Driving a wooden stake through his heart or breaking his neck sounded difficult to accomplish by himself.

Humanity streamed around him. He smelled not just their perfume and sweat now but the warm metallic/salty scent of the blood pulsing through their veins. It ignited a frenzy of hunger. His stomach churned. *Dear God, don't let me cramp again and attract attention!* Occasionally someone passed whose blood ran hot and strong and he turned toward her like a compass to north ... only to pull back, afraid. How long had it been since he last picked up a girl? Before he met Marti. He had been turned down a fair number of times in those days, he recalled. A refusal now meant more than a blow to the ego; it meant no supper. Worse, what if she came with him? What if he killed her?

He could not do it. He just ... could ... not ... do ... it!

In panic, he turned up a side street and ran, away from Broadway, away from the blood smells fanning his hunger, and did not stop until the next corner. There he leaned against the wall of a building, swearing at himself. Some vampire he made. What *was* he going to do?

Gradually, he became aware of voices around the corner, sharp, full of anger and fear. A man's: "And Richie says you're holding out on him. He don't like that."

"I'm *not*," a woman replied. "I just don't get the action. The johns want *young* girls. I do the best I can. I swear."

Garreth recognized Velvet's voice. Edging up to the corner, he peered around it. The hooker had been backed up against the building by a man waving a switchblade under her nose.

"Well, if you can't convince them you're sweet sixteen and a virgin, you better find something else they want, baby, because Richie says you're running in the red. You ain't cost-effective. So unless you get your act together, you *will* be running in the red. I'll fix your face so you can't get a job ushering at a dogfight."

Good old Richie, Garreth thought.

He came around the corner. In two long strides he was on top of the muscleman, clamping a hand on the wrist of the knife hand just as the man registered Garreth's presence and started to turn. Garreth bent the wrist back. The forearm gave with a sickening *crack*. He let go of the wrist and smoothly took the knife as the muscleman collapsed screaming to the sidewalk.

Garreth stepped over him and put a hand under Velvet's elbow. "Come on; let's get out of here." He hurried her back toward Broadway.

Her eyes looked the size of dinner plates. "Why'd you do that? He wasn't going to cut me this time. Now Richie will get mad."

"Tell Richie the muscle was getting carried away and was about to use the knife for fun when a friendly flatfoot came along. Better yet, drop a dime on him and we'll nail him to the wall before he *does* have you carved up."

She bit her lip. "Sometime, maybe. For now, thanks." She glanced sideways at him. "Say, what's the story on you? First I hear they found you stiff in an alley with your throat torn out, then the word is you sat up on the autopsy table and knocked the knife out of the doctor's hand; now here you are walking around breaking arms with one hand. You look younger somehow, too."

He restrained a grimace. *Drink blood, the Elixir of Youth.* "I owe it all to clean living and a pure heart," he said aloud.

The blood ran hot in her. He smelled it: fear-driven, richly salty, and with it, the near audible hammering of her heart, just now beginning to slow after the terror. He drew a deep breath and, folding the switchblade, dropped it in his pocket. His hand shook with the driving urgency of his hunger.

He felt her looking at him and glanced over to see her smiling knowingly. She had seen his increase in breathing and misinterpreted it, he realized .

"Hey, baby. Maybe you'd like to party?"

He shook his head. "Don't make me run you in for soliciting a cop, Velvet."

"Did I mention money? This is on the house. Call it saying thanks. Come on." She reached up to ruffle his hair. "Let me show you that blondes really do have more fun."

He started to say no, but something else in him, something controlled by the ravenous thirst, made it to his tongue first. "Okay. Why not?"

She tucked her arm through his. "It isn't far. You'll like this."

He hated it. Not the sex; that felt fine. But afterward, with the blood smell of her filling his head, making him dizzy with need, she looked up and said dreamily, "Did you know your eyes glow red, Mikaelian? They're like rubies."

Hunger overwhelmed him. He kissed her neck, exploring, feeling his canines extend. She sighed in pleasure when his mouth found the throb under her silky skin. The sound goaded him. He bit, and ... nothing! Only a drop of blood rose to tantalize him where each fang pierced. He had missed the vein!

A scream of frustration echoed through his head, and then it screamed *at* him, demanding that he tear at her throat until he found the blood he needed. Garreth recoiled, and scrambled off her in horror. *No!* The guilt he had felt coming up here paled beside the self-loathing flooding him now. He did not have to stop being the person he was? Like hell. Look at him, turning into a ravening damn animal!

He struggled into his clothes, desperate to leave before his hunger destroyed what humanity remained in him.

Velvet stirred drowsily on the bed. "Don't rush off, baby."

How could he explain? It was impossible. "I'm sorry; I have to go to work." He buckled his belt.

She sat up, frowning irritably. "Well, wham-bam-thank-you-ma'am."

He clipped on his gun, not daring to look at her, breathing through his mouth so that he would not smell the blood in her. "I'm sorry," he repeated. It sounded lame in his ears.

"Cops." She snorted. "Always in a hurry to come and a hurry to go."

He fled the room without even bothering to put on his coat. He finished dressing on the street while he walked away as fast as he could and gulped the night air to clear her scent from his head. He kept walking, paying no particular attention to the direction, as long as it was away from the crowds and bright lights.

Missed! He could not believe it. Who ever heard of such a thing? *See the vampire miss the vein. See him miss supper. Poor hungry vampire. Maybe he should hire a dowser to find veins for him.*

How many necks did a neo-vampire have to mutilate before learning the quick, clean bite? He could not do that. How did he eat, then?

A car's horn blared. Garreth scrambled out of its path. It was then that he noticed where he was going ... east, down to the Embarcadero. He stopped and stood looking across at the pier buildings, forgetting his problem for a moment to think about the ships moored over there, where they had been and where they might be going, exotic places. He had never even been out of the state.

A man passed him, jogging, with a sleek Doberman running easily at his side. They left the scents of sweat and blood behind them.

Garreth's spine tingled. He turned to watch the dog. They had blood, too. Could he live on animal blood? Lane drank human blood and all the books talked about vampires drinking human blood, but blood was blood, surely.

The idea of preying on dogs did not appeal to him; they were pets, usually loved by someone. Cats, too. Besides, he had no idea how much blood they could lose without dying. However—his eyes moved toward the pier across the street—the city did have one species that existed in profusion, that would not be missed, and that he would not mind killing. Over there lay a bounteous hunting ground.

The idea of touching a rat, let alone biting one, disgusted him, but a growing weakness in him and the return of his stomach cramps provided incentive for overcoming his squeamishness. People learned to eat many things out of necessity, even other people. Better rats than people.

He crossed the street ... only to find the gate across the entrance locked. He clutched at the grating in frustration. What now? The only open gates led onto piers with activity. He needed to find a way onto an empty pier ... somehow. He stared into the darkened building longingly.

Something moved in him, a gut-jarring wrench that sent pangs through him from head to hands and feet. He started to lean against the grating for support, to wait for the pain to pass. He almost fell onto his face. The grating had disappeared from in front of him. Looking around, he found, to his astonishment, that it lay *behind* him.

Another truth! Vampires could move through solid objects. He had not noticed that he became mist. How had he done it, then?

Garreth quickly ceased to care about *how*. His stomach said: *hunt*. He started down the length of the building, through a dark that appeared no more than twilight to his eyes, his ears tuned for every possible sound.

The building creaked around him. Outside, traffic mumbled and water slapped the pier and foundations. Then, amid other sounds, he caught the scrabble of tiny clawed feet and the high squeak of a rodent voice. One turn of his head pinpointed the sound. He moved in that direction, climbing over a customs barrier in his path. The rat's form appeared among the shadows under the customs counter.

It must have heard him because it grew suddenly still. Only its head moved, turning to look up at him. Garreth froze in place, too. The tiny eyes met his.

"Don't move," he said. Then he had a better idea. "Come here. Come to me." He would see just how far this control went.

The rat continued to stare.

Garreth concentrated on it. "Come here."

One slow step at a time, the rat obeyed. As it came within arm's reach, Garreth squatted on his heels. The smell of the rat reached him, a sharp rodent odor, strong but not quite strong enough to mask the tantalizing scent of blood. He steeled himself to touch the creature. *Blood is blood.* He drew a breath, smelling that blood … and reached for his prey.

The rat's fur felt rough and spiky in his hand. He waited for it to struggle, but the creature submitted to being picked up, hanging quiescent in his grasp. One wrench would break its neck, or a bend of his elbow bring it to his mouth, but he hesitated. Rats carry disease. How did plague and rabies affect vampires? Were they immune, or would the disease organism be destroyed by passing through his digestive system? This rat looked healthy enough, bright-eyed and fat.

The blood smell of it was overwhelming. Hunger maddened him. He had to risk drinking from it. He remembered the switchblade in his pocket. That would keep him from having to actually bite the rat. But what then?

The rat remained quiet. Garreth stood, carrying it, and looked around for inspiration. Draining the blood into the palm of his hand and licking it up from there sounded not only slow but primitive. He had never liked camping out with all the loss of physical comfort that meant: digging latrines, boiling water, bathing in a bucket. He wanted something more civilized now, too.

His gaze fell on a trash barrel. He carried the rat to it and looked in. Almost on top of the litter inside sat a foam cup of the type used for coffee carry-outs. Lipstick, looking brown in the twilight of his vision, printed one edge of the rim.

After this, he decided, he would bring a cup of his own, maybe one of those collapsing things for camping, something that fit easily and inconspicuously in a pocket. But for now, he set the cup on the customs counter, then, using both hands, broke the rat's neck and brought out the switchblade.

The blade opened with a snap. A pass of it opened the rat's throat, and Garreth held the rat by its hind legs, letting the blood drain into the cup. Its smell set his stomach churning in anticipation, though his brain still recoiled. *Blood is blood*, he reminded himself. *Blood is Life*.

And when the rat stopped dripping, he resolutely picked up the cup, lipstick away from him, and gulped down the contents before he had time to think further.

Any worry that he might throw up vanished immediately. The first swallow ignited a wild appetite for more. At the same time, though, it tasted flat, lacking, as though he drank simple tomato juice when he expected the peppery fire of a Bloody Mary. His skin crawled. What he really wanted, of course, was human blood. *But this will do and it's all you're getting, beast.* He drained the cup to the last drop and went hunting another rat.

8

"Mik-san!" Harry came up out of his desk chair grinning from ear to ear.

From around the room, other detectives converged on Garreth, pounding him on the back. Serruto came out of his office. "Is that our Lazarus behind those Foster Grants? You're looking pretty good, Mikaelian. Did you see the doctor today?"

"Yes, sir."

"What does he say about when you can come back?"

"I'm back now. Really," he added, handing over the evaluation form from the doctor. He took off his glasses and hung them on the breast pocket of his suit coat. "I checked out okay. I'm cleared for full duty." Or at least, he had been after "persuasion" helped the doctor perceive the readings for temperature, pulse, and respiration as normal.

Foreheads furrowed in surprise around him Harry looked concerned. "Only a week after the attack? You still look pale, and you seem thin."

"I'm on a diet. The doctor approves."

Serruto read the form. "He thinks your neck is healed?"

Garreth tilted back his head to show the scars above his collar, still livid but obviously in no danger of tearing open with exertion. "I agree it's incredible, but my mother's people were always fast healers, and I've been doing nothing since Saturday but sleeping and eating, and drinking an herbal tea my Grandma Doyle swears by."

He saw by their expressions that they put little credence in the herbal tea, but otherwise swallowed the lies. Garreth fought down a pang of guilt. He could not very well tell the truth, could he? That he had slept days but spent nights decimating the rat population on the Embarcadero, feeding the little corpses to the fishes in the bay. He hated admitting it to himself—it seemed like a savage, desperate way to be living, and he had come close to being caught last night by a watchman. He had had to crouch behind a pile of crates with breath held until the man walked out of sight. Garreth's chances of being seen increased with every night. He needed to find some way to hunt less often.

Serruto read the form again. "I don't know," he said doubtfully.

Garreth met his eyes as the lieutenant looked up and stared steadily into them. "I'm fit, the doctor says. You believe him, don't you?" It was a cheat and Garreth's conscience bothered him because of it, but he used it anyway. He wanted to be working.

Serruto stared back, then returned the form. "If the doctor says you're fit, who am I to disagree? Okay, everyone, the reception party is over. Back to work." He beckoned Garreth toward his office. "Come in. You, too, Harry."

It was about what Garreth expected, a short lecture which could be summarized as: "The doctors may think you're fit for full duty, but I think you should take it easy for a while. Make sure he does, Harry. Here's your new badge, ID card, and gun. Be sure to qualify with it on the firing range. Here's your temporary driver's license. Now, I suppose you want to know how we're doing on your redhead?"

"Yes, sir."

"We haven't found her," Harry said. "The APB is out with the names Barber and Alexandra Pfeifer. Odd alias, isn't it? I suppose it sounds more authentic than the standard Anglo-Saxon ones.

"It's all crazy. Did you know we dusted her apartment, but the only prints we found belonged to your name on the letter, Madelaine Bieber, but *she* turns out not to be Barber, but a sixty-seven-year-old woman who was arrested for assault in 1941? We can't find her, either."

Garreth bit his lip to keep from telling them that Lane and Madelaine Bieber were the same woman. Once he accepted Lane as a vampire, it followed that her apparent age bore no relation to her actual one. If he told them, and they believed him, then they would inevitably realize what he had become. He had no desire to learn how they might react to that.

Little wonder, though, that Lane hunted so efficiently; she had had decades of practice.

He asked, "Did you ever learn anything from the burned papers in the fireplace?"

Serruto shook his head. "The lab only managed to bring up a partial postmark with two of the ZIP numbers, a six and a seven."

"Doesn't that help?"

Harry sighed. "It might if we knew for sure whether they're the first or second two numbers. If the ZIP is sixty-seven something, the letter came from the middle of Kansas. If it's something sixty-seven something, it could have been mailed in any one of nine states. I had the fun of going through a ZIP directory to check the possibilities." He laughed. "Isn't being a detective exciting?"

"Show him the picture, Harry," Serruto said.

Harry brought it in from his desk. Studying the photograph, Garreth saw that most of the envelope had burned away. In what remained, he saw a postmark circle with the two numbers at the bottom. At the top of the circle, partials of three letters also remained, and below the postmark, an ornate M. He recognized the letter as part of the address on the envelope he had seen. Too bad they were unable to see the return address. Addressed to her real name, it must have come from someone who knew her well and from a long time back.

"Did you learn anything useful from her driver's license or car registration?"

"Just that the information given for the license was false," Harry said.

Serruto frowned. "We ran her through NCIC, even asking for Wants on anyone fitting her description. I know she's dirty. She stinks of 'fugitive.' She must be wanted somewhere for something."

Garreth found satisfaction in knowing that he was no longer the only one who felt that way.

"Anyway, that's where we stand now," Serruto said. "More is up to you two." He eyed Garreth intently. "Are you sure you feel like working?"

Garreth returned his gaze steadily. "I feel just fine."

Serruto waved them toward the door. "Then crack the whip over him, Harry."

Harry nodded, grinning. On the way back to their desks, he said, "I tried calling you a couple of times, to see how you were doing, but you never answered."

Garreth doubted a mere phone could wake him in the daytime. "I turned off the telephone bell so I wouldn't be disturbed." Even the small lie bothered him.

"Lien was so worried I almost drove over to check on you personally."

Garreth breathed a sigh of relief that he had not.

"She's down at City of Paris today. Why don't I give her a call to tell her what the doctor said about you, and ask her to make enough sweet-and-sour pork for three tonight?"

Garreth hoped the stricken plunge of his heart did not show on his face. He could never eat sweet-and-sour pork again, nor eat with Harry and Lien again, for that matter. He did not have to fake the disappointment in his voice. "I wish I could, but ... I have a date."

Harry's brows went up.

"A nurse I met while the doctor was checking me over."

Harry slapped his shoulder. "That's great. You get along well with nurses. Glad to see you back in the game."

"Does this mean you'll be playing Cock of the Walk with the rest of the boys now?" Evelyn Kolb eyed him over the cup of tea she was pumping from her thermos.

Garreth paused in the act of putting his glasses back on. "What a sharp tongue you have."

She smiled. He eyed her thermos. That might be how to reduce the number of times he had to hunt. After all, the ability to store food was supposed to be an advantage of civilization.

He walked over to her desk and picked up the thermos. "Does this work very well?"

"Very well. Tea I put in in the morning is still hot enough to burn my tongue twelve hours later."

He toyed with the pump spigot on the top. "How much does it hold?"

"A quart. Why?"

"I'm thinking of bringing tea to work the way you do. They come in larger sizes, too, don't they?"

"Sure, but how much do you expect to drink in a day?"

He shrugged, noting with dismay how easily he lied these days and to how many people. Why? Right now he could have replied truthfully that he was thinking of buying a thermos. *The wicked flee where no man pursueth*, he thought ruefully.

Garreth returned the thermos to her desk and watched her put it away in the kneehole. A thermos full of blood would keep him several days. The flaw in that struck him on the way back to his desk. Outside its owner's body, blood clotted. The thought of ordinary blood still sounded unappealing to his brain, but that of clotted blood turned even his stomach. If he wanted to store blood, he would have to use anticoagulants. Where to come by those, though?

Harry sat at his desk frowning at the lab photo of the postmark. "What do you think these letters are?"

Garreth peered over his shoulder. "The one in the middle has to be either an O or U. Isn't that a slanted foot to the left? That would be an A, K, R, or X."

"And on the right?"

It looked like the bottom end of a straight line. "Man, that could be anything." He checked the keys of the typewriter. "F, H, I, K, N, M, or P." A thought occurred which might solve several problems. "Why don't we ask the lab if they can work on making the letters a little more visible?"

Harry shrugged. "We can ask."

Garreth maneuvered Harry into doing the talking when they reached the Crime Lab. He put in a word or two, then slid away and wandered along the worktables to where a technician was checking bloodstains on a shirt.

The tech looked up with a smile. "Glad to see you back. I'm glad I won't be giving evidence on your bloodstained clothes at a murder trial. I see you got in a few licks yourself."

"Two kinds of blood on the clothes?"

The tech nodded. "Mostly A positive, but some B positive, too."

Casually, Garreth asked, "If you wanted to keep blood fresh, how could you do it?"

The tech shook his head. "I'd rather have it dried. It's easier to analyze. Blood cells decay so fast in liquid or clotted blood."

"What if you wanted to keep it from clotting? Would you use heparin?"

The tech rocked his row of slides back and forth, studying the blood on them. "Heparin? Probably not. That's about the most expensive product on the market. It's cheaper to use things like oxalates and citrates." He looked up. "I'd probably choose sodium citrate. That's inexpensive and available at almost any chemical supply house. It isn't a drug, so it isn't controlled like heparin."

"How much would you have to use?" Garreth crossed his fingers, hoping the tech would not ask why he was so interested in anticoagulants.

The blood on some of the slides looked clumped. The tech wrote letters on a report form, then stood and reached for a book on a shelf above the cabinet behind him. "Well, let's see. Anticoagulants ... Here we are. You need ten milligrams for a hundred milliliters of blood. I've bought it in a two and a half percent solution. That gives you twenty-five milligrams per cc. So a cc will keep two hundred and fifty milliliters. That help?"

"Yes. Thanks." Garreth hoped so.

9

Jubilation carried him into work on Friday. The citrate worked. Four quarts of blood sat cold and liquid in his refrigerator. A lot of drained rat bodies fed the fishes today but the slaughter was worth it. He would not have to hunt for several days. Rat blood still did not satisfy him; hunger continued to gnaw no matter how much he drank, but at least it took the edge off. He could live with what remained, like the time Marti took him off bread and he survived very well even though he never stopped craving the bread. His thermos of tea would help keep his appetite under control during the day. He was also learning to live with the pressure of daylight. The dream had been right; he could go on living a normal life and no one would ever have to suspect the changes in him.

Not even a useless interview with Lane's agent—*current* agent, Garreth qualified silently; she almost certainly changed them along with her identity—failed to dampen his spirits.

"She phoned and told me not to book her any gigs for an indefinite period of time," the woman said. "She said her mother is critically ill and she intends to stay with her until the crisis is over."

"Where's that?" Harry asked.

"I don't know. She never said."

Harry frowned. "You mean you don't have any background information on your clients?"

The agent frowned back. "Lane has a dozen backgrounds, all probably false. Look, Sergeant, I find her gigs and she pays me ten percent. That was our agreement. She gives me no trouble with performing drunk or strung out, or not showing up at all, and she brings me a small but steady income, so I don't pry into her life." The agent paused. "Once or twice I asked her personal questions and she changed the subject. She looks like a hot, foxy kid, but she's ice and steel underneath."

A very perceptive lady, Garreth reflected.

As they left, Harry asked, "Where do you want to eat lunch?"

The optimism in Garreth faltered only a little. "I'm on a diet, remember? We can eat anywhere you want, as long as I can buy a cup of tea there."

Harry grinned. "You're serious about the diet this time?"

"Of course." As though he had a choice.

"North Beach being our Italian Quarter, how about Italian food?"

"Fine." Garreth would hate it, whatever the restaurant. He hated all meals. Tea filled his stomach, but did nothing to neutralize the longings that food smells stirred in him. He envied Harry, happily putting away everything Garreth had loved but could no longer eat.

But the moment they walked in the door of the restaurant, Garreth lost all future appetite for Italian food. At the first breath of inside air, his lungs froze. Instant panic set in as he tried to breathe and could not. He clawed frantically at his tie and shirt collar, yanking them open.

"Garreth! What's wrong?" Harry shook him by the shoulders.

Garreth opened his mouth wide, straining, desperately struggling to suck in air, but he might as well have been trying to inhale solid concrete.

"Garreth!"

He would suffocate in here! Half dragging Harry, half carried by him, Garreth bolted for the street.

Outside, the air turned from concrete to cold molasses. Garreth staggered up the street until the last foul taint of garlic disappeared. Only then did the air return to normal consistency. He leaned against a building, head thrown back, gulping air greedily.

"Garreth, what happened?" Harry demanded.

Garreth had no idea what to say. Would any mention of garlic start fatal thought trains? "I'm all right." As long as he avoided garlic. Put one more piece of the legend in the truth column. "It was nothing."

"Nothing! That wasn't nothing, partner. We'd better—"

From the direction of their car, a radio sputtered. "Inspectors 55."

Harry hurried back to the car to roger the call. Garreth followed with unsteady knees.

"Public service 555-6116," Dispatch said.

Harry's brows rose. "Sound familiar?"

Garreth shook his head.

They drove to the nearest phone booth and Harry dialed the number. Garreth could not hear Harry's end of the conversation, only see his lips moving through the glass wall of the booth, but as he talked, Harry became more animated. He came back to the car at a run and jumped behind the wheel.

"Hey, Mik-san, are we still interested in Wink O'Hare?"

Garreth sat up straight. "Are you kidding? Did someone find him?"

"A lady who says she's Rosella Hambright's sister knows where he is. Seems he got peeved at his girl and worked her over. The sister doesn't approve and wants Wink's hide for it."

"Let's go get him," Garreth said.

They collected two black-and-whites for backup on the way. Garreth surreptitiously checked the house, a decaying two-story building with poverty ground like dirt into its facade, before they moved in. Wink was supposed to be in the second-floor apartment. Narrow, bare stairs led up from a front hall that reeked of garbage and broken plumbing. Two windows overlooked the street. Built against its neighbor, it had no side windows. In back, rotting stairs in two flights rose to a narrow back porch with one window into the apartment and a back door whose upper half contained nine small panes of glass.

The wages of sin is the hell of hiding in stinking holes, Garreth thought while walking back up the hill and around the corner to where Harry and the black-and-whites waited.

Harry deployed everyone, a uniform to be behind a black-and-white out front, covering the front windows, another around the corner of a building covering the rear window. A third uniform would go in the front with Harry, and the fourth, up the back with Garreth.

"You're sure you're all right?" Harry asked.

Garreth removed his glasses and looked him straight in the eyes. "I'm fine. Let's go."

"We'll give him a chance to come out. If he doesn't, you break in the back door. I'll go through the front at the same time. Back door and hall door are at right angles to each other, so we shouldn't be in each other's cross fire, but for God's sake be careful about that."

Garreth and his uniformed partner, a barrel-chested veteran named Rhoades, made their way around to the back of the building and eased up the stairs, checking each tread to avoid telltale creaks. Keeping low, they crossed the porch, then flattened themselves against the building on each side of the door.

With his ear pressed against the side of the house, Garreth heard Harry knock at the front door and call, "Wink O'Hare, this is the police." Nothing stirred in the apartment.

"Come out, Wink."

A board creaked inside. Listening carefully, Garreth made out the sound of stealthy footsteps. Garreth shifted his hand up on his gun so that he could use the handgrip to break the window. His eyes met Rhoades's. The uniformed officer nodded his readiness. Garreth, breaking the window, would go in high. Rhoades would dive in low.

"O'Hare, open up!"

The footsteps inside moved closer. "Garreth! Get him!"

At Harry's yell, Garreth smashed the handgrip of the gun into the pane directly above the knob. The glass shattered, but with it a wave of pain like fire burned up his arm and out through his body at the same time a shot sounded explosively inside the kitchen and glass higher up shattered under the impact of a bullet.

Rhoades swore. Garreth tossed his gun into his left hand and pointed it around the edge of the doorjamb to shoot back at Wink, tilting his head just enough to expose one eye for aiming. But his finger could not move the trigger. The gun mechanism seemed frozen.

"Shoot!" Rhoades yelled.

Garreth could not. Fire seared him.

What the hell was wrong with his gun? He remembered then, in dismay, that he carried a new one, one he had never fired before. *Damn*.

That did not account for the pain, though.

The thoughts raced through his head between one heartbeat and the next. Another followed, one that could explain both the pain and apparent failure of the gun, but he could not accept it. *No, that's just a legend! Besides, this is a hideout, not a dwelling ... just a hide-out!*

Wink disappeared from the kitchen doorway and two more shots sounded, this time followed by a man's agonized yell. Garreth could not tell whether the shots came from Wink's .45 or the hot-loaded Special that Harry carried. "Harry! *Harry.*"

"Don't just stand there!" Rhoades yelled.

The uniformed officer hurled himself at the door, shouldering Garreth aside. A third shot sounded. The aging door gave way under his weight. He hit the floor inside rolling, kept rolling back onto his feet, and vanished through the kitchen doorway.

With pain wrapping him in flame, Garreth pressed at the opening, willing himself through it. The hot metallic/salty reek of blood filled the apartment. *"Harry, are you all right?"*

"Get in here, Mikaelian," Rhoades's voice snapped.

The pain vanished instantly. Garreth stumbled forward, cold with fear. Fear justified. He found Harry sprawled groaning in the middle of the living room while the uniform who had come up the front with him tried to staunch the blood from a hole in the middle of Harry's chest. Garreth saw Wink, too, shoulder-wounded and screaming as Rhoades roughly cuffed his hands behind his back, but it was Harry he went to, dropping on his knees and pulling out his handkerchief to use as a compress on the wound.

A hand caught his collar and dragged him back. "What the hell were you doing out there?" Rhoades demanded. "If you'd fired when you had the chance, this wouldn't have happened. You froze, didn't you? This turkey shot at you and you lost your nerve!"

"I—" Garreth stared up at him. He could hardly admit his defense, that the apartment was a dwelling and that as a vampire, he could not enter it the first time without an invitation. It appeared that not even a bullet from his gun could violate the barrier around a dwelling.

Rhoades pushed him toward the telephone. "See if you can make yourself use that and call for an ambulance. If we get him to a hospital fast enough, maybe we can still save your partner's life."

Flushing from the lash of the sarcasm, Garreth picked up the phone.

The ambulance took a lifetime to arrive, and every minute of the wait, Garreth sat on the floor holding Harry's head in his lap, silently willing him to live. *Hang on, Harry! Dear God, don't let him die!* As though he, unholy creature, had a right to appeal to a power of Good for anything. Wink's complaints that he was bleeding to death, Rhoades's mutter as he read Wink his rights, the anger of the four uniformed officers directed at the one who failed them ... all existed somewhere beyond Garreth, not touching him. Only Harry felt real, Harry and fury at himself. What a fool he was! *See the vampire, funny beast, trying to act like a human.* Foolish, certainly, not to have systematically checked out every legendary condition of vampire existence. In the jungle, death is the price of error, only this time Harry might pay the price for Garreth's error. *Hang on, Harry. Don't let me destroy you.*

He rode with Harry in the ambulance to the hospital and rooted himself in the trauma unit's waiting room, smelling blood everywhere and sickened by it. Lien was not home. He could only give Dispatch the license number of her car and hope that some patrol unit found her before she heard the news on the radio or TV.

"Mikaelian."

Serruto's voice. Garreth knew he could not meet the lieutenant's eyes, so he kept his gaze riveted on the door through which Harry had disappeared.

"What happened?" The question sounded concerned, not angry.

Garreth kept his voice expressionless. "They say I froze."

"Did you?"

He could say no. He could say his gun jammed. Or he could say yes, and blame it on psychological shock, on suffering from the effects of his own recent experiences, on having come back to work too soon, after all. The first could be disproven by examining his gun and the second seemed too easy. He stared at the doorway and said, "It's my fault Harry was shot."

He heard Serruto sit down beside him ... smelled his mixed scent of soap, after-shave, and, beneath them, blood. "I have this feeling of being ignored. I didn't know what to tell the captain. Somehow I thought these operations needed to be cleared through me first."

Why did Serruto confine himself to mild sarcasm? He ought to be yelling. Garreth and Harry knew procedure. Why had they failed to follow it? Had his, Garreth's, eagerness to collar Wink persuaded Harry in the same way the doctor and then Serruto had been persuaded to let him come back to work? Was *all* of it his fault? "I got carried away and forgot to call in."

"And Harry? He's the sergeant. Why didn't he call in?"

Garreth sat angrily upright. "Harry's in there maybe dying and you're trying to blame *him*?"

Serruto sighed. "I know how you feel, but—"

Garreth stood. "How can you possibly know how I feel?" He heard the despair in his voice, a despair sharpened by the realization of how true the question was. Serruto could not know. No one normal, no one human, no one who was as he used to be could ever know exactly how he felt.

And it was looking across that now-perceived, unbridgeable gulf between himself and everyone he knew that Garreth saw Lien come running white-faced into the waiting room.

She stopped in front of him. "How bad is it?"

A constriction in Garreth's throat made speech impossible. He could only shrug.

Serruto answered her. "We don't know."

"How did it happen?"

"I'm sorry." Garreth forced the words out. "I'm sorry I didn't take better care of him. It's all my fault."

She, too, disappointed him by looking sympathetic instead of angry.

The doctor came through the doors from the trauma unit. They spun to face him. Garreth felt as though even his heart stopped, waiting for what the doctor would say.

The doctor spread his hands. "He's still alive. The bullet missed his heart. However, there's massive trauma and hemorrhage, so although we have the bleeding stopped now and the damaged vessels repaired, we'll just have to wait to see how he snaps back."

Her face like a china mask, Lien asked, "May I see him?"

"I'm sorry; not yet."

Pain twisted in Garreth. If Harry lived, it would be through no credit to Garreth Doyle Mikaelian. And if Harry lived this time, what about the next? Because there would be a next time, inevitably, another dwelling, another impenetrable barrier Garreth would face and fail. He might as well accept a hard fact … he could not continue playing cop when his own personal set of rules differed so much from those applied to the rest of humanity.

Garreth felt in his inside pocket for his badge case. Pulling it out, he turned toward Serruto and extended it. "I shouldn't be carrying this." The words pierced like a knife in his gut.

Serruto frowned. "Mikaelian—"

The lieutenant did not reach for the badge case, but Garreth let go of it anyway, before he lost his courage to give it up. It fell to the floor, flipping open.

Lien, Serruto, and the doctor stared startled at him. The badge seemed to stare, too … a seven-pointed star, the remaining half of his soul, shining up from the floor.

"Mikaelian."

"Oh, Garreth."

Their voices reached out for him, like nets or webs, seeking to snare him. Garreth fled the trap. He spun and bolted from the room. He fled down the corridor with their voices chasing him. An orderly reached for him but he jerked loose in one easy pull and escaped into the twilight.

Tears blinded him. He jerked his glasses off and wiped his eyes. What did he do now? Or should he do anything? He did not really want to live. He did not enjoy it, and his life, or undeath, had endangered the existence of people who could be integral, productive members of society.

He started walking, considering how he might kill himself. It must look like an accident, to spare his family. That made it harder than ever. He cursed the changes in him that did that to him. If Lane had used her strength to simply break his neck, it would have been over, finished with. *Damn you for not doing it!*

He stopped short in the middle of a street. Brakes screamed and horns blared unheard around him.

Because Lane had made him what he was, Harry was dying. Indirectly, she could be held responsible, too, for that fiasco in taking Wink.

An angry voice swore at him. Garreth finally heard and moved on across the street.

She had destroyed Garreth's life, killed his partner, taken away his job, and removed him from his friends. She had destroyed more lives than his, too, when he counted the families of Adair and Mossman. He had no way of knowing how many others she had killed in her lifetime. The tally must be high. All those lives over all those years, and she still went free, to kill and destroy again, laughing at law, sidestepping justice. Growing up with a cop father, working as a cop himself, Garreth believed strongly in law and justice as the foundation of civilization. Without them, nothing remained but barbarism and chaos.

Garreth took a deep breath. He knew now what he could do ... the same job he had been doing before. Before he ended his disliked unlife, he would hunt down the red-haired vampire. *It takes one to catch one* might be truer for this case than any. He would hunt her and he would bring her back to stand accountable for what she had done to Adair and Mossman and to Harry and him. If it took him to the end of the earth and time, he would find her.

Hunter

1

By lamplight, the liquid in the cut-glass tumbler had the rich, dark red of Burgundy. Since giving up regular food, Garreth had taken to gulping his meals, dispensing with the unpleasant necessity as quickly as possible. Tonight, however, he turned the tumbler in his hands, wondering sardonically what Marti's Aunt Elizabeth would think if she knew the end to which her crystal wedding gift had come. He sipped the blood almost idly, playing with it as a wine taster might. *This Rattus '83 is a bold vintage, speaking to the palate with lively authority, while ...*

Garreth ended the game abruptly by emptying the glass. He played not for amusement, he knew, but to delay, to avoid considering the problem he had set himself. How could he hope to hunt down Lane Barber alone when the combined facilities of the department were failing to find her? Refilling the tumbler, he wondered whether his melodramatic resignation had been premature.

No, he had no other choice, not when carrying the badge endangered fellow officers' lives. Besides, as a "free agent" he could spend his time exclusively on this one case, and since he knew what Lane was—his exclusive knowledge—he could think of leads that nonvampires would never consider. Perhaps he could learn how she thought, too.

The telephone rang, startling him. He stared across the room at it. Should he answer? He did not feel like learning that Harry had died or, if it was his parents, like admitting to his father how he had screwed up.

It went on ringing. After the ninth time, Garreth dived on the phone and unclipped the cord from it, then walked back to the table in the silence and sat down with his tumbler of blood again.

First question: Where could she go?

Unfortunately, probably anywhere. In forty-odd years of singing, she must have made many connections. She could no doubt travel to any large city in the country, or perhaps even around the world, and through those connections find a new job. Most of them would not be familiar with anyone named Lane Barber, either. She could change identity again; she must have that honed to a fine art.

Habits did not often change, though, the famous *modus oper-andi*. She drew her food supply from customers where she worked—small, intimate clubs which offered ample opportunity for meeting customers. The Barbary Now and several other clubs the agent named where Lane had worked were all that type. How many such bars and clubs existed in the United States? Thousands? Hundreds of thousands?

Garreth sighed. Finding her in North Beach had been simple compared with the task that faced him now. He had the time, of course—her bite had given him *that*, at least—but in another sense, he did not. He needed to find her before his money ran out and he had to take a job somewhere. He knew something about her, but, unfortunately, not enough to narrow down her possible avenues of escape.

Perhaps the place to start learning was the one where she shed all facades ... home.

He finished off his supper, washed the glass out, and left it draining on the sink while he grabbed his trench coat and let himself out into the evening.

One doubt troubled him on the drive to her apartment. It was her dwelling. Would he be able to enter?

He could not. Since he had no key, he tried to pass through the door as he did through the gates of the piers, but that same searing pain that had held him paralyzed outside Wink's hideout burned through him as he touched the door. Garreth backed hastily away and leaned against the porch railing while the flames cooled in him. The fact that she was a vampire and that he had been invited in before his transformation did not appear to cancel the prohibition. Now what?

He doubted he could talk Serruto into letting him in. Being officially off the case, his interest would probably be classed as interference, if not vengeance-seeking. *Isn't it?* He needed to use someone else.

He found a public telephone and called Lane's landlady. "Mrs. Armour, this is Inspector Mikaelian." Resignations took time to process; officially he could still be considered a member of the department. "We met at your home last week."

"Oh, yes. You were asking about Miss Barber." She paused. "The other officers said—did she really try to kill you?"

"I'm afraid so, ma'am. I—we need to look through her apartment again. I'm sorry to bother you this evening, but could you meet me there with the key?"

"I already gave a key to a very nice-looking lieutenant," she said in a puzzled voice.

"Yes, ma'am, but the lieutenant is out of touch this evening and the key is locked in his desk. It's an imposition, I know, but this is important."

Her sigh came over the wire. "All right."

Meeting him at the curb some time later, she said, "You detectives work long hours, don't you?" She handed him the key. "Will you try to return this as soon as possible? It's the only other key I have to the apartment."

He stared at the key and bit his lip. "I'd appreciate it if you could come through with me. You've seen the apartment before and I think you can help me."

She looked simultaneously interested and reluctant. "Will it take long?"

Try not to lie all the time, man. "It might."

She complained in a gentle way all the way up the steps, but she agreed to help. Unlocking the door, she moved through and began switching on lights.

Garreth waited on the porch, pain licking at him.

She looked back from the doorway of the living room. "Well, come on in; I don't have all night." The pain vanished. Garreth followed her quickly. "Look around and tell me if you think anything is missing. What she's taken might give us some idea where she's gone."

Mrs. Armour stood in the middle of the living room and turned. "She has lovely things, doesn't she? She's collected them from all over the world."

Spent good money on them, too, Garreth judged, if his term in Burglary had taught him as much as he thought about estimating the worth of objects. Though no art expert, he recognized the quality of the paintings and some small pieces of sculpture. Old toys resting on the bookshelves between sections of books drew more of his attention, however ... several old-looking dolls, a miniature tea set, a cast-iron toy stove. Hers, from her childhood? he wondered. He studied a tray hung on the wall, its sections turned into shelves holding an assortment of small objects that reminded him of the "treasures" he had collected in an old tin tackle box when he was a boy.

She had no broken pocketknife, but there was a top—wooden, not plastic—and some marbles—more beautiful than any he had had, he noted with envy—a giant tooth, a tiny rodent skull, and various stones: colored, quartzlike, or containing shell and leaf fossils. He could not identify one group of objects, though. He took down the largest to study.

Held by its flat base, its large central point and two flanking smaller ones reached jaggedly upward, like the silhouette of a mountain range. Its color was dark and glassy as obsidian. Except for size, each object in the group looked identical.

"Shark teeth," Mrs. Armour said.

He blinked at her. "What?"

"Miss Barber told me once that those are shark teeth."

Black? He shrugged. Very well. His tackle box had never held anything that exotic.

Garreth put back the tooth and turned his attention to the books. Nonfiction outnumbered the fiction, but of the several hundred volumes covering a wide range of subjects, including extraterrestrial visitors and medical texts on viruses, only music, dancing, and folklore were represented by any substantial number of books.

He glanced through the folklore. All the books contained sections on vampires.

The publication dates of the library as a whole went as far back as 1919. A couple of children's books—printed with large color plates tipped in and black-and-white drawings, not the large print and easy vocabulary of the books he bought to give Brian—bore inscriptions in the front: "To Mada, Christmas 1920, Mother and Daddy," and "To Mada, Happy Birthday, 1921, Mother and Daddy." The ornate penmanship looked vaguely familiar.

He went on to check for inscriptions in the front of other books. A few had them, written in varying hands with dates from the twenties to the midseventies: "To Maida," "To Della," "To Delaine," "To Mala." Some were also signed by the person giving the book, but never with more than a first name.

Mrs. Armour, peering over his shoulder, remarked, "It's odd that the books are inscribed to so many different people, isn't it?"

"Maybe she bought them in used-book stores," Garreth said. Now, why, he wondered almost immediately, had he covered for Lane? Guilt? Let no normal human have the chance to discover what Lane is, for by giving that away, he would give away himself, too?

He searched the desk. Not that he expected Harry or the lab boys to have overlooked anything useful, but he wanted to make sure. A slim chance existed that they might not recognize something as useful that he, with his special knowledge, would. But he found nothing except blank writing paper and some felt-tip pens ... no checkbooks, canceled checks, credit card records, or copies of tax returns.

Moving on to the kitchen, he found it as bare as Harry and Serruto had described, nor did the bedroom yield him information aside from the fact that she bought her clothes all over the world and with discrimination. He pursed his lips thinking of the price tags that accompanied labels like those.

"Can you tell me what clothes might be missing?" he asked Mrs. Armour.

She frowned. "Now, how should I—well," she amended as he raised a brow, "I guess I did peek in once. I think there used to be a blue Dior suit and some English wool skirts and slacks hanging at the end there." She described those and some other items in detail.

The dresser had been cleaned out. So had the bedside table and the bathroom medicine cabinet.

"Can you think of anything usually in the apartment that you haven't seen here today?" he asked.

From the bathroom doorway, Mrs. Armour considered the question. "I don't know. I haven't been here all that often, you know."

"Keep looking around, will you, please?"

He could understand Lane destroying papers but he had trouble believing that she would just walk away from all her personal belongings, an accumulation that she had obviously brought with her through the sequential changes of identity. She must have a few items too loved or revealing to be left behind.

He headed back for the living room. It had more of her effects than any other room. It also had the desk. He stared at it, pulled by some magnetism he could not explain. A letter had been on that desk the first time he saw it. He wished he had seen more than the address on it before Lane turned out the light.

He tried to visualize the envelope in his mind, picturing the ornate lettering. He paused. *That* was where he had seen the writing that matched that on the flyleafs of the children's books.

A letter from Lane's mother! He ticked his tongue against his teeth in excitement.

"I remember something," Mrs. Armour said. "There used to be two photographs on that top shelf."

Photographs. He turned his full attention on her. "Do you remember what they were?"

"One was of her grandparents. She never said so, but I assumed it. It was very old, that brown color, you know, and the woman's hair and dress were World War I style. I have a wedding picture of my parents that looks very much like it. The other looked old, too ... three little girls sitting on the running board of a car."

An outdoor picture? "What was the background behind the car like?"

"Background?" She blinked. "Why, just a street, I think. Maybe there was a house in it."

"What kind of house? Brick? Stone? Wood frame? Large or small?"

She stared at him. "Really, Inspector, I never paid that much attention. Is it important?"

"Perhaps." Little girls might well include Lane as a child. A close look at the background might have helped tell him where she came from ... and where she came from could give him someone who knew where Lane was now.

2

"I never thought we'd see you again, Inspector," Nikki said. The Barbary Now barmaid set a glass of soda water in front of Garreth, eyeing him with avid curiosity. "The cops who came in the other night, your partner and the handsome one, said you'd been killed."

Garreth smiled thinly. "I was, but death was so boring I gave it up. Can you stand to answer a few more questions about Lane Barber?"

She sighed. "Shit. More? I've told every frigging detective in the city every damned thing I know ... which is zip, *nada*. We never passed more than the time of day, little comments about music or fashions or some guy."

Garreth broadened his smile to a friendly, persuasive one. "People say more than you might think. You mention a toy you've bought for a nephew or child and they come back telling you about one they bought once. Did Lane ever do that? Or maybe she mentioned some game she liked as a kid, or a pet she had."

Nikki's fingers drummed on the bottom of her plastic tray. "No ... nothing."

Garreth could hardly believe that. Even someone with the experience and control Lane had must relax once in a while. Why should she avoid talking about pets and toys as long as the reference did not give away her age?

Then he thought about how he had lied needlessly to Evelyn Kolb about his interest in her thermos. Fleeing where no one pursued.

He paid Nikki for the soda water and sat back sipping moodily. Maybe Lane always avoided making personally revealing remarks. That was not much different from what someone like Chiarelli did, being undercover twenty-four hours a day every day. After so many years, caution may have become a reflex. Had that always been true, though? Maybe clues to her past lay in previous identities. As a younger, less experienced person, she might have been more open.

Her picture, with a different name attached, must be in the past files of agents here and in Los Angeles. Finding those agents would involve time and patience, but he was used to legwork. Eventually he could learn previous names and where she had worked. That would lead him to people who had known her.

The trouble was, memories failed. The further back into her past he went, the fewer people would even remember her, let alone recall specific conversations. The trail inevitably became colder and thinner. Except if someone had a good reason to remember her.

Such as an assault?

If he could find them after forty-odd years, the people involved in that assault back in '41 might give him the best chance he had at her past. The assault itself suggested a woman more hot tempered and less cautious than the one he had met. She even gave her real name when booked. Perhaps she told people about herself back then, too.

He wished he had written down the facts and names in that complaint when he had the file in his hands. Now he would have to go to Bryant Street in the morning and hope that word of his resignation had not reached the Records people yet so that he could see the file again.

He also wished he had had a closer look at that envelope on Lane's desk. He closed his eyes, trying to visualize it. He saw the address with its ornate penmanship clearly enough, but what he needed was the return address, and no matter how he concentrated, he saw nothing but a blur, a vague, peripheral smudge. He tried visualizing the postmark, too. That had not registered at all on his memory.

Finally, sighing, he gave that up. Scratch the luck of a return address. What else did he have? Names?

He considered names. All those she had used for herself professionally could be considered derivations from "Madelaine." Not unusual. Typically an alias bore a resemblance to the righteous name. He could almost bet that all her false surnames resembled "Bieber" much as "Barber" did. However, the name on the registration of the car and driver's license, Alexandra Pfeifer, was another matter. He still saw a resemblance, but an ethnic one. What were "Bieber" and "Pfeifer," Germanic? Could it be she chose "Pfeifer" because she was familiar with names like that? Could she have come from an area populated by people of German descent?

As if an answer to that helped. There had to be hundreds of Germanic settlements across the country.

Finishing his soda water, Garreth left the club and headed back for his car. What he needed to do was consult experts and find out where large Germanic groups had settled. It might help him.

At his car he was fishing in his pocket for his keys when a voice said, "Thank God. I was afraid I'd be sitting here all night, Mikaelian."

Garreth spun around.

Rob Cohen stepped from behind a nearby car. "This is getting to be a habit, turning out the force to find you. At least you're considerate enough to drive a conspicuous car. The lieutenant wants you at Bryant Street to talk to the shooting team."

3

A schematic drawing covered the blackboard. Garreth kept his eyes fixed on it while he answered the questions the detectives on the shooting team asked over and over again. His throat felt desert dry and his muscles almost daylight weak. Maybe dawn was coming. It seemed he had been here all night, endlessly repeating his version of the afternoon's nightmare.

"The gun wouldn't fire?" one of the team asked for the dozenth time. "Is that what you say?"

"No, sir," Garreth replied one more time. "I said I couldn't fire it."

"You said the trigger felt frozen."

"Yes, sir." He carefully told the truth. The team would pounce on evasions or lies.

"Is this the gun?"

He looked at it. It was the one he had surrendered when Serruto brought him in. "Yes, sir."

The four uniformed officers with Harry and him had undergone similar grillings earlier, he knew, but the knowledge in no way eased his own discomfort.

Pointing the revolver at the floor, the detective pulled the trigger. The hammer clicked on an empty chamber. "It's operating now. Had you ever fired this particular gun before?"

"No, sir. It was issued to me this morning."

"To replace the one being used as evidence?"

"Yes, sir."

"This is your first day back on duty?"

It went on and on. Please, Inspector, repeat as nearly as you can the exact events from the time you received the radio message to call that phone number. How was it neither of you called in for clearance to go after O'Hare? How did you determine the positions of the various officers at the scene? How many shots were fired? By whom? When? Over and over it, ending always in the schematic of the living room, where an outline indicated Harry lying bleeding.

Weariness dragged at him. Through the slits of the blinds he caught glimpses of reddened sky. Dawn.

Serruto came into the room, face grim, and whispered to one of the shooting team. Fear flooded Garreth. Was it about Harry?

Serruto backed against the wall by the door. The detective turned to look down at Garreth. "Describe what happened to you in the restaurant where you and Sergeant Takananda went for lunch."

Garreth stared at him. How could anyone have learned about *that*? The obvious answer took long seconds to occur to him, but when it did, Garreth came out of his chair grinning. "Did *Harry* tell you about that? Can he *talk*?"

"He told us," Serruto said soothingly. "He's going to be all right."

Garreth wanted to cry in sheer happiness and relief.

"Tell us about the restaurant," the detective repeated.

So overjoyed about Harry that nothing else mattered, he told them, scrupulously detailing all his symptoms, omitting only his knowledge of the cause. That gave them a whole new set of questions to ask, of course, but eventually they ran out of even those, perhaps in sheer exhaustion, and let him go.

Serruto walked down the corridor with him. "Mikaelian, until further notice, keep in touch. No more APBs, okay?"

Garreth nodded, too tired to talk. He could feel daylight outside the building. It made his head ache. He pulled the dark glasses out of the coat over his arm and put them on.

"I have your badge in my office. If you change your mind, you can have it back."

Garreth bit his lip. "Thanks, but I can't take it."

Serruto eyed him. Garreth sensed an emotional jumble in the lieutenant, but when Serruto spoke, it was only to say dryly, "Resigning doesn't get you out of the paperwork for everything up to now."

They stopped at the elevator. Garreth punched for *down*. "I know. Let me get a few hours in the rack and I'll type the reports."

"Why don't you see Harry before you do either? When they let us in to see him a couple of hours ago, the first thing he did was ask about you. He blames himself for everything."

Garreth shook his head. "No. It's my fault. I—"

Serruto interrupted. "You don't have to fight for the blame. I'm willing to spread it between both of you. You're not a child, Mikaelian; no one should have had to tell you that that attack indicated you weren't fit for duty. You should have seen a doctor immediately. Harry should have made sure you went and that I was notified of what happened." He grimaced. "My guess is, before the shooting board is finished, all of us will be wearing some egg."

4

The Records section clerk regarded Garreth with some surprise. "Well, good evening, Inspector. I heard you gave up your badge."

The grapevine worked as efficiently as ever, he noticed. "I did, but I have a few reports to finish before it's official. Would you have time to find this for me?" He handed her the case and serial numbers on Madelaine Bieber's assault charge.

"I think so. How is Sergeant Takananda?"

"He's doing fine."

Except for insisting on blaming himself for the O'Hare screwup. "I'm senior partner," he had repeated several times during Garreth's visit, his voice thin and weak but emphatic. "I let us go hot-dogging in there."

"Don't worry about it now," Lien had said, just as quietly and emphatically. "Neither of you died."

Garreth's and Harry's eyes met, mutually agreeing not to discuss the differences between her scale of priorities and that the shooting board would apply.

"What's this Lien tells me about you turning in your badge?" Harry asked. "You didn't have to do that. You just need more time to recuperate before you come back to work."

Lien's eyes begged Garreth not to discuss the issue. He gave her the barest nod in reply. Anything that might stress Harry should be avoided at all cost, and Garreth read serious anxiety in Harry over the resignation. "I see that now."

"Go ask for it back."

"I will," Garreth lied.

Harry relaxed. A moment later, a nurse appeared and chased them out of the room.

In the corridor, Lien had looked up at him and read the truth somewhere in his face. "Thank you for giving him peace. What will you do now?"

"I have some things to finish first. Then"—he shrugged— "maybe I'll go back to school and finish my degree."

The lies went on and on, he thought, leaning on the counter in Records. Did he think the web of them would help him bridge the gulf around him? Or were they building a protective fence to keep others from discovering that gulf and falling into it?

"I'm sorry, Inspector," the clerk said, returning. "That file is out."

Garreth sighed. Who else would want it after all these years? Unless ... "Did Sergeant Takananda check it out?"

"No. Lieutenant Serruto."

Thanking her, he went back to Homicide. He found the squad room nearly empty. The few detectives there crowded around him as he came in, asking about Harry. He repeated what he had told the clerk in Records.

Beyond the windows of his office, Serruto slumped tiredly at his desk, looking as though he had not slept in days. He glanced up and, seeing Garreth, beckoned to him.

"How do you feel?" he asked when Garreth reached the open door.

"Fine. I'll get started on the reports." He lingered in the doorway. "I wanted to check out this Madelaine Bieber whose prints were all over Barber's apartment. R and I says you have the file on her assault arrest."

"Yes." Serruto eyed him. "Why do you want to know about her?"

Garreth put on a faint smile. "Curiosity, I guess."

Serruto reached into his desk drawer and pulled out a badge case Garreth recognized. He laid it on top of the desk. "Mikaelian, if you want to play detective, you pick this up again; otherwise, forget about Madelaine Bieber and Lane Barber until you're called to testify at Barber's trial. They're police business." He yawned hugely and added almost as an afterthought, "I nail vigilante hides to the wall."

Garreth retreated to his typewriter.

Now what? he wondered, feeding a report form into the typewriter. He could wait out Serruto. He could sit here working all night until Serruto and the others left, then search for the file. His sharpened hearing could detect someone coming in time to avoid being caught burglarizing his lieutenant's office.

Is this how you uphold the law, an inner voice asked contemptuously, *breaking it for your own private ends?*

He bit his lip, suddenly ashamed. What was he thinking about? It might take a vampire to catch a vampire, but if he let himself become like her in the process, what right did he have to hunt her? *All right, no shortcuts,* he promised his conscience. *Somehow, even without a badge, I'll stay legal.* He rubbed aching temples.

"Why don't you forget that and go back home to bed?" Serruto asked from the doorway of his office. "On second thought, let's make that an order. Go home. You're on limited duty: desk duty only, daytime only."

"Yes, sir," Garreth replied, and obediently left.

Riding down in the elevator, however, he considered the problem of legally seeing the contents of the file. Could he ask Cohen or Kolb to look at it and pass on the information? They might expect him to say why he wanted to know. Worse, they might tell Serruto who asked them to look at it. Was there anywhere outside the file that he could find the same information?

He found the answer to that about the time he stepped out of the elevator onto the ground floor. Then he had to run for his car to reach the library before it closed.

"I need the October 1941 editions of the *Chronicle*," he told the librarian on duty in the microfilm section. He wished he remembered the exact date of that assault. It meant searching the entire month's newspapers.

He spun the film through the viewer as fast as he could and still read it. He felt closing time coming and sped up the viewer a bit more.

By concentrating so hard on small items, though, he almost missed what he wanted. Lane had earned herself two columns and a picture on the front page. There was no mistaking her, towering tall between the four police officers hauling her back from a woman who crouched with blood leaking through the fingers of the hand held over her left ear. "The Barbary Coast Still Lives," the headline proclaimed.

Garreth thanked Lady Luck for the lurid reporting of that day and pressed the button for a printed copy of the page. Maybe he had something here. This Madelaine with her face contorted in fury was a far cry indeed from the Lane Barber who stood him up against a wall years later and coolly proceeded to drink his lifeblood, then go back to work.

He read the story in the dome light of his car, writing down all names and addresses in his notebook. He smiled as he read, amused at both the gossipy style of the story, laden with adjectives, and what he saw between the lines, knowing Lane to be what she was.

A woman named Claudia Darling, described as "a pert, petite, blue-eyed brunette," was accosted in the Red Onion on the evening of Friday, October 17, by "a Junoesque" red-haired singer named Mala Babra—Lane could fill a phone book with her aliases—employed by the club. An argument ensued over a naval officer both had met in the same club the evening before, Miss Babra claiming that Miss Darling had caused the serviceman to break a date made previously with Miss Babra.

Garreth smiled. He could just imagine Lane's frustration … supper all picked out and some other lady walking off with it.

When Miss Darling denied the allegation, the story went on, Miss Babra attacked. They had to be separated by police hastily summoned to the scene. Four officers were needed to subdue and hold Miss Babra. Miss Darling suffered severe bite wounds to one ear and scratches on the face, but *"the popular habitue of the nightclub scene is reported to be in satisfactory condition at County General Hospital."*

Garreth eyed the last sentence, ticking his tongue against his teeth. He sensed a sly innuendo, something readers of the time had been meant to infer, but which he, a generation later, failed to understand. He studied the photograph: the four officers straining to hold Lane, obviously surprised by her strength; Lane ablaze with fury; and the Darling woman, showing what the photographer must have considered a highly satisfactory amount of leg as she crouched dazed and bleeding on the floor. The bare leg caught Garreth's attention, but the rest of the woman held it. Even with the differences in hairstyle and fashions, he recognized what she wore as just a bit flashier, shorter, and tighter than the dresses on the women in the background. Now he understood the innuendo and chuckled. Even a generation removed, she clearly signaled her profession to him: hooker.

That was a break. If she was in the life, she had probably been busted a time or two, and that meant a record of her: names, addresses, companions. Tomorrow he would run her through R and I.

Humming, he switched off the dome light and started the car, heading out of the parking lot toward home to pick up his thermos before hunting supper.

5

Danger! Even in the oblivion of vampire sleep Garreth sensed it. The heat of human warmth touched him, spiced by the scent of blood. Someone stood in the room with him ... stood over him! *Wake up, Garreth.* As though floating somewhere apart, he saw the young Englishman pick up a spade and bring it down toward the man lying in the coffin.

Fear dragged Garreth up from darkness, spurring him to open his eyes and roll away from the slashing spade, but sleep and daylight weighted him. His arms rose with painful slowness to ward off the blow.

"No, don't," he said.

A hand caught his arm and shook it. "Garreth, wake up. You're having a nightmare. It's all right."

The words reached his ears, but his brain made no immediate sense of them. His eyes, focusing, saw Lien's face above him and recognized that it did not belong to the spade-swinging man, but his mind spun in confusion, disoriented. Lien? Where was he? The pallet under him on the bed indicated that he must be home. So how—

Panic flooded through him. He sat bolt upright. Lien! She had caught him in his unorthodox sleeping arrangement! And naked, too, beneath the single sheet over him, he remembered, clutching the sheet and pulling it up to his chin.

"Lien, what are you doing here? How did you get in? What time is it?"

She sat on the edge of the bed. "It's past two in the afternoon. I came because your mother called me after church. She's been trying to reach you since Friday. When I saw your car out front, I knew you had to be home, but I pounded on the door for five minutes without any response, so I used your spare key to let myself in."

As of today, the practice of hiding a key outside stopped. What if an enemy had stood over him, like Jonathan Harker in his nightmare? He would have been helpless to protect himself.

"Why did you unplug your phone?" Lien asked.

Unplug his phone? Oh, yes … he remembered now. He had done it Friday. He sighed. "I forgot I did it."

"I've reconnected it. Now you'd better call your mother before she has a heart attack." Lien started to get up, but paused in the act. "Why do you have that air mattress on top of the bed? And how can you sleep with only a sheet? It's freezing in here."

He avoided the question. "I'll call … if you'll let me get up and dress."

She headed toward the bedroom door. "Don't take too long."

He pulled on the first shirt and pair of pants he found, which turned out to be jeans and a ski sweater. The jeans, always snug before, hung on him. He added a belt, taken up four holes tighter than usual, and slipped his off-duty gun into an ankle holster.

He was hurriedly shaving when he heard Lien call, "Garreth, how old is this food in your refrigerator?"

He dropped the razor and ran for the kitchen.

Lien stood before the open refrigerator, unscrewing the top from his thermos. "I thought I'd fix you something to eat, but everything seems to be either moldy or mummified."

"Don't open that!" He snatched the thermos away from her, then, as she stared open-mouthed at him, stammered, "It's … the liquid protein that's part of my diet. It … needs constant refrigeration." Carefully tightening the lid again, he returned the thermos to the refrigerator.

Lien frowned at him. "You don't mean to tell me that's *all* you're eating?"

"Of course not," he lied. "It's just all I eat here at home."

He shut the refrigerator and herded her out of the kitchen, sweating. Had she seen too much? Would it make her suspicious? He wished he could think, but his mind only churned, screaming at him to run.

"You should eat more," Lien said. "'Losing weight too fast isn't healthy, and you look positively gaunt."

As much as he adored her, he longed to throw her bodily out of the apartment. Her concern and solicitude terrified him. "Thanks for coming by."

"I want to hear you call your mother before I leave."

He did not sigh; that might tell her how anxious he was to have her leave. Instead, he made himself smile and pick up the phone.

After all the fuss, his mother wanted nothing more than to see how he was. "Mother keeps insisting that you're dead," she said, "and you know how unnerving her Feelings can be for everyone else. Why don't you come home for a visit? Actually seeing you should reassure her."

"Maybe this weekend," he said, "if I have time."

"Judith needs to talk to you when you're here, too."

"Judith?" A new fear touched him. "Is something wrong with Brian?"

"He's fine. It's something else; she'll tell you."

"Do you know?"

She hedged and wandered off on a tangent, which told him she knew, all right.

"Tell me. Don't let her hit me cold with it."

"Well." He heard her take a breath. "She wants your permission to let Dennis adopt Brian."

That single sentence buried all his impatience to be rid of Lien and on his way to the office to check the Darling woman through R and I. "She *what*! You can tell her—no, I'll tell her myself!"

He stabbed down the phone button. Releasing it again, he punched Judith's phone number. No one answered. Punching for Information, he asked for Judith's parents' number. She often spent Sunday afternoons there.

"Hello, Garreth," Judith said cautiously when her mother put her on the line. "How are you?"

"What do you mean, you want permission for your husband to adopt Brian? What the hell makes you think I'll ever agree to that?"

Her breath caught. "So much for polite amenities. No, it's all right," she said to someone on the other end. "Just a minute, Garreth." He heard her moving and a door shutting, with a diminution of background sound. "Now. I thought maybe you'd agree because you love Brian and want what's best for him. Brian and Dennis are already good friends, and—"

"They can be friends, but I'm his father. I stay his father."

"He needs one full-time, Garreth, someone he can feel he belongs to. What are you? He's lucky if he sees you four or five times a year."

"You were the one who insisted on moving back to Davis. My job doesn't give me enough time off to—"

"Your job is exactly what you choose to let it be." Her bitterness came clearly over the wire to him. "It wouldn't have to be twenty-four hours a day every day, but you wanted it that way. You chose that job over Brian and me."

Oh Lord here we go ... two minutes of conversation and down into the same old rut. "Judith, I don't want to start that again."

"With Brian adopted, you wouldn't have to pay child support anymore."

She thought she could *buy* Brian for her precious Dennis? "Forget it!" he said furiously. "Brian is my son and I'm not giving him to anyone else!"

He slammed down the receiver, shaking, and turned to find Lien regarding him with sympathy. All the anxiety related to her presence here returned in an icy flood. *Don't let her think too much.*

"I have to be going. I have stacks of paperwork," he said. "Thanks again for coming by. I appreciate your concern."

"You'll visit Harry sometime today, won't you?"

He picked up a ski jacket and hurried her out the door. "Of course. May I have my spare key back? Thank you." He clattered down the steps ahead of her and out onto the street, calling over his shoulder. "I'll come by this evening."

Pulling away from the curb, he saw Lien in the rearview mirror, staring after the car. He shivered. She had caught him asleep! She had almost found the blood in the thermos. If he remained friends with Harry and her, sooner or later he would slip, would give away something fatal. He had to find Lane just as soon as possible, take care of her, and leave the city before he woke some morning to find someone standing over him with a pointed wooden stake.

6

According to R and I, Claudia Darling had been born Claudia Bologna. Her yellow sheet listed eight arrests for prostitution in the years between 1940 and 1945. After that her only offenses were those of many good citizens: speeding citations. One had been issued in 1948, one in 1952— by which time her name had become Mrs. William Drum with a Twin Peaks address—and a final one in 1955.

He copied down the information and studied it as he rode up to Homicide.

Serruto's office sat empty, but otherwise the squad room looked like it looked any other day. Garreth felt almost like a civilian in his sweater, jeans, and ski jacket. He walked quickly to his desk, only nodding greetings to the detectives there. He felt better after he began the reports. They were easy ... just typed from his notes and memory, no real involvement required, no emotion. His fingers danced across the keys with almost self-volition, translating the thoughts in his head to words on paper. The rhythm soothed, draining away tension and anxiety, even when the report dealt with a dead-end lead or Wink's screwed-up capture. He typed steadily most of the afternoon, oblivious to the other activity in the room, only occasionally pausing to greet someone or let another thought creep in.

While proofreading, though, his mind slipped back to his conversation with his ex-wife. He fumed just thinking of it. Let Dennis have Brian? No way! Yet he recognized that Judith had a valid argument. Maybe that was what he found so infuriating. He had to admit that he had not been much of a father ... and what kind could he ever be now? *Come on, son; let's go out for a bite. You have a hamburger and I'll take the waitress.*

He tapped the reports into a neat stack and carried them into Serruto's office. That was enough for today. Now, to Miss Claudia Bologna Darling Drum. He closed the door of the office and sat down behind the desk with the phone book.

Three William Drums lived in San Francisco, none in the Twin Peaks area. Dialing the number of William C. Drum, he found a Mrs. Drum at the other end, but a young woman and not a Claudia. She had never heard of Claudia Drum.

No one answered William R. Drum's phone.

He dialed William R. Drum, Jr. A child answered. Hearing the high-pitched voice, Garreth grimaced. This did not sound promising. "May I speak to Mrs. Drum, please?"

"Who?"

Garreth tried another tack. "Is your mommie there?"

"Mommie?"

Garreth felt like an idiot, talking baby talk to make himself understood. But to his great relief, a woman's voice came on the line a few moments later.

"This is Inspector Mikaelian of the San Francisco police," he explained. "I'm attempting to locate a Mrs. Claudia Drum."

"I'm afraid I don't know anyone by that name."

"She's an older woman. Your mother-in-law isn't named Claudia?"

"No, Marianna. Wait a minute." Her voice became muffled as she called to someone with her, "Bill, what's your mother's name?"

Several voices murmured, unintelligible to Garreth, then the voice of an older man came on. "This is William Drum, Sr. You're looking for a woman named Claudia? I may know her. Can you describe her for me?"

"She's short, blue-eyed, brunette. Her maiden name was Bologna and in 1955 she lived in the Twin Peaks area."

"And you say you're with the police?"

Garreth gave Drum his phone number and invited him to call back. Drum did, then explained that Claudia Drum was his first wife. "We divorced in 1956."

"Do you know where she is now and what name she's using?"

Drum hesitated. "I'm curious, Inspector, what you want with her. If all you know is that name, this must concern something very old."

"We're looking for information on a woman who assaulted her in 1941."

A long silence greeted that remark. Garreth pictured Drum staring nonplused at the receiver, wondering why the police cared about a forty-year-old assault. Finally, with a shrug and a dry note in his voice, Drum said, "Her name is Mrs. James Emerson Thouvenelle and she lives on the wall." He gave a Presidio Heights address and phone number.

Garreth wrote them down, impressed. Claudia had done well for herself, rising from hooker to the mansions overlooking the Presidio. He wondered if Drum's dry tone indicated that he knew he had been a mere stepping-stone to that mansion. Garreth made sure he thanked William R. Stepping-stone Drum warmly before hanging up and dialing the Thouvenelle number.

How would his request to see her be received? As a rude reminder of her past?

When he mentioned Mala Babra, however, the rich voice on the other end of the line laughed. "That crazy singer? Are things so slow for you boys that you're digging into the basement files? Yes, I'll talk to you."

Garreth saw one problem: identification. It was all very well to tell her over the phone that he was from the police. She could call back and verify that. What did he do when she asked to see identification at her house?

His eyes dropped to the drawer where Serruta had put his badge case. His hand reached out for the drawer pull, then jerked back. *You were going to keep clean, remember?*

"Will this evening be convenient for you?" He would bluff his way in somehow.

"If you come before seven."

Garreth parked at the curb at a quarter till the hour. The heavy front door bore an ornate lion's head knocker in the middle. He reached out for it, but the door swung open even before he touched the knocker. A plump pouter pigeon of a woman looking the epitome of grandmother and matron studied him from the level of his shoulders.

"You're the young man who called? Mikaelian?" she asked.

"Yes. You're—"

"Claudia Thouvenelle. Well." She looked him over, relieved about something. "Please come in. Do you have a first name?"

"Garreth." He followed her to a set of double doors down the hallway.

She pulled one of the doors open and leaned into the library behind. "James," she said to the man sitting in a leather chair, "this is Garreth Mikaelian, the son of my old girlfriend Katherine Kane. You remember me telling you about her, don't you? Gary and I will be across the hall chatting if you need me."

She led an astonished Garreth across the hall to a living room and settled herself on a sofa. She met his eyes with her own, unnaturally blue—contact lenses?—and cool as ice. "I see no need to reveal the long-dead past to my husband, though understand that I'm not ashamed of it. I even find the idea of talking about those days after all these years a bit nostalgic. What do you want to know about that madwoman?"

"Everything you can tell me: who she was, where she came from, who her friends were."

She blinked, in disappointment, Garreth would have sworn. "I don't know anything except that she nearly disfigured me. She was crazy. It wasn't my fault if the naval officer preferred me to her. Who wouldn't prefer a woman-sized woman to that great gallumphing elephant?"

Garreth silently compared the matron with her blue-gray hair and sagging jowls to the slim, taut-bodied redhead who had her choice of men to bed and bleed. He could imagine that a woman so tall in those days might find the pickings a bit lean. Lane had the last laugh on her generation now, though.

"May I ask what your interest in her is after all these years?"

"We're trying to locate her. We think she has information we need on a current investigation."

"Have you checked the state mental institutions? She was quite unbalanced and should have been confined."

Garreth wrinkled his forehead. "Then why did you drop the charges?"

"As a favor for a friend, Don Lukert, the manager of the Red Onion. He was afraid that the owners might be upset by the bad publicity, so I agreed to drop the charges if he'd fire her and use his influence to see that she couldn't find another job in North Beach. He did and I did."

Vindictive bitch, Garreth thought. Aloud he said, "This manager. Is his name Donald Lukert?"

"No. Eldon."

"Do you know where he is today?" Mr. Lukert might have known something about his singer.

The woman shook her head. "I made enough during the war so that with some wise investments, I retired after Armistice and dropped out of my old circles. I went by the Red Onion a few years later but it had burned and another club had been built in its place. Don wasn't there. If he's still in the city, he's probably in a nursing home. He was in his late forties back then."

"Did Mr. Lukert ever talk to you about Miss Babra?"

"Oh, a couple of times, perhaps. We had some laughs over how ridiculous and grotesque she was."

Garreth decided he did not care much for Claudia Bologna Darling Drum Thouvenelle.

"She tried to make him think she was a Balkan princess. She carried the blood of ancient nobility in her veins, is how she put it. She gave him some fantastic story about having escaped from eastern Europe just ahead of Hitler's storm troopers. But she wasn't European. That Bela Lugosi accent she used disappeared the moment she started shrieking at me and before that, a client of mine I met at the club heard her speaking what she *claimed* was her language and he said it was nothing but a preposterous hodgepodge of German and Russian."

Garreth blinked. German matched Lane's choice of names, but where did the Russian fit in? *Possible German and Russian community?* he wrote. They would have to be groups insular enough to be speaking their own languages in addition to English.

After asking questions for another ten minutes without learning anything more that seemed useful, he closed the notebook and stood. "I think that's all I need. Thank you for your time."

She escorted him to the door, speaking in a voice pitched to carry. "I'm so glad to hear about Kate. I'd lost track of her and thought I'd never hear of her again. Give your mother a big hug for me, will you?"

Garreth sighed in relief as the door closed behind him. What luck. She had never come close to asking for his ID. *Lucky cop. Thank you, Lady Luck. Keep smiling, Lady.*

7

The final, formal steps of resignation took less time and hurt more than Garreth anticipated. Checking in all equipment issued to him by the department felt like the division of property in a divorce. Gun, theirs; holster, his. Badge and ID card, theirs; badge case, his. Call box and other assorted keys, theirs; receipt for items currently being kept as evidence, his. So it went, down to his signature on all the necessary papers and the receipt of his final check.

He put that away carefully in his billfold. How long would it last? Until he found Lane?

"Good luck, Mr. Mikaelian," the clerk said impersonally.

Mister. Civilian. Garreth turned away, biting his lip.

Cleaning out his desk felt like divorce, too … packing up what he felt like taking, giving or throwing away the rest. Some of it amazed him; had he really kept so much candy squirreled away in his desk? No wonder he had not been able to lose weight. And where had the Valium come from? For the most part, however, he worked numbly, feeling a chill like an arctic wind blowing through him … that despite the heat he had taken the past twelve hours. *See the heat getting the heat.*

First it had been Harry last night—someone Harry refused to identify had told him about the finality of Garreth's resignation—and then the shooting board this morning.

The officer going in the front with Harry had sighed in relief as the board ruled his shooting of Wink righteous, but no one else found any comfort. The board gave Harry and Garreth what amounted to the Starsky and Hutch Award for Hot Dog of the Month, but also named the four uniformed officers as accessories. Failure to clear the operation with Serruto headed the list of sins, followed by criticisms of the execution that left no doubt that the board felt only divine intervention prevented any loss of life.

They had reserved an entire section of their opinion just for Garreth. "Under the best of circumstances, even if all other procedure had been correctly observed, this operation would have been handicapped, if not compromised, by the presence of Inspector Mikaelian. From the evidence of his own statements and those made by Sergeant Takananda, it is clear that this officer should not have been on duty. The board questions the judgment of Dr. Charles in certifying him fit. We question the judgment of Lieutenant Serruto in accepting that certification. And in light of the particularly savage attack on Inspector Mikaelian such a short time before, its bizarre aftermath in the morgue, and the inspector's forcible departure from the hospital and refusal to return for proper medical observation and treatment, this board wonders why a psychological evaluation of this officer was not required before returning him to duty."

Behind his glasses, Garreth had glanced over to where Serruto sat with his handsome face grimly deadpan. Garreth burned in an agony of guilt. The lieutenant would be bearing the brunt of that last criticism. Under questioning, Serruto had stated that he planned to send Garreth to the department shrink, but could not explain why he had failed to do so. Of course he would not remember that the thought had disappeared the moment Garreth looked him in the eyes and declared himself fit.

In Homicide afterward, checking to be sure Garreth had all the necessary reports turned in, Serruto had said, "We can't make you see the shrink now, but you should go. Whatever brought on that attack in the restaurant and made you freeze at O'Hare's place is a time bomb ticking away inside you. You ought to have it defused."

"I'm fine," Garreth had said, declining, keenly aware that the advice and its refusal would probably be noted in his personnel jacket ... the final comments on his service.

He tried not to think of that now, as he went through his desk. "Tea, Mikaelian?"

He looked up to see Evelyn Kolb offering him her thermos. He nodded. Maybe it would help ease the cold inside him.

She pumped him a cupful. Sipping it, he reflected on Mr. Eldon Lukert. The phone book gave no listing for him, though a call to the phone company revealed that he had had one until five years ago. The county tax rolls still carried him. Garreth had managed to learn that much before the shooting board sat in judgment. Claudia Bologna etc. might be correct in her opinion that he was in a nursing home. Garreth planned to call them all to see.

Almost before he knew it, the tea was gone and the desk cleared. The box of belongings sat filled, ready to be removed. Reluctantly, Garreth put on his coat.

Serruto came out of his office, a hand extended. "Good luck, Mikaelian."

Garreth shook the hand. "Thank you." He thought about going around the room shaking everyone's, but a lump in his throat warned him that he might be in tears by the time he finished, so he shook just Kolb's and waved at the other detectives. "So long."

Their eyes reflected a common thought: *That could be me.* They said, "Good luck."

Garreth felt as though he stood on a ship pulling away fast from shore, watching the distance between himself and them growing ever wider. He ambled out of the room with the box, wanting to run, silently swearing at Lane. *These were brothers, lady. These were my family, and you took them away from me. Why didn't you just kill me straight out? Why couldn't you let me die clean?*

He drove home thinking: *Mr. Eldon Lukert, be good to me. Lead me to her. Please.*

He started with the A's in the nursing home section of the yellow pages and worked his way through the listings, one phone call at a time.

If necessary, he was prepared to call every home in the Bay Area, including San Mateo, Alameda, and Marin counties.

Halfway through the San Francisco listings, the woman answering said, "Eldon Lukert? No, we don't have a patient by that name now. It sounds familiar, though. Just a minute." She went off the line.

Garreth crossed his fingers.

She came back. "We did have an Eldon Lukert until last month … Mr. Eldon Wayne Lukert."

"That's the gentleman I need. Can you tell me where he went?"

She paused. "I'm sorry. He didn't actually go anywhere. He died."

8

Garreth stood at the window, staring out at the twilight-reddened sky. Lukert died last month. *The bitch Luck strikes again.* Dead end … literally. Finis. He rubbed his forehead. Now what?

Out of the churning in his mind, one thought rose: Lane's apartment. It still drew him. She had lived there, called it home. Pieces of her, collected and kept over the long years and many changes of identity, filled it. Those pieces must indicate what she was and where she had come from, if only he could put them together right.

Driving to the apartment, he approached the door with caution. He had been invited in once. Would it still hold good, as the legend said? Or would the fiery pain bar him again?

At the door, his body still felt cool and comfortable. He leaned against the door, willing himself to the other side. Still no pain touched him. There was only the wrenching that he had come to associate with moving through barriers, uncomfortable but not painful, and in a moment he stood in the hallway.

How dark it had looked that first time he walked down it behind Lane Barber. No more. Now he saw it as gray twilight. For once he felt grateful for his vampire vision; he could move around the apartment and study it all he needed without lights to arouse the curiosity and suspicion of neighbors.

He stepped into the living room … and stopped cold still. It had been stripped clean! The furniture remained, but the paintings, the sculpture, the books and objects on the shelves were all gone.

Garreth ran for the bedroom and jerked open the closet. Her clothes still hung inside. In the kitchen he found the few items in the cupboards untouched, too.

He went back to the living room to stare at the empty shelves. When had she come back? Sometime in the last few days, obviously. She had come back and taken the items that were important to her. How did she know the apartment was not being watched?

Perhaps because she herself had been watching?

He sat down in a handy chair. Could it be she had never left the city at all? He bit his lip. Never left the city. Why had they not thought of that?

Perhaps Serruto had and simply neglected to mention it to Garreth; after all, Garreth had not been deeply involved in the investigation since his injury. He found it easy to imagine how they missed finding her. After ridding herself of the car or hiding it, she probably checked into a hotel in some kind of disguise. With her height, she could even pass as a man.

She had stayed, and watched, and when it was safe, had picked up her belongings. This was one very cool lady. What was it her agent had said about her? All ice and steel inside. Really!

A shiver moved down his spine. *The maiden is powerful.* Beware of such a maiden. Made of ice and steel and with over forty years head start on him in vampirism and living experience, did he really stand a chance of finding her? What might she do if she suspected he was after her?

Then he shook his head. Personal danger should be the least of his worries. His life was already gone. All she could take away from him now was existence. On the other hand, she had the capacity to harm a great many more people if allowed to continue unchecked.

Very well, then … he must keep going. He needed a direction, though. Any help he might have gained from her belongings had disappeared. He had to proceed on what he already knew.

What *did* he know?

The writing paper still remained in the desk. He took out a sheet and itemized his knowledge. She came, probably, from a Germanic background. She sometimes used Germanic names. She spoke German and Russian.

He made a note to find out through one of the local universities the location of German and Russian groups near each other in the United States around World War I when she was born.

Could any of her belongings regionalize her? Too bad he did not know rocks well enough to describe those in the type tray to a geologist. If all of them were childhood "treasures" as other objects in the tray seemed to suggest, and if two or more came from a single geographic area, it might have been a lead. All he remembered, though, was the black shark tooth. Was that something he could use?

The apartment had given him as much as it was ever going to. He left, checking out the window beside the door to make sure the street was clear before passing through to the porch, and drove down to Fisherman's Wharf.

A few of the shops in the area remained open, catching late tourist trade. He wandered into one. "Do you have shark's teeth?" he asked the girl behind the counter.

She took him to a section where the wall displayed small circles of jawbone lined with rows of wicked teeth. He studied the teeth. They looked to be the same shape as the teeth he had seen, but were all white, not black.

"Do you have any black shark's teeth?"

She blinked. "Black? I've never seen black ones before."

He tried a similar shop farther down the street with the same results. The two clerks and a customer there had never seen or heard of black shark's teeth, either.

The time had come, he decided, to seek expert advice. In the morning he would call one of the universities and ask them where black shark's teeth came from.

Morning. He chafed at that. Why did it always have to be during the day when he could accomplish anything? He crossed Jefferson and began wandering through the arcades of the Cannery, peering into its shop windows fuming in impatience. Nothing was open when he felt most like working. Lane had taken convenience from him, too.

Then, in the window of a jewelry shop, he saw them ... earrings, hooped for pierced ears, with small black teeth dangling from them! The shop had closed, of course, but a light still burned and he could see someone moving around inside. Garreth rapped on the window.

A man came out of a back room. He shook his head, pointing at the sign in the window stating business hours.

"I just want to ask a question," Garreth called.

I'm closed, the man's mouth said.

"I just want to know where those earrings come from!"

Come back tomorrow.

Garreth groped in his jacket pocket, then swore when he remembered there was no longer a badge to pull out and dangle before the window.

"Sir," he called, "this is very important. I *must*—"

But the man shook his head a final time and walked out of the room, leaving Garreth swearing in frustration. The question would have taken only a minute to ask and answer. The shopkeeper would have opened up fast enough for a badge. So why did he refuse Garreth that minute?

Because I don't have a badge; I'm only a civilian now.

And as the implications of that beyond the present inconvenience sank in, Garreth saw how truly alone he stood against his quarry, and he shivered in the cold wind blowing down his unprotected back.

9

The TV morning news warned citizens to drive cautiously. Fog had rolled in overnight and blanketed the entire city so heavily that it lay in a dim, shadowless twilight. Foghorns sounded from Mile Rocks east to Fleming Point and from Point San Pablo south to Hunters Point. Traffic accident investigation units ran fifteen calls behind. Garreth, though, welcomed the fog. He still felt the sun above it, weighting and weakening him, but for once he could enjoy opening the shades and letting such daylight as there was fill the apartment. He could sit by the window wearing his trooper glasses, feet upon the sill, phone in hand, and look out at the billowing grayness while he dialed the number of the biology department at the University of San Francisco.

"My name is Garreth Mikaelian. I need to talk to someone who can tell me where certain kinds of shark's teeth are found."

He would have thought that was a simple request, but the phone went on hold for what seemed to be an eternity before a reedy male voice said, "This is Dr. Edmund Faith. You're the gentleman who needs to know where to find certain breeds of sharks?"

"I need to know where their *teeth* are found. Let me explain."

"By all means, Mr.—"

"Mikaelian. I found a shark's tooth in a shop on Fisherman's Wharf the other day. It's unusual because it's black. I'd like to find another and have a pair of earrings made for my wife. However, the girl in the shop had no idea where the tooth came from and neither did anyone else I asked."

"A *black* shark's tooth?"

"Yes. Do you know where in the world they come from?"

"Mr. Mikaelian, if you're interested in black shark's teeth, you don't want me; you want a paleontologist. I'm not sure of all the areas they're found, but I do know that the black ones are fossils."

"Fossils?" Garreth sat upright.

"Maybe I can give you a name," Dr. Faith went on. "Let's see." Over the line came the rustle of paper. "Yes. Try Dr. Henry Ilfrod in the geology department." He gave Garreth a phone number.

Garreth jotted the number down, then jiggled the phone button and dialed the new number.

Dr. Ilfrod, a secretary informed Garreth, was in class. Garreth remembered from his college days how difficult it could be to find a particular professor when one needed him, and with a sigh, said, "I need information on locating fossil shark's teeth. I'll talk to anyone who can help me."

"I'll see if the graduate students are in their office," the secretary said.

The phone went on hold again. Garreth drummed his fingers. As much as he preferred phoning to running around in daylight, perhaps he should have driven to the campus. Listening to a phone in limbo, he found it too easy to imagine the secretary finishing a letter then going on coffee break, forgetting about him.

Before long, though, another voice came on the line, pleasantly female, inquiring if she could be of help. Garreth patiently repeated his question. "Can you tell me the areas where black shark's teeth are found?"

"Well." She drew out the word. "Fossil shark's teeth can be found in about seventy-five percent of the country. It's almost all been under water at one time or another."

Garreth sighed. Seventy-five percent? So much for the tooth as a lead to Lane's background.

"But," the young woman went on, "most of the teeth are white. The only places I know to find the black ones are on the eastern seaboard and in western Kansas."

Garreth scribbled in his notebook. "Just those two places? How easy are the teeth to find there?"

"I think you have to dig back east, but they're on the surface and accessible in Kansas."

Accessible. "Could a kid find one without much trouble?"

"I'm sure he could. I've been told it's possible to pick them up just walking across a plowed field or in the cuts along roads and streams."

Which should be how she acquired it, if the tooth in the type tray were a "treasure." He recalled the other fossils in the type tray. "Are there many kinds of fossils available in the Kansas area, say in limestone?"

"It's wonderful fossil country"

He thanked her and hung up, then sat staring at his scribbled notes. Kansas. The postmark the lab brought up on the burned envelope had a 6 and 7 in it. Harry had said that the Kansas ZIPs used those numbers. He ticked his tongue against his teeth. Did the trail smell warmer?

He went through the phone book again, this time for the number of the sociology department. "I need to talk to someone who can tell me where immigrant German and Russian groups settled in this country."

That brought him more interminable time on hold while the secretary hunted for a likely prospect. She came back suggesting he call in two hours, when a Dr. Iseko would be in his office.

Hanging up, Garreth sat looking out the window. A partial Zip code and—when he reached this Dr. Iseko—areas of German and Russian settlements would still not pinpoint Lane's home exactly. He needed a town. Three partial letters had also been visible on that postmark. What were they? An O or U preceded by A, K, R, or X and followed by any letter beginning with a vertical stroke. He hunted through the bookcase, but had nothing like an atlas, nothing with a detailed map of Kansas in it. It appeared he would have to go out, after all.

He drove down to what had become his best source of information lately, the public library. There he spent an hour, with the zip directory, finding towns with 67 as the first or second two numbers and whose name contained letters in the right combination to match the postmark. Halfway through the list of towns, a name leaped out of the book at him: *Pfeifer.* Pfeifer! Eagerly, he raced through the rest of the names. Ten fit. He looked up their locations in an atlas. Of the ten, two possibles lay in the immediate vicinity of Pfeifer, Dixon to the southwest and Baumen to the northeast.

Then he went looking for a telephone to call the university back. This time he found Dr. Iseko in his office.

"I'm a writer doing research for a book," Garreth told him. "I need to know if Kansas has communities of German immigrants living in close proximity to Russian immigrants, and if so, where."

"I'm afraid there are none quite like that in Kansas," the anthropologist replied.

Garreth's stomach dropped. He swore silently in disappointment. "But what about towns like Pfeifer?"

"That's the Ellis County area? Pfeifer and the communities around it like Schoenchen and Munjor don't have German and Russian immigrants; they were settled by the so-called Volga Germans, Germans who immigrated to Russia and lived along the Volga before immigrating to this country in the latter quarter of the nineteenth century."

Something electric sizzled through Garreth. He felt all his hair stand on end. "They're a kind of mixed German and Russian, then? Does their language have both German and Russian in it?"

"It most certainly does. It's a very unique language. An acquaintance of mine wrote his dissertation on it."

Claudia etc. had said: *It was nothing but a hodgepodge of German and Russian.*

"How large an area did these Volga Germans settle?"

"The Catholic group is mainly around Ellis County. However, there was a Protestant German-Russian group who settled in Bellamy and Barton counties, and some of them extend into Rush and Ness."

Garreth wrote it all down. After thanking the doctor and hanging up, he went back to the library and the atlas. Dixon lay in Rush County; Baumen, in Bellamy County.

Back to the telephone, calling Information in Kansas, calling Information in Dixon and Baumen. Did they have listings for Biebers? Yes. Both had Biebers.

Excitement rose in Garreth. He might be completely wrong, Lane might come from the East, but Kansas looked good. Very good. He had a feeling about it. A Grandma Doyle-quality Feeling? Or perhaps blood called to blood. After all, in a sense, he was Lane's son; she had made him.

However strongly he felt the key to her lay in those two small towns, though, he would never know for certain without further investigation. He could not do it by phone, either. If she were in touch with people there, they might warn her that she had been traced. To be effective needed subtlety.

He would have to go there.

10

The country did not have the dinner-plate flatness Garreth expected, but its gold-brown hills, so unlike either the yellow ones of California or those in San Francisco, stepped with streets and houses, rolled to an almost unimaginably distant horizon, only sparsely dotted with trees and human constructs. The sky arched overhead, a cobalt bowl of infinity broken only here and there by wisps of cloud. The sun burned Garreth's eyes even behind his glasses. Driving south toward Dixon out of Hays, he felt overwhelmed, a mote crushed between the immensity of earth and sky. He wondered whether it might have been wiser to drive during the day instead of only at night, sleeping in his little tent at public campsites by day. Then he could have gradually accustomed himself to the broadened horizon instead of being suddenly hit by it on this drive.

To take his mind off his unexpected agoraphobia, Garreth thought ahead to Dixon, rehearsing his cover story. He wanted to hunt his relatives. When his grandmother died last year, she had left a letter revealing that she was not the real mother of Garreth's father. Phillip Mikaelian, the letter said, had really been born to a young girl who roomed with them and became pregnant out of wedlock. After the birth, the girl ran away, abandoning the baby, and rather than send it to an orphanage, Garreth's grandmother had raised the boy as her own. She had no idea where the real mother was, but she had a photograph and remembered that the girl used to write letters to a town in the Ellis County area of Kansas. As he was currently between jobs, he had decided to trace his real grandmother's family. He looked young enough to pass as the grandson of a woman born around 1916.

The photograph he carried was actually of Grandma Doyle, taken in the late twenties when she was seventeen and fresh from Ireland. The hard cardboard square stiffened the inside pocket of his coat. Feeling it, Garreth remembered two weekends ago, when he asked for it.

Handing it to him, his grandmother had said, "May it bring you she who killed you, and then a peaceful sleep."

She had known what he was from the moment he walked in the house. She said nothing, but beyond his parents, he saw her reach for the silver Maltese cross she always wore around her neck.

"Garreth," his mother had exclaimed in horror, "you're becoming skin and bones!"

His father said, "What the hell is this I read in the paper about your partner being shot and you quitting the department?"

But his eyes and attention were on Grandma Doyle. "Grandma?" He reached out to hug her but she hurriedly backed away and left the room. Garreth stared stricken after her. "Grandma!"

His mother touched him on the arm. "Please forgive her. I think she's getting old. Ever since you were attacked, she's insisted you're dead. I think she just needs time to accept that, for once, her Feeling was wrong."

Garreth had given silent thanks that his mother misinterpreted the reason for his distress. "I understand." Which did nothing, however, to lessen the pain of having someone in his family fear him.

"What's been going on out there with you?" his father asked.

Garreth's jaw tightened in resentment. Could they have at least a little of: *How are you, son?* and: *It's good to see you home in one piece*, rather than immediately moving into: *Up against the wall. Spread those feet. You* don't *have the right to remain silent, and anything you say or don't say will be used against you.*

Explaining was not only going to be difficult; it would be impossible. Nevertheless, Garreth tried.

His mother went white, listening. "Will you go back to college now?"

He heard the relief in her voice. Of course she was glad to have him out; now she did not have to fear phone calls about him.

But his father said, "Shane never gives up. They've operated on that knee four times and sometimes he has to play filled with painkillers, but he always plays. He never quits because he's been hurt a little. He's never walked out of a game because he was going to be penalized, either."

That stung. Garreth protested, "I didn't resign because of what the shooting board might say or do!"

"Are you going to see a psychiatrist like they suggested?" his mother asked.

His father snorted. "He doesn't need a shrink; he just needs to quit feeling sorry for himself." He leveled a hard stare at Garreth. "You ought to ask for reinstatement, take your lumps from the shooting board like a man, and get back to work."

Garreth had not argued. "Yes, sir," he said, and escaped from the house into the backyard. Even sunlight was preferable to further conversation with his father.

Why did this have to happen? He loved his father dearly. If only the man could ask a question without making it sound like interrogation and offer an opinion that did not seem to be an order. The worst part was, Garreth could not help wondering if his father was right.

The earth welcomed him as he sat down in the shade of the big cottonwood where he and Shane had built a tree house years ago. The platform still sat in the fork, a little more weathered each year but sound enough yet for Brian and for Shane's kids to play on it when they visited.

Garreth had lain back against the trunk, rubbing his forehead as he thought about Brian. As soon as he visited the boy the question of adoption was bound to come up again. He closed his eyes wearily. What should he do about it this time?

Feet whispered down the back steps and across the lawn toward him, but he left his eyes closed. The scent of lavender overwhelming that of blood told him who it was.

The feet stopped a short distance away. "*Dearg—due*. Undead," his grandmother's voice said quietly. Fighting his eyes open, he saw her lower herself into a lawn chair. "Why is it you're walking?"

He sat up. "Grandma, I'm not dead! Look at me. I walk; I breathe; my heart beats. I reflect in mirrors. I can touch your cross, too."

"But what do you eat? Do you still love the sun?" She pointed at his glasses.

He could not answer that. Instead, after a hesitation, he said, "Whatever else I am, I'm still your grandson. I won't hurt you."

She regarded him uncertainly, then, with a quick touch on the cross around her neck, patted the side of the chair. "Come to me."

She sat in the sun, but he moved to the ground beside her.

She reached out hesitantly to touch his cheek. "Is it to avenge yourself on she who did this to you that you can't sleep?"

He considered several answers before sighing and giving the one she appeared most ready to accept. "Yes."

She stroked his hair. "Poor unquiet spirit."

His inner self protested, denying that he was walking dead, but he swallowed it as useless to say—she would expect the refusal to believe—and leaned his head against her knee. "I need your help."

"To find *her*?"

Garreth nodded.

"What will you be wanting me to do?"

At the fierce tone of her voice, he looked up and had to laugh. She looked so righteously angry, so ready to go into battle against the fiend who had done this to her grandson, that Garreth regretted needing only the photograph from her. Coming up onto his knees, he hugged her.

She hugged him back and then, to his dismay, began sobbing. He knew he was hearing her cry over his grave.

He held her until she quieted, wondering … could she be right? Was he nothing but a temporarily animated instrument of revenge?

It made a hell of a thought to take with him when he visited Brian. Thinking it, he stood at a distance from himself and the boy. He noticed for the first time a certain formality in the boy's attitude toward him, a reservation not exhibited toward his stepfather. Logic told Garreth that was natural; Brian saw Dennis every day, whereas, for six years, since the boy was two years old, Garreth had been no more than a visitor. How much less would Garreth be from now on?

"Judith," he said, "I've been thinking about the adoption."

She looked quickly at him. "I'm sorry I brought it up when I did; I didn't realize the kind of stress you were under."

He shrugged. "It doesn't matter. If you and Dennis want to go ahead—"

She shook her head, cutting him off. "Of course we want to, but can you be sure *you* really want us to? Why don't we let it ride for a bit, until you have things straightened out for yourself."

He had regarded her with surprise, but nodded, and for once, a visit had ended amicably.

He wished he could have said as much for the rest of the week-end, which became a test in ingenuity in avoiding meals and dodging questions about how he had changed and what he planned to do now. Altogether, returning to San Francisco had been a great relief.

A relief which, unfortunately, had not lasted long. Harry, feeling better every day, began nagging him during Garreth's daily visits. "Kansas? What in the world are you going to Kansas for? Come on, Mik-san; why don't you see the shrink and come back to the department where you belong?"

Only Lien kept silent on the subject, quietly helping him sublet the apartment, sell what he no longer wanted, store what he chose not to take with him, and buy a few new clothes to replace the ones that no longer fit. She had said nothing until the day she helped him pack his car. Then, as he closed the back, she said, "I don't know what's happened to you. I wish I knew how to help. I asked *I Ching* for advice to give you. Do you mind listening to it one last time?"

He leaned against the car, smiling fondly at her. "What did the sage have to say?"

"The hexagram was number twelve, *Standstill*. It says that heaven and earth are out of communion and that all things are benumbed."

He bit his lip. That was certainly true enough for him.

"Inferior people are in ascendancy but don't allow yourself to be turned from your principles. There are change lines in the second and fourth places, advising that a great man will suffer the consequences of a standstill and by his willingness to suffer, ensure the success of his principles. However, acting to re-create order must be done with proper authority. Setting one's self up to alter things according to one's own judgment can end in mistake and failure."

Garreth listened soberly. "What else? The change lines make a new hexagram."

"The second one is number fifty-nine, *Dispersion*." She smiled. "It suggests success, especially after journeying and, of course, perseverance. Persevere, Garreth, and be true to yourself. And don't forget about us."

He had hugged her hard, promising to keep in touch. Lien, Harry, San Francisco, and his family seemed so far away from these Kansas plains he drove across now that they might have belonged to another lifetime, but *I Ching* lingered with him. Persevere. Yes, he would, to the end of the earth and time ... whatever it took to find Lane. That threat of failure if he set himself up as judge bothered him, however. It smacked too closely of the warning regarding powerful maidens. He was not making himself judge, was he? He only intended to find her and take her back to San Francisco.

The highway entered Dixon. After asking directions, Garreth found the high school. As he was climbing out of the car outside the small building, the warm wind struck him. It had some of the same qualities as a sea breeze, a pushiness, an aggressive wildness, a singing contempt for the land and that which crawled there. It buffeted him, bringing the scents of fresh-watered grass and dusty earth, and pushed him up the steps into the building.

He located the office, an expanded broom closet bearing the word OFFICE on the frosted glass panel of the door, and the principal, a Mr. Charles Yoder. Yoder listened to his story with interest.

"People are more and more interested in their roots these days. I'll be happy to help you if I can."

What he did was take Garreth to the Board of Education building and down a steep set of stairs to a dim basement. There they hunted through file envelopes stacked together on metal shelves and through ancient metal and wooden filing cabinets. A secretary joined them eventually. "Graduation pictures? I know I've seen them somewhere ... a whole stack of them."

They finally located the pictures on a top shelf, all still framed, the glass so dusty as to render the sepia-toned photographs behind all but invisible. The principal went back to the high school, leaving Garreth and the secretary to bring the pictures up into the light and clean them. But when all that had been done, and Garreth compared the picture of the girls in the 1930 to 1940 classes with his mental image of Lane Barber, he found no match.

The secretary wiped at a smudge on her nose "I'm sorry," she said.

Garreth shrugged. "It would be almost unbelievable to find the right town first off, wouldn't it?"

Still, he would have liked that much luck. Now he had to check all the high schools in the area, both to maintain his cover and on the slim chance that even if the letter came from Dixon, Lane's family lived somewhere else in the area.

"I met a Bieber in San Francisco," he said to the secretary. "Madelaine Bieber. She was a singer. I wonder if she came from somewhere around here, too."

"Madelaine? The name doesn't sound familiar."

He dropped back by the high school to thank the principal and managed to work in the remark about the singer with him, too ... but with no more luck. The name meant nothing to Yoder.

Back in his car, Garreth spread the Kansas map on the steering wheel and studied the area around Dixon. He had time yet today to visit another town. Or maybe two? Was it possible to cover three a day? A whole cluster of towns sat at no more than ten-mile intervals and he needed to work as fast as possible. Every day depleted his dwindling cash reserves still further.

He started the car and headed down the road west toward the next town.

A name on a map did not necessarily mean a town there, Garreth discovered. It could indicate no more than a gas station and a grain elevator—a row of huge, melded columns which he found an odd but fascinating structure. There had once been a real town, but it had dried up over the decades until just the elevator remained, a massive tombstone to mark its passing. The former town had once boasted a high school, too, in that bygone era, but the records had disappeared into limbo. The best a withered old man tending the gas station could suggest was for him to check the county seat.

"They might've moved the town records there."

Garreth visited the county courthouse and the local high school, as long as he was in town—but the county clerk knew nothing about any school records transferred from the defunct town. She advised checking back the next day.

The high school had its records, but they were not immediately available, either. They, too, suggested that he come back the following day.

Tomorrow. Garreth sighed. Why always tomorrow? Lane's mother had to be elderly, and if he did not find her soon, he might be in the same position he had been in when looking for the manager of the Red Onion, with only a grave to question.

Gloomily, he wondered at the real chances of finding Lane this way. Between dead towns and lost records, he could so easily miss the traces of her. And then what would he do? Question every Bieber in the area? Word would certainly find its way back to her then, and knowing a hunter had come this close, she might stop communicating with her family and disappear forever.

On that depressing note, he headed the car back toward Hays.

11

One nice thing about bad days, Garreth reflected ironically, was that something else always came along to offer an alternative worry … in this case, hunger. The four quarts of blood he had collected to keep him fed on the way east were gone. Tonight he needed to find a new source of food.

Rinsing out his thermos in the washbowl of his motel room, he considered the possibilities. He had already concluded that rats would not be as common in a small town as along the Embarcadero, a fact he faced with mixed emotions. As much as he detested being dependent on rats to live, at least he knew where and how to hunt them. He knew nothing about jackrabbits and prairie dogs, the two comparable species he most associated with the plains, and after driving across this country today, he wondered whether the creatures *could* be considered a viable alternative. Not one rabbit had appeared anywhere near the road during the drive, nor had he seen a single sign of a prairie dog town. The sound of distant and not-so-distant barking told him the town supported a canine population, but he still found himself reluctant to use dogs. People cared about them.

Outside, the sky blazed scarlet, then darkened. A series of violent cramps doubled him, goading him into action. Garreth headed for his car. He had learned to hunt rats, after all, by hunting them. Why should rabbits be any different?

The highway took him out of town almost immediately. Somewhere north a few miles, he turned off the highway onto a graveled road and pulled over. On both sides of the road lay rolling fields. He studied them, alert for any signs of life, but nothing moved. Still, it must be there. The night wind brought him a faint scent of something warmly blood-filled.

Garreth considered the fence around the pasture on his side of the road. Instead of planks, four taut strands of barbed wire enclosed the pasture. He tested the ends of the bars with a cautious finger. Sharp. Crawling through the fence could ruin his new jeans, not to mention putting holes in his hide. Then it occurred to him that a fence presented less of a barrier than a gate across a pier entrance. With a sigh for his mental slowness, he moved through the fence.

Once inside and walking across the pasture, he found plenty of life, mostly mice and quail, too small to do him good. He literally stumbled over the quail. They leaped skyward around him with startled cries and a storm of wings. Ahead, though, a rabbit leaped out of the brush and bounded up a rise, frightened into flight by the panicking quail.

Garreth followed cautiously, just close and fast enough to keep the rabbit in sight while he waited for it to halt. Once when it zigged across in front of him, he dropped to a crouch and waited motionless until the rabbit turned away again. The stalk gave him a vague sense of déjà vu, which turned to amusement when he identified the reason for the feeling. He laughed silently. *See the ex-cop shadowing the rabbit. Isn't it nice he can put his training to good use?*

Moments later Garreth gave thanks he had not gone flat out in a footrace after the rabbit. It disappeared over the crest of the rise, and when he followed it, he found himself face-to-face with a cow that loomed huge as an elephant and pale as a ghost in the twilight brightness of his vision. If he had been moving fast, he would have run head-on into it.

The cow snorted in surprise.

Garreth backed away. He had better get the hell out of here.

Then he stopped, nostrils flared, nose filled with the blood scent that the wind had brought him at the pasture fence. He stared at the cow. Cattle had blood, too ... in great quantity. If Lane could drink from a man and not kill him, would a cow even miss a quart or two?

On the other hand, could he control a cow as he did rats? This one seemed docile, but he knew nothing about cows, had, in fact, never been this close to one before. Did they often grow so terrifyingly large?

Another doubt assailed him, too. Could he find a vein? That neck was far thicker than Velvet's had been.

The cow snorted again and lowered its head. Garreth sensed that he must either act or retreat. He licked his lips and wiped suddenly sweaty palms on his jeans. Moving enough to catch the cow's eye, he focused on it. "Hello, friend. Listen to me. Stand still for me. Don't move."

The animal's eyes widened, showing white rims that glistened in the night. Its ears wagged.

"I need a little of your blood, enough to feed me. It won't hurt." He kept his voice low and even.

The cow relaxed visibly.

So did Garreth. "Lie down for me. Lie down."

The white rims still showed around the cow's eyes, but its legs began to sag, the forelegs folding first, followed by the hind ones. Its nose dropped to touch the earth.

Still talking, Garreth moved toward the cow. He reached out and gingerly touched the massive head. The hair felt warm, soft, and curly under his fingers. The cow did not flinch or resist. Murmuring soothingly, Garreth knelt and moved his hand back along the head past the ear, toward the throat. He probed the neck behind the jaw, searching for a pulse.

He found it, beating strong and slow. Keeping the fingers of one hand on it, he pushed at the thick shoulders with the other. "Roll," he said softly. "Lie flat."

With a sigh, the cow did so. Garreth, still on his knees, bent over the outstretched neck and, extending his fangs, bit where his fingers touched.

But found only flesh and the barest taste of blood. *Not again!* He wanted to scream in frustration.

The cow twitched. Panic boiled up. Garreth needed all his will-power to control it. He thought frantically. The pulse throbbed under his fingers; he smelled the blood running hot under the pale hide. It had to be in there somewhere. He made himself try again, biting in a slightly different position.

This time blood spurted. The twin gushers filled his mouth. After his usual refrigerated diet, its heat startled him. He nearly let go. But the driving hunger in him quickly overcame surprise, followed, however, by more frustration. Despite its heat and volume, the blood still did not satisfy him, only filled his stomach. He sat back, holding thumbs over the punctures with longing snarling in him. Tears of fury gathered in his eyes. *No. It isn't fair! Blood is blood. Why isn't this enough? Why do I never stop wanting human blood?*

The cow lay quiescent, its eyes closed, snoring. Garreth removed his thumbs. The punctures had stopped seeping blood. A handful of earth rubbed into the hide covered the marks. Then Garreth stood.

The cow opened its eyes and rolled onto its chest, but made no further attempt to stand, just closed its eyes again. Still, Garreth eyed it as he backed away. It was a very large animal. He did not turn until he was over the hill, then, once out of sight, he ran … partially to put distance between himself and the huge animal, partly in a vain attempt to run away from the longings racking him. But there was enjoyment, too, in the nighttime strength and energy clamoring for release.

He ran, his lungs and heart pumping. The ground streamed beneath his feet as power surged through him. Soon exhilaration drowned all other thoughts and he gave himself up to the unthinking joy of motion. He had never been able to run this fast before!

The fence stretched ahead. Should he stop for it? *Hell, no.* He hit it without even slowing down-*wrench*-passing through like the night wind.

At the car he stopped and to his delighted astonishment, found his heart and breathing barely above normal. He whooped. At this rate, he could run for miles without even trying. What a kick.

Headlights found him there beside the car.

He froze in their glare, throwing up an arm to shield his eyes. The action came reflexively but even as his forearm rose between his eyes and the lights, Garreth realized it served another purpose as well, to keep the driver of the car from seeing his eyes reflecting red.

The lights halted as the car stopped. A door opened.

Not being able to see who climbed out of the car, Garreth assumed the worst—a drunk or bully who thought a man alone on a country road made easy pickings—and prepared to fight. Since resigning, he had had to stop carrying a gun, but tonight's run had given him some hint of the strength his vampire change had brought him, and between that and police hand-to-hand combat training, surely he could tie any assailant in knots.

"Howdy," a voice said from behind the lights.

Garreth heard the hard edge of authority beneath the amiable greeting. He lowered his arm enough to peer over it at the shape of a light bar on top of the car. Relief swept through him. No drunk or bully but a local cop. Then, remembering times on patrol with a few partners before Harry, he wondered if he might not have been better off with a drunk or bully.

"Good evening, Officer," he said.

"Deputy sheriff," the voice corrected him. "What's your name?"

"Garreth Mikaelian. My driver's license is in my pocket. Would you like to see it?"

"Yes." As Garreth fished his billfold out of his hip pocket and extracted the license, the deputy said, "You have California plates. You a student at the college, son?"

College? Yes, he did seem to remember some sign naming a college in Hays. He debated his answer and chose honesty. "No."

The deputy moved into the headlights to take the license. "Visiting someone in town?"

"I'm here on personal business ... staying at the Holiday Inn."

"What are you doing way out here?"

What answer would the deputy accept? What would *he* accept if their positions were reversed? The easiest solution was to look the man in the eyes and persuade him to find nothing suspicious in Garreth being out here. Conscience stopped him, however. The last few times he had persuaded people, he could not help but remember, it brought nothing but trouble to people he cared about. In any case, who could be sure of the long-term effects? If nothing else, the deputy had surely called in before leaving his car and an inconsistent report would raise questions Garreth might not care to answer. No, somehow he had to satisfy the deputy here and now in a straightforward way.

"I'm a night person and your town goes to sleep before I do. Since there was nothing else to do, I took a drive. This is a spectacular sky."

"I saw you in that pasture."

Garreth kept his voice casual. "I wanted to see what the countryside looked like from the top of that hill. I did, and then I came back to the car."

"Running in the dark? What was your hurry?"

He could hardly tell the deputy how well he saw in the dark. "Look, Deputy, maybe I trespassed, but I didn't hurt anything. I'll take you where I went and you can see for yourself. There's nothing but a cow asleep on the other side of the hill."

"Cow?" The deputy laughed shortly. "The Good Lord looks after fools, I guess. Son, that 'cow' is Vale's Chablis of Postrock, Postrock ranch's prize Charolais show bull, or he was until he got too mean to handle."

Garreth swallowed. "Mean?"

"He's put three men in the hospital. You could have paid for that walk with your life." The deputy handed back the driver's license. "Suppose you forget about looking at the night sky and go on back to town."

Garreth went, shaking in retrospective fear. But gradually, new feelings replaced the fear. He had found a plentiful source of blood, and he had controlled the bull. Best yet, he had not had to kill for his meal. He had better find a cover for his nocturnal hunting trips, though. The next deputy might not believe that he was driving for lack of anything better to do.

He would take up "jogging." Everyone ran these days. Tomorrow before he set out south to look at more school records, he would buy a pair of running shoes and a warm-up suit to lend his story credence. But maybe he should be a bit more careful, too, about what cattle he fed on.

12

One day ... two ... a week. Garreth combed the records of the towns around Hays, places with exotic names like Antonino, Schoenchen, Liebenthal, Munjor, Bazine, Galatia, and, of course, Pfeifer. He could hardly afford to overlook Pfeifer. But in all of them, he drew a blank. Deciding that mentioning Lane's name in any connection might leak back to alarm her, he revised his questions to ask about any Bieber girl who had left home late in her teens during the thirties, possibly to go to Europe or one of the coasts. That should sound innocent and expected in light of his cover story to directly question as many Biebers as possible.

The question brought some response. A number of older people said, "I remember that. She went to the college in Hays and ran off with one of her professors. Caused a big scandal." They spoke with a curious accent, hissing final *s*'s, turning *w*,'s to *v*'s and *v*'s to *f*'s.

"Do you remember her name and where she lived?" Garreth asked.

One old woman said, "She was one of Axel Bieber's granddaughters, I think. Axel was my mother's half brother's cousin. They lived in Trubel up in Bellamy County."

Trubel? Garreth checked the letters. No, the B would not fit the postmark. Still … Heart pounding in hope, he headed for Trubel.

It proved to be another dead town … six houses, a general store-cum-gas station and post office, and the inevitable grain elevator. The high school had burned near the close of World War II, destroying all its records, and had never been rebuilt.

Garreth tried to swallow his disappointment. "There used to be a family here headed by a man named Axel Bieber. Are any of them still around?" he asked the man at the general store.

"There's Rance and Ed Bieber farming south of here about six miles," was the reply.

Garreth lost his way twice before finding the farm. Rance Bieber turned out to be a man in his thirties, a great-grandson of Axel Bieber. He knew nothing about one of his father's cousins running away with a college professor. His father, Edward, was off in the state capital at a meeting protesting grain prices. His mother had been dead for twenty years.

"Where can I find one of your father's brothers or sisters who might know this cousin I'm looking for?"

"Well, the closest are an uncle in Eden and an aunt in Bellamy."

Garreth took the names and addresses and went to see them. Both said essentially the same thing, that they knew *of* the cousin—the scandal had set the family on ear—but they did not know the woman personally.

The aunt in Bellamy said, "My Grandpa Bieber wouldn't have anything to do with Uncle Ben—that was her father. My grandfather was a Lutheran, you see, and Uncle Ben married a Catholic woman and joined her church. Grandpa never forgave him for becoming a Papist."

"Where does your uncle live, do you know?"

"He's dead now, I think."

Graves and more graves. Disappointment settled in a cold lump in Garreth's stomach. "Where did he *used* to live, then?"

"Oh, up in Baumen in the northern part of the county."

The lump in Garreth's stomach dissolved. Baumen was one of the towns on his list from which the letter to Lane might have been mailed.

That day he paid off his motel bill and moved his base of operations to Baumen. After checking the cash he had left, Garreth bypassed the single motel to check into the Driscoll Hotel downtown. Fortunately, while old, it was clean, but even at its low prices, he could not afford to stay there long … not unless he found a job soon.

He swore unhappily, resenting the time that working would steal from his hunt. Still, what else could he do? He had to have money for gas and his room. He would check the local high school, he decided. Maybe that would end his hunt for Lane here and he would not have to stay any longer.

13

For a change, the records for the Baumen High School were stored in an attic instead of a basement. Like the basements, the attic was dusty, but unlike a basement, it was also hot and stuffy. The school principal, a man named Schaeffer, had not been able to find the graduation pictures for the years 1930 to 1936 and Lane had not been in the '37 to '40 pictures, so he took Garreth up to the files. "There's a picture in their school records. That cabinet should hold all the Biebers."

Garreth stood at the cabinet, bending down to go through its second drawer and praying for the principal to leave. As long as the man breathed down his neck, he had to check each and every file instead of being able to go straight to where Lane's file would be located.

"How can you see up here with those glasses on?" Schaeffer asked.

Eyes. Garreth thought carefully about that, then took off the glasses and hung them on his shirt pocket. He twisted around, blinking in the light, to look straight at Schaeffer. "Don't you think it's hot and dusty up here? I know you'd be more comfortable in your office. You don't have to stay with me."

Schaeffer's face went blank for a moment, then he mopped at his brow. "It's a shame we can't afford air conditioning for this building. Mr. Mikaelian, if you don't mind being left alone, I think I'll go back to my office."

"I'll be fine."

He watched Schaeffer leave, and the moment the door closed behind the principal's figure, he slammed the drawer shut and pulled open one on the bottom. He flipped through the files, past the Aarons, Calebs, Carolyns, and Eldoras. His hand paused at Garrett Bieber out of simple reaction to the similarity to his own name, and then went on, through the letters of the alphabet to the M's.

The folder there came to his fingers like iron to a magnet. BIEBER, *Madelaine.* He pulled it out of the drawer and spread it open on the floor. First the picture. He studied it. Though obviously of a young girl and brown with age, it was recognizably Lane. A sigh of satisfaction came up from his soul. He had found her origin. From here, hopefully, he could reach out to capture her. He paged through the record of her four years in the school, looking for anything more he might learn about her from it.

She had been a good student, he saw, earning straight A's. She had graduated first academically in her class of ten, but had not been valedictorian at graduation. The grades he somehow expected, but the lack of honor surprised him; that is, it did until he noticed the long list of disciplinary actions against her. She had, various teachers stated, an uncontrolled temper and frequently became involved in fights—the knock-down, tooth-and-claw variety—with both other girls and an occasional boy. Garreth saw the young woman who had attacked a prostitute for stealing her supper … but a very different person from Lane Barber. Could any of those teachers still be alive to appreciate how well Lane had learned to control her temper?

The record also gave her parents' names, Benjamin and Anna, and her home address, 513 Pine Street. Garreth made a note of it, though he doubted that it remained valid after all these years.

When he had all out of the file that he thought he could use, he returned it to the drawer, then he had only to sit in the stifling, dusty heat to wait until enough time had elapsed for searching the files before leaving the attic.

He headed for a phone. The phone book listed five Biebers, one of them an Anna living at 513 Pine. Smiling at the clerk in the high school office, he copied down the addresses of all the Biebers. "I guess I'll talk to a few people. Thanks for the help."

He started, of course, with Anna Bieber at 513 Pine, just a few blocks from the high school. A middle-aged woman answered the door. Her face bore similarities to Lane's. "Mrs. Bieber?" he asked. If she was not Lane's mother, perhaps she was a sister.

"Come on in," the woman said. "I'll get Mother."

Mrs. Bieber turned out to be a tiny, frail-looking wisp, nothing like the strapping woman Garreth would have expected to spawn an amazon like Lane. Like her daughter, though, she looked younger than her years. Though she moved slowly, she still walked straight, without the bend of age, and her eyes met Garreth's face directly, undimmed. For a moment, the similarity to his own grandmother seemed so strong, panic fluttered in him, and he wondered if she, too, possibly recognized him for what he was.

But her hand did not touch the crucifix around her neck and she cordially invited him to sit down. At the end of listening to his story, she looked him over with searching eyes. "My daughter Mada ran away at the age of eighteen with a professor from Fort Hays. May I see the picture you have?" She spoke with the distinctive accent he had heard so often these past days.

"It isn't your daughter," he said, handing over the photograph of Grandma Doyle. "I've been to the high school, and your daughter's school picture doesn't match mine. But I thought maybe you would remember a relative who looked like the girl in my picture."

She studied it. "I'm sorry. No." She handed it back.

Now what? How did he bring up Lane without asking questions that would arouse suspicion, and without appearing to pry?

Garreth pretended to examine his photograph. "I wonder how anyone can just leave home and never go back. I hope you hear from your daughter?"

The old woman beamed. "Mada calls every week, no matter where she is. She's a singer and she travels a good deal, even to Mexico and Canada and Japan. I'd be satisfied with a letter; calling must be terribly expensive, but she says she enjoys hearing my voice."

His breath caught. Jackpot! He did not have to pretend delight. "Every week? How lucky you are."

"I know." She launched into stories about friends who had children who hardly ever called or wrote.

Garreth only half listened. Called every week. Could he reasonably ask where Lane had called from the last time? Knowing even just a city— Belatedly he realized Mrs. Bieber had said Lane's name again. "I'm sorry. What was that?"

"I said, for someone so huge and awkward as a girl, Mada became a very attractive woman. She's still handsome."

He blinked. "You see her often too?" Could she be somewhere
near?

"Every Thanksgiving or Christmas," Mrs. Bieber said with pride
"She always comes home for one of the holidays."

Garreth wanted to yell with happiness and hug the old woman—
Lane *came home. Lady Luck, you're a darling!* Instead of running around
the world looking for her, all he had to do was wait ... find a job here,
make friends with Mrs. Bieber so he would know when to expect Lane
... and let the fugitive come to him.

Spider Game

1

The Help Wanted section of the local paper had little to offer Garreth. The jobs advertised all appeared to be day positions. "Is there night work available anywhere in town?" he asked the Driscoll Hotel's desk clerk.

She pushed her glasses up on her nose. "Well, there's the drive-ins, but high school kids usually work there. I suppose you could try the Pioneer Cafe up the street and the Main Street Grill across from us. They stay open late, until nine o'clock, and until eleven weekends."

That late? Gee whiz. Aloud, he said, "Thanks." And left the hotel.

In the street outside he stood orienting himself. Baumen was a far cry from San Francisco. He had never seen a main street with railroad tracks down the middle. With two lanes of traffic and two strips of diagonal parking on each side, the far side of the street looked almost as distant as the far end of Baumen's three blocks of stores. Like the grain elevators, though, the buildings intrigued him. Everything here seemed to be built of that buff sandstone: barns, houses and stores, high schools, courthouses, even fenceposts. He rather liked it, both for the easy color and the way it gave human habitation an appearance of having grown organically from the prairie around it.

Heading up the street toward the Pioneer Cafe first, he found himself almost alone in the late afternoon. With the stores closed for almost half an hour now, the street lay empty of all but a scattering of parked cars. A placard in the ticket window of the Driscoll Theatre next to the hotel announced showtimes on Friday, Saturday, and Sunday. Garreth eyed it in passing. A weekend theatre? What did these people *do* nights?

Three-quarters of the way up the block, all thoughts of entertainment were wiped from his mind. The breeze carried a foul taint, a smell that turned the air turgid in his lungs. Garlic! He spun away. So much for the Pioneer. But would the Main Street be any better?

He crossed his fingers.

Across the tracks and down the other side of the street, he stopped at the drug store, which also served as the local news stand, but they carried no papers from San Francisco or anywhere in California. A few doors farther down, a display in Weaver's Office Supplies included *I Ching* along with other books, Bibles, religious jewelry, and stationery. The book brought a stabbing pang of homesickness.

Give it up, a voice in him urged. *Go home and tell Serruto where to find Lane. Let him handle it. You don't belong here.*

The very logical, sensible suggestion tempted him, but he shook his head. *Get thee behind me, angel. It's my case; she's my collar.*

At the doorway of the Main Street, he paused, cautiously sniffing. The air smelled of grease but no garlic. He went in. The menu, stuck in a holder in the middle of the table, offered a range of meals from breakfasts and hamburgers to chicken-fried steak, but nothing even vaguely Italian.

"Take your order?" the single waitress asked.

"I'd like to speak with the manager, please."

She raised a brow. "You mean the owner? Verl," she called to a man at the grill, "someone to see you."

Garreth came up to the counter and introduced himself.

"Verl Hamilton," the stocky, balding man replied. "Aren't you the kid looking for his relatives?"

Word had spread. He nodded. "And I need a job in order to afford the search. Do you have anything open?"

Hamilton eyed him. "I like to see a man's eyes when I'm talking to him."

Garreth took off the trooper glasses.

"You know how to cook?"

He considered lying, then shook his head. "TV dinners and hot dogs and marshmallows over an open fire is about all."

Hamilton sighed. "I could sure use an evening cook."

"I'm a fast learner. I was a police officer for eight years and a couple of times had to learn new skills in a hurry for an undercover assignment. And I really do need a job," he finished earnestly.

The waitress said, "Verl, I've subbed on the grill. Let him wait tables and I'll cook."

Hamilton pursed his lips and tugged an ear, then nodded. "We'll give it a try."

Garreth grinned. "When can I start?"

"Tomorrow. Come in at three o'clock."

"Verl, tomorrow's Thursday," the waitress said.

"Damn." Hamilton frowned. "How about starting right now? It'll only be a few hours but you can see what's going on. Tomorrow you can give me your social security number."

"What's wrong with Thursday?" Garreth asked.

The waitress replied, "The stores stay open late. Everyone comes in to town to shop and they stop here for coffee and dessert. It's no time to break in."

So Garreth quickly found himself in his shirtsleeves, sitting at a table with Sharon Hagedorn, the waitress, nodding while she explained the table numbering and how to write up orders. They went through it twice, then she turned him loose.

The job seemed easy enough, barring the tiring drag of daylight on him. Sunset helped that. The plates lightened and his step quickened. The novelty soon wore off, though. He saw that it would be a job, something to earn money. Nothing more.

Shortly before closing time, a cop walked in to a chorus of: "Hi, Nat," from Hamilton and Sharon. Garreth had seen the car park outside, a tan-and-dark-brown compact with a sleek Aerodynic light bar on top. The uniform of the stocky cop had the same colors as the car, a tan shirt with shoulder taps and pocket flaps of dark brown to match the trousers.

The cop, whose name tag said TOEWS, slid onto a stool at the counter, eyeing Garreth. "You're new."

Garreth nodded. "Coffee?"

"With cream. Throw on my usual, Sharon," he called toward the waitress at the grill, then he set his radio on the counter with the volume adjusted to make it just audible. He smoothed his mustache—red like his sideburns though his hair was dark—and looked Garreth over some more. "Is that your ZX with California plates in front of the Driscoll? You're the one looking for your relatives."

Garreth nodded and poured the coffee. He longed to sit down and talk. Seeing the officer was like meeting a cousin in a foreign country, but the brusqueness of Toews's voice warned him away.

Hamilton rang up the ticket of the last customer and locked the door behind the man. "This is Garreth Mikaelian, Nat. He used to be a cop out there."

Garreth winced. Now he felt as though he had just badged an officer who stopped him in a strange town, to keep from being ticketed.

But Toews immediately thawed. "You were? I'm Nathan Toews." He pronounced it *Taves*. "Where did you work?"

"San Francisco. Homicide."

Toews raised a brow. The unspoken question was obvious: *Why did you quit?*

Garreth felt compelled to answer it. "My partner got shot up pretty bad and it was mostly my fault. It shook me up."

"Order up," Sharon said.

Garreth picked up the cheeseburger and fries.

Toews pour catsup over the fries. "Too bad you're transient. We've lost an officer and god knows how long it'll be before we find a replacement."

Hamilton snorted from where he sat counting receipts. "Latta's no loss. He deserved to be canned for a stunt like blowing out the window of the patrol car with the shotgun and claiming someone took a shot at him."

Garreth stared at Toews for a long time before shaking himself. *Forget it, man.* He thought about the officer's remark, though. A permanent job would give him an excuse for staying past the end of his alleged search, and being official would help when arresting Lane.

"What's the job like?"

Toews shrugged. "Door rattling, traffic, refereeing domestic disturbances, and picking up drunks weekends, mostly."

Which did not really answer the big question: Could Garreth handle the job? How much would his limitations handicap, if not outright endanger, other officers? And in view of the circumstances under which he had quit at home, why should these people even want him?

Still, he continued to think about it all the way back to the hotel and while pulling on his running suit for "exercise."

He followed the main street north. From four lanes it narrowed to two on the west side of the railroad tracks, passed the railroad station and stock pens with a sale bar and fairground east beyond them, then crossed the Saline River and angled west as Country Road 16. The countryside, which had dropped from the plateau Bellamy sat on into the river valley around Baumen, rose again to rolling plateau, pastureland brightly lighted by the waxing moon and broken only occassionally by a stretch of barb wire fence. Cattle dotted every section, block-square beef cattle, sleek black or curly red-and-white. All, he noticed, appeared smaller than the white behemoth he drank from that first night, but like the Charolais bull, the black steer he finally approached yielded to him, and he fed, wishing he had some way to refrigerate his thermous so he could bring it along and fill it up.

Patting the cow's head in thanks as he stood, Garreth became aware of something else near him. He turned to face another pair of glowing eyes. The animal looked like a small, thin German shepherd. A coyote?

The creature eyed him, and the supine cow beyond. Garreth shook his head. "No. Don't bother it."

The coyote's eyes burned into his. Garreth held them until the cow scrambled to its feet.

Leaving, he found to his surprise that the coyote followed, trotting about ten feet off to the side. When Garreth broke into a run, so did the coyote. It followed like a shadow, not threateningly, he decided, reading curiousity in the cock of the carnivore's ears. Puzzled by his not-quite-human scent? Whyever, he enjoyed the company.

The coyote paced him most of the way back to town, until Garreth passed through the fence onto the country road just north of the river. Then it dropped back and faded into the darkness of the prairie. Garreth jogged on into town alone.

He heard a car coasting in behind him as the passed the railroad station. Glancing over his shouler, he identified the light bar of a patrol car and stuck up a hand in greeting.

The engine revved. The car shot past him to swing across his path and come to a tire-screeching halt. A spotlight flashed in his face. Garreth threw an arm up in front of his eyes.

"In a hurry to go somewhere?" a voice asked from behind the light.

Damn! "I'm jogging." Garreth plucked at his jogging suit.

"In the middle of the night? Sure. Come over here. Put your hands on the car and spread your feet!"

What? Garreth opened his mouth to protest, and snapped it closed again. Resisting would only make trouble. Angrily, he spread-eagled against the car.

The spotlight went out. Moving up behind Gareth, the cop began frisking him. Garreth glimpsed an equipment belt polished to a mirror shine. The cloying sweetness of aftershave masked any scent of blood. "You do this like someone with a lot of experience at it, friend," the cop said.

Which was more than Garreth would say for the cop. Almost any of the scumbags on the street back home could have turned and taken the man in a moment. The cop's idea of a frisk missed half the places a weapon might be hidden, too.

Keeping his voice polite, Garreth explain who he was.

"Oh, the ex-cop Nat met. No wonder you know the routine." The cop stepped back. "I'm Ed Duncan. Sorry about the frisk, but you understand we can't be too careful with strangers. There's a lot of drug traffic through the state. No hard feelings?"

Garreth understood that Duncan had probably been bored out of his skull and used the first opportunity to create some activity. He resented being the subject of it. "No hard feelings."

Turning, he discovered that Duncan bore a faint resemblance to Robert Redford. From the way the cop walked and wore his uniform, Duncan knew it, too.

The car radio sputtered. Duncan leaned in through the window for the mike. "505 here as always, doll. What do you need?"

Someone had reported a prowler.

Duncan rolled his eyes. "It's probably just the Haas dog again but I'll check it out."

Watching Duncan drive away singing a country western song, Garreth thought again about Toews remark. If someone as cavalierly careless as Duncan could survive here, maybe Garreth's limitations would not cause trouble. In the morning, he decided, he would drop by the station and check out the job more closely.

2

Chief Kenneth Danzig had the build of an ex-football player, and though, he was now in his forties and his waistline was trying to match his shoulders for width, he still looked capable of battering through a defensive line or a felon's door. His blood smelled warm and strong. Scated behind his desk in the office he shared with the padlocked evidence locker, he made the room seem even smaller than its actual limited dimensions. He fingered Garreth's application. "I take it you regret resigning?"

"Yes, sir." Garreth had stated the checkable facts of the resignation frankly. He wished he could read the chief, but small town cop though he was, Danzig wore a city cop's professional mask. "Law enforcement is my life. It's the only kind of job I know or want."

Danzig's face never moved. "Why apply here, though? Why not ask for reinstatement in San Francisco?"

Garreth had been expecting that question. He had a half-true answer ready. "I need a change and this is nice country. I like it more every day I'm here."

Danzig leaned back in his chair. "Do you think working in a small town means a soft job? Or that you'll never face a shoot/don't shoot choice again? Remember the Clutter murders in *In Cold Blood*? Those were here in Kansas. York and Latham were another pair of turkeys on a murder spree who came through here. We tried them just over in Russell. We're on the drug traffic pipeline and almost every year there's a hi-po trooper killed making a routine stop on I-70. You get into trouble out here and you're often on your own, with no backup close enough to do you any good."

He made the job sound as dangerous as any city. Garreth drew a deep breath. "I don't expect a soft job. Of course I hope I'll never have to draw my gun again—who doesn't—but I'm not running away from the possibility." *I'm just running away from kicking in doors.*

"We work semi-permanent shifts. As a new man, you'd have to work nights, and be stuck there until we have a daytime opening and you have enough seniority to claim it. Any objections?"

"No, sir." None at all! "I prefer nights."

Danzig leaned forward. "Considering your history, I wish I could send you to a shrink for a psychiatric evaluation, but the taxpayers of this town can't afford luxuries like that. We're lucky to find officers willing to work here at all. But I don't hire anyone without at least a physical exam. I'll set up an appointment for you with Dr. Staab at the medical center."

He had been expecting that, but cold still slid down Garreth's spine. A doctor he could probably handle, but ... what about bloodwork? Using his powers, he had talked the doctor in San Francisco out of running bloodwork on that checkup before sending him back to work. The same trick could not work where it was required as part of the physical. He would have to think of something else. *Are you crazy, man? Be safe; give it up.*

He sat frozen in the chair while Danzig made the phone call and handed Garreth a memo sheet with the appointment time. "We'll contact San Francisco for your records while you're taking care of this. Now let's fingerprint you to make sure you're who you say you are."

Walking out of City Hall later, Garreth toyed with the memo slip and debated whether to forget the whole thing. *Now you see why Lane keeps her head down. She's smart. You're courting disaster, Garreth Doyle Mikaelian.* But perhaps he wanted to be found out, he mused, to be destroyed finally and for always.

He stared at the appointment slip for a long time, thoughts churning, before folding it and putting it in his pocket. He might be a total fool, but he wanted the job, and not just to kill time waiting for Lane. He wanted it for himself, wanted a badge again. He wanted to come home.

3

The Lord watched out for fools, even damned ones, Garreth reflected. A week after he stewed over it so much, his stuck-out neck not only remained unchopped but here he stood in a suit and tie, carrying copies of the Kansas Criminal Code and Vehicle Code to study, beginning six months probation. Even the physical had gone smoothly, the bloodwork problem solved by catching the lab tech's eyes and intructing her to destroy the samples she took from him, replace them with samples from herself, and forget she had made a substitution.

The chief introduced him to the day office staff, a tiny wisp of a secretary named Nancy Sue Schaefer and a pretty but broad-beamed dispatcher, Geri Weaver. Then Danzig led him over to a slim, dark-haired young woman in uniform at a typewriter. "And this is Margaret Lebekov, our Afternoon officer and expert with juveniles and domestic disputes. Maggie, this is Garreth Mikaelian."

Garreth held out a hand, smiling. "Glad to meet you."

She looked up, stared at his hand, and returned to typing. "Yes."

Garreth examined his fingers for frostbite. Terrific. Six officers in the department and one of them hated him on sight. In a sudden spasm of fear he wondered if she, like Grandma Doyle, sensed his unhumanity.

"When you go on your own you'll be on Nights, from eight, taking over from Lebekov, until four AM," Danzig went on. "That overlaps Toews's and Duncan's shifts. Until your uniforms come and you know the town, though, I want you to ride with Sergeant Toews."

"Yes, sir."

"You'll need a Kansas driver's license. The examiner is in Bellamy on Thursdays. Drive down then and take the test."

"Yes, sir."

A look at the three cells and drunk tank upstairs completed the station tour, by which time Lebekov had left, Toews was coming out of the combination interview/locker room buckling on his equipment belt, and a voice on the radio announced that 102 would shortly be 10-19, coming into the office.

Garreth sucked in a deep breath. Shift change. Despite the vast differences in place, the rhythm of it felt as familiar as the beat of his heart ... Day Watch coming in—one Lieutenant Byron Kaufmann, a beefy veteran with fading red hair—a briefing for Garreth and Toews that differed only in size from every other Garreth had ever attended; checking equipment and the car; pulling out onto the street. It *was* like coming home.

Toews eyed Garreth sidelong as they rolled down Oak toward Kansas Avenue. "Have you found your grandmother yet?"

"No." He had made daily trips to surrounding towns, keeping up the cover. Perhaps the time had come that he could quit. "I'm beginning to doubt I will."

"But you still want to stick around here?"

Garreth shrugged. "There's no reason to go back to California."

Toews peered in his outside mirror at a battered pickup which passed them going the other direction. "That gives us two city boys. Danzig used to be on the Wichita P.D."

The radio mumbled sporadically, but little of the traffic had local call numbers. Garreth quickly gathered that all the area law enforcement agencies used the same frequency. The loudest voice kept drawling, "Bellamy S.O.," the sheriff's office.

Toews saw Garreth listening. "That's Lou Pfeifer, the sheriff. He's usually patrolling somewhere in this end of the county so he can look in on his ranch and his wife and daughters."

"206 Baumen," a woman's voice said. "Requesting a 10-28 on local K-king, five-five-three."

Toews shook his head. "That's the fourth registration I've heard Maggie run since we came on. She's on a rip tonight."

"She didn't seem in a very good mood when Danzig introduced me to her at the station," Garreth said.

"Oh." Toews shifted in his seat. He watched a driver slow but roll through a stop sign across the street. He honked the horn as the car came at them, and when he caught the driver's eye, shook his head. "It says stop, Walt," he called. To Garreth he said, "That's because you have the shift she wants."

Garreth winced. "Damn."

"It isn't your fault. Danzig will never give it to her because he doesn't believe in women patrolling at night. Do you ride?"

The change of subject threw Garreth. He blinked. "Ride what?"

Toews's brows rose. "Horses, of course. I have a great little mare out of Skipper W that I use for calf roping. I'll take you by to see her in a little while. What *do* you do when you're not on duty, then?"

The game of Get Acquainted had begun, a friendly mutual interrogation that they sandwiched between calls ... an elderly woman whose daughter in Hays had been unable to reach by phone all day proved to be healthy, only working in the yard with her hearing aid turned off ... a motorcycle stopped for speeding had a driver operating on an expired license ... checking businesses along Highway 282 at the east edge of town they found the Gfeller Lumber gate unlocked. The search for mutual interests went on while they waited for the owner to come out and lock up.

To Garreth's disappointment, they shared almost nothing in common but law enforcement. Between that and the obvious emnity of Maggie Lebekov, Baumen P.D. did not look quite like home after all. On the other hand, it made a decent bivouac and would keep him busy enough not to brood over the uncertain, perhaps nonexistent future beyond collaring Lane.

4

The house was two stories and large by Baumen standards, white-painted brick with a driveway running under a portico on the side. Large old trees shaded it, oaks and maples whose leaves, turned lemon yellow and scarlet, glowed almost incandescent in the autumn afternoon sunlight.

Flame touched Garreth, too, but it was inside, licking at him as they stood before the door.

Toews pushed the bell. A small, elderly, white-haired woman answered the door. Toews touched the visor of his cap. "Hello, Mrs. Schoning. Is Helen home?"

The woman nodded. "I'll get her. Please come in."

They followed her into a wide hallway flooded with rainbow light from a stained-glass window at the turn of the stairs. Mrs. Schoning left them there to disappear into the rear of the house.

"You ought to have a good chance," Toews said. "I don't know who else in town she'd have to rent to."

Garreth crossed his fingers.

He needed somewhere besides the hotel to live, somewhere free of the fear of a maid coming in to find his earth pallet on the bed or in the closet and gossiping about it. A town this size had no apartments, though, just houses. Except maybe one over the garage of Helen Schoning, the Clerk of the Municipal Court.

Miss Schoning appeared, a slender woman in her late forties with only a trace of gray in short chestnut hair. Blood-smell eddied warmly from her. Garreth fought a sudden surge of hunger.

She smiled at them. "What brings you here, Nat?"

"This is our new officer Garreth Mikaelian. He's interested in the apartment."

"Ah, yes, the Frisco Kid." She studied him keenly for a minute, then extended her hand. If the coolness of his skin surprised her, she did not show it. "Welcome to Baumen. The garage is this way."

Out a side door into the portico and back along the drive to a large two-car garage. She led the way up a set of steps on the side to the second floor.

"It's small. I take it you don't have a family."

"No, ma'am."

Unlocking the door, she stood back to let him enter first. "Call me Helen, please. Here you are."

Half the area had been furnished as a den, with wood paneling, built-in bookcases, and a large leather couch and chair. A rear corner was partitioned for the bathroom. Between it and a set of french doors leading out onto a deck above the garage doors stretched the cabinets and small appliances of an apartment kitchen.

Helen opened the couch out into a bed. "I can provide sheets and blankets. The phone is an extension from the house. You can use that and pay part of the bill or put in a private line. Half the garage is yours to use, too. It's $75.00 a month."

"Baumen 303," the radio on Toews's hip muttered. "See Mrs. Linda Mostert at 415 South Eighth about a missing person."

"En route," Toews said. "It sounds like Mr. Halverson is out again, partner. Come on."

Following him out, Garreth called back, "I'll take it. May I move in tonight?"

"Just knock on the side door and I'll give you the key."

He waved thanks.

Mr. Amos Halverson turned out to be Mrs. Mostert's father, a healthy but sometimes confused old man who regularly took walks and forgot his way home. By talking to people in yards along the street, they learned the old man had headed north. Twenty minutes later they located him working on his third beer in the Cowboy Palace and drove him home.

Returning to patrol, Garreth said, "I wonder if he's all that confused. Do you realize we just paid for his beer and gave him transportation home?"

Toews grinned. "He's earned it. He ran a grocery store when I was a kid and I remember a lot of times when he gave me and my sisters free candy. Where do you want to eat tonight?"

Not that they had a great deal of choice. Garreth said, "The Main Street."

"We ate there last night. How about the Pioneer?"

Garreth's lungs clogged just remembering the garlic reek from it. He thought fast. "I ... got sick once in an Italian restaurant and since then I haven't been able to stand the smell of garlic."

Toews grinned. "So how long have you been a vampire?"

Every nerve in Garreth overloaded. He gaped at Toews, feeling the bomb explode in him ... unable to move, scarcely able to think. "A ... what?" *He guessed; he knows! What an idiot you are, Mikaelian, to ever have opened your mouth about garlic.*

The other's grin broaded. "You're a little slow on the uptake, city boy. Vampires can't stand garlic, so if you can't, you must be one, right? Tell me, how do you manage to shave without a mirror?"

Garreth groped in confusion for almost a minute before he realized Toews was joking. Then he cursed himself. *A guilty conscience obstructeth logic* ... not to mention strangled the sense of humor. He had better say something quickly, though, before the lack of reply betrayed that he had taken Toews seriously. "I use an electic razor."

Toews chucked. "The benefits of technology. Okay, it's the Main Street again."

Garreth drank tea and pretended to study the Criminal Code. Inside he still shook. That had been a near call.

Toews wolfed down a cheeseburger. "You better eat something more than tea, partner. Friday and Saturday are our busy nights."

Garreth quickly learned what he meant. As dark approached, every parking space along Kansas Avenue and up the side streets filled with locals coming downtown to the bars and private clubs, the latter the only place dry Kansas allowed hard liquor. Garreth and Toews wrote up two accident reports for fender benders resulting from trying to park more cars than intended in the diagonal spaces along the tracks.

Every teenager in the area also appeared to be downtown, but since they could not drink, the ones not attending the movie theatre drove, making a loop that went north on Kansas to the Sonic Drive-In, across the tracks, south seven blocks to the A & W, and back across the tracks to go north again, endlessly. They drove cars, pickups, and vans, and carried on conversations by driving alongside each other and leaning out the windows to shout across the space between.

Toews ticketed only flagrant violations, the most flagrant being a blue van weaving wildly through the traffic, and broke up a couple of impending fights. They also checked businesses along Kansas. Later came drunk-and-disorderly calls, and an accident in the parking lot outside the VFW. Taking a report from one driver while Toews talked to the other, watching a couple pass non-too-steadily toward their own car, Garreth shook his head. This was a *dry* state?

5

Garreth had intended just to pick up the key, but Helen Schoning insisted on coming out with him. She raised one of the garage doors. "This is your side. If you want to work on your car, feel free to use my tools. Just ask first and put them back afterward."

He stared around the garage. She looked as though she could open her own auto repair shop. "You use these?"

She smiled and went over to stroke the fender of the car in the other half of the garage. "Someone has to keep this running."

He felt his jaw drop. It was a gleaming old Rolls Royce.

"My father bought it in 1955 when his first wells came in. He was so proud of it. It was the only car like it in Bellamy County. Still is." She paused, chin down, looking at him through her lashes. "Mr. Mikaelian, I do have one favor to ask. If you should come home some night and find a car in your side, will you please park in the drive behind my side so the other car can get out? And say nothing about it to anyone?"

He felt himself staring again and closed his mouth with a snap. "No problem."

She smiled. "I hoped you'd understand. I enjoy my solitude— which is not the same as loneliness despite what most people around here think—and am single by choice, but I also like companionship from time to time. Discretely, of course. This is a small town and some of my friends are married."

Garreth regarded her with amazement. She was not what he would have expected to find here. "You don't miss the stability of a long-term relationship?"

She laughed. "What stability? Nothing ever stays the same. People, either. Each of my relationships has suited my needs at the time. What more can I ask? Good night."

Moving in did not take long, just luggage and his pallet. Then he sat back in the deep leather chair and sighed happily. Privacy. Better than that, a refrigerator. He would take his thermos with him on the run tonight and fill it.

Helen had made up the couch. Laid under the bottom sheet, the pallet would fold conveniently, safely out of sight with the bed.

All that remained was to buy some health foods, even if he had to go to Bellamy or Hays for them ... stage dressing so his cupboard would not look as oddly empty as Lane's. Then like a spider in the center of his web, he would sit and wait for his red-haired vampire fly to appear.

6

Mrs. Bieber greeted Garreth with delight and invited him in. "How nice to see you again. Have you found your grandmother yet?"

He shook his head. "No, but I think I've found a home." While they drank tea he told her about the apartment and job. It was overcast outside, which made the room enjoyably dim. After a while he asked casually, "How are you? What do you hear from your singer daughter?"

"Mada's in Mexico. Following the herds south for the winter, is how she put it." Mrs. Bieber looked apologetic and embarrassed. "People, she means. I'm afraid she's not always very polite."

"Do you know which holiday she's coming home for?"

"No." The bright eyes probed him. "Why do you ask?"

Garreth shrugged. "No particular reason."

Mrs. Bieber frowned. "You don't have to lie to me, young man."

He froze. *Damn.* What had he done to give himself away? "I don't know what you mean."

She leaned toward him over her teacup with a sly smile. "Deep down don't you think she's your grandmother?"

Amazing. The cup remained steady in his hand despite a surge of relief that left him feeling limp as low-test spaghetti. "How can I? The pictures are nowhere alike."

"Maybe your picture is wrong. I can ask Mada a few questions the next time she calls."

"Good god, no!" Garreth lowered his voice as her eyes widened in surprise at his passion. "Please don't. That would be so embarrassing to both of us." Not to mention fatal to his hopes of trapping Lane here. "Please don't say anything about me to her."

Her eyes danced but she agreed and he changed the subject to casual conversation about his job. What he wanted most to talk about, though, he could not ... his run the previous night.

He had taken the thermos with him. Filling it involved more than he anticipated ... biting a large hole in the cow's carotid artery, then spending the extra time necessary holding off the place until the blood clotted. By that time he had collected an audience of three coyotes who stayed back at his orders but later accompanied him most of the way back to town. Memory of the run still exhilarated him ... the stars brilliant in the black velvet of the moonless sky, his breath white on the night air, the coyotes running like ghosts around him. He would so love to be able to discuss it with someone. How could Helen think solitude was not lonely?

He stood finally. "I'd better go. I'm due at the station for roll call in a few minutes."

She saw him to the door. "Thank you for coming. Visit again if you like."

Hell and garlic could not keep him away.

7

The thick layer of clouds, drooping in dark, waterlogged folds, prevented Garreth from seeing the sun, but he felt it set, felt the welcome cessation of pressure and the renewed flood of energy through him. In the distance, thunder rumbled. He stretched, drawing a deep, contented breath. "Nice evening."

Nat rolled his eyes. "Californians have strange taste. It ain't nice at all for someone who wants to rope calves tomorrow afternoon, partner. Say, why don't you come over for Sunday dinner? You can meet my wife and kids and then watch Skipper Flint Jubilee and me work."

Before he stopped eating food, Garreth had never realized how much social activity revolved around it. He hunted a diplomatic refusal. "Thanks, but I intend to sleep in late. Give me a time and I'll meet you at the fairgrounds for the roping, though."

They moved down the street trying the doors on the Light House electrical shop and Sherwin-Williams paint store. The Saturday night parade of cars rolled past in a bright string. The blue van they had cited the evening before slowed down opposite them long enough for the adolescent boy driving to lean sideways and flip them off. They pretended not to see him.

"I got a guy for that once," Garreth said.

Nat tried the door of Rivers Hardware. "How?"

"I wrote him up for an illegal signal. He was using his left arm and indicated a right turn which he then failed to make." Garreth grinned. "And the judge fined him."

Nat's radio said, "Baumen 303. 717 Landon. Tom Loxton."

Nat rogered the call and sighed as they hurried up the street to where they had parked the car. "Damn. He's right on schedule."

"With what?"

"Tom's half Indian. Every time he gets liquored up, about twice a month, he sits on his front porch taking pot shots at passing cars. He's never hit anything yet, but there's always a first time."

They parked the car across the intersection at one end of the block and walked down to the house. "You wave off traffic at the other end of the block while I talk to him," Nat said.

A reed-thin man with long hair and a red bandana tied around his head lounged in a porch swing at 717, pointing a rifle at them. Garreth eyed him. "Maybe I ought to stay with you."

"I'll be all right. You just stop cars from coming past here."

Garreth went reluctantly, itching to reach for the .38 on his belt under his coat. He kept Nat and Loxton under observation while he watched for cars.

Nat leaned on the gate and called casually, "Hi, Tom. Why don't you put the gun down?"

"Not 'til I get me some whiteyes." Loxton's voice slurred.

The silhouette of a woman appeared in the doorway from the

porch. Loxton yelled at her.

"Tom, let's talk about it," Nat called, and started to open the gate.

"Guard, Cochise!" Loxton yelled.

A huge black-and-tan dog hurtled around the corner of the house to plant himself barking and snarling in the middle of the sidewalk.

Nat jumped back, slamming the gate.

The woman said something Garreth could not hear. Loxton swore at her and she slammed the door.

Along the block neighbors came out onto porches to watch. Garreth grabbed the nearest man and stationed him in the intersection, then cautiously moved back to join Nat.

"Tom, call off the dog and put down the rifle," Nat said.

"Go to hell!"

The dog snarled.

"What do you usually do with the dog?" Garreth asked.

"He's never been loose before. Tom must really be loaded tonight."

Garreth thought about the coyotes. He sidestepped and when the dog swung toward the motion, caught its eyes. He said, "Cochise, sit down and be quiet."

Whining, the dog backed up a step.

Loxton yelled, "Guard, Cochise!"

Garreth held its eyes. "Sit."

The dog whined again, but sat. Loxton leaped to his feet in rage. "You damn mutt! Guard!"

"Your dog respects the law, Mr. Loxton," Garreth said. How close did he need to be to exert influence? He considered what he wanted to do, tried to decide if there could be consequences as negative as the ones of influencing the doctor and Serruto to let him come back on duty. He saw no obvious ones. Pushing through the gate past the dog, he focused all his attention on the drunken man. "Why don't you just put down the rifle and show us you respect the law, too, sir?"

Loxton stared back at Garreth, his expression smoothing from rage to blank, then slowly laid the rifle on the swing.

Climbing back into the patrol car later, Nat said in awe, "No one but Tom and Millie has ever been able to control that dog before."

Cold chased up Garreth's spine. Had he been a fool to draw attention to himself with one of his vampire talents? Or could he joke it away as they had the other night? He made himself grin at Nat. "The Dolittle Animal Talk course was one of the electives offered when I went through the Academy."

Lightning arced across the clouds overhead, followed a few seconds later by a crack of thunder. More lightning followed, and thunder so loud it shook the car.

"Shit," Nat sighed. "There goes the calf roping."

More and more lightning chased through the clouds. Garreth's skin crawled. The awesome show went on for ten more minutes before the rain started. That came first as a light rattle of drops on the roof of the car, then in blinding sheets.

The rain did not noticeably thin the traffic downtown, though, just transformed it into a glittering light show, headlights and reflections of lights off wet cars and rain-slicked paving.

Over the radio came weather reports from surrounding sheriff offices. Some places high wind was bringing down tree limbs and electric lines. Maggie Lebekov announced she was coming into the station. "Tell 303 the town is all theirs."

Minutes later, though, her voice came over the radio again, high with excitement. "206 Baumen. 10-48, Kansas and Pine. One victim is trapped. I need an ambulance and the fire department's extracting equipment."

Nat switched on the light bar and siren and threaded the car through the traffic. "This is bad weather for traffic accidents. We'd better help."

At Kansas and Pine three vehicles sat jammed together, two pickups with a Volkswagen accordioned between them. A yellow-slickered Lebekov and a tall boy in a cowboy hat yanted at the driver's door of the Volkswagen. Inside the car a girl screamed and pleaded for help. Garreth smelled blood and leaking gasoline even as he came piling out of the car.

"It's jammed," Lebekov yelled above the thunder. "The steering wheel is pinning her, too."

The blood smell flowed thick and hot around Garreth, stirring a storm of hunger. The girl must be bleeding. Peering into the car he saw what the dark-blink eyes of the others could not, bone protruding from the flesh of one leg under the dash and blood running from around it.

He fought down a cramp of craving. They had to free the girl before she bled to death! Could the fire department's equipment arrive soon enough? Minutes might be too long.

"Turn your face away," he called into the car.

The girl did not seem to hear. She went on screaming and pounding on the steering wheel. Garreth wrapped the tail of his suitcoat around one hand and drove his fist through the window. Breaking out enough glass to give him a hold on the frame of the door, he braced a foot against the side of the car and pulled.

"Garreth!" Nat yelled, "you can't—"

The door tore loose in a scream of metal. Garreth reached in and levered up the steering column, then scooped out the girl. Some part of him saw a crowd of people staring dumbfounded but his main attention remained on the girl. She bled profusely.

He laid her on the paving out of fire range, in case the cars went up, and whipped off his tie. "Loan me a baton."

Lebekov handed him hers, and used her slicker to keep rain off the girl's face while Garreth make a tourniquet. "Nice work, Mikaelian."

Nat said dryly, "I see the Hulk Course of Accident Assistance was one of your electives, too."

Garreth gave him a fleeting smile. He had acted without thinking. Would it set people to wondering? "Amazing what adrenalin will do, isn't it?" Not that it mattered. Whatever the cost, he had had to do it. He could not let the girl die.

She began sobbing hysterically. He reached down to catch her chin and force her eyes to his. "You're going to be all right, miss. Just relax. If you breath deeply, the pain will ease up. Come on, try it. Take a few deep breaths for me, will you?"

She took one, then another.

"See. That's better, isn't it?"

She nodded. In the shelter of Lebekov's slicker, her face relaxed in relief.

Garreth felt his own tension loosen. He savored the clean wetness of the rain streaming down his face, drowning the blood smell. So this vampire ability to control others could be used for more than personal gain. It might actually serve others. So could his strength. In the sound and fury of the storm, that brought a little comfort to his personal corner of hell.

8

"That's Mada in the middle," Mrs. Bieber said.

The photograph showed three little girls sitting on the running board of a twenties-style touring car in front of a house that looked like this one minus an addition and part of the porch. The description Mrs. Armour had given of the photograph in Lane's bookcase made it sound like a copy of this one.

"The other two are my daughter Mary Ellen, who's a year younger than Mada, and their cousin Victoria. Mada and Victoria were about seven then." She cocked her head, smiling at him. "Are you sure you don't have anything more exciting to do with your evenings off than visit an old woman who isn't even a relative?"

Not when he needed to learn everything possible about his quarry. It meant using this friendly old woman, though, which filled him with guilt even as he smiled at her. "You're a friend, aren't you?" He bent over the photo album. "She's about the same size as the others."

"She didn't start growing so tall until later. Here's a picture of her at ten."

There was no mistaking her now, towering over her younger siblings. With the October night chilly and windy outside, Garreth leafed through the album and easily picked Lane out in the subsequent photographs, head and shoulders above any other child she was with.

"She's the brightest of my children. Let me show you something." Mrs. Bieber led him into the dining room and pointed proudly to rows of plaques on one wall, each announcing a First Place in spelling, debate, or archery. "Mada won all those, but she would have given up every one in a moment to be six inches shorter. My heart ached for her so often. She used to come home crying because the other children taunted her about her height. I never knew what to say. Maybe if I'd been older and wiser, but I was barely more than a girl myself, just sixteen when she was born. Later she stopped crying. She developed a terrible temper, flying into a rage at the least remark. She was always fighting someone. That only made matters worse, of course."

Of course. Children, and even adults, turned like animals on someone who looked or acted different. Lane must have made an easy target, too.

Mrs. Bieber said, "'I hate them,' she would sob to me, with such savagery in her voice. 'Someday they'll be sorry. I'll show them they don't own the world.' I tried to teach her to forgive, to be kind to her enemies, but it was many years before she could."

Garreth doubted that Lane ever did. She simply gave up threatening. After all, she *had* her revenge ... living off their lifeblood, reducing them to cattle, leaving some of them nothing but dead, dry husks. When she had been bitten by the vampire who made her, whoever it had been, wherever it had happened, how had she felt? Had she cursed, or wept in confusion and dismay, loathing her body for what it had become? Looking at the pictures in the album, imagining the world through the eyes of the tortured child she had been, he thought not. He suspected that she had seen instantly what the change would bring her and embraced hell willingly, even happily, greedily. In her place, perhaps he would, too.

In sudden uncertainty, he snapped the album closed and thrust it back at Mrs. Bieber. Maybe this visit was a mistake. He wanted to know Lane, not sympathize with her, to understand how her mind worked, not feel echoes of her pain in him.

"Is something the matter?" Mrs. Bieber asked in concern.

He gave her a quick smile. "I was just thinking about your daughter's childhood. No wonder she ran away."

She laid her hand on his arm. "It wasn't all that bad. We had happy times here at home. It's still good when everyone gets home together. There's a tenseness and ... distance in Mada when she first comes that makes me wonder if she's really any happier in all the glitter of those exotic places she goes, but at least she's content and happy here."

He carried the last remark away with him, echoing through his head, chewing at him. She enjoyed coming home. Only this time, instead of a happy family reunion and carefree holiday, she would find a cop waiting, a date with retribution and justice. Mrs. Bieber would be hurt, too, when he arrested Lane.

Unbidden, Lien's quotation from *I Ching* the day he left San Francisco came back: *Acting to recreate order must be done with proper authority. Setting one's self up to alter things according to one's own judgment can end in mistake and failure.*

Driving home through the windy night, Garreth felt a nagging doubt and wondered unhappily about the rightness of what he was doing.

9

Handing the keys to the patrol car over to Garreth, Maggie sighed. "Are you sure there isn't any way I can talk you into going on Afternoons? What if I give you my body?"

He grinned. "Danzig is the one to sell yourself to if you want Nights. What's the matter—rough shift today?"

She grimaced. "Aside from breaking up another major assault between Phil and Eldora Schumacher, there was a ten-minute lecture from Mrs. Mary Jane Dreiling on how we're harrassing her precious little Scott and I am single-handedly dooming the sanctity of the American Family by not sitting home breeding babies like a normal woman! My teeth still ache from smiling at her."

"What did you ticket little Scott for this time?"

"Playing Ditch'em at fifty miles an hour in that hopped-up van of his. I wish you'd had the watch. Nat's told me that every time some turkey starts giving you a bad time you just peel off your glasses and say, 'It's a nice day, isn't it?' and suddenly you're dealing with a pussycat. What's your secret? Come on, share with a needy fellow officer."

Did he really use his hypnotic ability that much? Frowning, Garreth hefted his eqipment belt, readjusting it. The worst part of being back in uniform was becoming reaccustomed to all the weight around his hips. He made himself smile. "It can't be told. The trick is my Irish blood, Maggie darlin'." *Dearg-due* blood. "It's the gift o' blarney."

She sighed. "I might have known. Well, have fun tonight. You're all alone. With Nat off, Pfannenstiel's working and you know he'll be on his butt somewhere all night working nothing but his mouth." She disappeared through the station door of City Hall.

Garreth checked the equipment in the car and trunk before sliding into the driver's seat still warm from Maggie's body and smelling of her blood. He did not dread the shift. Bill Pfannenstiel, who worked Evening and Morning relief, liked to talk and could be maddeningly slow, but he had twenty-five years of experience and knew every inch of the town. And unlike some of the older generation of officers Garreth had met, he was always willing to try talking through a situation before resorting to force. Garreth suspected that Maggie's dislike stemmed from Pfannenstiel's tendency to call her *Maggie-girl honey.*

Maggie's remarks about persuasive ability echoed around in his head while he patrolled. *Did* he use the vampire ability too often and without thinking? He tried not to, no more than necessary. He preferred to act like normal people.

He moved through the business district, checking doors and keeping an eye on the Friday night traffic. He spotted the Dreiling boy's blue van in the thick of it as usual. The kid saw him, too, and leaned out to give him the finger before pulling away.

Later as his and Pfannenstiel's cars parked together in the Schaller Ford lot while they watched traffic, Garreth asked, "What is it with the Dreiling kid? He's inviting someone to come down on him."

Pfannenstiel grunted. "Daring us is more like it. He doesn't think we can touch him. After all, his folks are plank owners."

Garreth blinked. "What?"

"One of the founding families. The town belongs to them."

Garreth eyed the passing cars. "We'll see. The first chance that comes along, I'm writing him up good. It'll cost him his license."

Pfannenstiel sighed. "That badge is a pretty big stick, but you want to be careful you don't trip over it."

While Garreth digested that bit of philosophy the radio came to life, putting them back to work. He checked on a barking dog, then rounded up three juveniles who had ripped off two six-packs from a local liquor store. Their parents met him at the station. With the beer paid for, the liquor store owner dropped charges, but watching the boys being dragged away by enraged parents, Garreth wondered if juvenile proceedings might not have been gentler and more humane than what what waited for them at home.

"Like some cookies?" Sue Pfiefer asked. "They're fresh chocolate chips."

He shook his head.

The Evening dispatcher looked down at her plump self and sighed. "I envy your will power." The phone rang. "Baumen police." Her expression went grim listening. "We'll be right there." She slammed the receiver down. "That was the Brown Bottle. Bill Pfannenstiel went over to break up a fight and someone hit him. He's unconscious."

Garreth raced for the door.

He found a crowd at the sidewalk outside the Brown Bottle and sounds of breakage coming from inside.

Each crash made the bartender wince. "Mr. Driscoll will be mad as hell about this. Get that lunatic out of there."

"Where's Officer Pfannenstiel?" Garreth demanded.

"Still inside."

Garreth eased around the door, keeping low, baton in hand. He spotted Pfannenstiel immediately, sprawled against the bar with blood running down his face. Anger blazed up in Garreth. He would nail the bastard who did this.

A few patrons still remained ... but flattened against the walls, too frightened to move toward the door.

With good reason. In the middle of the barroom floor, methodically reducing tables and chairs to kindling, stood a colossus of a man. Garreth guessed his height at near seven feet. His biceps looked bigger around than Garreth's thighs.

"Who is he?" Garreth whispered back at the bartender.

"I don't know. Part of the road crew repairing 282 south of here. His buddies smoked out when he hit Bill with a chair."

Some times talking was *not* the answer. This was one of them.

"You, Hercules!" Garreth barked. "You're under arrest. Down on your knees!"

The big man whirled. "Another goddamn pig." He sneered drunkenly. "A wimp kid pig. Here, oinker." Picking up a table, he threw it.

Garreth smiled grimly. *Two can play that game, turkey.* Dropping his baton into its ring on his equipent belt, he caught the table and threw it back.

The gasp from the bartender behind him matched the big man's open-mouthed astonishment. Staring at Garreth, the man almost forgot to duck as the table went by … and Garreth used the opportunity to trap the man's eyes with his.

"I said, you're under arrest." He felt the other resist him, saw denial in the big man's eyes. He met the drunken hatred with his own anger-driven will, however, and held him. "You *will do* as I say. Now, stop where you are!"

The man froze, clenched fists half raised, as though he had suddenly become a statue or store-window mannequin.

"Down on your knees!" Garreth snapped. "Hands together on top of your head! Cross your ankles! *NOW!*"

The man went down so hard the floor shook. Fierce satisfaction flared in Garreth. He felt resistance beneath the compliance, but the man's body still obeyed. Garreth controlled this behemoth. He could make him do anything.

Garreth handcuffed him. "Up." He pointed him at a remaining chair. "Sit … and stay."

The prisoner did so.

Garreth was heading for Pfannenstiel, who had pulled himself up to sit with his back against the bar and was fingering the gash on top of his head, when one of the patrons against the walls called, "Hey, that's a good trick. Can you make him heel, too? Or roll over and play dead?"

The words brought Garreth up short. Suddenly he heard himself as those in the bar must have, giving commands in the same tone used on a dog. More, he saw the expressions on the faces. One waited with glee to see what might be next in the show but others showed varying states of fear. He did not need to read minds to know what they feared: him; someone in his position who would treat one man that way could do it to anyone else.

He carried, he realized, a bigger stick than a badge. He carried the biggest stick of all, the power of absolute control, bestowed and limited by no regulatory body. The responsibility for it rested in just one person, Garreth Mikaelian. The thought awed and frightened him. He felt the stick between his ankles, tripping him.

To lighten his step, Garreth said dryly, "The gentleman is through entertaining tonight. Now, I'll need all of you to remain until I can take your names." He crossed to Pfannenstiel and squatted on his heels beside the older officer. "How do you feel?"

Pfannenstiel grunted. "Stupid. I should have known to duck."

Garreth smiled in relief. Pfannenstiel did not appear seriously injured. "You take it easy. The ambulance will be here as soon as Sue rousts out the driver."

Standing again, he worked his way around the room taking names. And while he did, he slid glances at his prisoner. The big man remained motionless in the chair, staring straight ahead. The biggest stick. *Walk softly*, a voice whispered in his head. *Walk very softly*.

10

"How I envy you young people sometimes." Mrs. Bieber pointed at Garreth's windbreaker. "It feels like winter today but I see the children out around the high school in nothing more than that. You're so thin, too; aren't you cold?"

"Not as long as I keep moving," he lied.

She pulled a shawl tighter around her shoulders and moved into the living room. "The older I get, the more I hate winter. Mada keeps talking about moving me somewhere like Arizona or Florida."

"It's an idea."

She sighed. "But this is my home. All my children were born in the bed upstairs. The few friends of mine still living are all in this town. Mada called last night and offered to give me a vacation in Mexico as a Christmas present. I wouldn't mind *visiting* there for a while."

Garreth's stomach plunged. "You mean, go to *her* this year instead of her coming here?"

She nodded. "Mada said Acapulco is touristy but warm. I'd like that, though of course I would miss not spending Christmas with my grandchildren. Maybe I could go after Christmas."

Garreth's mind churned. Could he get to Acapulco? He tried to think of all he would need … a visa, and a plane ticket, which might be hard to come by with no money. *Dracula, where are my bat wings when I need them?*

Maybe he could find money for driving down, or sell the car and fly. Enough people had eyed the ZX longingly that he should be able to find a buyer. As a place to arrest Lane, aside from the problem of being a foreign country, Acapulco had its attractions … principally that it would save Mrs. Bieber the distress of having her daughter taken in her own home by someone the old woman thought was a friend.

"Acapulco sounds nice," he said. "Let me know if you're going, and where you'll be staying." He made himself smile. "I'll send you postcards from the shivering north."

She laughed. "I will."

Silently, he swore. Of all the lousy luck, just when he had himself settled in his web. He had better start planning for the trip now so he could leave the moment he knew where to find Lane.

11

Given the tendency of cops to hang out with other cops and the fact that he and Maggie were the only single officers in the department, Garreth supposed it was inevitable that they should start dating. It also provided a good chance to get out of Baumen. Not that seeing *Sudden Impact* in Bellamy was very much of an escape, but at least the movie theatre there ran seven nights a week.

Once in the theatre, though, Garreth wondered if the movie was a mistake. He felt as though he were drowning in a sea of blood. The reek of it surrounded him, leaving him fighting cramps and shaking in longing. Someone had been eating Italian food, too; a taint of garlic eddied intermittently, each whiff bringing a moment of suffocation.

Maggie peered anxiously at him. "Are you all right?"

"Fine." But even saying it he knew the tremor in his voice betrayed the lie. "I … get a little claustrophobic sometimes." Not the best excuse in the world with the theatre just half full this Monday night, but it would have to do.

Maggie appeared to believe him. "Do you want to leave?"

He shook his head and put an arm around her. "I'll tough it out."

Somehow he did, though the effort cost him the satisfaction he usually felt watching Dirty Harry blow away bad guy after bad guy with blithe disregard for civil rights, due process, and public safety. It was a relief to escape to the car. There he could at least roll down the window and let the wind dilute the warm blood smell coming from Maggie.

She snapped her seatbelt and settled back. "A little gratuitous violence is good for the soul, don't you think? Have you ever wanted to act like Harry?"

He shrugged. "Sure, especially after spending two weeks tracking down some punk who cuts up girls or old ladies only to learn that he's back on the street before I've finished the paperwork on the arrest."

A nasty whisper in the back of his head asked him if he might not be doing a Callahan now with this self-appointed hunt of his. *Setting one's self up to alter things according to one's own judgment can end in mistake and failure.* He shook his head inwardly. No. After all, he was not looking to kill Lane, just arrest her, all perfectly legitimate since there was a warrant out on her.

"Did you ever find yourself sympathizing with someone playing vigilante, like Harry did that girl hunting down the men who'd raped her and her sister?"

He shook his head. "I might sympathize, but I'd never let them go like he did. If someone chooses to kill another person, no matter how strong or justified the motive, they should be willing to accept the consequences of their act."

Lord that sounded self-righteous. Would he apply it to himself, too? There was probably no way to know until it happened.

They passed the city limits. Garreth floored the accelerator. The car leaped forward like a wild thing unleashed.

Maggie whooped in delight. "This thing really moves. Just don't overrun your lights too far. Cows sometimes get out on the highway along here."

"No problem." Even on this moonless, overcast night the highway stretched in a shining gray ribbon, clearly visible far beyond the edge of the headlights.

He sighed. Nightsight. Vampires. Lane. What was Mrs. Bieber going to do? Here it was nearly Thanksgiving and no word yet about whether she was going to Acapulco or not. Belatedly he realized Maggie had asked him a question. "What?"

"I said, what are you doing Thursday?"

He bit his lip. Was she going to invite him to Thanksgiving dinner? "Nothing in particular. Sleep."

"Not going to pollute your body with delicious, fattening carbohydrates and preservatives and additive-filled plastic side dishes?"

A flood of Thanksgiving memories rose in him, bringing a wave of homesickness. He could never enjoy another feast like those again. Would he even see another holiday? A nagging suspicion had haunted his dreams lately that once he had settled with Lane he would simply cease to exist. "I'm not going to feast, no."

"Then could I talk you into talking Danzig into letting us trade shifts just this once, oh golden-tongued one? Dad and I have been invited to Aunt Ruth's in Victoria and I'd love to be able to spend the whole day there."

Garreth did not know whether to be relieved or disappointed that she was not inviting him to dinner. "I'll talk to Danzig." Without his glasses on.

"Great!" She leaned over and kissed his cheek. Sitting back, she glanced out the window and said, "Look, it's starting to snow."

What? He pulled the car over to the side of the road and switched off the lights. Fat, feathery flakes drifted down around them, and with them the darkness lightened, as though each snowflake brought a bit of moonlight with it. Garreth leaned out the window to stare up, fascinated.

Maggie grinned. "I don't suppose you've seen much of this before. The ground's too warm yet for it to stick, but isn't it pretty?"

"You know what I'd like to do? Run in it. Want to? Just a couple of miles to that rise over there and back."

"Garreth!" She laughed. "Run? Just a couple of miles? Look at my shoes. I can't run anywhere in them. Even if I could, we'd break our legs running in the dark. Let's go on to your place. We can sit out on the deck in the snow there, if you like, and think of some way to warm up afterward."

Pleasure at the snow faded. He put the car in motion again and sighed inwardly. Sitting on the deck would be all right, but ... he wanted to run. It seemed he and Maggie could date and talk about everyday things. It sounded like she was inviting him to make love later, too. But they could not talk about the things deep in him, could not even share some of the physical activities he had come to take for granted. She could not run through the magic of falling snow with him. Tonight he would just about sell his soul for someone who could.

12

Baumen felt like a ghost town. Garreth saw almost no one. Kansas Avenue lay completely deserted. Which did not disturb him a great deal. With luck nothing would happen on the shift. Even beneath an overcast sky threatening snow that might manage to stick in today's near-freezing temperature, and wearing his trooper glasses, the light still gave him a headache. Somewhere above the clouds the sun pressed down on him, draining his energy. *I hope you appreciate what I'm doing for you, Maggie. I wouldn't take on the sun for just anyone.*

He tried not to think about what she was doing at the moment, for fear it might bring on more memories and homesickness. But those came anyway. Would calling home after the shift help or just make the pain more unbearable?

"Baumen 407," the radio murmured. "Public service a Mrs. Anna Bieber at 555-7107."

Mrs. Bieber? Garreth drove to the telephone outside the A & W and dialed the number. Background voices almost drowned out conversation with the woman who answered. Garreth had to shout to make her understand who he wanted to talk to.

But finally Mrs. Bieber came on the line. "I tried calling you at home but Emily Schoning said Helen said you were working. Can you come to the house after you're off? I have the address of the hotel in Acapulco where I'll be joining Mada after Christmas."

He sighed. So it was decided. At least he had several weeks to sell the car and make other arrangements. "It may be eight-thirty before I'm through. Is that too late for you?"

"I'll be expecting you."

He hung up the phone and leaned against the side of the booth, staring out at the patrol car. Guilt stabbed him at the thought of walking out on Danzig and the department. He could give them a story about a critical illness in his family, but it was still unfair to everyone. Doubt at the correctness of his chosen course nagged him again. It spread pain from one temple across his forehead to the other, a headache which not even sunset cured.

At the watch change, Maggie took the car keys from him and said, "You look terrible. I think you're right about being a night person. Would you like it if I come over after I get off and show my appreciation for the favor?"

Monday night seemed to have started something. Would she be amused or insulted if he told her he had a headache? No, headache or not, he wanted her to come. He needed someone, however wide the gulf between them. "The bed and I will be waiting."

He raced through his reports and drove straight to Mrs. Bieber's, still in uniform except for the equipment belt left in his locker at the station.

The old woman answered the door. "My, you look nice. I've never seen you in uniform before. Come on in the living room." She led the way.

He smiled at her despite the lump in his stomach. "I hope you had a good Thanksgiving."

"Oh, yes. My daughter Kathryn hosted this year. It was noisy, of course, but I loved every chaotic minute." She stopped and turned to face him. "I'm afraid I have a confession to make."

A chill of unease moved down his spine. "Confession?"

"I have a hotel address, but that was just an excuse to get you here. Come on." She moved on into the living room.

He followed, only to stop in the doorway. A woman sitting on the couch stood up.

Mrs. Bieber grinned. "I wanted to surprise you. Garreth, this is my daughter Mada."

Mada! His stomach plunged. But this was not Lane! The woman had the right height, legs that seemed to stretch forever and looked even longer with the high heels on her black boots and her snugly fitting dark green slacks. Mahogany hair swept the shoulders of a scarlet turtleneck, but … gray streaked the red and her skin had the coarseness and creases of middle age.

He felt numb with shock. All these weeks he'd been lying in

wait for the wrong woman? But—his mind stumbled trying to think—
the postmark, the school picture, Mrs. Bieber's description of her daughter
as a singer; how could all that match so well and yet be so totally *wrong*!

"I ... am very glad to meet you," he managed to force out. He
must not betray his disappointment.

"And I you," Mada said in an amused voice.

He stiffened. It was Lane's voice.

Looking at her again more closely, this time he saw her eyes.
His heart jumped. The eyes were hers, too. They reflected the light,
vampire eyes, and they glinted cold and blood-red, recognizing him ...
measuring him.

Duel

1

A jumble of emotions and thoughts jostled each other in Garreth's head:

Admiration ... *That's a really convincing make-up job.*

Relief ... *I don't have to go to Acapulco after all.*

Anxiety ... *Oh, lord, we're in the middle of her mother's living room; I can't arrest her here.*

Concern ... *This is going to make the department short for the weekend.*

Dismay ... *So soon? I thought I wouldn't be dealing with her until after Christmas. I don't want to leave here yet.*

Apprehension ... *What will happen to me now, when she's in custody and my reason for living is gone?*

From somewhere beyond the mindstorm, Mrs. Bieber's delighted voice reached him. "Isn't this nice? Mada got tired of Acapulco and decided to come home. We picked her up at the airport in Hays this morning."

"Not tired, Mama," Lane said. "I was there with a friend who had a terrible accident and I just couldn't enjoy it any longer." The middle-aged mask smiled at Garreth. "Mama says you're from San Francisco. Are you the same Garreth Mikaelian the papers were calling Lazarus?"

"Accident? You didn't say anything about that before," Mrs. Bieber said.

"I didn't want to spoil Thanksgiving, Mama. My mother has been telling me something about you, Mr. Mikaelian," Lane said lightly. "It's a very interesting story, but also a little puzzling. Baumen is a long way from San Francisco. How did you happen to come here?"

He took off his glasses and met her eyes. "Good police work."

"What kind of accident?" Mrs. Bieber asked.

Lane shrugged. "He was found at the bottom of the cliff with his neck broken and throat torn out. The police said he must have been attacked by some dogs and fell over the cliff trying to escape from them."

Garreth reached automatically for his own throat, for the now almost-indistinguishable lines of scarring.

"He?" Mrs. Bieber's forehead furrowed in distress. "You were there with a—I'm sorry," she said as Lane started to frown. "I just can't imagine you as part of this modern morality. I'm so sorry about your friend. Are you all right?"

Satiated, Garreth thought angrily. *Replete.* She had come home to wait for Acapulco to cool.

"I'm fine, Mama. He wasn't a close friend, and there was nothing improprietous." She smiled at her mother without taking her eyes from Garreth. "Men don't have wild affairs with women my age. I shared a room with his teen-age grandaughter in order to help him chaperon her. So you've decided to settle here because it's a pleasant change from the city, my mother tells me. But you're still a policeman."

The mockery underlying the pleasant tone irritated Garreth. He said evenly, "It's what I know how to do best, enforce the law." See what she made of that.

Her eyes flared red.

Mrs. Bieber glanced from him to her daughter, her forehead furrowed, obviously sensing the tension between them but unable to understand the reason for it. In a determinedly cheerful tone, she said, "Why don't you two sit down and get acquainted while I go make tea. Garreth doesn't drink coffee, either."

She left the room.

Garreth took off his jacket but continued to stand, eyeing Lane.

She broke the silence first, raising her brows and laughing. With the sound of it he seemed to see through the mask to the ever-young face beneath. "You amaze and delight me, Inspector. I've been looking forward to our next meeting, but I confess I never expected it to be here. Tell me, how *did* you find your way?"

He blinked, nonplussed. She looked forward to their next meeting? What made her think there would be one? "I'll tell you all about it on the way back to San Francisco."

Lane turned away, walking in a wide arc toward a widow, where she peered out into the night, toying with the jaw-high collar of her turtleneck. "Ah. So that's the reason for your remark just now about enforcing the law. You came to arrest me."

The arc took her well around a crucifix on the wall, Garreth noticed. "Hunting killers is my job and you killed Mossman and Adair. You tried to kill me."

She whirled. "No, Inspector; I did *not* try to kill you. If I'd wanted you dead, rest assured you would have been found with your neck broken."

So it had not been a mere oversight. "Why didn't—" he began. "Tell me, how do you propose to take me back?"

He frowned. How did she think? "There's a warrant for your arrest. Extradition will be arranged and you'll—"

She hissed, interrupting him. "Are you really so dense? I mean, *how* will you take me back? By what means do you propose to force me to accompany you and remain confined: rosestem handcuffs? A cell with garlic on the bars? May I remind you that anything used against me hurts you equally, if you can even convince your law enforcement colleagues to agree to such nonsense."

The words echoed uncomfortably through his head. It had not even occurred to him there would be problems with taking her back and jailing her. Even given his concentration on finding her, how could he have been so blind, so unforesighted. *Dumb, tunnel-visioned flatfoot.* There must be a way to handle her, though. He could not just let her walk away.

The crucifix caught his eyes. "Maybe I can drape a rosary around your wrists."

Lane's pupils dilated. "Superstition," she said smoothly.

But Garreth watched her breathing quicken and pupils dilate. Superstition, yes, since crosses and holy water did not bother him, but superstition still affected those who believed in it ... and the look of this house told him she had been brought up in the bosom of the Roman Catholic church. "Then why did you tear the Christian fish symbol off Mossman's neck?"

"I detest tacky jewelry." She came back to him, again swinging wide around the crucifix. "Open your eyes, Inspector. It's useless to arrest or try me. Our kind are beyond the reach of mere human laws."

"No." He shook his head. No one could be beyond the law. Without law there was only chaos. "I don't believe—"

He broke off as Mrs. Bieber came in with tea and slices of pumpkin pie. "Mada, you didn't eat a bite at Kathryn's. You must be starved by now. Have some pie. You, too, Garreth."

Garreth and Lane exchanged quick glances. He laughed wryly inside at the irony of finding himself on the same side of a problem as his quarry.

"If you don't think I ate, you didn't see me snacking out in the kitchen while we were cooking," Lane said. "You know I don't have a big appetite anyway, and I never eat dessert."

Garreth smiled but shook his head, patting his belt. "Sweets have been my downfall for years. Now that I've finally gotten the weight off, I don't dare relapse. Thank you for the tea, though."

Shaking her head, Mrs. Bieber poured the tea. "In my day, a good appetite was considered healthy. These days it seems everyone wants to starve to death. Well, have you two been getting acquainted?"

"Yes," they both lied, and sitting down, accepted tea from her.

"I'm so glad. And I'm glad you came home after all, Mada. Will you be able to stay through Christmas?"

Lane glanced at Garreth. "I plan to stay until I take you back to Acapulco."

Daring him to make her a liar? Garreth sucked in his lower lip. What *could* he do about her? Sipping his tea, he listened to Lane tell anecdotes about people in Acapulco. Opposing feelings warred in him ... his belief in due process and justice against the obvious impossibility of following proper established procedure. He must violate the latter to accomplish the former, and that itself violated what his badge said he stood for. *I Ching* insisted that one must act with proper authority or end up in mistake and failure.

The delicate blood smell drifting from Mrs. Bieber set hunger gnawing at him. Before he did anything, he would eat and think the problem over. If he appeared to be retreating, Lane might not feel it necessary to bolt. Garreth stood and reached for his jacket. "I'd better go. Thank you for asking me over, Mrs. Bieber. And it's nice to meet you, Miss Bieber." He pulled on the jacket. "I hope we'll see each other again."

Lane raised a brow. "The night isn't over yet. Mama, I'm going to impose on this nice young man of yours to drive me around for some fresh air. I'll be back before too long."

He stared at her.

She kissed her mother on the cheek and smiled at Garreth. "Shall we go, Mr. Mikaelian?" She led the way into the hall, where she picked a coat off the huge mirrored coat-and-umbrella rack, then fairly pushed Garreth out the front door before surprise gave him time to think or react. "We got sidetracked from our conversation about the nature of reality and I'd really like to finish it."

2

The door closed behind them. Garreth said, "There's nothing more to say except to read you your rights."

"Oh, I think there's a great deal to say yet. That ZX is your car? Of course it is; I saw it outside my apartment." She took his arm. "Let's go for a drive."

I Ching had also said: *The maiden is powerful.* Beware of that which seems weak and innocent. "I don't think so."

She scowled. "How paranoid cops are. What can I do to you? Anyway, do you really think I'd be careless enough to try something in my hometown, where everyone sees everything? Where my mother would see it? I won't foul her nest. I don't even hunt here, one reason I never stay too long."

Somehow he found himself propelled toward the car. "How do you eat?"

"Even during the holidays there are young men around the college campus in Hays. They're always willing to pick up an attractive young woman and demonstrate what superstuds they are. I hunt in disguise, of course ... in my own face." She slid into the passenger side of the car and closed her door. "When I was a girl the most popular spots for couples to park were behind the Coop elevators across 282, around the fairgrounds and sale barn, and in Pioneer Park. I think these days you police hang out behind the elevators waiting for speeders so let's go to the park."

Thinking about it, what *could* she do to him? Garreth wondered. He was strong enough to resist a physical attack and in the reverse of what she had said to him, anything she could use that would hurt him must also hurt her. He walked around the car, climbed in, and started it.

Lane leaned back in the seat. "I have always loved beautiful cars, though I've never dared own one. They're too conspicuous. Though I was once seriously tempted by the Bugatti Royale a friend of mine in Europe had years ago, and lately I've thought about Porsches. My favorite lovers have always been men with fine taste in cars. Yours is passable. Is this stock, Inspector?"

Now why did he feel ashamed to admit it was? "You didn't come to talk about cars." Hunger gnawed at him. His stomach twinged in the threat of a cramp. *Damn!* If only he had taken time to eat before going over to Mrs. Bieber's. "We're here to talk about law."

Lane sighed. "I told you, human law doesn't apply to us, but ... I don't intend to talk about anything more just yet, except maybe the weather." She leaned her head out her open window and blew. Like steam from a locomotive, her breath blew back past her in clouds of billowing white. "Fairy wreaths. I hope it it snows. I love snow now. I didn't used to because I hated being cold. Isn't it a relief not having to care whether it's hot or cold out anymore?"

The sudden shift from world-wise woman to child left Garreth groping in mental confusion. Like a child, too, she leaped from the car at the park and raced from the parking lot up a path toward the swinging bridge. The bridge connected to an artificial island made by digging a channel looping from the Saline River around a large oval of land and back.

She danced across the bridge in a rapid tap of boot heels, pausing only to laugh over her shoulder at him. "In case you haven't already discovered it, yes, vampires can cross running water. It's amazing the superstitions humans have dreamed up to convince themselves they're protected from their nightmares."

In the center of the island lay an open stone pavilion with a raised bandstand. Garreth caught up with her there, and found her peeling off the middle-aged face she wore, so that he truely faced Lane Barber again, youthful face shining pale in the twilight of his nightsight. She raised her brows. "No lights and yet not a misstep anywhwere. Isn't it wonderful being able to see in the dark?"

What was she trying to do? "It has its uses, yes."

She stuffed the latex bits of her mask in a pocket, grimacing. "How solemn you are. Too bad I couldn't have brought you here in the spring, with tulips and crocus and daffodils everywhere, and peonies later in the summer. They used to have a band on Friday and Saturday nights. Lights lit up the pavilion so you could see it from miles away. Everyone in town came. Mama and Papa would polka and waltz until they were almost too tired to walk home."

The ghosts of those dancers haunted the pavilion. He could see them in the leaves the wind whirled across the paving. The ghosts and the sudden wistfulness on the girl-woman face sent a pang through him. Maybe there were things she could do to him that had nothing to do with physical assault. He regretted having come. "Whenever you're ready to talk, let me know."

She sat down on the steps of the bandstand. "All right; let's talk." It was the woman's voice again. "You can't beat me, so why try? It isn't worth it for a couple of arrogant, self-centered humans. There's no reason for you to care about them. There's no reason for you to care what happens to any humans any longer."

He sat down at the other end of the steps from her. "The way you don't care about your family?"

She flung up her head, eyes flashing, and in the motion he saw another ghost ... of the girl in the photo album, and the singer who attacked Claudia Darling in 1941. Then she laughed. "Touché. But ... family is one thing, the rest of humanity another."

"Not to me. I'm sworn to protect them, and all my friends are human, of course."

Lane snorted. "Friends are people you can do things with and bare your soul to. Do you have anyone who fits that description, anyone you can sit and talk with as openly as we're talking? Is there a someone you'd trust to tell what you are without being afraid that the next time you saw him he'd be carrying a sharp wooden stake?"

That stung. He remembered the morning he woke up to find Lien above him and had wondered about that very thing.

She leaned toward him. "Reality, Inspector ... humans are only one thing to us: a source of food."

He sat up straight. "Not to me. I've never drunk a drop of human blood."

Her eyes narrowed. "You drink only animal blood?" She shook her head mockingly. "No wonder you're so thin. You really ought to eat properly, Inspector."

His jaw tightened. "I refuse to prey on people!"

"Oh, really." Her lip curled. "How righteous. But I notice you have no scruples against using my mother as an informer and tricking her into thinking you're a friend to get to me."

That stung even harder. He felt faint heat crawling up his neck and face. "I'm sorry about that. I didn't like doing it. I like your mother."

Her voice flattened to a hiss. "I could kill you for that. It almost makes me sorry I didn't break your neck when I had the chance."

"I keep wondering why you didn't."

For a minute he wondered if she were going to answer. She leaned back against the steps and looked away. But after a bit, she said, "I intended to, but ... you bit me."

He blinked. She sounded as though she expected that to explain everything. "So?"

Lane sighed. "The drawback to immortality is that while we go on, nothing else does. I hold on to my possessions because I lose the people. They die or are left behind when I take a new identity. I'm enjoying my family while I can because when they're dead, I won't have anyone left in the world I give a damn about. Everything I know best, the world I was born into, will be gone forever. It'll happen to you, too."

Without wanting to, Garreth saw it … his parents dying, even his son passing him in age. Eventually, he could become the contemporary of his grandchildren and great-grandchildren, except they would be alien to him, looking at the world through different eyes and even speaking a different language. Look at how the little slang Lane permitted herself—like calling him a mick—dated her.

"Immortality and vampirism are very lonely, Garreth."

The words echoed through him. Almost desperately, he thought of Helen Schoning. "It doesn't have to be. There's nothing wrong with serial relationships. Every time period ought to offer at least several people who can meet some of our emotional needs."

"And what if you could find someone like that, someone just right, like your late wife, say?"

That hit like a knife in the ribs. Garreth shot to his feet with the pain. "How do you know about Marti?"

Lane smiled. "I asked around about you. Your neighbors were only too happy to talk to a reporter about the Man Who Came Back From The Dead. They told me you and Marti had a very special relationship. Her death must have been extremely hard for you."

His throat closed tight, trapping the pain suddenly filling his chest. "Leave my wife out of this."

"But that's just the point." Lane leaned toward him. "What if you found someone else like that. You'd know from the beginning that you were going to lose her eventually. And what if you found another soulmate, then another, always to lose her. How long could you endure that kind of pain?"

Agony wracked him now just thinking about it. He clenched his fists and whispered hoarsely, "God damn you!" Then he laughed bitterly. "Except you already are, and me, too."

She raised her brows. "Surely you don't believe that nonsense. Damnation has nothing to do with us. We're neither demonic nor Undead. We're as alive as humans, only in a different, superior way. What mechanism do you think actually produces a vampire?"

The question surprised him. He thought about it for a minute and had to shrug. "I never thought about it."

"Well I have, and I've studied. I'm convinced there's a vampire virus."

He remembered the medical books on her shelves. "Like rabies."

She laughed. "Close enough. It's carried in blood and saliva like rabies. A person bitten receives a small innoculation of the virus. In a normal, healthy person the immune system destroys it. If there are repeated innoculations, though, some viruses survive to set up house-keeping in the host's cells, and when the body becomes very weak—dies—they take over, modify the host to suit their needs, and reanimate it." Lane's eyes gleamed as she warmed to her subject. "It would appear to take very little to just reanimate the body. The amount of virus from several bites or one long drinking session ending in death are sufficient for that, but apparently there has to be a large colony to affect the brain enough to restore higher intellectual functions."

He stared at her, suddenly understanding. "Blood would carry the most, and I received your blood by biting you."

She nodded. "I knew you would reanimate with higher functions intact, unlike Mossman or Adair." She stood and came over to reach toward the scars on his neck. "Flesh of my flesh. Blood of my blood."

The light spicy-musky scent of her perfume curled around him. He jerked away. "I don't believe you, lady. I'm a cop and you're a killer and you thought you'd make me your companion? How in hell did you ever think I'd agree? Didn't it occur to you that once I realized what had happened to me I might tell everyone what you were and destroy you?"

Her smile was knowing. "You didn't, did you? You haven't told anyone anything, just come after me on your own."

Something he had done once before, he remembered with a sudden chill, and had died for the error. He bounded up the steps into the bandstand. "But not to become your companion. I'm taking you back, even if I have to tell everyone everything."

She followed him up. "And destroy yourself, too?"

He turned his back to the rail and leaned against it for support. "Why not?" he said steadily. "I detest what you've made me. You destroyed my life; you almost destroyed my partner's. You've brought misery to the lives of Mossman and Adair's families. All I care about is seeing you face judgment for that, then I want to die ... finally and for always."

Lane's breath wrapped white around her and melted away into the night air. "Do you? When there's so much you've never seen or experienced?" The musical cadence of her whisper filled the bandstand. "You lived on the bay for years, but did you ever once climb aboard one of the ships that dock there every day and sail away with her? Do you really want to die before you've seen wonders like the Himalayas above Katmandu or climbed to the temples of Tibet? Or walked the Great Wall of China and explored the ancient ruins of Karnak and Zimbabwe? Poling through the Okavanga Delta in Africa at flood time there is such beauty and richness of life that it makes your throat ache, and there's nothing more awesome than the migrations in the Serengeti, when the plains stretch like a sea of grass and there are wildebeest and zebra as far as the eye can see. There's a city in northern China that holds a winter festival every year and fills the city with ice sculptures, not just snowmen but pure, clear ice chiseled into a wonderland of heroes and mythical animals and castles, and ice arbors with ice benches to sit on."

The whisper sang on, naming cities, describing mountains and rivers and caves, most he had never heard of but all sounding awesomely breathtaking ... sang on and on until Garreth's head swam and he ached in longing. He had looked at the ships along the bay, yes, and thought about the places they sailed, but he could never afford to board one. "Most people don't ever see those places," he said. "There isn't time for them all in a life."

Garreth did not recall seeing her move, but Lane suddenly stood beside him. The scent of her perfume filled his head. "Not a human life, no, but we have all the time in the world. We can explore every wonder completely before moving on to the next."

Yes, he thought with a slow wonder. "You can afford a trip like that?"

She slipped an arm through his and laughed—a low, rich sound. "My dear, a woman with hypnotic powers can learn a great many investment tips from the business giants she beds." She sighed happily. "It will be the grand tour of grand tours. Vienna and Rome and Copenhagen. They aren't like they were before the war, but they're still beautiful, and Peking, Mecca, and Sri Lanka. Carrara, where the best marble in the world is quarried, and Venice, where all the greatest glass craftsmen work. And there are pleasures I'll show you that are beyond your imagining, pleasures no human can appreciate. I'll teach you survival techniques it's taken me decades to learn. Garreth, my love, we will bestride the world like a colossus."

The bandstand felt like a carousel, with the night spinning dazzlingly past them. But uneasiness still stirred beneath his growing excitement and anticipation. What? Something he had forgotten? No matter; he would remember it later.

He shook his head. "I'm surprised you've waited this long to go. Wasn't the vampire who made you interested?"

Lane sighed. "We were going to. All the signs indicated Europe was about to fall apart, though, and we couldn't leave until the Polish property was secured or sold off. Another week and we'd have been clear, but ... Hitler pushed in so much faster and more brutally than anyone ever anticipated." She shuddered. "*Blitzkrieg* isn't just a word when you've lived through it. Warsaw was in chaos. Irina and I got separated and I never saw her again, not even when I went back to look for her after the war."

Garreth blinked. "Irina? Her? A *woman* made you?"

"Don't sound so scandalized, love." Lane squeezed his arm. "Human blood is human blood; we don't have to drink from the opposite sex. That's usually the choice and Irina normally fed only on men, but ... I begged her to take from me and let me drink from her. She called herself Irina Rodek and she had a Polish passport."

He felt his brows hop. "Polish."

Lane giggled. "All vampires aren't Transylvanian, you know. Not that she was really Polish. She once told me she was nearly five hundred years old. She'd been Russian for a while, an aristocrat, but had to flee during the Revolution. We met in Vienna." Her voice went dreamy. She leaned her head down on his shoulder. "July, 1934. Vienna really wasn't the place to be that month with Hitler's *putsch* and Dollfuss's killing, but Matthew was stubborn. What were politics to us, he said, as long as the cafes and museums stayed open? That was when he had his reservations and that was when we would use them."

"Matthew? That's the professor you ran away with?" Garreth said.

"Matthew Carlson, yes, but it's more accurate to say I ran *after* him. I'd had him for history that spring and knew he'd be going to Europe on his sabbatical, and I wanted so much to get the hell away from Baumen and Kansas. I threw myself at him. He was middle-aged with a middle-aged wife so the idea of some coed, even an over-sized, clumsy one, finding him sexy turned him to putty. He left his wife and took me with him instead. We were sitting in a cafe and I noticed his eyes going past me. I turned around to see what he was looking at. It was a who, a woman at the next table." Lane laughed. "I hated her on sight. She was so exquisite, like a Dresden figurine, small, perfect cream complexion, hair like sable, and violet, violet eyes. And she was looking at Matthew, flirting with him. Worse, he looked back, all goggle-eyed. Suddenly I was furious. I threw myself at her, fully intending to ruin her beauty for life."

Garreth remembered the photograph in the *Chronicle*. "You have tended to react violently to other women interfering with your meal ticket, haven't you."

She grinned. "Oh, yes. And this would have been another nasty scene except she looked straight at me and said very calmly, in the most charming accent, 'Please don't be angry. Sit down. It would delight me to have you join me for tea.' And suddenly I wasn't angry any longer, and Matthew and I did join her."

The scene played in Garreth's head. He glanced sideways at Lane, fascinated. "How did you come to find out she was a vampire and ask her to make you one, too?"

"I found out by observation, watching her with men, always a different one, including Matthew once, and seeing the man afterward. She sort of took me under her wing after that afternoon. 'I sense you are a very unhappy young woman,' she told me several days later. 'You think you are ugly.' She taught me to dress and walk properly. 'You cannot be small and cuddly so don't waste your youth longing to be. Think of yourself as a goddess, a queen, and move like one.' Irina was the one who showed me that I had a singing talent. She even paid for coaches to train my voice. But that was later. At first she was just kind and when I saw how much men fawned over her, I wanted to be just like her, so I watched her closely in order to imitate her." Lane frowned. "*Why* I realized she was a vampire, I don't know. Even though I had always been fascinated by werewolves and vampires and ogres while growing up, dreaming of becoming one and wreaking revenge on all my tormentors, I didn't believe in them. If I'd been back in Kansas, the idea would never have occurred to me; it would have seemed preposterous. But I was in Vienna, where it seemed all the fairytales in the world might be true. I'd found myself a kind of fairy godmother, hadn't I? I figured it out and when it came time for Matthew and me to leave, I refused to go with him. I went running to Irina, weeping, claiming he'd been overcome with remorse and guilt about the way he'd treated his wife and had abandoned me. I begged to stay with her, as her maid if nothing else."

"And she let you."

A complacent smile lifted the corners of Lane's mouth. "Yes, but as a companion, not maid. I was useful to her, you see. She quickly realized I knew what she was and didn't care. She also saw that as I gained self-confidence, I attracted men ... meals for her. After a couple of years, I begged to join her in her life. She refused at first, saying how hard and lonely a life it is, but when I pointed out that she wouldn't have to be lonely anymore, she agreed. I think she was sorry. She kept scolding me and threatening to leave me on my own if I killed another man. 'It is excessive; it is dangerous. You must learn control,' she would say."

The uneasiness, the feeling that he should be remembering something, stirred again in Garreth. "Irina was right," he said.

Lane snorted. She flung herself away from him, pacing across the bandstand. "Not if it's done right, like a wild animal did it, or a fanatic cult. I knew what I was doing. Irina came from a superstitious age, when people believed in vampires, and was careful out of habit. Even so, sometimes ..." She turned back to face him. "Sometimes I wonder if she comprehended how much power we have. And how much safety in this age of logic and technology. We can do whatever we like with no fear of reprisal."

The chill inside him exploded outward, shattering the warm spell her plans had woven around him, reminding him why he was here and what he had to do. "No. We can't. We still have to be accountable."

Her frown told him she saw she was losing him again. Lane hesitated, mind churning visibly, then shook her head with an indulgent smile. "Ah, we're back to that again, are we?"

"I'm sorry, yes."

She shrugged. "I'm sorry, too, but I suppose it's too much to forget what you were so soon. You have to grow out of it. Then let me start you on your way by dispensing with this foolish illusion you have of returning me to San Francisco. It can't be done. Rosary handcuffs and a garlic cell might hold me, but you'll never get me from here to there. I'll kill you first, even though I adore you and long to show the world to you. Now lay down these wisps of humanity you cling to and come with me. Enjoy the power that is ours."

Cold and dread sunk into his spine, bones, and gut. Dread? Or maybe just uncertainty. What she said carried a ring of truth. "Power? Something I've learned as a cop, and maybe as a vampire, too, is that power always carries responsibility, and the greater the power, the greater the responsibility for not abusing it."

Lane snorted. "A human notion. For us there is no responsibility because there is no one with more power who can punish us."

The dread grew. The latter was certainly true. Garreth felt leaden, as though daylight pressed down on him. Very soon, he feared, he would see what the dread was, and he did not want to. That she was right? That he must forget Lien and Harry, Maggie and Nat, everyone he cared about, and look on them as no more than walking bottles of blood?

"And we certainly have no responsibility to humans," Lane continued coldly. "They are only food. We prey on them. We must. It's our nature."

The words cut like a knife, but to his surprise, the knife did not stab him. Rather, it sliced through his uncertainty, suddenly releasing him. He straightened like a drowning man finding a bottom under his feet and his head out of the water. "Bullshit! It's the vampire nature to need blood and prefer darkness and sleep on the earth, and that is *all*! The rest we choose: our source of blood, killing or not in obtaining it, the way we use our power. I may be new to this life, but I can recognize the difference between what I *must* do and what I *may* do. So don't do any numbers on me about predestination and compulsive behavior!" His voice was rising. With an effort, Garreth dragged it down again, to keep the whole town from hearing. "You abuse people because you hate them. You kill because you enjoy it. I understand why you do it, but that doesn't mean you have to do it, and it sure as hell doesn't justify it! You're a killer and you have to answer for it."

Her eyes flared. "You've decided that, have you? Tell me, how do you justify *that*? What gives *you* the right to judge *me*? That badge?"

The dread burst in him, like ice, like hunger cramps. He wanted to turn away and throw up. "No, not the badge." There was no responsibility, she said, because there was no one with greater power to punish her ... the same principle punks like Wink lived by: *get away with everything you can until you're caught*. And of course they never thought they would be caught. There was another principle, though, one that worked in human law and could apply equally to vampires. An awareness of it must have been working at him since the evening's first mention of the difficulty of taking her back to San Francisco. He drew a deep breath and said steadily, "I'm your peer."

She froze. "A jury of one?"

Acting to recreate order must be done with proper authority. He leaned back against the rail, fingers biting into it. "I'm all there is."

Lane stared at him. He avoided her gaze. After a moment, she gave up trying to trap his eyes and shrugged. "Very well. How does the jury find me? Guilty?"

He felt as though he were suffocating. "Yes."

"Then what sentence do you pass?"

The question stunned him. Something else he had not thought through. What *could* he do? Have her make some kind of anonymous cash gift to compensate the dead men's families? But that did nothing to restrain her from killing again. "I ... have to think about it."

"Poor baby." She strolled back and reached out as though to stroke his cheek.

But before she touched him, her hands dropped to grab his upper arms. A knee drove hard up into his groin.

Pain exploded through Garreth. The world disappeared beyond a raging blue haze and he dropped to the floor, writhing and gasping in anguish.

Dimly, he felt her hands going through his jacket pockets, and heard the jingle of keys. "Dumb mick," she hissed. "The world could have been yours. Now *I'm* imposing a sentence on *you*. Actually I'm doing you a favor by granting your wish. You will die, finally and irrevocably."

The heels of her boots rapped down the steps and away toward the bridge.

Garreth struggled to stand, to pursue her, but could not even make it to his knees, only continue to huddle groaning and cursing. Through the pain paralyzing him came the distant snarl of the ZX's engine. With it rang a grim echo in his head. *Setting one's self to alter things according to one's own judgment can end in mistake and failure ... mistake and failure ... failure.*

3

A decade later he managed to drag himself up the railing of the bandstand, and a couple of years after that the pain finally subsided enough for Garreth to walk. Anger helped, even directed at himself. *Dumb mick, all right. The maiden is powerful. When the hell are you going to get that through your thick skull and quit underestimating her, man?*

Reaching the bridge, he paused to breathe deeply and push self-recrimination aside. It did not solve the problem at hand, which was what to do now. With any other fugitive he could call for back-up and count on help from every other officer in the area. But not this one. It would only needlessly endanger their lives. He really was the only one to deal with her.

But maybe he could let them help find her.

He broke into a run, angling through the park so he came out on Seventh Street and raced down it toward City Hall. The wind had swung around to the north, he noticed, and it felt damp. A sign of snow coming?

A patrol car rolling up the street toward him braked to a stop. Maggie rolled down her window. "Garreth, I passed some girl driving your car a couple of minutes ago. When I realized it *was* your car, I swung around the block to catch her again, but by that time she was gone."

"That was La—Mada Bieber, Anna Bieber's daughter." He scrambled into the passenger side. "Will you call Sue and have her ask Nat to be on the lookout for the car and woman? I need to talk to her."

Maggie raised an eyebrow. "She looked a whole lot younger than Mada Bieber."

"The night is kind to aging faces." He gave her a quick smile.

Maggie continued to eye him. "How does she happen to have your car?"

Garreth grimaced. He would probably have to give some kind of explanation sooner or later. "She snatched the keys while we were sitting on the steps of the bandstand."

The curious stare became a suspicious frown. "What were you doing on Pioneer Island with a woman old enough to be your grandmother?"

He groaned inwardly. The last thing he needed to deal with now was jealousy. "Finding out she *is* my grandmother ... and not very happy about the past crashing in on her." He reached for the microphone. "206 Baumen. Ask 303 to watch for a red 1983 Datsun ZX, local—"

"Baumen 206," Sue Pfeifer interrupted. "Be advised that vehicle is 10-19."

He blinked at the radio. The car was at the *station*?

Before he could ask about it, though, Sue went on, "206, will you please check the high school? 10-96 reported around the gymnasium."

Maggie grimaced. "Even on Thanksgiving someone has to be out making trouble."

They both checked all around the high school, but neither saw any sign of the reported prowler. All the doors and windows were secure. After ten minutes, Maggie called off the search and they drove on to the station, where Sue handed over Garreth's keys.

"This woman stuck her head in through the door and tossed the keys at me. She said to tell you she's sorry for stranding you and that she'll see you later."

Cold slid down Garreth's spine. He heard Lane's voice beneath Sue's cheerful tone and the words rang with threat.

Maggie said, "Sounds like she's cooling down."

He smiled grimly. "Yes." Cooling to sub-freezing. The lady of ice and steel was out there planning how to kill him. He tried to imagine possible methods. Throw garlic at him and break his neck while he struggled to breathe? Wait and attack while he slept?

No matter. She was not going to have the chance. Lane had victimized him for the last time. He intended to find her first, and while he hunted, would think of some way to deal with her.

Blood smells from the two women swirled around him. His stomach cramped, reminding him sharply that he still had not eaten today. That had better be taken care of before he started the hunt.

Calling goodnights over his shoulder, he headed for the door and his car.

His watch read midnight as he turned in the drive. Leaving the car running, he went to peer in through the windows on his side before opening the garage door. It was empty. The tool drawers caught his eye. Might there be something in them that would make an effective weapon? His gun was no good unless the bullets had suddenly transmuted to wood.

Wood. His gaze slid to the stack of firewood against the back of the house, and to the smaller pieces left from tree trimming during the summer and saved for kindling. Garreth's gut twisted. No! He turned away. Not that. It *would* be setting himself up as judge. It would also be murder. There had to be another answer, even if it meant becoming her companion after all, in order to be her keeper.

He bent down for the garage door handle.

A flat thrum and hiss sounded from the direction of the shrubbery separating Helen's property from that next door. Garreth reacted with all his cop's training and instincts … spinning and dropping. Not quite fast enough, however. Pain exploded in his right shoulder. He fell backward against the garage door.

With shock, he saw the feathered shaft of an arrow pinning uniform jacket to his shoulder. But even then his training carried through. He rolled for the cover of the car.

There he pressed against the front fender and wheel and pulled at the arrow, gritting his teeth against the pain as the shaft grated on the underside of his collar bone. At the same time he listened, straining for any sounds that would give him Lane's position. The assailant must be Lane. But the rumble of the car's engine drowned out all other sound.

The arrow came free in a spurt of blood … and fear. The arrow confirmed his assailant's identity. Among those plaques on the Bieber dining room wall were several for excellence in archery. The arrow also told him how vulnerable he was to her. Its metal point had been broken off and the shaft sharpened in hurried, rough knife cuts. An arrow, Garreth realized with sudden chill, throwing it aside, was essentially a wooden stake.

He pressed the jacket against his shoulder, using the thick pile lining to soak up the blood, and scooted toward the car door. The car would protect him. He could also use it to escape.

Then a sharp hiss sounded above the engine and the rear of the car sank. Garreth swore. She had put an arrow in a rear tire. No matter; he could still drive. Tires were replaceable. He reached for the door handle.

Heels rapped on the concrete of the driveway, approaching the car. Garreth froze. The moment the door opened, she would know what he intended to do. Could he open it and thow himself in faster than she could circle the car? He licked his lips. He would have to try.

He reached for the door handle again.

"Don't move, lover," came a whisper. "Stay very still."

To his horror, her voice dragged at him like daylight. He wanted to obey. Grimly, he fought the power of it, fought to reach for the door handle.

The heels tapped closer, circling the rear end of the car. "You're weak. You're hurt, poor baby. You want to curl up and wait for the pain to go away."

No. Move, you stupid flatfoot. Move! But his body, shocky from pain, blood loss, and hunger, would not listen to his mind. With all his will pushing his hand toward the door handle, the hand still fell back.

Lane appeared around the car. She held the bow with another arrow nocked, the bowstring half drawn.

Could two play the power game? Panting in gasps of pain and with the steam of his breath fogging his vision, he stared hard at her. "You don't want to shoot me." He crouched, presenting as small a target as possible, protecting his chest. He poured his will at her. "Put down the bow and arrow. Lay it down."

She continued drawing back the bowstring. "Good try, but it won't work, lover. I've had more practice. Now, sit up," she crooned. "Give me a good target so it'll be over quick."

No. No! his mind screamed. His body slowly, inexorably straightened.

She smiled. "That's a good boy."

Desperately he fought to look away, fought to think of his pain, to become angry, but nothing worked. She held him, pinned him with her eyes like a butterfly specimen.

A second floor window opened. "Is that you, Garreth?" Helen's voice called.

Lane's gaze shifted fractionally.

Free! He flung himself sideways.

The bowstring thrummed again, but this time *she* was late. The arrow clattered across the paving where he had been.

"Garreth?" Helen leaned out.

Like a shadow, Lane leaped for the shrubbery.

"Garreth, what's going on!"

He scrambled to his feet. "Stay inside where you're safe."

Lane was headed east. Garreth blocked out the pain in his shoulder and raced after the fading sound of her footsteps. Vampires healed fast, he reminded himself. The bleeding had stopped; the pain should disappear soon, too, then. In any case, he had no time to bother with it. He must catch Lane.

He saw only glimpses of her between trees, shrubbery, and buildings. His vampire hearing let him follow the sound of her flight, though. Minutes later he saw Maggie, too, headed west on Oak with light bar flashing. Helen must have called in about him.

Between the medical center and the hospital lay only open lawn. There he saw Lane clearly, but could not gain on her. Still well ahead of him, she raced past the doctors' offices and across the street into a yard. On the other hand, he was staying with her.

Three blocks later, approaching downtown, he remained just over half a block behind. Then she dodged north behind the Prairie State Bank. When he reached the alley entrance, she had vanished.

Obviously she had passed through the rear door into one of the buildings along the alley. The question was, which one?

The Prairie State Bank had no alley door but the library on the back side of the block did. Might she have gone in there? He could imagine her lying in wait among the stacks.

He touched the door—*wrench*—and stood on a landing, between short flights of stairs leading down into a basement and up behind the circulation desk on the main floor. Garreth grimaced. The passage had renewed the lessening pain in his shoulder. With an effort, he ignored it and sniffed the air. It smelled of dust and paper and the musky odors of humanity which had been sinking into the walls and tables since Carnegie money put up the building. Traces of glues carried up from the basement. There was no fresh blood scent, though. Then it occurred to him that he had noticed no blood scent all the time he was with Lane. It would make sense that vampires could not scent blood in each other; they were not potential food sources. But he smelled no trace of her spicy-musky perfume, either.

He held his breath and listened. There were only the creaks and sighs of an aging building, and for a few minutes the roar of the furnace ... no footsteps, no hiss of breathing. No Lane.

Wrench. Pain sliced through his shoulder again. Garreth grimaced as he peered up and down the alley. This constant aggravation of his wound was going to make the search a really fun one.

Would she have gone into one of the stores? The main sections were all lighted and their interiors visible from the street, but back rooms and office space would not be. J.C. Penney lay closest.

Wrench.

But this time triumph helped him forget the pain. She was here ... somewhere! The scent of her perfume hung fresh among the stale, fading odors of daytime occupancy. The entire main floor stretched before him with no sign of her, but he could not see it all. Clothing racks sat close enough together to use for cover.

He dropped to a crouch behind one so he could not be seen, either, and listened for any sound which should not be here. Nothing. Only the normal building creaks. The household goods section lay downstairs. Could she have gone there, or up to the offices on the second floor? His hand itched for a gun, though he knew it would be useless. Old habits die hard. He had had one on every other building search like this.

Running, crouched, for the stairs up to the offices, he wondered why she had come in here. It was not as though she were a simple fugitive who wanted just to hide so she could escape.

The scent of her perfume in the stairway faded halfway up. Garreth continued the climb just to satisfy himself that she had not come this way. He smelled no trace of her in the upper hallway.

Downstairs, plastic hangears rattled.

Garreth raced down the steps on tip toes, cat-silent. Just in time to see a figure carrying a bundle under one arm vanish at the rear door.

Lane had changed clothes, to running shoes and a dark blue man's work coverall. Her hair was all pushed up under a dark stocking cap. The bundle must be her own clothes, then, wrapped up in her jacket.

He ran for the door, too, then hesitated. Outside metal rang softly, like the lid of a trash dumpster being stealthily lowered ... or someone crawling across the top. Garreth had a sudden mental image of Lane crouching atop the dumpster in wait for him.

He quickly considered his options. Opening the door would set off alarms. Try going through low and rolling? Not having tried it before, he could not be sure that was even possible.

He turned away and moved from rack to rack for the front door. Better to go around and head her off.

A glance out the window from the cover of the last rack showed him the street was clear.

Wrench!

He leaned back against the door, clutching his shoulder and breathing through clenched teeth. That had been the worst one yet. It took most of a minute for the pain to subside to just a fierce throb.

"What's this—drinking on the job?" a voice sneered. "An outrage."

Garreth looked up to see a familiar blue van coasting to a stop opposite him and the Dreiling boy leaning across to the passenger window. He made himself stand up and let go of his shoulder. "A little late for you to be out, isn't it, Scott?"

"Oh, I'm on my way home right now, officer. Gee, I hope the chief doesn't see you patrolling without your hat on, and without your gun, too. I didn't know cops ever took their guns off."

Snickering, the boy pulled back into the driver's seat and gunned the van away. Garreth glared after him. *Laugh on, punk; one of these days I'm going to have your head.*

Something brushed his face. He looked up ... snow, not the feathery flakes of Monday but small and hard, rattling against the paving and store windows like icy grains of sand. He raced through the rain of it around the end of the block for the alley.

Each step of the way, he tried to put himself in Lane's place, to guess where she might go next, what her plan was. She had one. Her route, into Penney's first for a change of clothes, indicated that. But what it might be, he had no idea. Maybe just to keep him running until he wore down too much to resist. The way he felt, light-headed, nauseated, shaky, that would not be much longer.

Garreth reached the alley in time to see her at the rear door of the library. A moment later, she had disappeared.

"Damn."

An ear against the door brought him the whisper of footsteps running up steps and away across wooden floors. At least she was not trying an ambush just inside. Steeling himself, he pressed against the door.

Wrench!

He made himself keep moving, but the effort brought a cold sweat, the first Garreth could remember since the alley in North Beach. His right arm felt heavy and numb. And ahead of him among the stacks, he heard the light dance of Lane's feet.

Her whisper carried clearly through the silence. "This is a nice place to play hide-and-seek, don't you think, Inspector?"

He leaned against the end of a stack. "Let's talk."

"What's the matter? Haven't you found a weapon to use on me yet? Too bad, lover. You should have tried the hardware store. I think they have hammers and wooden stakes. Sport and Spinner up the street have bows and arrows. We could be armed equally ... except those arrows have metal points, which can't hurt me, and I'm probably a better archer than you are."

He moved along the ends toward the sound of her voice. He stopped long enough to talk. "I had a chance to think while I was lying there in the bandstand and you're right, I can't beat you. So I want to join you."

"Would you join in the spirit of the hunt, though? I think not. You're too much like Irina ... cautious, worried about human feelings and that they'll discover what you are."

While she talked, he moved again, following her voice. If he could get close enough, perhaps he could surprise her and grab her bow. But even as he formed the thought, he realized she was moving, too. By the end of her speech the sound of it came from somewhere above and behind him.

On top of the stacks? Garreth flattened against the books and peered up, hoping to catch some sight of her. "I thought you cared about your mother, at least, and wouldn't foul her nest."

"Don't worry, lover; I won't." Her voice was moving, coming closer. "Do I look like Mada Bieber to you?"

Not in her true face and new clothes. He backed away, around another stack. "Then you're not worried about the questions that'll come up if I die?" A weapon. He needed something to defend himself with. "People know we were together and that we had a disagreement which ended with you taking off with my car."

A book. At least it might deflect her aim. He chose a moderate-sized one from the nearest shelf.

Her laughter floated around him. "No one will ever connect Mada Bieber with your death." Suddenly she was there, arching above him as she stepped from the top of one stack to another. She knelt, nocking an arrow. "I promise they won't."

He threw the book and dived sideways. She pulled back to dodge the book and he scrambled up around the cover of another stack.

Lane laughed. "Run, rabbit, run. Catch me if you can."

She vaulted off the stacks, but instead of coming after him, sprinted for the rear door. Cursing wearily, Garreth followed.

This time the pain of passage nearly knocked him to his knees. Only stubborn determination and anger kept him on his feet. Did she want to kill him or not? She could have managed it in there if she had really tried, but she seemed to be just playing with him. To torment him first?

Too late he happened to think that she might try to ambush him, but she did not. She was running across the street toward the alley in the next block south. He staggered after her.

Engines roared on Kansas Avenue. Across the intersection raced a blue van and a red pickup jacked high on its axles. Another engine rumbled to the other side of Garreth. Headlights flashed across him. Above the glare of the lights, he caught a glimpse of a lightbar.

He dived across the street for the alley.

The patrol car braked and swerved after him, fishtailing on the snow crystals. "Mikaelian," Ed Duncan's voice called. "Are you all right?"

Garreth swore and kept moving. "I'm fine. You go after the Dreiling kid."

The car pulled up alongside him and halted. Duncan jumped out. "Maggie said someone took a shot at you with a bow and arrow and you were on a foot chase after—"

"I said I'm all right! Get out of here; I'll handle it!" Garreth shouted.

"Maggie said one of the arrows had blood on it."

"*Damn it! Will you get the hell out of here!*" He shoved Duncan toward the patrol car.

"Imperialist pigs!"

The hoarse scream startled both of them. They spun in the direction of the sound.

Lane leaped squarely into the headlights of the car, an arrow nocked, bowstring drawn. "Is death to all bourgeois yankee dog pigs!"

Duncan clawed for his gun. The bowstring sang. With a scream, Duncan went down, hip impaled by the arrow.

Lane streaked away up the alley. Garreth hesitated, torn between her and the wounded officer, then started for Duncan's car.

"No, you go after him," Duncan gasped. "I'll call in. Take my gun."

Garreth left the gun. After *him*. Yes, with her height and those clothes Lane did look male. The voice had been hoarse enough for a man, too. Suddenly he understood her confidence that she would escape suspicion, and why she had been playing with him. She had been waiting for another officer, someone to be a victim and a witness to the fact that a crazy foreigner was shooting police officers in Baumen.

Anger boiled up in him. Chance brought Duncan, but it could just as easily have been Maggie.

The icy chill of fear followed. With her witness ready, play time was over. They had arrived at the finale and she lay in wait for him somewhere. Not in the Lutheran and Methodist churches on the back side of the block, nor did he think she would choose lighted stores or the Driscoll Hotel.

His eyes fell on the rear exit of the Driscoll Theatre. There. Certainty rang like a bell in him. But of course the door was locked. He would have to go through it.

Garreth gritted his teeth.

Wrench!

A vestibule stretched between the door and curtained archway into the theatre proper. Garreth huddled on the floor of it waiting for the pain to ease. Triumph and anger threaded through the anguish, though. Lane was here; he smelled her perfume.

While he fought down pain, he thought, his mind racing. Just chasing Lane with no weapon, no way to catch her, was suicidal. Worse, the whole Baumen Police Department and sheriff's deputies from who knew how many surrounding counties would be descending on the area any time. She had a plan. He had better come up with one, too. He must think of a way to fight her, and must settle the matter quickly, before anyone else could become involved or endangered.

Only one weapon occurred to him. Could he reach it? Maybe … if he could make it through two more doors.

Grimacing, he stood and moved cautiously out into the theatre. The spicy-musky odor died among the others lingering there, popcorn and butter and candy mixing with the scents of sweat and human blood. The creaks and moans of the old building hid any footsteps or breathing, but ... she was here. He felt it in every nerve and bone as he moved up one of the two aisles. She waited with a final arrow ready for him. *Welcome to the William Tell Sitting Duck Shooting Gallery.*

A bowstring thrummed. From above him. Balcony!

Garreth flung himself up the aisle under the balcony. The arrow sliced along the carpeting behind him.

"That's the trouble with a bow, Lane," he called. "There's no silencer on it. Now you catch *me* if you can."

He ran for the lobby and the front door, heart thundering in terror. He was, he freely admitted, scared shitless. Lane had all the advantages: a weapon, experience, no injuries, and no conscience.

Wrench!

He staggered forward, fighting to stay on his feet. *Don't fall, damn you; don't fall!* What did he have in this contest? *Just my pure heart.*

He sprinted for the tracks and the far side of the street.

The bowstring sang its deadly song behind him. Fire burned across his left ribs.

Garreth stumbled. He struggled half a dozen steps on feet and both hands but managed to avoid a complete fall, then he was up again, running as hard as he could.

The snow fell harder, sheeting the street like graphite. Garreth slipped twice, once scraping his palms as he came skidding down on them. The nerves over his ribs and in his shoulder spasmed. He gasped in anguish ... kept moving, not daring to slow down, not daring to look back.

Weaver's Office Supplies loomed before him. He hit the door—*wrench*—and landed heavily on the floor inside. His head spun and he felt sweat running down his face and underarms. On hands and knees, he crawled around the back of the cash register counter.

Inside the display case lay a row of open boxes, each holding a crucifix and rosary. Garreth tried the case. It was unlocked. He slid the glass open and reached in. His hand hesitated over a rosary, though, as he might over a bare wire suspected of carrying electric current.

Come on, man, pick it up. Church and holy water didn't hurt you, remember. The avoidance is only psychological.

Quickly, he scooped out the rosary, then crawled on through the store, past the steps leading up to the mezzanine like second floor with its stock of office furniture, past the bookcases and shelves of stationery and envelopes. He flattened against the wall just beyond the door of the stockroom in the rear.

Only then did he take the time to examine the wound in his side. The arrow still stuck in his jacket but not in him. He pulled it loose from the fabric. The shirt, however, clung to his ribs, wet with his blood. Two holes and so much blood. The shirt would be ruined.

He laughed wryly at himself. *Worry about a new shirt when you're sure you'll need one.*

Footsteps whispered across the floor.

Garreth's heart lurched. He peered around the door. Lane stood just inside the front door, an arrow ready in her bow, her head tilted, listening. Garreth forced himself to breathe slowly and softly.

"Hello, Inspector," Lane said. "I smell you, and I see blood on the floor. Are you badly hurt?"

He needed to get close to her ... behind her. *Come to me, blood mother.* He groaned softly.

Lane's head turned, hunting the source of the sound.

Garreth allowed himself a whimpering gasp.

Lane moved forward, silently now ... past the stairs and bookcases, past the stationery shelves.

Garreth tossed the arrow into the far corner of the stockroom and gathered the rosary in both hands. Breathing as little as possible, ears straining for sounds of Lane's approach, he waited.

The clatter of the arrow brought her through the door swiftly, bow ready to fire. She spun toward the corner where the arrow had landed.

Garreth tossed the loop of beads over her head and drew it snug.

Lane reached for her neck, snarling. Then her hand touched the crucifix in the middle of the rosary. She screamed, shrieking the high, tearing sound of someone in mortal agony. Garreth needed all his control to keep the rosary tight.

"Garreth, let loose!" Lane cried. "I can't stand the pain!" She clawed at his hands. "I'll do whatever you want ... anything ... just take this thing off me. Please. *Please.*" She began sobbing.

Weakness and dizziness swept through him. He bit his lip. Was this capture too late? Had he become too weakened to stay on his feet?

He thought of Duncan bleeding in the alley, Duncan, who might have been Maggie. Grimly he said, "We're going to walk out of here and back to my place."

"Yes. Whatever you want, if you'll just take this thing off! Inspector, it's burning me! It's a hundred times worse than the barrier around dwellings. Help me. Take it off!"

He thought of Harry, of Mossman and Adair's families, of his own shattered life. He thought of *I Ching*. *The maiden is powerful.* He kept the rosary tight.

"Garreth, *please!*" Lane screamed.

He adjusted his hold to give him a free hand for picking up the bow and arrows. "We'll go this way." He hoped. His knees felt weak.

Wrench!

Only his grip on the rosary kept him on his feet. The street spun around him. He shivered, suddenly feeling cold, a sensation he noted with dismay. Could he hang on long enough to reach his place?

Lane started screaming. "Help! Someone help me!"

Garreth jerked the rosary. "Stop that!"

She subsided, but he knew from the hiss of her breath that she remained in pain. Her hatred beat at him.

He angled for Maple Street. Police activity would be centering initially at the north end of the block near Oak. If they hurried past the south end, then stuck to alleys and back yards, they should reach his place without being seen. And then?

There was only one answer. But the deaths had to look like an accident, and it had to destroy their bodies completely. A car crash with the car burning should work best. It would solve everything. Lane would be punished and he would pay for her blood with his. He could stop fighting blood hunger; Grandma Doyle would be relieved; Brian could be adopted in clear conscience.

They crossed the tracks. Lane whimpered. He fought to keep his balance on the slick paving. His only regret was that he would not live to see this country under a good layer of snow. Running in it might have been fun.

Lane still reached for his hands, but each time her nails touched his skin, Garreth jerked the rosary and she subsided with a sharp gasp of anguish. He gritted his teeth, fighting dizziness and weakness.

Up the street, motors roared. Garreth looked around to see the Dreiling boy's van gunning up the street again, just in front of the red pickup. Garreth sucked in a breath of relief. He did not have to take her all the way home.

Before he could debate the rightness of the action, or change his mind, he dropped the bow and arrows and caught Lane's chin with his freed hand. A quick jerk snapped her head around backward on her neck with a *crack* like a gunshot. Too fast for her to know what happened, he hoped. At the same time, he lifting the sagging body and leaped directly in the path of the van.

It had no chance to stop. The Dreiling boy tried. Brakes screamed. His tires found no traction on the icy paving, though, and the van spun end for end. Garreth kept moving, pushing himself and the slack Lane in its path. The gamble was that the van would hit something before it stopped, but the gamble paid off. In front of the hotel, better than a ton and a half of hurtling metal wrapped itself sideways around a solid old light pole, with Lane and Garreth directly between the two.

Wrench.

Garreth rolled on the sidewalk, shoulder and side burning with pain. "No!" he howled. He was not supposed to pass through the pole! He was supposed to die in the crash and fire *with* Lane.

But in spite of himself he felt ... relief. Did he not really want to die, then? He had been relatively content here the past couple of months, he suddenly realized.

He realized something else, too ... there was no fire, only the smell of spilling gas.

Lurching to his feet, Garreth scrambled for the driver's seat. He ripped open the door and reached for the dazed boy. "Come on. It's going to blow!"

One hand searched the boy's pockets as he dragged him out. Good. There were the cigarettes and lighter Garreth expected to find. Flicking the lighter, he tossed it under the van and hauled the boy backward.

Flame engulfed the van.

The driver of the pickup ran up with a fire extinguisher. Garreth reached for it. "I'll do this. You take Scott into the hotel and go for the police officers who are in the alley."

He contrived to fall as he aimed for the van. The extinguisher "came apart" in his hands, spreading its contents all over the paving but not the flames. After that, he and the people who materialized out of the hotel could only stand back and watch the van and Lane burn.

Lane! Desolation swept Garreth, bringing another startling realization about himself. In spite of his outrage at her lack of respect for law and life, in spite of burning hatred for what she had done to Harry and him, her death hurt. Pain closed his throat, grief ... grief for the child whose torment had driven her to seek the power of the vampire life and use it to vent her hatred on humanity, for the waste of intellect, for the voice that would never sing again. He wondered, too, if there might not also be regret for what might have been ... companionship, the grand tour with so many wonders to delight the child still in her.

God he hurt, and was so tired.

Garreth sat down against the wall of the hotel and leaned his head on up-drawn knees.

4

"What do you mean, you're calling the supervisor to find a room for me?" Garreth frowned at the emergency room doctor. "I'm not stay-ing." Hunger cramps wracked him.

The doctor scowled back. "You most certainly are. You may call those flesh wounds, but you've bled heavily. It's given you the most bizarre blood picture I've ever seen. You need to a unit of blood and several days' observation."

Knots raced through Garreth's gut. "Make the blood To Go. I'm signing myself out."

"I'm ordering you to stay." Danzig appeared in the doorway, regarding Garreth narrow-eyed. "Or would you assault another orderly and go over the wall again?"

Garreth set his jaw. "I hate hospitals."

Danzig and the doctor exchanged glances. The chief sighed. "Skip that for a moment, then. Just tell me what you know about Mada Bieber."

Garreth froze. "What does she have to do with this?"

"Nothing as far as I know, but Anna Bieber has been calling the station frantically. It seems she hasn't seen Mada since the two of you drove off together around eight-thirty."

Garreth closed his eyes. The one loose end. Everyone believed that the person who died in the van accident was a stranger, the man who shot Ed and him. How did he explain Mada Bieber's disappearance? Then again, it occurred to him, why should he try? She had run away once in her life once before.

He opened his eyes again. "Sue Pfeifer saw her last, turning in the keys to my car at the station."

Danzig frowned. "What?"

Garreth sighed. "It's a long story, the short of which is, in talking we discovered that she might well be my grandmother after all. That upset her. I don't know why. Am I such a terrible person to have as a grandson? Anyway, she took off with my car. I was going to go looking for her. I thought maybe she'd decided to walk around thinking. This archer business made me forget all about her, though." He frowned in concern. "I hope that psycho didn't have friends who took her hostage or something."

"Hostage!" Danzig's eyes widened. "Oh, lord."

Garreth caught the chief's gaze. God, how he longed for bed, and for the blood in his refrigerator. The smell of blood here was driving him crazy with hunger. "Please get my jacket; I'm going home. Helen can look after me, or Maggie can after she's off duty."

Danzig's face lost expression for a moment. "If you're going to be that stubborn about it, all right."

"Chief!" the doctor exploded.

Danzig shrugged. "You can't hold a man against his will if he's able to walk out under his own power."

Please let me be able to stand and walk.

"But when you're home"—Danzig turned on Garreth with a severe scowl—"you get into bed and stay there. I'll call Helen and have her make sure you do."

Garreth dropped his eyes. "Yes, sir," he said meekly.

5

Where do they end, the roads that lead a man through hell?

Maybe with the realization that the only hell is what people make for themselves, Garreth thinks, lying with his arms around Maggie three nights later, breathing in the sweetness of her blood smell and the musky scent of their lovemaking. Maybe it ends with retribution. He has penalties to pay for killing Lane and the manner in which he has used the Dreiling boy to destroy her; that is only just. As much as he dislikes the boy, he felt sorry for him at the hearing today, no longer looking arrogant but white-faced and frightened at the consequences of his recklessness, clinging to his parents' hands. Garreth commits himself to making friends with the boy. It might even help straighten him out. He commits himself, too, to giving Anna Bieber friendship and support, to becoming a great-grandson. He regrets that the cemetery plot containing Lane's ashes cannot be marked with her name, but he will tend the grave. That should keep him reminded of responsibility and accountability.

Maggie stirs in his arms. "Why don't we move more to my side of the bed. Your side is so lumpy, like you have rocks in the mattress."

"Nothing would be wrong with that," he answers, though he carefully shifts to her side, off his pallet. "Earth is healthy. It sets up positive vibrations with the human body." Grinning, he adds: "My veins carry the blood of an ancient lineage who always keep close contact with the earth and, barring accident or murder, live very long lives."

She sighs. "You're crazy, Garreth."

"Ah, yes, but it's part o' me charm, Maggie darlin'."

She giggles and snuggles against his still-bandaged shoulder.

He smiles down at her. Maggie is not Marti—how can there ever be another Marti?—but she fills some of his needs, as he does some of hers. If he cannot share his soul with her, perhaps that will save him future pain when he has to give her up. His differences cannot be laughed away forever.

A gulf stretches between him and normal humans, but perhaps it is not as wide as Lane tried to make him think, and a few slender bridges can span it if he makes the effort to maintain them.

"What did you talk about with your ex-wife today?" Maggie murmurs.

"Brian." Dennis will adopt his son. Not that Garreth intends to give up all strings on him, though; he wants to keep track of his descendants. "Go to sleep. I want to run."

"You can't lay off until your shoulder and side finish healing?" She shakes her head and pulls the blankets over her head. "I always knew runners have a cog missing. Happy anoxia."

The bandages are nothing but props any longer, of course, hiding the fact that only slight scars remain of his wounds. But he does not tell her that. Sliding out of bed, he dresses in a warm-up suit.

The night outside is clear, the stars and sliver of moon bright as crystal in the icy sky. Garreth draws the air deep into his lungs and blows it out in an incandescent cloud of steam. He runs easily, taking quiet pleasure in his strength and endurance and in the vision that turns darkness to twilight. Briefly, he still wishes he could share it with a companion, then shrugs. Nothing is perfect and the solitude has a loveliness he is coming to enjoy.

The frozen ground streams beneath his feet. When something moves in his peripheral vision, he smiles. Three coyotes are falling in behind him, tongues lolling in predatory laughter.

He glances back. "Hi, gang."

Facing forward again, he lengthens his stride. Far ahead, a herd of cattle lies dozing. With his shadow escort pacing him, he aims for them. Nothing is perfect, but this is not bad. It is enough.

Bloodlinks

Burning
Bridges

1

He dreamed of death, and Undeath. Inspector Garreth Mikaelian stood backed against the wall of an alley in San Francisco's North Beach, pinned by the hypnotic gaze of eyes glowing like rubies, unable to move even enough to ease the pressure where the handcuffs looped over his belt pressed into the small of his back. Red light glinted in the vampire's hair, too ... not a beautiful woman, some distant part of him noticed, but she used her long, showgirl legs and mahogany hair to seem like one.

"You're going to like this, Inspector." She gave him a sultry smile. "You'll feel no pain. You won't mind a bit that you're dying."

There was pleasure in the touch of her soft, cool lips, and it persisted even after the kisses moved down his jaw and became bites pinching his skin in hard, avid nips. High-heeled boots made her five-ten tower even higher above his five-eight. Lassitude held him passive while she tipped his head back to reach his throat better.

Her mouth stopped over the artery pounding there. "Lovely," she breathed. "Now, don't move." Her tongue slid out to lick his skin. She stretched her jaw. He felt fangs extend, then she bit down.

A spasm of intense pleasure lanced through him. Catching his breath, he threw his head farther back and strained up against her sucking mouth.

Presently, though, as cold and weakness spread through him, concern invaded the ecstacy, a belated recognition of something unnatural, wrong. Evil. Fear stirred. He started to twist away sideways, but to his dismay could not move. Her body slammed into his, pinning him helpless against the wall ... despite the fact that he outweighed her by a good fifty pounds. The fear sharpened.

Use your gun, you dumb flatfoot, a voice in his head snarled.

Her grip blocked him from reaching the weapon. He sucked in a breath to yell for help, but her hand clamped over his mouth. In desperation he sank his teeth into it. Her blood scorched his mouth and throat ... liquid fire.

The vampire sprang away, ripping out his throat in her retreat.

He collapsed as though drained of bone as well as blood.

She laughed mockingly. "Goodbye, Inspector. Rest in peace."

Her footsteps faded away, leaving him face down in his blood. Leaving him to listen in helpless terror to heartbeats and breathing that gradually slowed, stumbled, and stopped.

Garreth woke shaking.

Sitting up in bed, he leaned his forehead against updrawn knees, waiting for the adrenalin rush to subside. Shit. How many times did that make for the damn dream this week?

Except that it could not be called a dream exactly. A dream was something one woke from, returning to the ordinary. For him that would be his San Francisco apartment, and joining his partner Harry Takananda in the Homicide squadroom at the SFPD's Bryant Street station. Instead ...

Garreth raised his head to look around the den-come-efficiency above Municipal Court Clerk Helen Schoning's garage in Baumen, Kansas ... wood paneling, leather chairs, kitchenette, and closet forming one side of the corner bathroom. The uniform hanging on the open door, tan shirt with dark brown shoulder tabs and pocket flaps to match the trousers, belonged to the Baumen Police Department. Despite heavy drapes which left the room in midnight darkness, he saw every detail clearly, even to the lettering on the shirt's shoulder patch. The daylight outside pressed down on him like a great weight. And his throat already tickled with building thirst.

He did not wake these days, merely exchanged one nightmare for another. The vampire was memory, not dream. She had existed ... Lane Barber, born Madelaine Bieber seventy years ago in this little prairie town where he tracked her, where he had killed her. But not destroyed her.

Falling back against the pillow to the accompanying grit of dried earth in the air mattress beneath the sheet under him, he sighed. In all honesty, he had to agree that Bauman probably deserved better than to be called a nightmare. Everyone believed the cover story he used to justify asking questions about Lane, that his father had been her illegitimate son. They accepted him as one of the Biebers, albeit a strange one, no doubt because he came from California. The 8:00 PM to 4:00 AM shift despised by Baumen's five other officers suited his needs perfectly and the rolling hills around town pastured plenty of cattle who never missed the blood he took from them.

Vampires did not *have* to drink human blood.

It was a quiet town, unnoticed by the rest of the world, a good place to hide, to bury himself—he smiled wryly—at least until someone began wondering too much about his quirks, and why he never aged.

And then? When he wanted to leave this nightmare, what did he wake up to? Where did he go?

The pressure of the unseen daylight outside shifted. Approaching sunset. *Rise and shine, my man.* Garreth swung out of bed and after folding it back into a couch, headed for the bathroom.

He shaved without turning on the light so his eyes would not reflect red. A sharp-boned face with sandy hair and gray eyes stared back at him from the mirror, boyish-looking despite the mustache he had grown and still a stranger's face even a year and half after replacing the beefier one he had grown up with. *No, boys and girls*, he mused, running the humming razor around the edges of the sandy mustache, *it isn't true vampires don't reflect.*

As he dressed, the tickle in Garreth's throat grew, flaring to full-blown thirst. Taking a thermos from the little refrigerator, he poured some of the contents into a tall glass and leaned against the counter to drink.

The cattle blood tasted flat and bland, like watered-down tomato juice, never satisfying the appetite, no matter how much he drank; but he refused to become what Lane had been, preying on people, drinking them dry whenever she felt it safe to do so and breaking her victims' necks to keep them dead. He scowled down into the glass. Since he got along on animal blood, that was all he would use! He just wished ...

Garreth finished off his breakfast in a gulp and rinsed out the glass in the sink. *I just wish I could like it.*

2

Garreth's key let him in through the back door of the police department's end of City Hall. Chief Danzig and Lieutenant Kaufman had both been gone since four o'clock, when Nat Toews—pronounced "Taves"—the Evening officer, came on duty, but as usual Danzig had left a written briefing. Sue Ann Pfeifer, the evening dispatcher and clerk/typist, looked up from the communications desk dividing the office and reached across it to hand Garreth the notes ... warrants issued by the sheriff's office down in Bellamy and in surrounding counties, requests on activity to be watching for, a bulletin on a nationwide manhunt for two men who had robbed a bank in California then killed a highway patrol trooper in Nevada, a synopsis of the day's activity ... items the shift sergeant in a larger department would have covered verbally at rollcall.

"Nat's rattling doors downtown. Maggie radioed that she's on her way in," Sue Ann said. "Have a cookie."

Garreth grimaced. "I'm allergic to chocolate, remember?"

"I wish I was." She sighed, patting a generous hip.

The smell of her blood curled around Garreth, warm and tantalizingly salty-metallic, pulsating with the beat of the dispatcher's heart. Thirst flared in him.

Pretending to become engrossed in the briefing notes, he unzipped his fur-collared winter uniform jacket and strolled away from her back to a desk by the locker room, where the other odors permeating the office drowned the blood smell: sweat and gun oil, coffee, the eternal plate of donuts and chocolate chip cookies by the coffee urn, scents of urine and disinfectant in the four cells upstairs.

Item Ten brought a groan of dismay. The bloodmobile visited Bellamy in two weeks. Not that again? "Does Danzig really want every one of us to drive down and donate?"

On the other side of the communications desk, Sue Ann smiled. "He says it's good public relations."

Vampire blood dripping into the veins of someone with a weakened immune system would *not* be good for the public, Garreth thought.

Lane had believed in a vampire virus carried in the blood and saliva. According to her, a healthy person's immune system easily destroyed small innoculations of the virus. The virus triumphed, however, in a severely weakened body, invading every cell and altering the host's DNA. Anyone transfused with Garreth Doyle Mikaelian's blood would certainly live, but at what a price. Worse, some nurse or doctor might discover what the patient had become, might realize that far from being just myth, vampires actually existed.

He had to find some way out of donating.

A key clicked in the lock on the back door. Moments later Baumen's best-looking officer strolled up the short hallway between the locker room and Danzig's office. Grinning at Garreth, Maggie Lebekov tossed her cap onto a desk and combed the fingers of both hands through her curly cap of dark hair. "You'll have fun out there tonight."

He pushed aside the problem of the bloodmobile. "Rough shift?"

Her blue eyes crinkled. "Mine wasn't, but … it's the first Friday after Easter and all those virtuous abstentions for Lent are over with. Business is booming at the bars and private clubs. By midnight, you'll have your hands full of DUI's. Oh, and take your slicker; there's rain headed our way."

"Damn." Kansas spring storms could be exhilirating with their roiling purple clouds sweeping in from the west in a spectacular play of lightning and thunder, but on a night like this shift promised to be, rain meant only headaches.

Maggie followed him to the locker room. As he took his equipment belt and clipboard out of his locker, she wrapped her arms around him. The speedloader cases on her belt pressed into his back below his jacket. "What say I set my alarm for 0400 and come over to your place in time to soothe your aching body after the shift?"

The scent of her blood enveloped him, beating at him. Pretending he needed the room to buckle on his equipment belt, he moved out of her arms.

He ought to tell her not to come, he knew. It would be in her best interest to break off the relationship entirely. Over the year and a half that they had been seeing each other her nearness and the blood running warm and salty beneath her skin increasingly brought the hunger boiling up in him with such a fierceness that the effort of denying it left him shaking. And yet ... he could not face the thought of always coming home alone.

Hating himself for his weakness, he said, "I'll look forward to seeing you," and dropped a kiss on the tip of her nose. Maybe her presence would chase off the nightmares.

3

Rain coming in indeed. Thunder grumbled to the west while he checked the equipment in the patrol car's trunk. Climbing into the car, Garreth racked the shotgun and switched on the ignition prepatory to testing the lights and siren.

All hell broke loose. Above him the siren screamed. Red and white lights flashing across the building and the other cars in the lot told him the light bar was on, too, and the left turn signal. Both the car and police radios blared at top volume and the windshield wipers scraped across the windshield at full speed. The air conditioner blasted him with cold air. A knee cracked against the steering column as he jumped in startlement. With the pain, though, panicky confusion—what did he turn off first?—gave way to a return of rational thought. He switched off the key, then opened the door to lean out and glare back at the department's rear door.

"You're dead, Lebekov."

Maggie grinned wickedly from the top of the steps and jumped back inside.

Shutting off all the switches before he tried the ignition switch again, Garreth chuckled. But amusement faded by the time he pulled onto the street. The problem of the bloodmobile seeped back up. What could he do? He had manufactured a bout with flu the last time, so the excuse of illness had been used up. He needed something else this time.

"*Bellamy S.O.*," Sheriff Lou Pfeifer's voice drawled on the radio, calling his office. "*Emma, call Dell Gehrt and tell him he has cattle out on 282 north of the river again. I almost hit one of his steers.*"

Garreth swung the car onto Kansas Avenue. The motorcade was in full swing, two lines of traffic on each side of the railroad spur running up the middle of Baumen's main street, teenagers from the Baumen and surrounding farms and smaller towns driving cars, pickup trucks, and vans on an endless loop that stretched north to the Sonic Drive-in this side of the railroad station, across the tracks, and south past Baumen's three-block shopping area to the A & W near the edge of town before turning north again. The vehicles parked down both sides of the street and along the tracks belonged to patrons of Bauman's movie theater, open only on weekends, and to adults drinking and dancing in the local bars and private clubs.

Garreth cruised south. His radio muttered sporadically, mostly with traffic from the Bellamy PD and sheriff's offices in Bellamy and surrounding counties. Around him kids honked horns at each other and shouted back and forth between cars. A few cars zigged around others to catch special friends and he kept an eye on one pickup he remembered citing twice last month for jumping lights, but for the most part, traffic remained orderly, following its ritual pattern.

He passed Nat Toews checking the doors of businesses and honked a greeting at the stocky cop.

When the cruise circuit crossed the tracks and turned north, Garreth did, too. Presently a sleek black Firebird with four girls inside pulled up beside him on the inside lane. A blond girl in the passenger seat rolled down her window and leaned out, smiling.

"Hello, Garreth."

Garreth sighed. Amy Dreiling. Well, it was inevitable that he run into her sooner or later this evening. "Good evening, Miss Dreiling."

"Do you have to be so formal?" She pouted prettily. "You always called my brother by his first name."

Only to his face. For a long time Garreth had other names for the banker's son he used in private and with fellow officers. "Scott and I shared what you might call a professional relationship."

"If I buy a customized van and drag race and run stop signs with it like Scott did, will you call me by my first name, too?"

Mention of the van abruptly took Garreth back to another night on this street, an icy one two Thanksgivings ago with him struggling across the treacherous, deserted thoroughfare, bleeding and weak from arrow wounds Lane had inflicted. He held the beautiful vampire prisoner, helpless in the rosary he had managed to wrap around her neck. At the roar of a motor he looked up to see Scott's van and a pickup dragging on the far side of the street. Inspiration flashed ... a way to destroy Lane by using this boy who continually dared the police to arrest the son of a city father. He hurled himself and Lane across the tracks into the van's path, snapping Lane's neck as he did so.

Brakes screamed in memory, followed by the shriek of metal as the skidding van wrapped around a telephone pole in a vain attempt to avoid hitting the two of them. Then fire enveloped it, set by Garreth to incinerate Lane's body.

Later, however, he had made friends with the boy, stabbed by guilt at the sight of a pale, frightened Scott facing charges of vehicular homicide in juvenile court. With the arrogance knocked out of him, Scott was not a bad kid. Garreth had actually come to enjoy having him ride along on weekends.

Garreth smiled politely at Amy. "You'll do better driving carefully. Good night, Miss Dreiling."

He turned right at the next corner and patrolled the side streets. It netted him two cars with expired tags and one without handicap identification parked in a handicap zone. It gave him satisfaction to call for a tow of the latter, then while waiting for the truck, he also wrote the car up for a broken outside mirror and a missing lens on a tail light.

Thunder growled louder in the west.

Nat's voice came over the radio announcing he was back in his car.

The pace of the evening picked up. Garreth answered a complaint of a barking dog and vandalism on parked cars in a residential area. Between calls, his mind churned. What *was* he going to do about the bloodmobile?

Lightning flashed in the west, now, accompanying the nearing thunder.

On a swing back down Kansas Avenue Garreth spotted Nat parked at Schaller Ford and turned in to pull up window-to-window with the other officer's car.

Nat grinned beneath his mustache, a red bush matching his sideburns, though his hair was dark. "How's the groupie? I saw you flirting with her."

Garreth grimaced. "I don't know what's worse, a juvie daring us to pick him up, or one inviting me to. Oh, speaking of juvies, our antenna-twister struck again. Three cars on Poplar. One of the neighbors saw some kids in the area, one matching Jimmy Pflughoff's description."

Nat scowled. "The little shit. If only we could catch him at it."

"He's hit Poplar three times out of five. How about planting a car there, something flashy and inviting, with fairy dust on the antenna?"

Nat arched a brow. "Fine. Now if we can find a night dry enough not to wash off the marker, what car do we use ... a certain flashy red ZX?"

"You go to hell."

"Not devoted enough to sacrifice you own car, huh?" Nat grinned. "Speaking of flashy cars, there's someone new in town you ought to meet."

"What's he driving?"

"A Continental, but that isn't why you ought to meet him. The car just reminded me of him. He was at the Driscoll Hotel when I went by, asking Esther at the desk if a Madelaine Bieber lives around here."

Garreth fought an irrational desire to run. *Don't be ridiculous. What do you have to be afraid of?* Nothing ... except questions that might revive others he preferred everyone to forget. He knew Lane was dead but to everyone else she had mysteriously disappeared. She had been disguised as a man that night. After the fire, of course, what remained of her body had been unrecognizeable and Garreth never volunteered her identity. Why should Anna Bieber have to learn her daughter was a killer?

Garreth forced a casual tone. "Did he say why he's looking for Mada? Who is he?"

"He's English. His name's Julian Fowler and he's a writer. I told him no one's seen Miss Bieber for over a year but he still wanted to talk to her family. I sent him over to your great-grandmother."

Despite the knots in his gut, Garreth felt a rush of relief. Now he could stop pretending calm. "What! You sent a stranger we don't know anything about to visit an old woman who lives alone? You should have had him talk to me!" He slammed the patrol car into gear and gunned backward in a tight Y-turn.

"What could you tell him?" Nat yelled after him. "You only met her the once. I'm not stupid, though. I looked over his identification before I gave him the directions. He's—"

"I'm still checking on Anna," Garreth interrupted.

4

The Englishman must have rented the car in Hays. Pulling up at the curb in front of Anna Bieber's house, Garreth's headlights shone on an Ellis County tag on the sleek gray Lincoln in front of him.

Garreth keyed his mike. "407 Baumen. I'll be out of the car on high band at 513 Pine." Sue Ann would recognize the address.

He moved up the walk and climbed the steps to the porch in long, urgent strides.

Anna Bieber answered his knock, her face lighting with surprise and pleasure. "Garreth! How nice. I wasn't expecting to see you until Sunday."

The radio on his hip muttered. Garreth smiled through the screen at the old woman ... thin with age but still straight-backed and sharp-eyed. "I thought I'd just drop by for a minute. This Englishman is visiting for a long time this evening, isn't he?"

Her smile went knowing. "Ah. That's why you're here." She shook her head. "Thank you for your concern, but Mr. Fowler is a charming gentleman." Like so many people in the county descended from the Volga Germans who settle the area, her accent gave "is" and other *s*'s a hissing pronounciation. "Don't be such a suspicious policeman all the time."

"Con men are also charming." A distant part of him noted wryly that his anxiety for her had become genuine ... as though he were actually her great-grandson and not just playing a role. "Grandma Anna, what does he want with Mada?"

"He's a writer researching for a book about World War II."

Lightning flashed, brightening the yard, followed several seconds later by a long drumroll of thunder. The wind picked up. Garreth's radio spat a report of a tree knocked down across a road by lightning in Ellis County.

"Why don't I come in and meet Mr. Fowler?" Garreth said.

"Why don't you," Anna replied dryly. She unhooked the screen and pushed it open.

Garreth followed her through the hall into the living room. He left his jacket on for the appearance of huskiness its bulk gave him, and did not regret the choice when the visitor on the couch set his teacup on the coffee table and stood. Julian Fowler stretched up a good six-foot-plus, an athletic-looking man in his late forties with light brown hair, pale blue eyes, and the kind of peculiarly English face that had probably been pink-cheeked in his youth but had now aged enough to gain character and masculine edges. He looked vaguely familiar, though Garreth could not imagine where he had seen Fowler before. The Englishman's gaze raked him, too.

"Mr. Fowler," Anna said, "I'd like to have you meet my great-grandson, Garreth Mikaelian … Mada's grandson."

The visual autopsy ended abruptly. Fowler grinned in delight. "Really?" He pumped Garreth's hand. "Splendid. I don't suppose you'd know where your grandmother's got to?"

"I'm afraid not." Garreth rescued his hand and gave the Englishman a tight smile. "Excuse me, Mr. Fowler, but I don't quite understand what you want with Mada when you're doing a book about World War II. Shouldn't you be looking at military records?"

Fowler chuckled. "The book isn't *about* World War II, it just takes place during it. It's fiction. All my books are."

All his books? Garreth started. Fowler. Of course! Now he remembered where he had seen the face … on the back of a book his first wife Judith was reading. "You write under the name Graham Fowler."

The Englishman shifted his shoulders, as if embarrassed. "Actually it's as much my name as Julian is. Julian Graham Fowler. I use it because my publisher is of the opinion that Graham sounds more appropriate than Julian for a writers of thrillers. It's just for books and promotional tours, however. Otherwise I'm Julian."

Garreth raised his brows. "I'd think using Graham would open more doors."

"That's quite true. Unfortunately, it also attracts attention when I need solitude." Fowler grimaced. "Tell me, what do you think happened to Mada? Mrs. Bieber says the chief of police believes she was abducted by accomplices of a man killed in town that night."

"As a hostage in case they were pursued. That's what he thinks, yes."

"And you?"

Garreth shrugged. "I can't see abduction. We never found a body."

"Could she have simply run away?" Fowler frowned thoughtfully. "It's rather a habit of hers, isn't it … first haring off to Europe with that college professor, then abandoning him in Vienna, not to mention dodging Hitler's army and all."

Cold knotted Garreth's gut. "How do you know so much about her?"

Fowler blinked. "She told me. I met her once, you know, in the south of France after the war. That is, my parents did. I was just six at the time." He smiled. "I went mad over her. She was the most smashingly magnificent creature I'd ever seen. When she visited with my parents, I was underfoot the whole time, hanging on her every word. She had marvelous stories about traveling around Europe with a Polish woman just before the war."

Garreth caught his breath. That would be Irina Rodek, the vampire Lane told him had brought her into the life.

"But the story I remember best was the one about escaping from Warsaw just ahead of Hitler's forces. She made it so real, like being there. When my publisher suggested that I try a World War II story, naturally I thought about her." Garreth had the feeling that Fowler had forgotten everyone else in the room. He stared dreamily past them. "We have a young girl coming from a sheltered, insular background, suddenly exposed to the sophistication and desperate glitter of pre-war Europe and then caught up in the violence of the war itself. Everything would be through her eyes, a romantic vision at first, then increasingly sophisticated, but still politically naive. Gradually, though, she understands what's happening and is terrified by it until finally, stripped of all innocence, honed into a practical, shrewd woman by the needs of survival, she triumphs." He focused on Garreth. "So I dredged up every detail I could remember her mentioning about her background and came looking for her, to talk to her and learn more about—" A clap of thunder shook the house, interrupting him. Fowler jumped. "My god. We're under seige."

Garreth had to smile. "Of a sort."

Lightning crashed outside, making the lights flicker. Rain drummed against the house. Garreth kicked himself for not bringing the slicker in with him.

The radio on his hip sputtered: *"Bauman 407. 10-93, Gibson's."*

An alarm at the discount house. The lightning had probably set it off, but it had to be checked out.

He backed toward the door. "Sorry we can't help you. I wish you luck luck on the book." Just not enough to learn what had really happened to Lane in Europe.

5

Wind drove the rain before it in blinding sheets. Swearing, Garreth dived down the steps and across the lawn toward his car. But even that short a distance left him soaked. In the car he pushed dripping hair back out of his eyes with a grimace and peeled off his jacket, tossing it into the back seat. With his broadened temperature tolerance, the chill of the rain did not bother him, but water running down his neck did, and he hated the feel of the sodden trousers plastered to his legs.

None of which improved at the Gibson store. His slicker and hat did nothing to protect his cuffs and Wellingtons from further soaking while he walked around the building checking doors amid the crash of thunder and the shrill clamor of the store alarm. For a wistful minute he considered how much drier and more comfortable it would be searching the building from the inside, but with regret discarded the idea as too risky and waited outside until Mel Wiesner, the manager, arrived to shut off the alarm. If Weisner had found him inside, it would be impossible to explain how he had managed that with all the doors locked.

The shift wore on ... two bank alarms, both, like the Gibson's alarm, apparently set off by lightning; power lines pulled down by a fallen branch, where Garreth sat until a KPL truck and crew arrived to take care of them; fights in two bars; opening a car for a woman who had locked her keys inside the Shortstop, Bauman's single convenience store. None of the activity could quite make him forget about the writer or the bloodmobile, however. Through everything, both problems gnawed in the back of his mind.

Lightning and thunder eased. The rain settled into a steady drizzle.

Toward midnight the cruisers along Kansas Avenue had thinned to a last stubborn few. But the closing bars had begun emptying their customers onto the street and the combination of alcohol and wet pavement produced two minor fender benders and several near accidents. One of the latter erupted into a fight as the drivers, both big, burly men, piled out of their cars, enraged by the damage almost inflicted.

Garreth broke up the fight by stepping between them and while they stared down at him, astonished at being pushed apart by someone so much smaller, caught the eyes of each man in turn. "Don't you think that's enough? There's nothing to be upset about."

Rage faded from the men's faces. "I guess you're right." They eyed Garreth with puzzled frowns, clearly aware that something had happened to them, but not sure what or how.

Garreth gave them no time to figure it out. "Then why don't you both go home?"

With pats on their shoulders, he steered the two sodden men toward their cars and stood in the street watching until they drove away.

Someone chuckled behind him. "The Frisco Kid strikes again. I'd sure like to know how you make them roll over and wag their tails for you."

Garreth glanced around. It was after midnight already? Ed Duncan grinned at him from the other patrol car. The grin made the Morning watch officer look strikingly like Robert Redford, a resemblance Garreth knew Duncan cultivated. Garreth sent him back a wry smile. "It's a gift that comes with me blood."

"Okay, if you don't want to share with—hey, podner, we've got a live one!"

Garreth followed Duncan's gaze to a car weaving its way down the lane line on the far side of the tracks.

The light bar on Duncan's car flashed to life. "I'll pull him over. You test him and breathalize him."

Garreth frowned. "Me? It's your stop. You do it."

Duncan grinned. "But you're already drowned and I just got a trim and blow-dry this afternoon."

Usually Duncan did not bother him, but tonight the remark scraped the wrong way across Garreth's nerves. He said shortly, "Tough nuts. You want the fucking DUI, you haul your pretty blow-dry out of the car into the rain and write him up yourself."

He turned away.

"You got an attitude problem, you know that, Mikaelian?" Duncan snapped after him. "You think you're so goddamn much better than the rest of us, a real hotshot, because you were a detective and worked in a big city department! But *I* never froze and let a partner get shot."

The jab hit dead center. Garreth stopped short, pain twisting his gut.

"And I wonder about you ... skinny like that and coming from San Francisco. Maybe we ought to warn Maggie to watch you for night sweats."

With that parting shot, Duncan gunned the car away across the tracks, lights flashing.

6

The rain either sobered everyone up on the walk to their cars or inspired cautious driving. After the private clubs closed at two their parking lots cleared without incident. Garreth checked the Co-op, Gfeller Lumber, and other businesses along 282 on the east side of town, then made a sweep through the city park up by the river and around the sale barn and rodeo grounds, disturbing half a dozen parked couples.

The rain continued unabated but radio traffic faded to near zero. For five and ten minutes at a stretch, only the soft hiss of static came over the air. Garreth yawned. Now came the hard part of the shift ... staying awake.

He turned around to head back south on 282.

Then in the distance, brakes and tires screeched.

Garreth held his breath, straining to hear through the drum of rain on the car. The sound stretched out for what seemed infinity before ending abruptly in a scream of crumpling metal and an animal shriek of agony.

Swearing, he flipped the light bar switch and stamped on the accelerator. The sound came from the north. Over the bridge was out of city jurisdiction but something cried out in pain-edged grunts and who else was there to check it out?

"407 Baumen. Investigating possible 10-47 on 282 north of the river. Advise S.O."

Half a mile past the bridge his stomach jolted floorward. Dark, square shapes loomed through the rain on the road, shapes the human eye would never see until on top of them. Angus cattle. Those Lou Pfeifer had reported earlier? One sprawled on its side groaning, rumen and intestines spilling onto the asphalt.

Garreth swung onto the shoulder, radioing for a wrecker and ambulance. The car that hit the Angus lay upside down in the ditch, a little Honda, or what remained of it after ploughing into a ton of beef at fifty-five or more miles an hour. And north beyond it, a human form hung across a barb wire fence … feminine in outline … motionless.

The stench of rumen contents and blood washed around him with the sound of the cow's agonized grunts as Garreth scrambled down into the muddy ditch to peer into the car. He ignored the thirst they triggered in him. The ditch carried two or three inches of water and another girl remained in the Honda. She did not move either. He smelled no more than the normal blood smell about her, though. By lying flat and reaching in through the slot left of the front window he could reach her wrist. A faint pulse fluttered under his fingers.

She was alive at least.

He splashed up out of the ditch to the girl on the fence, and cursed softly. This one must have gone out through the windshield. Her face had turned to bloody hamburger. With only pulp remaining of her nose, she gasped for breath open-mouthed … in liquid, bubbling sounds and a blast of blood smell on each expiration. Cold bit into Garreth's spine. The girl's throat was filling with blood draining down from her nose.

"I need that ambulance *now!*" he shouted into his portable radio.

"*It's on its way,*" Doris Dreiling, the Morning dispatcher, came back.

But how long before it arrived? Baumen had no regular ambulance service, just one owned by the hospital with a couple of personnel assigned to it on each shift, and when a call came those individuals could be in the middle of other duties just as pressing.

Garreth gnawed his lower lip. Maybe if he laid the girl on her side the blood would drain out of her mouth and let her breathe.

All the warnings against moving accident victims echoed loudly in his head as he gingerly lifted the girl loose from the barbs impaling her and eased her to the ground. On her side she did seem to breathe more easily. He covered her with his slicker against the rain.

A shrill cry mixed with the groans of the injured cow. "Help! Someone help!"

He whirled. The girl in the car had regained consciousness. He slid back down beside the vehicle and stretched out in the muddy water where the girl could see him. "Take it easy, miss. I'm a police officer."

"Get me out, please!"

Not even vampire strength could move this car, the way it had wedged into the ditch. What might moving it do to the girl inside anyway? He had no way to assess her injuries.

"There's a wrecker on the way, miss. We'll have you out in a few minutes."

"No! Please, I want out now! My legs and back—this thing!" She began thrashing, pounding at the steering wheel pinning her.

"Don't move! It's important that you lie still and wait for—"

But panic left her deaf. She continued fighting, and screaming. And up near the fence, the bubbling of the other girl's breath grew worse.

"Miss. Miss!" God, if he could only catch this girl's eyes. Where the hell was Duncan? He needed help. Grabbing the girl's arm, he shook it. *"Goddamn it listen to me!"*

Miraculously, her screams softened to whimpers. But she continued pushing at the steering wheel and would not look in his direction.

He lowered his voice soothingly. "What's your name, honey?"

It seemed an eternity before she answered. "Kim." The nails of her other hand dug at the wheel. "Please, please help me."

"Kim, listen to me. I know you're scared but you'll be all right if you just lie still and wait for the wrecker. Will you do that while I go help your friend?"

"Sheela?" The arm in Garreth's grip jerked. "Oh, no! Where is she?"

"She was thrown out of the car." He let go of the girl's arm. "That's why—"

"No!" Her fingers clamped around his wrist.

"Kim, don't worry. I'm not going far, just up the bank. Your friend—"

"Don't leave me!" Her fingers dug in with fear-driven strength.

The gasps by the fence became gurgles.

His heart lurched. Tearing loose from the girl in the car Garreth scrambled backward and clawed his way up the slippery ditch to the fence. Lying on her side no longer helped.

He groped for his radio. "Baumen, *where's ... that ... ambulance!*"

The girl needed immediate suction to clear her airway.

"*En route. It should be there any time.*"

The girl's breath gurgled.

Garreth stared down at her in anguish. His own breath rasped through a throat closed tight. Below, her friend in the car continued to scream in hysteria. "Any time" would be too late. "Any time" now she would be dead, drowned in her own blood.

She choked.

Unless he did something.

He bit his lip, and grimaced at the prick of his unextended fangs. *No.* Rain washed down his face and splashed on the slicker covering the girl.

The injured cow grunted, each cry punctuated with a thrash of its legs.

Garreth pushed sodden hair out of his eyes. No, he could not do that. He would not touch human blood. Must not.

Desperately he peered toward town, but no emergency-vehicle lights showed through the rain.

The girl choked again.

His gut knotted. He should not touch her, and yet ... if he did not, she would die.

"All right!" he shouted, though at whom Garreth had no idea. Fate, perhaps, or Lane's ghost. "All *right*. Just this once."

He knelt at the girl's head, lifted her chin, and crouched over her. His mouth fastened over hers, sucking. He would spit out the blood, would—

Then it filled his mouth.

Every cell of him screamed in joy. The hot, salty-metallic liquid flowed over his tongue with a richness animal blood never had. A richness his instincts had been craving since the moment he woke in the San Francisco morgue. Garreth could not turn away and spit. Something else snatched control of him. He swallowed.

The blood burned like fire in his throat, but a fire that cooled, not seared, soothing the other fire of thirst. And from it warmth spread outward through the rest of him, warmth and a crackling surge of energy. All awareness of the rain, the mortally injured cow, and the screaming girl in the car faded to the distant edge of perception. Garreth sucked and swallowed again, and again, ravenously, greedily relishing every drop.

Then, also dimly, he became aware of a siren wailing, rising above the cries of the trapped girl.

The chest of the girl at his knees heaved, drawing in a convulsive breath.

A hand touched Garreth's shoulder. "We'll take over now."

Fury boiled up in him. *No, not yet!* He clung snarling to his prey.

The hand pulled at him. "Mikaelian!"

The sound of his name ripped through the thing controlling him. Garreth suddenly saw what he was doing. In horror he flung away, jumping up and backing until the fence stopped his retreat. Barbs pricked him but he barely felt them. *Animal! Is this the way you serve and protect, feeding on a helpless girl?*

One of the ambulance attendants glanced up from examining the girl. "You've got her airway clear. Good work."

Good work? Garreth grimaced bitterly. They had no idea how he had done it, or that he had taken such pleasure in the act. A pleasure that part of him still felt, savoring the taste lingering in his mouth. That part of him also pointed out with some smugness that for the first time since he entered vampire life all hunger had been satisfied.

Red lights flashing on the highway toward town caught his eye. The wrecker. That reminded him of the car in the ditch.

The girl in it was still screaming. He hurriedly slid into the ditch and lay down beside the car again to reach in and catch her hand. "Kim, honey, it's all right. I'm back."

To his ears the reassurances he murmured at her sounded inane, but perhaps all that mattered was the sound of his voice and being touched by someone. The girl calmed. He made no attempt to leave again, just lay holding her hand, the two of them alone in the rain and cold and mud. Thank god the wrecker was coming. The water in the ditch felt deeper, and the girl's hand had gone icy.

Then abruptly the solitude vanished. The ditch swarmed with people: the wrecker crew, one attendant from the ambulance, a deputy sheriff from Lebeau, the town north, and a tall, beefy man Garreth recognized as Dell Gehrt. Someone put the cow out of its agony.

Garreth continued holding the girl's hand through the jolts and bumps of winching the car up on the shoulder and while it was cut apart to free her.

Finally the ambulance screamed away with its two patients. Garreth collected his slicker from where it had been pulled off the girl and slipped back into it to protect the seat of his car from his messy uniform, then leaving the deputy to finish up at the accident scene, he headed back to town.

7

Garreth had never been so glad to finish a shift. Despite the energy from the girl's blood, exhaustion dragged at him as though the sun has risen.

Doris Dreiling's plump, motherly face peered at him with concern over the top of the communications desk. "Are you all right? You look like you could use some fortified coffee."

That meant brandy in it. She kept a bottle in her desk—against regulations—for just such occasions. Lien used to meet Harry and him at the door with rum-laced tea, he remembered wistfully. What a lifesaver that had been sometimes. Now— He smiled wryly. *Now I'd have to have Doris drink the brandy and take the shot from her.* "Thank you, no. I'm fine."

"How are the girls?"

The girls. He sighed and peeled off his slicker. "The one from the car just has a broken ankle and some broken ribs. For which she can probably credit her seat belt. The other one ..." He grimaced at the blood and mud smearing both sides of his slicker. It would have to be washed thoroughly before it could be worn again. "They don't know yet. She might have brain damage, or never regain consciousness. X-rays showed a severe skull fracture with fragments in her brain. The heliocopter from Fort Riley picked her up a few minutes ago to fly her to the KU Med Center for surgery."

Mud crusted his equipment belt, too. And probably filled his holster and gun. He dropped it all on the floor to deal with later. Right now— He sat down at a desk and rolled a form into the typewriter to start on his reports.

A key clicked in the back door. Duncan stamped in. "God what a miserable night. Doris, sweetie, would you consider making up a thermos of your fortified coffee to go. Jesus!" He stared at Garreth. "You're a mess, Mikaelian. It must have been some fun up there."

Garreth typed on without looking up. "Where were you? I could have used some help."

"Sorry. I was on the way when I got a flat, and by the time I changed the tire, you didn't need me anymore. I could hear on the radio that the ambulance and wrecker and a deputy sheriff were there. So, kind of tough out there on your own, is it ... even for the Frisco Kid?"

Garreth stiffened, anger flaring in him. The smug tone told him there had been no flat. It was merely Duncan's alibi for not backing him up.

He looked up, and either the anger showed in his face or his eyes reflected the light because Duncan retreated several steps. Garreth made no attempt to follow, however. He just said with deadly quiet, "I think the question is the ethics of letting personal differences between officers jeopardize civilian lives. Now if you'll excuse me, I'd like to finish this paperwork and go home."

Bending over the typewriter again, he saw by the flush rising in Duncan's face that the shot had hit dead center. But as Duncan slammed out of the office, Garreth wondered unhappily whether he had solved their problem or only made it worse.

8

Rather than mess up the inside of his car, he left the ZX in the City Hall lot and walked home. What did being wet a little longer matter? Halfway to the Schoning house he realized he did not really want to go home. What would he do there but think about the accident and remember the taste of the girl's blood?

He turned south at the next corner. Minutes later he walked up the main drive of Mount of Olives Cemetery. Obelisques and other ornate headstones of the older graves near the gate bore names like Dreiling, Pfeifer, Pfannenstiel, and Wiesner. And Bieber. Garreth passed them all, striding on until he reached a grave on the far west side which bore no headstone or name, just a metal stake with a laminated card reading: *Unknown male d. 11/24/83*.

Garreth knelt beside it. How small a grave it seemed for so tall a woman. Not that much of Lane remained after the fire. He began pulling the new spring growth of dandylions and other weeds sprouting in the grass around the edge of the plot. The rain-softened earth made the task easy; even dandylion taproots came up. Garreth still worked carefully, avoiding the thorns of rose bushes on the grave.

The memory of Maggie's voice whispered in his head. *"This is crazy, Garreth. The man was a cop hater. He tried to* kill *you and Ed Duncan. Yet you look after his grave like your mother is buried there. Why?"*

A lot of people wondered the same thing, Garreth knew. *"He was also someone's son,"* he had replied for Maggie's and everyone's benefit.

New leaves showed on the canes of the rose bushes planted on top of the grave. Soon there would be buds, then, hopefully, a profusion of blossoms. Blood red American Beauties. What more fitting for Lane?

Thinking about her here, he usually pictured not the vampire, the killer, but Mada Bieber, the child she had been ... angry and tormented, her unusual height and quick temper making her a pitifully easy target for the ridicule of other children. He ached for the child and for all she might have been if hatred had not driven her to beg Irina Rodek for the vampire life as a way to wreak revenge on the humanity she despised. He talked to the woman, though.

"You would have laughed seeing me tonight." He carefully worked a weed free, making sure he had its roots, too. "I can just hear you: *'See, lover; that's what this life is about. Human blood is what we're* meant *to drink.* They're *our cattle, not the four-legged kind. So stop being so stubborn and unnatural. Stop trying to be human and join your people.'* You'd like me to become like you." He jerked out a dandylion. "It would mean you'd won after all."

With her rich, mocking laughter echoing in his head, he continued cleaning the grave until growing light and a sudden drag at him announced dawn. Garreth sighed. Time to go, before he fell asleep on the cool, inviting earth, or early-bird citizens saw him and wondered why one of Baumen's finest was running around looking as though he had wallowed in a pig sty.

He might already be too late for the latter. The sound of running footsteps carried across the cemetery. By the time Garreth managed to push to to his feet, a man in sweats appeared out of the drizzle up one of the paths. So intent was his effort, though—blowing steam at every step, face grim with eyes focused inward—that he passed close enough to touch without ever seeing Garreth.

Surprise made Garreth call out. "Good morning, Mr. Fowler."

The writer started violently and flung around white-eyed, then let out a gusty breath of relief. "It's you, Officer Mikaelian. You gave me a bit of a turn. Disheartening, isn't it? We think we're such civilized, rational beings and then something appears out of nowhere in a cemetery and we jump right out of our bloody skins."

"Yet you chose to run through the cemetery. Isn't it a cold, wet morning for exercise?"

"Yes, well, I suppose, but I'm British, aren't I?" Fowler smiled wryly. "I'm used to weather like this. And I've been addicted to running since Alistair Cooper."

Garreth blinked. "Who?"

"A spy character of mine who used marathon running as a cover. I started running to learn what it feels like." He peered at Garreth. "What about you? Surely it isn't part of your normal patrol to be out here dressed and looking that way. If you don't mind a personal observation, you look like hell."

"It's the way I always look when I've been walking in the rain after pulling sixteen-year-old girls out of what's left of their car."

Fowler sucked in his breath. "Bloody shame. I keep a flask in the car for myself after a run on a day like today. You're welcome to a nip."

His gaze slipped past Garreth as he talked. Garreth turned but saw nothing except Lane's grave. His chest tightened. "Something wrong?"

Fowler blinked. "What? Oh. No, nothing. The rose bushes just caught my eye. You know that's how legend says you keep a vampire in his coffin."

Garreth hoped his start looked like surprise and not guilt. "I thought you used garlic or drove a stake through his heart."

"That's all the cinema shows, yes," Fowler said, and snorted, "but real vampire lore says to drape the coffin or grave in mountain laurel or roses. The thorns supposedly have magical power against vampires."

Garreth kept his face expressionless. "I'll remember that."

Fowler circled around him to lean down and touch the new green growth on one bush. "The word *vampire* is Balkan in origin, of course, but vampires aren't. They can be found mentioned as far back as Babylonia under the name *Ekimmus*. The Greeks had them, and the Chinese." He turned to lift a brow at Garreth. "Your Irish forefathers had them, too."

Dearg-due. Yes, I know. It still hurt remembering Grandma Doyle hissing the term at him. "Interesting. I take it you're into vampires?"

Fowler smiled. "It's purely professional interest. I used to write horror novels. But what a fool I am, nattering on when you're standing there looking positively frozen. Why don't you come back to my car for that nip. Then I'll give you a lift home."

Garreth grimaced. "I haven't eaten anything in hours. I'm afraid alcohol would put me flat on my butt and you'd have to *carry* me home. I'd rather walk anyway. Home is close; everywhere in Baumen is close. Thanks anyway."

"As you wish. Well, then, I hope there's someone warm at home waiting to help you thaw—what is it?"

Garreth stared at Fowler in horror, suddenly remembering. *Maggie!* He had completely forgotten about her! "I'm in deep shit. Pray for a miracle, Fowler, or the next time you see me, I may *really* be a ghost."

He spun away, and despite the exhausting drag of daylight on him, began to run.

9

His single hope all the way home was that Maggie had not come over after all, but one quick look through the garage door windows shot that down. Her Bronco with its "SHE-PIG" license sat parked in his side. *I'm dead.*

He crossed his fingers and silently climbed the outside steps. Maybe she had fallen asleep waiting and did not realize how late he was.

No such luck. The door opened even before his key touched the lock. Maggie stood in the opening, fully dressed.

Garreth opened his mouth. Only no words came out except a guilt-stricken: "Maggie ..."

"Garreth!" She threw her arms around him. "Where the hell have you been?"

He gaped at her in surprise. "You're not angry?"

"Angry? Of course I am. I'm furious. I've been frantic. My god, you feel like ice. Come in and get out of those clothes and into a hot shower this instant." Hauling him in by the shirt front, she shut the door and began unbuttoning his uniform shirt. "When you didn't come home, I called the office. Doris said you'd left ages ago and she was worried because you'd left both your jacket and slicker and when she looked out at the parking lot, your car was still there, too. Where did you go?"

The scent of her blood curled around him, bringing up the taste of the girl's blood in his mouth. He pulled loose and bolted around her for the bathroom. "Just walking. Did Doris tell you about the accident I worked tonight?"

She followed him. "She told me. Walking where, for god's sake? I got dressed and drove all over town, too. You weren't anywhere."

The smell of her was making him dizzy with longing. He shut the door between them. "I ended up in the cemetery."

"Again? Why? Isn't that what we have each other for, to talk to and work out these job stresses?"

"Yes, but … I forgot you were here."

As soon as the words were out he wanted to kick himself. *Open big mouth; insert big flat foot.* An ominous silence answered from the other side of the door. Garreth stripped off his clothes and jumped into the shower.

The bathroom door banged opened. Maggie jerked back the shower curtain and turned off the water. "You *forgot* I was here?" she said quietly.

He grimaced. "I'm sorry."

The blue eyes bored into him. "What else happened besides the accident?"

"I don't know what you mean." He could not talk about the writer and bloodmobile with her.

Her lips tightened. "Okay, you want to shut me out, I guess I can't do anything about it."

The hurt in her voice ran through his gut like a knife. "Maggie, I'm not—"

"Yes you are," she said sadly. "You always do. Somewhere in every one of our conversations there's a wall and part of you is shut away on the other side. You're very skilled at putting up diversions to hide the wall, like when you worm out of dinner invitations, but I see it anyway. I keep hoping that one of these times we'll mean enough to each other that the wall will come down. But maybe not."

He hugged himself. "Maggie, I'm sorry." He wanted to hug her, to take her in his arms and soothe her hurt and somehow make it up to her for not loving her as well as she deserved, but the scent of her blood beat at him. He was afraid to touch her. "I don't know what else to say."

She sighed. "I don't either, Garreth. Maybe until we do—"

"Maybe what we both need is sleep," he interrupted. "There's that movie in Bellamy you've been wanting to see."

"*Witness.*"

"Yes. Why don't we go Monday, just have a good time, and then we can talk afterward."

She stared hard at him for several minutes before replying, but finally she nodded. "All right; we can try."

When she had gone Garreth turned the cold faucet and leaned back against the stall with the icy water pelting him. *We can try.* Her tone held no optimism. He bit his lip. He was going to lose her. It would be better for her, but ... he would lose one of his fragile ties with humanity, and he would have nothing to come home to but the apartment and the ghosts waiting there.

Lane's laughter echoed in his head.

10

He dreamed of fire. He stood in the shade of a tree at the edge of the artificial island in the city's Pioneer Park. High overhead a summer sun blazed in a heat-bleached sky. Lane lounged on the railing of the old-fashioned octagonal bandstand in the island's center. A blood-red dance costume cut up to her hip bones showed off the full length of her showgirl legs. Even in the shade her hair shone rich mahogany, and her eyes gleamed red as fire.

"Come here to me, inspector," she crooned. "Blood son. Lover. I need you. We need each other."

"The hell I need you," he yelled at her. He wanted to leave the island, but the wooden bridge lay in the full blaze of the sun. Just looking at it made him feel weak. If only he could find his mirror-lensed trooper glasses. Somehow he had mislaid them, though. He searched all his pockets in vain. The thought occurred to him that perhaps Lane had taken them.

"But you do need me, lover," she called. "You don't want to be all alone."

"I'm not."

She laughed. "You're referring to your human friends? Don't be foolish. They don't want you. See?"

She pointed. Following the direction of her finger, he caught his breath. Massed at the shore end of the bridge stood Duncan, Maggie,

Maggie's father in his wheelchair, Anna Bieber, Nat, Sue Ann, Chief Danzig, and Helen Schoning. And Julian Fowler, too.

"All in favor, say *Aye*," Duncan said.

"*Aye*," the rest of them chorused.

"Carried." From a box of kitchen matches in his hand, Duncan struck one and tossed it onto the bridge.

"Maggie, stop him!" Garreth yelled.

Maggie turned away.

Smiling thinly, Duncan struck another match. "What's the problem, Mikaelian?" He tossed the match. The plank it struck began to smolder. "All you have to do is come over and stamp them out."

Garreth tried, but the moment he stepped out of the shade, the sun struck him down like a sledgehammer. He reeled back into the shade, pain blinding him.

Duncan struck and tossed another match. A second plank caught fire. "I don't see what's so difficult. Just walk over the bridge and join us. Anyone can do that. Any human."

But Garreth could not. The sun held him pinned in the shade of the tree. He could only stand and watch helplessly while his single link to those on shore blazed up.

"You see, lover?" Deceptively soft arms wrapped around him from behind. Sharp teeth nipped his ear. "You're mine. I'm the only one who'll have you. I'm the only one who understands. Now aren't you sorry you murdered me?"

11

Sunset woke him. Garreth scrambled gratefully out of sleep and stumbled out of bed. In the bathroom a note on the mirror greeted him: *Maggie tonight. Don't forget* this *date*.

As though that would save the relationship. True, she had been friendly enough when he saw her Saturday and Sunday, but there had been a certain reserve.

At least he had done better with her than with Duncan. An attempt Saturday to smooth things over with the other officer when he found Duncan parked in the Schaller Ford lot had met a chilly reception. "So the department is too small to afford a feud?" Duncan snapped.

"Too bad." Gunning his car, he pulled away in a scream of tires.

Then there had been Sunday and Julian Fowler. Garreth found the writer in Anna Bieber's livingroom when he arrived after dinner to take her to evening mass. The fact that the writer accompanied them to church did not bother Garreth. As usual, he found the service soothing, quite the opposite from the physical agony which Lane, raised in a strict faith, had experienced around religious objects. Afterward, though, having tea at Anna's, Fowler kept asking questions about Lane. What had Mada been like as a child? How had she changed when she finally came home again? Did she ever mention the names of friends in Europe or fellow performers she worked with? Did Anna save letters from her? Did she remember the return addresses and postmarks?

Cold crawled down Garreth's spine. The man asked questions like a detective. In the right quarters, the answers were likely to bring him too much knowledge ... too much for Garreth's safety and peace of mind.

"You sound like you're planning a biography," he had said. "I had no idea you had to know so much to write fiction."

Fowler smiled. "Oh yes. I have to make it sound realistic, after all."

Garreth had spent the evening sidetracking Anna into reminisces of Lane's childhood and come home exhausted.

And today had one strike against it already. After two days of feeling no hunger, thirst burned in his throat with a fierceness that the entire remaining contents of the thermos scarcely blunted. The cattle blood tasted even thinner and more unsatisfying than usual.

He surveyed himself wryly in the mirror on the closet door ... black turtleneck shirt, tan corduroy sport coat and slacks, mirror-lensed trooper glasses to protect his eyes. *What the well-dressed vampire wears to a goodbye date.* Saluting his image, he turned and left to wait at the station for Maggie to get off duty.

12

The late show ended around eleven. They walked out of the theater into an overcast night that although chilly, smelled of spring ... damp earth and hints of green. Clean smells, free of any blood scent. Garreth drank them in.

"Did you like the movie?" Maggie asked.

"Of course. It's a good flick." He lied, but how could he tell her the truth, that movies were always difficult at best, sitting there drowning in the smells of blood from other patrons, tortured by thirst and sometimes by deadly whiffs of garlic which left him suffocating, the air in his lungs hardened like concrete. Tonight, too, one of the blood scents had carried the sour flavor of disease. Its touch set him itching. But most uncomfortable had been the painful chords the movie rang in him as the big-city detective hid in the alien culture of a rural community. Detective John Book had one big advantage, though, which Garreth envied. When it became clear he did not belong, at least that cop had another world to return to.

Garreth had parked in the next block. They started to cross the street ... only to stop short at the wail of a siren. A Jeep wagon painted with the sheriff's star shot past them from the side street and into the parking lot of the courthouse across from the theater. The stocky driver vaulted from behind the wheel to race into the two-story Law Enforcement wing of the courthouse.

Maggie stared after him. "That's Tom Frey."

The undersheriff. The hair twitched on Garreth's neck. "I wonder what the trouble is."

Serious dicussions of their relationship could wait. As one, they changed direction toward the courthouse.

Both the Bellamy PD and Sheriff's Office shared the wing. A broad counter with glass and metal grilling along it partitioned the main office. Behind it Tom Frey's black Amerind eyes glinted grimly as he glanced from a walrus-mustached PD officer to a tall, lean man who looked as though he belonged on horseback working cattle—Sheriff Louis Pfeifer.

"... heard the trouble buzzer," the officer was saying, "and ran down from the jail, only as I came out the stair door, someone hit me from behind. By the time I could get up again, this turkey had fished the car keys out of my pocket and was dragging Emma outside with him. He had a gun. I called Wes in 512 on the radio right away and he's tracking them. They're headed northwest."

The sheriff spun. "Tom, get on the horn to the Russell and Rooks SO's, then call our deputies. Have them spread out north and west, but keep back. We don't want Emma hurt."

The undersheriff reached for a phone.

"Can we help, Sheriff?" Garreth asked.

The tall man looked around through the glass at them and smiled. "Who says there's never a cop around when you need one? Our dispatcher's been kidnapped. Why and how he got past the counter, we don't know. Give me your radio, Clell."

The PD officer lifted it out of the case on his belt. Pfeifer handed it to Maggie through an opening in the glass. "Head toward Schaller and help 512 keep track of that car."

Garreth and Maggie raced for the ZX.

As they reached it the radio crackled with alerts issued by the Russell and Rooks SO dispatchers for the Bellamy PD car carrying a male of unknown description and a female which the dispatchers described.

Then another voice said, "*512 Bellamy. Subject is headed north from County 9 at Droge Corner.*"

"Lincoln Street takes us out to 9," Maggie said. "But I don't know where Droge Corner is."

With no siren or lights to clear the way for him, Garreth drove carefully as far as the city limits, then stamped the accelerator. "Watch for anything that looks like a corner."

"That ought to be fun in this dark." Maggie tightened her seat belt.

A harsh male voice came on the radio. "*If that pig following me comes anywhere near, I'll kill this bitch.*"

A woman yelped in pain.

Garreth's headlights caught a sign with names and distances to various farms. The top name read: *Droge.*

"Garreth—" Maggie yelped as they hurtled past.

He was already hitting both gas and brake and hauling at the steering wheel to spin the car in a one-eighty turn. He gunned back for the corner, reached it still accelerating, and somehow still made the turn anyway, wheels screaming, gravel from the new road scattering beneath his wheels. Maggie whooped like a banshee.

"*512, turning east five miles from last turn.*"

"*Get away from me! I'm warning you!*"

Garreth swore. He had not noticed his mileage at the turn. "How are we going to know which corner it is?"

"Relax," Maggie said. "These roads are section lines, remember, exactly one mile apart."

She counted crossing roads; he concentrated on keeping the car on theirs and, when it came, making the turn without piling them into a heavy stone fence post at the corner of the field.

"I see them!" Maggie hissed.

He did, too … small ruby points of light far ahead, and two more points half a mile beyond those. The farther lights swerved and vanished.

"*512. Turning north*—"

Maggie hit the transmit button on the hand radio. "We have you, 512."

"*You've got one last chance to get away from me or this cow dies.*"

A female voice came on moments later. "*Bellamy SO. Fall back, 512.*"

The tail lights grew larger and brighter as Garreth gained. He watched them swerve into a turn. He followed, and shortly after that, drew up alongside.

"Roll down the window, Maggie." When she did, Garreth shouted across to the Bellamy officer, "Drop back and mark that corner. I'll follow him from here."

"Orders are—"

"He won't see me, I promise." He shut off his headlights as he passed the PD car.

Maggie gasped.

The road stretched before him in a distinct gray ribbon, as though through twilight. On it ahead of him, growing ever brighter, shone the tail lights of the stolen police car.

Maggie clung to the radio. "I can't see a thing. How can you?"

He hesitated only a moment before answering. "I never told you but I'm a werewolf."

"Terrific. I've been dating a fruit loop." The car fishtailed and she swallowed audibly. "How fast are we going?"

"I'm afraid to look."

Her stream of language had to come out of her father's oilfield days.

The lights ahead swerved off onto another road, then another, and finally into a lane which consisted of two wheel ruts with a grass-grown center. Far up the lane, perhaps half a mile, Garreth made out the blocky shapes of buildings, one tilting crazily.

He down-shifted to slow the car, then stopped with the hand brake to keep the brake lights from giving their presence away. "Maggie, I'll follow on foot from here."

"On *foot*! Garreth, you can't—"

He climbed out. "Take the car and go back to wait at that last corner for the others. I'll leave my jacket on his fencepost to mark the lane. Get going."

"Do you have a gun?"

"Of course." He patted his ankle holster, and before she could protest further, took the radio from her, peeled off his sport coat, and dropping it over the fencepost beside the gate, sprinted up the lane after the fading lights of the car. His breath swirled thick and white around him in the chilly air.

The lights vanished.

Garreth stretched his stride. Had they gone over a rise? Around a corner? He had almost reached the buildings. He slowed, still looking around for the car. The lane led on past. Could the kidnapper have continued?

No, voices carried on the night wind, whispers so low no normal ears could have heard them ... a woman's, frightened and weeping, a man's hissing angrily. "Stop whining, you bitch, or you're dead."

Garreth tilted his head, testing for direction of the sound. The house with its multiple doors and windows gaping empty, or in the dark cave of the tilting barn? A car could be hidden from sight in there. The barn, he decided. The wind brought him scents of human blood and sweaty fear mixed with the odor of moldering hay.

Circling behind the house, he climbed through two barb wire fences to the rear of the barn. The windows, empty of glass, were high and small. The doors had been blocked up some time in the past. Garreth nodded in satisfaction. The kidnapper should feel himself safe from the rear, then. The sealed door gave no protection from a vampire, though.

He pressed against the door. Everything in him wrenched sharply, then he stood inside between disintigrating stacks of hay. A tall, rawboned man with a heavy thatch of dark, wiry hair sat against the bales in a position where he could watch the lane. Beside him huddled the dispatcher, a short, plump woman in her late thirties, held down by an arm twisted behind her back.

Now what? Garreth plucked at his mustache. As soon as he revealed his presence, the man would open fire. The trick was to make sure he did not shoot his hostage first.

But what would happen if the kidnapper shot and hit *him*? Theoretically, if a vampire could pass through a door, an object could pass through him without harm. Wooden stakes excepted. Theoretically.

There was only one way to learn. *Watch the idiot cop put his head in the lion's mouth.*

Laying the radio on a hay bale, he stepped forward. "You're under arrest, turkey."

The kidnapper whirled, the muzzle of his gun flashing fire.

He shot well for having only sound to aim at. A small, wrenching pain lanced through Garreth's chest. Reflex brought his hands clutching at the point of pain, but a moment later he realized he felt nothing else, no weakness, no bleeding.

The kidnapper fired again, and once more Garreth felt only that single small pain similar to the one of passing through doors. Good enough. He grinned—"Try again, turkey,"—and charged.

Cursing, the kidnapper tried to empty the gun, but had time for just two more shots before Garreth reached him. Wrenching the gun away, Garreth rapped the butt across the side of the kidnapper's head. The man dropped in his tracks.

Beyond him the dispatcher huddled on the floor. She had to be terrified, hearing the gunfire and collapsing body but unable to see who had gone down.

Garreth spoke before touching her. "Emma, it's all right. You're safe. I'm Garreth Mikaelian, Baumen PD." Then he picked her up.

"Mikaelian. You're 407." Burying her head against his shoulder, enveloping him in a smell of blood and terror-sweat, she burst into tears. "What an idiot I am. When he went down in the waiting area, I thought he'd fainted. I didn't even think; I just opened the counter door and ran out. Of course it was a trick. He grabbed me around the neck and dragged me back inside the office. He demanded the keys to the cells, to get his brother out, he said. I pretended to be getting them and hit the button that rings an alarm at the guard's station up in the jail. I knew Clell Jamison had just brought someone in and was up there, too. The bastard figured out what I'd done, though, and he dragged me over to the stair door and hit Clell when he came down. Did he kill him?"

"Jamison is fine."

Garreth led her back to where he had left the radio. "Mikaelian to Bellamy S.O. Situation resolved. Hostage unharmed."

In minutes the old farmyard had filled up with cars and flashing light bars, representatives of law enforcement agencies in three counties … police, sheriff and deputies, highway patrol.

His ZX was there, too, and Maggie, throwing her arms around him, drowning him in the smell of her blood. "You took him by yourself? Are you all right?"

"Of course." He slid away from her so she would not smell the powder burns on his shirt. "He fired a couple of shots at me but he's a lousy shot in the dark." Luckily the powder burns did not show up on the black turtleneck. "Do you have my coat?"

She handed it over. "Are you sure you're all right? There are holes in your shirt."

"Front and back. Yes, I know. I had to crawl through two barb wire fences." Smiling, he carefully buttoned his coat across the holes.

13

Pounding woke him. At first he thought it was part of his dream, hammering on the barn being unaccountably built by a swarm of Amish men at the land end of the bridge from Pioneer Park's island. He did wonder when the entire group turned and began shouting in unison: "Mikaelian! Mikaelian, goddamn it, wake up!" Amish would surely not curse that way. These could not be real Amish.

Then he noticed that though they stopped pounding when they yelled at him, the pounding noise went on. Their voice sounded familiar, too.

"Mikaelian!"

The voice and pounding were real ... outside his door. He clawed his way up out of sleep to squint at his clock ... and then stare in outrage. Eleven-thirty!

The pounding sounded ready to break through the door. "*Mikaelian*! MIKAELIAN!"

"I'm coming!" He staggered to the door and opened it half the width of the safety chain.

Through the crack and the glare of light outside he recognized the burly form of Lieutenant Byron Kaufmann filling his porch. "Helen Schoning and her mother weren't kidding about how sound you sleep," Kaufmann grumbled. "I've been making enough noise to wake the dead."

Garreth leaned his forehead against the crack, sighing. "So you have. What do you want, lieutenant? I just got to sleep."

"Sorry, but I'm supposed to bring you down at the station."

"At *this* time of day?" While he unchained and opened the door, Garreth's mind raced, hunting serious transgressions.

"Relax." Kaufmann strolled in past him. "There are just some reporters waiting for you."

"Reporters?" Garreth's gut knotted. He shoved the door closed. "Shit."

"Jesus it's dark in here."

Garreth switched on a lamp. "Why do they want to talk to me?"

Kaufmann grinned at him. "Don't you realize who you collared last night? Frank Danner."

The name sounded vaguely familiar. Garreth had shaved before he identified it, though. Then he stared at Kaufmann. "One of the bank robbers who killed that Nevada trooper? They're in Kansas?"

Kaufmann rolled his eyes. "Don't you read your briefing notes?"

"I've been off for two days."

"Don't you watch the news? Two days ago Frank and his brother Lyle shot a Colorado trooper. Every cop in the country wants them. And you nailed Frank without a scratch to you or his hostage. Danzig says wear something professional looking."

Garreth reluctantly put on a suit and tie, and after a moment of hesitation went to the refrigerator. Instead of filling a glass, though, he drank directly from the thermos, freshly refilled from the Gehrt Ranch herd after taking Maggie home last night.

They never had talked.

Kaufmann eyed him. "That's health food stuff I suppose."

"Liquid protein and additives." Perfectly true. He added sodium citrate to keep it from clotting. But let Kaufmann think he meant vitamins and brewers yeast. Despite the knots in his stomach, Garreth could not resist adding slyly, "Try some?" He held out the open thermos. "It's very healthy. Makes you live forever."

As he hoped, Kaufmann refused with a shudder and he returned the thermos to the refrigerator.

They trotted down to the patrol car in the driveway. "Why don't I just follow you in my car?" Garreth asked.

"Danzig remembers how camera shy you were after our round with the bow-and-arrow cop killer. He wanted to make sure you showed up. I'm also supposed to brief you on the way."

Why became obvious as Kaufmann filled him in. The Bellamy PD had arrested Lyle Danner without realizing who they had. Early in the evening he had tried to rob a liquor store, only the owner had been in the back room when Danner pulled a gun on the clerk, and the owner had called the police from an extension then sneaked out to jam a shotgun in Danner's back and hold him until the police arrived. Danner gave the name William Dane when he was booked, which came back negative when checked through the National Criminal Information Center in Washington.

"So the arresting officer tossed Danner in a cell to wait for the fingerprint check and his court appearance and thought nothing more about him," Kaufmann said. "But when Pfeifer and Chief Oldenburg saw 'Dane' and the guy you collared together in jail, their descriptions clicked. Someone woke up the editor of the *Bellamy Globe* to tell him what had gone down and in nothing flat he had it on the wire and people to collect more details. A whole group of reporters complete with minicam showed up at our office half an hour ago asking to talk to you."

Minicam. Garreth slunk down in the seat. *Damn.* "Does the chief want me to say something in particular?"

"Just avoid making us sound like hick cops who stumbled over these fugitives in spite of ourselves."

There should be nothing to this interview, Garreth told himself. With all the mass murderers, serial killers, and terrorists in the news, no one cared about a couple of men who had only robbed a bank and killed two law enforcement officers, let alone had any interest in a small-town cop who happened to be part of capturing one of them. At most this would be something for the local news out of KAYS in Hays. Still, he felt like a prisoner marching to execution.

At City Hall Danzig charged out of his office, a big man still built for the football he had obviously played in school, still impressive despite his waistline trying to match the width of his shoulders. "What the hell took so long? I have them waiting in the city commission meeting room." He led the way through the door connecting the office to the rest of City Hall and down the corridor.

To Garreth's relief, the group consisted of only five, and he already knew Jeanne Reiss from the *Baumen Telegraph*. The others were from the *Bellamy Globe*, the Hays paper, and KAYS.

"Would you mind removing your sunglasses so we can see your face better?" asked the TV cameraman.

And record the flare of his eyes if he tilted his head wrong? Garreth left on the glasses. "I work a night shift. My eyes aren't photogenic at this time of day. Just why do you want to talk to me anyway? Frank Danner's capture resulted from a coordinated effort of several law enforcement agencies. I was just one of many officers involved."

From his place by the door, Danzig nodded approval.

The *Globe* reporter, an attractive brunette woman named Catherine Heier, raised an eyebrow. "You were the one who followed the kidnapper's car without headlights to keep him from spotting you behind him, and then tracked him to that farmyard on foot and faced his gun in the dark. That was very brave."

Garreth shrugged. "It's my job and no more than any other officer would have done in my place."

Each reporter took a turn. Had he realized at all who he was after? Would he have changed his tactics if he had? How had he felt with the kidnapper shooting at him? Predictable questions, he thought. Stupid ones. He did his best to answer politely.

Then the *Globe* reporter said, "You seem to have as many lives as a cat when it comes to brushes with death."

Garreth tried not to stiffen. "You mean that incident with the killer archer a couple of years ago?"

"And the one in San Francisco where you were found in North Beach with your throat mutilated and erroneously thought dead."

How the hell had she found out about that? He glanced at Danzig, who frowned a denial.

"No, your chief didn't tell me," Heier said. "I came into town before dawn and met one of your fellow officers. In the course of chatting, he made remarks about the circumstances of your departure from the San Francisco Police Department that piqued my curiosity."

Duncan! It had to be. Garreth held his face expressionless.

Behind the reporters, Danzig did not bother. He stiffened, mouth thinning to a grim line. Duncan would pay for talking to a reporter instead of referring her to the chief, Garreth saw, but that did nothing to help right now. Damn the man! Garreth said evenly, "Are there more questions about Frank Danner?"

But the reporter was not about to be distracted. "I called a friend of mine who knows someone on the *Examiner* out there, who in turn knows someone in the police department, and it turns out that your colleague misunderstood the facts. Which delights me, because the true story is much more interesting than the one I thought I'd get. I'd like to talk about that with you, Officer Mikaelian."

"I *don't* wish to talk about it," Garreth replied. "It's totally irrelevant to Danner's capture. Now if you'll excuse me, I need to go home and sleep before I come on duty tonight."

Heier tried to follow him. "We have a great human interest story here."

Which would make life in Baumen very awkward if she turned up the difference between his actual recorded parentage and the one he claimed locally. He produced a weary sigh for her benefit. "I don't think much of it, Ms. Heier. I lived it. It was painful; it was traumatic; and I prefer to forget about it."

14

He should have known that that was too much to ask. It was obvious the moment he walked into the office before his shift.

Sue Ann grinned at him over the communications desk. "Hello, celebrity."

And Danzig still sat in his office. "Did you see the news?"

Garreth stopped in the open door. "No. How bad was it?"

Danzig smiled. "Not bad at all … a minute of KAYS footage on the national news, mostly Sheriff Pfeifer and Chief Oldenburg, but they did mention you as the officer who disarmed Frank Danner, and showed you for a couple of seconds, saying how you'd only done what any other officer would have done. Locally," —his smile broadened to a grin— "you rated about the same amount of time, but Ms. Heier managed to get herself on with a guest editorial about how people forget what a dangerous job law enforcement can be and how dedicated we cops are to stick with it. You, needless to say, were her prime example."

Garreth groaned.

Danzig shook his head. "I don't understand you. Most people would love a moment of fame."

"I'm not most people."

The saving grace was that tomorrow everyone would forget it. In the meantime there was tonight to survive. Bill Pfannenstiel, the aging officer who worked relief and replaced Nat Toews tonight, teased him every time they passed, and everyone else he met wanted details about the incident in North Beach. Why had he ever thought he could hide in a small town? Lane knew what she was doing sticking to cities. In San Francisco only colleagues and a few close friends would have known or cared about his part in the arrest.

Here even Julian Fowler stopped him in front of the hotel. "I saw you on the news. That's fascinating. It'd make a great novel, *The Lazarus Incident* or some such title. May I talk to you about it sometime?"

"I'll think about it," Garreth replied.

Maggie tracked him down, too, at the Shortstop buying a cup of tea. "Hey, TV star. You looked great." She followed him back out to the car and when he climbed in, leaned down to the window. "Very professional."

Her blood scent coiled tantalizingly around him. The smell of it brought back the memory of the girl in the accident. He fought hunger. "Thanks. I wish they'd picked on someone else, though."

Her stare showed the same disbelief Danzig expressed. After a moment she said slowly, "What *is* behind that wall you're so afraid of someone seeing, I wonder."

"I'll talk to you later," he said, and backed out of the parking space.

In the rearview mirror he saw her staring after him. Was it imagination that she seemed to be standing at the far end of a bridge going up in flames?

15

A note waited on Garreth's door when he reached home after the shift: Helen Schoning's bold, square handwriting in dark green ink on pale green paper.

> Garreth,
> Your old partner in San Francisco called after you left for work. No wonder you were such good friends. He's a delight-ful man; great fun to flirt with. He wants you to call him back as soon as possible.
>   Helen

Garreth pulled down the note and smiled at it as he unlocked the door and went inside. He had opted to keep his phone an extension of the Schoning's instead of putting in a private line, and times like this he never regretted the choice. Having missed Garreth, Harry Takananda had probably found it much more pleasant talking to Helen than he would have leaving his message on a machine.

Only one small chill marred the pleasure of talking to Harry, wondering what he wanted. Call him back as soon as possible did not sound like a social call.

Garreth glanced at the clock. It was too early yet; they would still be asleep.

He changed out of his uniform, showered, and drank a glass of blood, then settled into the easy chair with a book and read until he knew Harry would be getting ready for work. He punched Harry's number.

Lien Takananda answered. The sound of her voice spread warmth through Garreth and brought a quick image of her ... wrapped in her comfortable old terry robe, her black helmet of hair streaked with gray but her face still smooth as a girl's. Her voice also brought back the hours she had spent patiently talking at the wall of misery enclosing him after Marti died, battering through it, forcing food into him ... dragging him back into life.

"Lien, this is Garreth."

"Garreth?" Her voice warmed even more. "Hello! Oh it's good to hear your voice. How are you?"

Guilt stabbed him for not having called more often.

Harry's voice came on another extension. "Is this really Garreth Doyle Mikaelian? So you still remember our number after all. I wondered if maybe you'd forgotten since you never call and now you're a nationally famous cop."

Garreth pictured Harry, too, black eyes glinting with mischief, belt straining to hold in a waistline spread by Lien's excellent cooking and the copious amounts of sugar Harry always added to his coffee. Garreth winced. "You saw that story out there, too?"

"Oh, yes, Mik-san, though I have to admit you were a bit hard to recognize with that funny stuff on your upper lip. When did you grow that?"

"I think you're thinner than you were in the last picture you sent us," Lien said. "Are you taking care of yourself?"

"Lien, you sound like a mother; quit fussing at him," Harry said.

"I'm not fussing. I just want to be sure he's all right. You looked so uncomfortable, Garreth."

"What he looked like, honorable wife, was the stereotype of the hard-assed cop. Garreth, couldn't you have taken off the dark glasses? You've sure become addicted to those things."

"Terrific," Garreth said in pretended disgust. "Is this what you wanted me to call you for, insults?"

"Call. Oh. No. I called because after the item about you and the Danner brothers, I thought you might be interested in another fugitive who's surfaced: Lane Barber."

Shock jolted Garreth. Lane! "Surfaced? What do you mean?" That was impossible. Neck broken, burned, buried under roses. Impossible! He sat bolt upright, fingers digging into the phone receiver. "Has—has someone seen her?"

"Not her personally," Harry said, "but last week we found the apartment she moved into after lamming out of the one on Telegraph Hill. There's been a man in and out and it's only a matter of time until she shows up, too."

Guilt pricked him again, but this time because he could not tell Harry they were wasting time and manpower. "That's great," he lied.

"Yeah. I wish you were here. You deserve to be in on the kill ... so to speak."

Garreth started again, prodded by an idea. Time away from here might be just what he needed ... to avoid the bloodmobile and Fowler and that reporter, to think about his relationship with Maggie. "Maybe something can be arranged. I'll get back to you this evening."

Not until he had already hung up did it occur to him to wonder: if Lane's ghost haunted him here where she had lost to him, what might it do where she had been strong and triumphant?

Echos and
Shadows

1

In the morning light San Francisco rose bright and inviting above the waters of the bay. A feel of homecoming enveloped Garreth as he drove across the Oakland bridge, countering day's lethargy and the headache from sunlight sneaking around the edges of his trooper glasses. At the same time, however, he felt as though he drove into cold and shadow. Lane's laughter echoed in his head and foreboding lay like lead in his gut. Was he wrong to be coming back?

He had refused to think about it until yesterday, and the question was easily shoved aside in the rush of preparing to leave Baumen, in the strain of trading shifts with Maggie and working a day shift on Saturday in order to leave that evening. Certainly he had no time to doubt while driving cross country, not with watching the rearview mirrors and road ahead for cars with light bar silhouettes. The vast open stretches of I-70 and I-80 had been too tempting to resist and he turned the ZX loose, slowing down only for the mountains and when instinct suggested troopers might be around.

Which had brought him rolling into Davis and up to his parents' house early Sunday evening, and to his surprise, into the middle of an unexpected family reunion.

"Hey, we couldn't waste this chance to celebrate the current family hero," his brother Shane said, and dragged him from the car into the crushing hug that always made Garreth pity anyone meeting Shane on the line of scrimmage.

Not only had Shane come from Los Angeles with his wife and daughters to join their parents and Grandma Doyle—Shane looking content and healthy, obviously satisfied with giving up playing end for the Rams for a position on their coaching staff—but his ex-wife Judith was there, too, with his son Brian and her husband. The scents of blood, and sweat from the inevitable Sunday family scrimmage, washed around him, making Garreth glad he had taken a long drink from his thermos before reaching the house.

Phil Mikaelian wrapped a beefy arm around his shoulders. "That was a damn fine piece of police work catching Frank Danner, son. I'm proud of you."

No praise meant more than those few words from this cop Garreth had grown up worshipping. He grinned happily. "Thank you, sir."

"But it doesn't look like you're taking time to eat," his mother said. "Or can't your Maggie cook?"

"Mom, I eat enough."

"His sport is running, remember, not football," Grandma Doyle said.

"Not football?" Shane's wife Susan pretended shock. "Esther, are you sure you brought the right baby home from the hospital?"

Judith and Dennis greeted him less boisterously, Judith with a light kiss, her husband shaking hands. Brian, so tall and husky now that he looked twelve instead of ten years old, held out a hand, too. "Hello, sir. Congratulations."

Such formality from his own son stung, even as Garreth recognized that he could hardly expect more when he saw so little of the boy. Judith had been right to have Dennis adopt Brian.

Still it felt like—it felt like someone had tossed a match on his bridge. Suddenly all pleasure drained from the evening. Even at home surrounded by laughter and chatter, he stood alone.

By the end of dinner the swirl of blood scents and the strain of playing with his food to hide the fact he ate none of it left him feeling suffocated. He fled to the dark and peace of the back yard. Sitting down in one of the lawn chairs, he breathed deeply. Out here the air smelled wonderfully of nothing but flowers, grass, and earth.

Presently the back door clicked and footsteps moved across the porch. The scent of lavender drifted to him on the night air.

He looked around. "Hello, Grandma."

She crossed the lawn to sit in the chair next to his. "It's a lovely night."

That was all she said for a long while. They sat in silence, not the strained one there would have been with his father or Shane, who both treated silence as a void to be filled, but a sharing of solitude, each wrapped in separate thoughts and reluctant to intrude on the other. If he had to be alone, Garreth reflected, Grandma Doyle was a comfortable person to be alone with. If she felt any horror at what he had become, she was careful never to show it, yet she did not appear to be afraid of mentioning it either.

She broke the silence by mentioning it. "You handled dinner very well. I hardly noticed meself that you weren't eating anything."

He smiled wryly. "Thanks. I'm glad I don't have to keep it up for more than a couple of meals in a row, though."

"You're going on to San Francisco in the morning then?"

"Yes."

She reached out to lay a hand on his arm. "Don't."

Cold slid down his spine. "Do you have a Feeling about it, Grandma?" Grandma Doyle's Feelings had been a source of amusement for friends and neighbors over the years, but no one with any experience with them ever laughed, not even tough cop Phil Mikaelian. "What kind of Feeling?"

"There's danger waiting there, and maybe death."

He smiled wryly. "I thought you said I'm already dead."

Age had not slowed her hands. She thumped him on the head with her knuckle just as fast and hard as she had when he was a boy. "I won't be taking backtalk from you even if you are grown and *dearg-due*. Perhaps you're dead, or it's as you say and just a different kind of living, but there is a true, final death for even your sort, and it's waiting in San Francisco."

"From what? Can you see?" He rubbed the sore spot on his head.

She sighed. "No, I can't. There's a woman involved, though, a woman with eyes the color of violets."

The words echoed in Garreth's head as San Francisco loomed nearer across the bridge. A violet-eyed woman, and death. He stared across the bay. Was he a fool to go there? He could still turn around on Treasure Island. But the city called to him, echoing with the past ... Marti, Harry and Lien, good times and love, friendship. Bridges whole and strong.

He kept driving.

2

Leaving the terminating I-80 at Bryant Street and pulling into the police department parking lot was like slipping into familiar old clothes. All the months away might never have existed. His feet automatically followed the familiar path into the building and up the elevators to the Homicide section, where the faces were exactly as he remembered: Rob Cohen with half-glasses riding the end of his nose, Evelyn Kolb with her ever-present pump thermos of tea on the corner of her desk, Art Schneider. Schneider appeared to be wearing the same brown suit he had worn the day Garreth cleaned out his desk. And the room smelled the same beneath the blood scents ... of coffee and cigarette smoke and the acid tang of human bodies sweating in frustration and anxiety.

One new face at a desk near the door looked around from talking to a red-eyed female citizen. "May I help you, sir?"

"I'm looking for Harry Takananda."

The detective glanced around the room. "Sergeant Takananda and Inspector Girimonte aren't here right now. Can someone else help you?"

Girimonte must be Harry's new partner. Garreth did not recognize the name. "Maybe. Thanks. Hi, Evelyn, Art," he called.

The double takes around the room were classics. "Mikaelian?"

"My god." A grinning Schneider loped around his desk, with Kolb and Rob Cohen close behind. He pumped Garreth's hand. "Harry wasn't kidding when he said we wouldn't recognize you."

Cohen slapped his shoulder. "If you're an example of Kansas cooking, remind me not to eat there."

"*I* think he looks *great*," Kolb sighed. "What's the name of your diet?"

Garreth grinned back, warmth spreading through him. This was like another family reunion. And why not? The department had been his family, too, the Homicide inspectors his brothers and sisters. "You're all looking great, too."

"Well, well. The wanderer." Across the room Lieutenant Lucas Serruto had appeared in the doorway of his office, as dapper as ever and still with the dark good looks of a TV cop-hero. "Of course we all want to welcome Mikaelian, but remember that we're here to serve and protect the taxpayers of San Francisco. Let's get back to it as soon as possible. Mikaelian, grab a cup of coffee and join me when you're through saying hello." He disappeared into his office again.

Garreth followed in five minutes or so with a mug of Kolb's tea.

Serruto motioned him to a chair. "That Danner business was a good piece of work. I take it you're enjoying rural life?"

"Oh, yes." Garreth sank gratefully into the chair. Lord he hated daylight. "You might say cattle are in my blood now."

As Serruto's brows rose Garreth kicked himself for the wisecrack, but the lieutenant did not pursue the subject. He leaned back in his chair. "Don't think I'm being hostile, because it really is nice to see you again, but let's have something straight from the beginning, Mikaelian. Despite the understandable score you have to settle with Lane Barber, she isn't your case any longer. You don't work for this department now. You're just a guest, a ride-along. Remember when you resigned and we had a chat about how much I dislike vigilantes? I still do. So leave all action in this case to official personnel. Is that understood?"

No, the lieutenant had not changed a bit. "Understood." Garreth sipped the tea. Its heat soothed the burning in his throat. "Do you mind if I ask how you found the apartment, though?"

Serruto smiled wryly. "The way we get most of our really big breaks ... sheer blind luck. We had a hit-and-run and when we found the vehicle and checked it against the list of cars involved in other accidents and crimes, lo and behold, the computer announced that the Vehicle Identification Number matched the one on the car you found in the Barber woman's garage. We hoped we'd get a lead backtracking the car through the used car lot where the hit-and-run driver bought it, but she sold it the day after she attacked you, using her Alexandra Pfeifer alias and the Telegraph Hill address. So that went nowhere. But when the lab examined the car for evidence on the hit-and-run, they found a section of apartment rentals from the want ads down behind the passenger seat. The yellowing indicated it had been there a while so we took a chance and checked every apartment listed."

Garreth leaned forward. "Some neighbor or leasing agent identified the Barber woman's picture?"

Serruto grinned. "Give the man a cookie. We found a guy she'd sweet-talked into carrying a box of books up the stairs for her. She hadn't even disguised herself, just used an alias, Barbara Madell, and put her hair up under a kerchief." He paused. "That bothers me. It's like she wasn't trying to hide at all. Like she wanted to be found."

The words reverberated in Garreth. Lane *had* wanted to be found, he realized suddenly ... only not by the police. She had known that by just tearing out Garreth Mikaelian's throat instead of breaking his neck he would become a vampire. She was expecting him to come after her, was waiting for him. By finding her he would prove his suitability to be her lover and companion. Only she had over estimated him. He never thought to look for her car, had never found the planted apartment listings.

Garreth sipped his tea without either tasting it or feeling its warmth any longer. If he had done as she had expected, had followed the trail she laid and found her here in San Francisco while he was still frightened and confused by what he had become, and she so knowledgeable and assured, so seductive ... how different the outcome of their confrontation might have been. A twinge of regret stirred in him. Whatever she might have made of him, he would at least not be alone now.

Belatedly, he realized that Serruto had said his name several times. "I'm sorry. What?"

An elegant dark brow rose. "That's my question. Did you fall asleep? It's impossible to tell through those glasses. I thought you'd want to know there's someone trying to attract your attention." He pointed toward the squadroom.

Harry waved wildly from the other side of the glass forming the upper half of Serruto's office walls.

Garreth leaped out of the chair for the door.

Outside it Harry enveloped him in a fierce hug. "I wasn't expecting you until tomorrow, Mik-san. What did you do, confuse the highway numbers with the speed limit?"

With the arms also came the scents of Harry's aftershave and the salty-warmth of his blood. A vein pulsed visibly in the older man's neck. Garreth broke away, covering by pretending it was to eye his old partner with mock concern. "Lien's still starving you I see, Taka-san."

Grinning, Harry slid his thumb inside his belt. "Not lately, as she would say. Oh, I'm forgetting introductions." He turned toward a woman behind him. "Old partner, meet new partner. Garreth Mikaelian, Vanessa Girimonte."

Girimonte made Garreth think of a panther ... long, lithe, and mahogany dark with hair cropped to velvet shortness. Even her name purred.

He held out his hand. "Glad to meet you."

"Likewise." She shook the offered hand, then stepped back, dark eyes dissecting him. Reaching into the breast pocket of her slack suit jacket, she pulled out a pencil thin cigar and lit it. "I don't know, Harry. For me the lean, hungry look and mirror glasses add up to menace, not boyish charm, but I suppose you can still be right. If the old adage about cold hands holds true, he definitely has to be warm-hearted."

Garreth winced. "Harry, don't tell me you've been trying to sell her on me."

Harry grinned. "I want you two to be friends." He picked up his coat. "Come on; we'll show you the hideout."

Girimonte frowned. "Now? Harry, we—" She broke off as he raised his brows. "Go ahead. If you don't mind, though, I'll stay here to get our woman's description in circulation and see what possibles Missing Persons has."

"Sounds good." Harry headed for the door. "See you later. A fine officer," he said in the corridor, "except maybe a workaholic. A bit like you that way, Mik-san. I think she also has ambitions of being chief some day."

"She didn't seem too happy about you leaving. What are you working on?"

Harry grimaced. "The usual assortment ... a liquor store clerk shot during a holdup, some nut case who walked into a clinic in the Mission district Friday afternoon and opened fire with a shotgun—killed a nurse and wounded three patients—and a woman found in Stow Lake this morning."

"Then you shouldn't have to bother with me right now. I'm tired from the drive to Davis anyway. I'll find a hotel, then this evening we—"

"Hotel!" Harry interrupted. "Nothing doing. You're staying with us." He punched for the elevator button.

Visions of a solicitous Lien plying him with an endless succession of the dishes he used to love ran through Garreth's head. The situation would not be like last night at home, where everyone was so busy talking that they paid no attention to anyone else's appetite or lack of it. Lien would notice he ate nothing. And she would try to find out why. Panic flickered in him. "I don't want to put you to any trouble."

Harry rolled his eyes. "You're not putting us to any trouble. You'll be saving my hide, in fact, because Lien will have it if you *don't* stay with us."

The argument echoed familiarly in Garreth's head. Harry had always said the same thing when dragging him home to dinner with them. He found himself reacting the same, too; mention of Lien melted away his resistance. How could he refuse anything to someone he owed so much?

He sighed as the elevator doors opened and they stepped inside. "All right. You have a guest." He would work out something ... perhaps hypnotize her into thinking he ate normally. "Now tell me about Lane's apartment."

3

She had gone to ground almost under their noses, just moving west of her old Telegraph Hill area apartment into the residential section of North Beach. Harry parked with his wheels turned into the curb to keep them from rolling down the steep street and pointed at a house half a block below, a two-story blue Victorian structure with bay windows and white gingerbread.

"She has the second floor."

Seeing the house gave Garreth a sharply uneasy feeling, compounded of a sense of being late for an appointment and a feeling that he stood on the edge of a trap. The knowledge that the trap could no longer be sprung somehow changed nothing. Perhaps it was still a trap. The house tugged at him.

"She hasn't been around for months but you still think you're close to catching her. Why?"

"Her downstairs neighbor, a guy named Turner, the guy who ID'd her, says there's a guy with a key who had been coming in Sunday afternoons to collect Barber's mail and check the apartment, and once a month with a cleaning woman. Then starting just before we found the apartment Turner noticed the mailbox being emptied every couple of days. It was still the guy and not Barber doing it—he knew because he met the guy at the mailbox one evening. The guy didn't say so but Turner got the feeling he was hoping to find Barber in. He must have some reason to think she might showing up."

Garreth started. Lane had a friend? Someone close enough to entrust with keeping an eye on her apartment? His pulse leaped. Another vampire? He could not understand a vampire choosing daylight visits, but would Lane trust one of the humans she despised and preyed on? Vampire or human, though, neither jibed with her claims of loneliness when she was asking him to become her companion.

She could have lied, of course.

"Have you talked to this guy?"

"We will as soon as we find him." Harry sighed. "So far all we have is a description: fifties, five-ten, 180 to 190 pounds, gray at the temples, blue eyes, mustache and glasses. He's never given Turner his name and since we've been around Turner hasn't seen him to get a car description or license number. I was about to talk Serruto into a stakeout for him when I called you. After you said you were coming out—"

"You thought you'd let me volunteer for the job," Garreth interrupted dryly.

Harry grinned.

"You know Serruto's told me I'm only riding along on this. Period."

"So we won't tell him." His ex-partner's eyes widened with innocence. "It isn't as though you'll actually be *doing* anything, just sitting here for a couple of days until you get a license number, or happen to tail the car home. Any citizen might do the same. Of course you'll pass the information on to me for action."

"Of course." Would he? Did he dare give Harry someone who knew Lane well? "Let me trade cars with you. My red beast isn't exactly inconspicuous."

"You don't say." Harry grinned. Digging into his trousers, he produced the car keys. "We'll go back for it as soon as we've visited Armour, Hayenga, and Kriszcziokaitis."

Garreth blinked.

"Accountants," Harry said. "I started wondering how the rent and other bills are paid with Barber gone. Maybe this guy does that, too. So I contacted the landlord to find out." He started the car. "His accounting department finally called back on Friday. The rent check comes from Armour, Hayenga, and Kriszcziokaitis. I was going to talk to them then, but—"

"But a wacko walked into that Mission clinic with his shotgun and upset your schedule," Garreth finished for him.

Harry nodded. "Let's go see them before anything else interferes."

4

The accounting firm's tastefully understated offices occupied most of a skyscraper floor in the middle of San Francisco's financial district, and judging by the directory inside the double glass doors included several generations of Armours, Hayengas, and Kriszcziokaitises.

Harry eyed the sculpture and original oils around the reception area and dragged in a deep breath. "Smell the money."

The stunningly beautiful receptionist directed them down the corridor to the office of one Magrethe Kriszcziokaitis, a handsome woman in her forties, to argue out what they wanted.

Ms. Kriszcziokaitis smiled politely. "Sergeant Takananda, I understand your situation and I would like to help, but I just don't know what I can tell you. I know nothing about this Barbara Madell."

Harry sent back an equally professional smile. "But your firm has been paying her rent for over a year and a half. I respect your desire to maintain the confidentiality of your clients, but I remind you that the woman is a suspect in a murder case."

Ms. Kriszcziokaitis tented her fingers. "The woman isn't our client, strictly speaking. We only pay her bills."

"Then you must know where she is. How does she give you her instructions?"

"She gives us none, sergeant. The instructions come from another party."

Harry straighted. "Someone else's money is paying her bills? Whose?"

The accountant leaned back in her chair. "I'm sorry. I'm not free to divulge that information, sergeant. Unless, of course, you come back with a court order."

Harry's expression never changed but his body language told Garreth how hopeless Harry considered that possibility. He stood. "Perhaps we will. Thank you." Leaving the office he muttered to Garreth, "Do you think it's the guy?"

"She's a beautiful woman. What do *you* think?" But this time Garreth knew he lied. There could be only one person paying, the person who had so much money to spend. *A woman with hypnotic powers can learn a great many investment tips from the business giants she beds*, Lane had told him. "Damn." He felt his pockets. "I think I dropped my notebook in there. Go on and I'll catch up with you at the elevator."

He stepped back into Kriszcziokaitis's office. As she looked up with a frown, he pulled off his glasses and caught her gaze. "A moment more of your time, please. Tell me, is a Madelaine Bieber paying Madell's bills?"

The accountant's pupils pulsated with an inner struggle. It lasted only a moment, however, before she surrendered. "Yes. She's a very old and respected client."

"How old?"

"She's been with us since 1941."

That sounded about right. "And in that time she's paid the bills for a number of young women, hasn't she?"

"Yes."

All of them Lane herself with different aliases. What a convenient solution to the problem of finances through numerous identity changes.

"Please write down the name of her bank for me." The money belonged to her family; they should be able to find it.

The accountant scribbled on a memo pad and ripped off the sheet.

Folding the sheet and putting it away in the inside pocket of his sport coat, Garreth smiled at her. "Now please forget that I came back and we had this conversation."

He slipped out of the office.

Outside the reception area Harry held the elevator, calmly ignoring the glares of the passengers. "Hard time finding the notebook? Strange. I don't remember you having one in there at all."

The doors closed and the car started down.

Garreth grinned while conscience stabbed him over the lies and half lies to come. *I'm sorry, Taka-san; you deserve better.* "What sharp eyes you have, grandpa. No, it was just an excuse to spend more time in there and hint that we know who Lane's patron is. She didn't turn a hair, though. She's one cool lady."

Harry glanced sideways at him. "Why didn't you ask her before we left?"

Garreth gave him a thin smile. "You don't want to know I'm doing anything except riding along." *And I don't want you hearing Lane Barber and Mada Bieber's names together. You'd go hunting the connection between them.*

5

Watching Lane's apartment had to be the most uncomfortable stakeout of his career, Garreth reflected. Between the boredom of inactivity and weariness from the sleep he had missed since leaving Baumen, daylight dragged so heavily he felt as though he moved through molasses. Despite his glasses and the shade of Harry's car, his head also throbbed from the sunlight. Oh to have come in summer, when heat in the central valley would be pulling sea air in through the Golden Gate and blanketing the city in thick, beautiful fog.

That might make the day bearable, and the jumble of police calls coming over Harry's scanner interesting instead of irritating.

What are you doing here anyway, Mikaelian? The object of agreeing to this was to fail, so the police would not learn the name of Lane's friend. He would do that best by being somewhere he could not possibly see the man arrive, such as at Harry's house. With Lien gone, either working at her studio or teaching her grade school art classes, whichever she did on Mondays, the house would be empty. He could be sleeping. He ought to be. So why was he suffering this daylight vigil in Harry's car up the hill from the blue house?

A rich laugh echoed in his head. *Because I want you here, lover.*

Staring down at the house, he knew it was true. Lane had meant him to find it, and her trap still retained its power.

Garreth fought the house's pull by lying back in the seat, closing his eyes, and forcing himself to listen to the scanner. For a while it worked. The radio traffic brought a flood of memories, of patrolling in uniform, of becoming an inspector and working for Robbery, then Homicide. The radio and car sounded and felt so familiar he could almost believe he had never left. An: "*Inspectors 55,*" Harry's and his old number, even brought him automatically upright, groping for a mike to roger the call.

That shattered the illusion. He had no mike. Inspectors 55 were now Harry and Girimonte. And the blue Victorian house sat down the street whispering its siren call at him.

Garreth climbed out of the car and sauntered down the street. What the hell. Without Lane around, what harm could there be in going down for a look?

At the house steps he resisted the urge to glance around for anyone watching him. Few people questioned someone who appeared to be assured— going about his business. Hesitancy or furtiveness, however, caused suspicion. Passing the door of the lower apartment, pain burned at the edge of perception, warning him of the fire that would sear him if he attempted to enter the dwelling uninvited. Upstairs, however, the hallway and door remained cool. Rooms ceased to be a dwelling if they were empty or the occupant died.

Still, he hesitated outside. *Watch the visiting cop get arrested for breaking and entering.*

But he was not breaking in. He pressed against the door.

Wrench.

Darkness fill the apartment, delicious cool darkness without a single ray of daylight leaking in through the blackout drapes over the bay window. That alone told him a vampire lived here. The darkness of

Lane's other apartment the first time he visited her in his human days remained indelibly imprinted in memory. He had been blind, groping his way uncertainly until she turned on a lamp.

Now he saw perfectly well and reveled in relief from the sun. Despite feeling Lane around him. She might not have lived here long, but she had imprinted herself firmly on the room, from her old-fashioned taste in furniture—overstuffed couch and chairs, a wicker basket chair, colonial-style desk and chair—to personal belongs. The typetray on the wall held an assortment of stones, animal teeth, marbles, a rodent skull, and other small treasures she had collected as a child. Books and toys filled bookcases built in on either side of the fireplace ... children's books, others on the occult, on music, history, and medicine; old dolls; a cast-iron toy stove; a miniature tea set. Original oils and watercolors Lane had bought around the world hung on the walls while several small sculptures stood between old photographs on the mantel. Anna Bieber had identical photographs in her home, a wedding picture of her and her husband and another of Lane seated with her next youngest sister and a girl cousin on the running board of an old touring car.

The room echoed so strongly of Lane's presence that Garreth found himself holding his breath, waiting for her to appear, smiling seductively and offering him the world if only he would give up his ties to humanity.

An envelope leaned against one of the sculptures on the mantel. He noted it and started to turn away, then stopped short. Precise, square handwriting on the outside said: *Mada*. He stared, his breath caught somewhere in the middle of his chest. Someone had been here who knew her real name?

Even as he imagined Harry coming in with a search warrant and stumbling across the note, his hand reached for it.

The square handwriting continued on the sheet of thick, cream-colored stationery inside.

> Dear Mada,
> I wish I could bring this myself, but since I have not yet been invited in, Leonard is delivering it. Contact me as soon as possible. It is urgent. I regret not being able to be more specific, but this is a matter better not detailed in writing. For the moment, I can be reached at Leonard's.
>
> Irina

Garreth shoved the note into his coat pocket along with the memo bearing the name of Lane's bank. No, this note must not be left where Harry might find it. It had clearly been written by another vampire.

Another vampire.

Remembering Lane talking about the vampire who made her, he took the note out to read the signature again. Could this Irina be Irina Rodek? A beautiful woman, Lane had said, describing her, exquisite as a Dresden figurine, with sable hair and eyes ...

His grandmother's warning rang his head and cold trickled through him. Irina Rodek had eyes the color of violets.

Now the echoes in the apartment seemed less those of Lane than the clang of a closing trap.

It took several seconds to realize that the metallic sounds were real, but not in the apartment. They came from the lower hall. Garreth caught his breath. Someone had closed a mailbox. Leonard?

Footsteps hissed across tile.

Garreth spun, looking for a place to hide. The man must not find—

The thought broke off at the bang of the front door. Cursing, he sprinted for the apartment door. The man was leaving!

Wrench!

In the hallway, he vaulted over the railing onto the middle of the stairs and half scrambled, half fell down the rest of the flight to the lower hall. A car started outside. Jerking open the front door, Garreth raced across the porch and down the steps. As in his dreams, the brilliant sunshine slapped him like a hammer. He fought through it to the street, swearing every step of the way. The visitor was the man Harry wanted. What he saw of the man as the car pulled away matched the description Harry had given him. But there was no chance to reach Harry's car in time to tail the man, no time for anything more than catching the BMW's license number.

Only when he had it written down on the envelope Irina's note came in did he remember that his object had been to miss the man. He laughed wryly. Foiled by cop reflexes.

Or had he done the right thing after all? Garreth fingered the envelope. If Irina really posed the threat his grandmother's Feeling indicated, he dared not stumble around in ignorance. He must learn something about her ... what way she might be dangerous, and exactly how deadly. So he needed this Leonard after all.

He trudged up the hill to the car and started it. The scanner crackled to life. If only he had been able to tail the man. Then he would know who Leonard was and still be able to pretend the stakeout had failed. With just a license number, though, he had to tell Harry so his old partner could run a registration check on the car for the name and address of its owner.

Then again, he reflected, listening to the scanner ... maybe not.

6

It took almost fifteen minutes to locate a black-and-white unit with a familiar face in it. Pulling up alongside on the passenger side, he rolled down his window and shouted across at the patrol car's driver, "Kostmayer. Dane Kostmayer. Hey, remember me, Garreth Mikaelian?"

The driver glanced over, frowning, then started. Another classic doubletake. Grinning, he motioned Garreth to turn up a side street. Once parked, both officers climbed out of their car and Kostmayer loped back to meet Garreth at the rear bumper with a staggering slap on the back.

"Mikaelian, you old devil. What've you been doing with yourself? I heard you quit after your partner got shot."

Garreth nodded. "I'm still a cop but in a smaller department." He pulled out his Baumen badge and ID.

"I'd say smaller," Kostmayer snorted. "So what are you doing back here? Vacation?"

Garreth nodded again. "Visiting Harry Takananda and looking around ... and until I spotted you and got distracted, I was tailing one gorgeous lady."

"Tailing?" Kostmayer's partner said.

"We were drinking coffee at tables next to each other at Ghirardelli Square and started talking. We hit it off great, but when she left I realized she hadn't given me her name. So I jumped in my car—"

"Your car?" The partner pointedly eyed the California plate on the front bumper.

Garreth shrugged. "Harry's car. He loaned it to me to use while I'm here. I was hoping to catch her and ask her her name, but then I spotted you and got distracted. Now it looks like I've lost her."

Kostmayer shook his head. "That's too bad. Sorry."

"Except …" Garreth smiled. "I got her license number. It's a personalized plate: PHILOS. Do you suppose I could ask for a little favor?"

Kostmayer and his partner exchanged glances and grinned. "Sure thing. Run it, Ricardo."

The partner slid into the car. Garreth heard him call Dispatch.

"I really appreciate this, Dane."

"A favor for an old friend. What's it like working in Baumen, Kansas?"

They chatted until the partner climbed back out of the car. "You didn't tell us she was driving a BMW. She also has a Pacific Heights address. That's nice taste in women, Mikaelian." He handed Garreth a page from a notebook, scribbled with a name and address. "But it looks like your lady is married. The car is registered to a Leonard Eugene Holle."

Garreth eyed the paper with pretended disappointment. "Maybe she's his daughter? Anyway, however it turns out, thanks again. I owe you one."

"We'll get together some evening before you leave and you can buy me a beer."

He stood watching while the two officers climbed back in their car and drove away, then grinned in satisfaction, headed for his own car. Now to have a little chat with Mr. Holle.

7

The short burp of a siren behind him several blocks later brought a quick rush of anxiety—was Kostmayer coming back for something?—which quickly escalated to low panic with a glance in the rearview mirror. The flashing light behind him came not from a light bar but the pop-on bubble of an inspector's car. Had Kostmayer's partner used Garreth's name in checking the registration? Had word of it reached Serruto?

Biting his lip, he pulled over. The other car stopped alongside. He found himself looking into the long face of Dean Centrello, and beyond him to a grinning Earl Faye at the wheel, hair as much of an unkempt mane as ever.

"Small world, isn't it?" Faye said.

Garreth groaned inwardly. A chance meeting. That bitch Lady

Luck. He had had to *hunt* for someone to talk into running his registration but when the last person he wanted was a fellow cop, two former colleagues fell over him before he even managed to leave North Beach.

He forced a smile. "Hi, guys."

Centrello shook his head incredulously. "It really is you, Mikaelian."

Faye said, "I told you so. If you'd watch the evening news like a normal person instead of insisting your family eat supper around a table and talk to each other, you'd have recognized him, too." He grinned at Garreth. "Hey, man, it's good to see you again. Where you headed?"

Garreth shrugged. "Just driving."

"Oh, I thought maybe you'd made the guy who's been visiting the Barber chick's apartment. Harry said you were watching the place this afternoon."

A string of profanity ran through Garreth's head. So much for secrecy. With Faye's motormouth, Serruto would know about this meeting before the end of the day. "All right, yes. I got lucky, too. I have the man's name and address. I was just headed back for Bryant Street to tell Harry."

"That's two breaks for Takananda today," Centrello said.

Garreth raised his brows, and breathed a sigh of relief that neither man appeared to notice that driving west was a strange way to reach Bryant Street to the south.

"Someone dropped a dime on the Mission clinic shooter," Faye said. "He and Girimonte are out now picking up the turkey. Hey, we're headed downtown, too. Follow us on in and we can catch up on old times while you wait for Harry."

Garreth saw no way to refuse without arousing curiosity, if not suspicion. He gave them his broadest smile. "Sure. Great."

Riding up in the elevator at Bryant Street, he felt the same prisoner sensation he had felt when meeting the reporters in Baumen. Faye and Centrello seemed oblivious to his discomfort, though. If anything, Centrello's expression contained envy. "Harry says you're into running these days. It's sure thinned you down."

"Sometimes I think about running," Faye said, "and then I start wondering why should I deliberately inflict pain on myself and deprive my brain of oxygen. I remember this case last year. We were called out to the Great Highway early one morning for a body in the northbound lane by Golden Gate Park. More of a grease spot, really. The dude is squashed flat. Almost every bone broken. And the first car must have dragged him ... smeared blood and skin down the highway for a good hundred feet."

Garreth could not help smiling. Faye always relished a story with gory details.

The elevator stopped. They stepped off. Faye never missed a syllable. "He must have been hit by a dozen cars before people realized what was going on and someone blocked the lane so the traffic would go around. He turned out to be a runner. Went clear around Golden Gate Park every morning. Had for years. We figured he was a hit and run, but you know what the post turned up? He'd died of a heart attack. He was dead before the first car hit him. Can you beat that? Here's this dude running miles every day and in great shape, then all of a sudden ..." Faye snapped his fingers. "Think about it, Mikaelian."

Garreth chuckled.

The amusement died in an icy drench of dismay as they walked into Homicide. He stopped short, staring.

In Serruto's office Julian Fowler stood up, smiling.

Garreth swore silently. What was the writer doing here?

Fowler came out of the office, followed by an attractive young woman and a poker-faced Serruto. "I dare say this is a bit of a surprise, Mikaelian."

The height of understatement. Garreth dragged his feet loose from the floor to move farther into the room. "I ... thought I left you in Kansas."

Fowler grinned. "Sorry, no. I followed you. Or to be perfectly accurate, I preceded you. I flew out on Friday, after Anna told me you were going on holiday. Thanks to Miss Kirkwood here and the rest of the Public Relations section, who have been a marvelous help, I'm ready to start my research."

The young woman smiled. "It's a pleasure to work with such a well-known writer."

The air in Garreth's lungs felt thick, as though tainted by garlic. Research! That had to mean records of the case ... the report of finger-prints found in Lane's Telegraph Hill apartment, prints identified as Madelaine Bieber's from the records of her 1941 arrest for assault, and photographs of Lane obtained from her agent. "You don't mean you're still thinking of writing about this case?"

"Too right!" Fowler's light eyes glittered. "It's absolutely fas-cinating. You're going to make a marvelous protagonist."

Every detective in the room turned to stare. Except Serruto, who leaned against the side of his office door with arms crossed and gaze fixed on the far corner of the ceiling.

Panic welled up in Garreth. His one protection against someone realizing that Mada Bieber and Lane Barber were the same person was their apparent age difference. Fowler's background in horror legends, though, made him the one man capable of seeing the real truth in the facts, of seeing how Lane could be Mada and what she was ... and by extention, what Garreth Mikaelian had become. He made his voice casual. "What about the war story you came over here to research?"

Fowler shrugged. "That'll wait." He raised a brow. "You're bloody reluctant, I must say. Most people would love to be written about." One brow arched. "I can make you immortal, you know." Both brows skipped. "You find that amusing?"

Garreth bit back his wry smile. "No." *Just redundant.* "Mr. Fowler, I'm not most people. Count me out of your project."

The woman from Public Relations frowned. "Officer Mikaelian, the department has agreed to extend Mr. Fowler every possible courtesy."

"I don't work for this department," Garreth pointed out. "Lieutenant, may I wait for Harry in your office?"

One corner of the lieutenant's mouth twitched. He waved Garreth by, then followed him in and closed the door. "I'm glad someone else doesn't want to join the circus." He eyed Garreth. "You look exhausted. Are you that out of shape for stakeouts?"

Garreth started. "What stakeout?"

Serruto ticked his tongue against his teeth. "What stakeout. Mikaelian, I can see the parking lot from my window. I watched you drive out in Takananda's personal car. Why would you use a vehicle other than your own except to be less conspicuous, and why would you want to be inconspicuous except—"

"All right." Garreth sighed. "Yes, I was watching the apartment for Harry."

"And?"

Garreth showed him Holle's name and address. "Here's the guy who's been looking after the apartment. I swear I did not accost him and interrogate him, Lieutenant sir. I didn't even tail him. I only took down the license number and ran a registration check."

"Good boy." Serruto glanced toward the squadroom. "Ah. Ms. Public Relations has taken her pet away and the conquering heroes have returned." He opened the office door.

Harry and Girimonte swaggered into the squadroom. Harry shook clasped hands above his head. "We got the turkey! He's signed, sealed, and delivered to the jail."

Thumbs went up around the room.

"Did you get the gun, too?" Serruto asked.

Girimonte lit one of her sleek cigars. The sweet smell of it drifted past the lieutenant to Garreth, temporarily drowning the blood scents. "Of course. It's at the lab." She blew a perfect smoke ring.

Harry headed for the coffee pot. On the way he caught Garreth's eye. "How was your sightseeing this afternoon, Mik-san? Has the old town changed much? Glad to see the cable cars back?"

Garreth grimaced. "Forget the subterfuge, Harry; Serruto knows everything." He slid around Serruto out of the office to hand the notebook page to Harry. "However, I did see the individual we hoped I would."

Harry's sheepish wince vanished into a grin. "The luck of the Irish." He passed the page on to Girimonte. "Well, partner, let's run Mr. Holle through Records and pay him a visit, unless you're hot to start on the shooter's paperwork?"

"Hot for paperwork?" Girimonte blew another smoke ring and bared her teeth. "Harry, honey, I have absolutely no interest in starting any of it without you. We've got all night to write reports." In one sinuous motion she stubbed out her cigar and headed for the door.

8

Holle's house matched the BMW for quiet elegance ... faintly gothic, three and a half stories of red brick with pointed windows gleaming gold in the late afternoon sunlight and an entrance of broad double doors set into a pointed stone arch. Eyeing it, a sharp pang of apprehension stabbed Garreth. He found himself reluctant to leave the car. A reaction to his grandmother's warning, or perhaps a Feeling of his own? Or was it more from this sense of indeed being just a ride-along that had grown in him as he rode in the back seat, like a civilian or prisoner, while Harry and Girimonte up front gleefully rehashed their capture of the Mission clinic shooter, reliving a shared experience of which Garreth had no part. Another match burning on his bridge.

Garreth forced himself out of the car. Misgivings or not, he had to hear Holle's answers, and head off dangerous ones.

Fire licked at him as he approached the doorway.

A middle-aged woman in a light gray dress answered the bell. A strong scent of perfume drifted from her. After studying Harry's indentification with a frown, she opened the door wide. "Please come in. I'll see if Mr. Holle is available."

The flames in Garreth snuffed out.

She left them waiting in a baronial-looking hall with wood paneling and a soaring ceiling while she disappeared up the broad staircase.

Girimonte rolled her eyes. "Jesus. I like Emeraude, but that woman smells like she bathes in it. I wonder how a servant gets away with so much perfume."

A few minutes later, when a man matching Harry's description of Lane's caretaker came down the stairs, Girimonte's question had an answer. Leonard Holle reeked of cologne himself, a spicy male scent but still so strong it overpowered even the blood smells around Garreth. Holle could not have smelled a pig sty next to him.

He put on his glasses to take their badge cases and read the identification. "Inspector Girimonte, Sergeant Takananda, and ..." His brows rose at Garreth's silver oval shield with its blue Seal of Kansas in the center, so different from the seven-pointed stars the other two carried. He looked up with a smile. "You're a long way from—" Both sentence and smile died in a start.

Panic washed through Garreth. That was recognition flaring in Holle's eyes, and since it had not come until he looked up from the ID to Garreth himself, it had to be recognition not of who but *what* he was. And it could not be because Holle himself was also a vampire. Beneath the heavy scent of his cologne lay a blood smell. Lane had had none.

"... from home, Officer Mikaelian," Holle finished. He handed back the badge case.

"Officer Mikelian has special knowledge in this case and is working with us as a consultant," Harry said.

Holle's eyes did not leave Garreth's face. "What case is that, Sergeant?"

"Do you suppose we might sit down somewhere to discuss it?" Girimonte asked.

Holle blinked. "Oh. Of course." He glanced toward an archway and the living room beyond, golden in the late sun shining through the front windows. "I think we'll be most comfortable in the library." Turning toward the stairs, he led the way up to the next floor.

Breathing came no easier. Holle *did* know. The library had drapes as heavy as those in Lane's or Garreth's apartments. With the doors slid closed, the only light came from a lamp Holle switched on.

He waved them to deep, leather easy chairs around a fireplace and took another for himself. The leather, smooth and cool and smelling faintly of saddle soap, squeaked as Garreth settled in. Around them bookshelves filled the walls from floor to ceiling.

Holle leaned back with another squeak of leather, stroking his mustache. "Now, what's this about, Sergeant?"

"You've been collecting the mail at an apartment in North Beach belonging to girl named Barbara Madell."

Holle hesitated only a moment before replying. "Yes. Is there some problem with that? I have her keys and can show you a letter from her asking me to look after the apartment while she's gone. I've done it often before."

"She's a friend of yours then?" Girimonte asked.

Holle considered. "More a friend of a friend, but she needed someone who could be expected to stay in one place so I ended up with the job."

"That's a bit unusual, isn't it?" Girimonte said. "Asking a near stranger to look after your place?"

Holle frowned. "Not among my circle. What *is* this about?"

"How long has it been since you've seen her?" Harry asked.

The frown deepened. "I'm not sure. About a year and a half I suppose. Sergeant—"

"She's been gone that long and you've never worried? Or is *that* common in your circle, too?"

"It is with Lane. She's a singer and a footloo—"

"Lane?"

Holle rolled his eyes. "That *is* her name ... Lane Barber."

"Then how do you explain the name on the mailbox?"

"Oh for god's sake! Names are a game with her. She's always changing the ones on her mailbox. Sometimes there are groups of them, all outrageous. Surely that can't be what this is about. As far as I know, using different names is no crime if there's no intent to defraud."

"What this is about, Mr. Holle," Girimonte said with a thin smile, "is murder."

Holle stiffened. "I beg your pardon?"

Harry leaned forward. "On August 30, 1983, a visiting businessman named Gerald Mossman was dumped in the bay with his throat cut and neck broken. We have evidence linking Lane Barber to the death."

"Lane?" Holle's jaw dropped. "That's impossible."

"Before he was killed," Garreth said, "someone drained him of blood. The autopsy found two punctures in his neck that the pathologist said could have been made by large-gauge hypodermic needles."

Holle stared hard at Garreth. "And you think a charming young woman like *Lane* would do such a ... barbaric thing? Ridiculous! You should be looking for some demented cultist."

"On September 7th she attacked and attempted to kill Officer Mikaelian here, who was a member of the San Francisco Police Department at the time," Harry said. "She bit him savagely on the throat."

"I can hardly be mistaken about who attacked me. How could you not be aware that we were looking for your friend? The papers were full of news of the case at the time, complete with pictures of Miss Barbar as a suspect."

"I—" Holle swallowed. Sweat gleamed on his forehead. The acid smell of it cut through the spicy sweetness of his cologne. "I was in Europe from the middle of August to the middle of September. I never heard anything about the case, I swear. When I came home, there was an envelope with keys and a letter from Lane saying she was leaving and would I look after her new apartment. I had no reason to think it was any different from the other times."

"Did she say where she was going?" Harry asked.

Holle shook his head. "I doubt she knew. I gather she just travels where the urge, or some man she's attached herself to, takes her."

"Suddenly you're visiting the apartment more frequently according to her neighbors. Have you received word that she's due back soon?"

"No." Holle shook his head emphatically. "I haven't heard anything from her."

"Then why the increase in visits?"

For a moment Garreth wondered if he were going to answer. Holle's eyes flickered behind his glasses, as though his mind was racing frantically. His gaze slid back toward Garreth. "A friend of hers came to town and wanted to reach her. So I kept going over hoping Lane would have come back."

"What's the friend's name?" Girimonte asked.

Garreth held his breath. Holle had not contradicted him at the mention of hypodermic needles, though he must know that Garreth knew what made those punctures, and he was being evasive about the reason for checking Lane's apartment so often. Still, there was always a chance he might mention the name Irina.

"I—I'm sorry, I don't know," Holle said.

In relief, Garreth resumed breathing.

Harry frowned. "How the hell can you not know? You talked to this person, didn't you?"

To Garreth's astonishment, the panic in Holle evaporated. His face smoothed and his voice steadied. "I never met her before. Mutual friends in Europe had told her that I might know where to reach Lane."

"Exactly what is this circle of people you run with, Mr. Holle?" Girimonth asked.

Holle sighed. "Before my parents died and left me this house, I worked for one of the airlines as a ticket agent. There is a subculture among airline employees. Since we had free flight privileges, we often flew different places for weekends, to a jazz festival or the Mardi Gras or the opening of a new opera. Just about anything. We stayed with friends when we got there. Except very often the friend wasn't someone we knew directly. Sometimes the friend's friend wasn't even home. It isn't uncommon to be given a key, stay in the house, and leave without ever meeting the people who live there. By the same token, friends and friends of friends of friends stay here with me while they're in San Francisco. I've stopped working for a living but I've kept my friends."

Harry's almond eyes narrowed. "And Lane's friend came by one of these indirect connections?"

"Exactly."

Garreth glanced around the darkened library. All those friends of friends could not just be airline employees.

"Yet she never told you her name?" Girimonte asked.

Holle sighed again, this time in exasperation. "Of course she told me, but I have a terrible memory that way. I don't know it would help you anyway, since if she had had any idea where Lane is, she wouldn't have come to me. If I remember her name, or I hear anything from Lane, I'll contact you immediately. I really can't believe Lane is involved in anything so ... psychotic, and the sooner she can clear her name, the better." Holle stood. "Is there anything else you need?"

"Not for the time being, no." Harry gave him an inscrutible oriental smile. "But we'll keep in touch."

Holle's steps faltered only a moment as he crossed to slide open the doors. "Of course."

Smiling politely, he saw them down to the front door.

As it boomed closed behind them, Girimonte bared her teeth. "We ought to have leaned on him, Harry. You know he's lying."

And hiding a hell of a lot, Garreth thought. "But not lying about knowing where Lane is."

Harry nodded. "I'm pretty sure he didn't know anything about Mossman's murder or the attack on Garreth, either."

Girimonte scowled up at the house. "I'll bet he believes Barber did it, though, and what about that story of some friend looking for her?"

"Oh, I think that's true enough," Harry said. "The lie is he doesn't remember the friend's name. We may have to chat with him again about that, but for the time being, since Records says he's clean, we'll leave him alone. Besides, we have reports to write, partner ... which we'd better start if Garreth and I want to make it home before Lien's dinner dries up in the oven."

9

Lights by the front door and shining through the dark from the living room windows above the garage welcomed them. *Another homecoming*, Garreth reflected, squeezing the ZX into the driveway beside Harry's car. How many evenings had he spent here? Dozens. Hundreds. After Marti died it had been more of a home than his apartment had been ... a sanctuary from the stress of the job, from personal pain. He climbed over the gear shift and out the passenger door.

"Harry! Garreth!" Lien rushed out of the house with her salt-and-pepper hair flying around her face, throwing herself into her husband's arms first, then breaking loose to circle the front of the cars and give Garreth a fierce hug that almost smashed the trooper glasses in his breast pocket. The warm, salty scent of her blood flooded him.

Thirst seared his throat and closed like a fist around his stomach. Garreth fought for the control not to push her away.

Fortunately she released him and drew back, smiling. "It's so good to see you. This is just like old times ... the two of you home after dark to a dinner kept from total mummification only by arcane Eastern cooking arts." Catching both their arms, she propelled them toward the door. "Honorable husband, you could at least have sent Garreth on ahead instead of making him wait while you finished your reports. I would have had time to find out all the personal news that bores you, like what his Maggie is like, and we could have finished off four or five rum teas and gotten comfortably smashed."

Harry grinned. "See the virtue of a Chinese wife? She still scolds, but with respect."

Lien pinched him through his suitcoat.

Longing twisted in Garreth. The welcome and the fond banter-ing echoed so many other evenings. If only this one *could* be like those others.

Inside, Lien steered them past the stairs into the family room. They had changed it a little but the general flavor still remained ... sleek, contemporary American furniture surrounded with oriental touches ... a Chinese vase here, a Japanese flower arrangement, shoji doors closing off the dining area, paintings by Lien with brush strokes as clean and elegantly simple as Chinese calligraphy.

Lien vanished through the dining room into the kitchen, calling back, "Your rum teas are on the coffee table. Relax while I rescue dinner from the oven."

Dinner. Garreth grimaced inwardly. *How are you going to fake your way through* this *one*?

He and Harry kicked off their shoes, shed their coats, and unclipped holsters from their belts. Harry plopped onto the couch. Pick-ing up his cup of tea, he leaned back and propped his feet on the coffee table. "It really is like old times. Cheers."

Garreth curled up cross-legged in an easy chair. "Cheers." The odor of the rum wafted up from the tea, setting his stomach churning. He pretended to start a sip, yelped, and put the cup back down.

"Too hot?" Harry said. "Sorry."

"No problem. I'll just let it cool a bit." In the course of which he could "forget" to drink it at all. But there was still dinner to face. Could he even tolerate being at the table? The tantalizing smell of Lien's sweet and sour pork flooded the room, leaving him torn between longing at the memory of the taste and the nausea of his new preference's rejec-tion of it.

Harry mentioned something about an evening several years be-fore. Garreth nodded automatically, eyeing the patio doors. Perhaps a few breaths of night air would help clear his head and settle his stomach.

"Garreth," Lien called, "will you please come help me?"

Harry winked at him. "Careful, Mik-san. She just wants a chance to cross-examine you about your girlfriend and you love life." He heaved to his feet and trailed after Garreth, still holding his tea cup. "I'll come along to protect you."

Lien raised her brows at them. "I might have known both of you would come in. Very well, but no snitching bites before everything is on the table."

"Snitching bites? Us?" Harry said innocently.

Garreth smoothed his mustache. That was an idea.

He feigned passes at the food while he and Harry helped move it into the dining area and sat down. And he kept talking, answering all Lien's questions about Baumen and Maggie at great length, telling every amusing anecdote he could think of, including Maggie setting up his patrol car. Lien seemed to have relaxed her rules about forbidding shop talk, but he did not want to push his luck.

Lien shook her head. "I really believe the biggest danger you face on the street is other cops. I remember when this one was in uniform." She pointed at Harry. "Nickles glued over keyholes, lockers turned upside down, windows and doors of other patrol cars sealed with fingerprint tape with the officers inside, and then, of course, we mustn't forget the Fourth of July, that wonderful holiday when he could throw bottle rockets into other patrol cars as he passed them."

Harry grinned.

Garreth winked at him. "I guess I'd better not tell her about the time you and I unplugged the mike in Faye and Centrello's car and it took them most of the morning to figure out why they couldn't roger their calls or reach Dispatch."

Lien rolled her eyes. "*Boys* in blue indeed."

Miracle of miracles, she did not appear to notice that he only stirred his food around on his plate instead of eating it.

Then Harry, reaching for the pork a third time, stopped with his hand on the serving spoon to raise a brow at Garreth. "Hey, Mik-san, you're falling behind. Better clean up your plate before you lose your chance for seconds."

Now they were watching him. Garreth cursed silently. Could he possibly swallow one bite and keep it down for a few minutes? The lurch of his stomach said no. So did memory. That last solid meal he had eaten, in the hospital after Lane attacked him, had done an instant reverse. "That's all right. This is plenty. My eating habits have changed since I left." The understatement of the year.

Perfectly true, though. Yet guilt pricked him as though he had lied. *Well, didn't you?* By implication, by omission, hiding the truth and separating himself from two people he cared about. Starting a fire on his bridge he could blame only on himself.

10

He tried to sleep. With people here expecting him to live by daylight, he had to make himself rest at night. Surely he could manage that for a few days; he had before, in the beginning. The earth pallet and sheer tiredness should have helped, but his mind kept churning, tossing up images of Lane, Fowler, his grandmother, and Holle, of a small woman faceless but for violet eyes, of burning bridges and gothic houses full of shadows and chill with danger. Garreth rolled over and pulled the top sheet up over his shoulders, but the images continued to spin behind his closed eyes, mixing together in endless varieties ... Lane and the bridge, Fowler and the bridge, his grandmother and violet eyes, Lane and Fowler, Fowler and Holle.

Fowler and Holle! Garreth came wide awake, sucking in his breath. He sat up in bed. That could happen. Harry had no probable cause for requesting a search warrant for Lane's apartment, but Fowler's passion for details about his characters might well take him to Holle to charm his way into accompanying Lane's friend on the next visit to her apartment. Cold crawled up Garreth's spine. One look around, at the photographs duplicating some of Anna Bieber's, at the books inscribed to "Mada" and "Madelaine," and Fowler would know what the police file on Mossman's murder might have already suggested, that Lane Barber and Madelaine Bieber were the same person.

Garreth had not looked in this kitchen, but in her other apartment the kitchen had been empty, its cupboards barren of anything to cook in or eat from, not even a drinking glass. Lane, he knew, considered it a backstage area she never expected anyone to see and therefore not worth the trouble of stocking with props. What would it suggest to a horror writer, though, after reading the autopsy report on Mossman and seeing file photographs of Garreth's body and the wounds on his throat?

Garreth sucked in his lower lip. Fowler must not see the apartment. How to stop him, though? Attempting to keep the writer away from the apartment might draw his attention to it instead.

"Damn." His gut knotted. Throwing off the sheet, Garreth swung out of bed and paced the room. His grandmother was right; he should never have come back to San Francisco.

The urge to run beat at him. His suitcase sat invitingly by the dresser. All he had to do was slip away. Except it was too late to pack up and retreat. The very act of coming had brought the means for his destruction, and Fowler would still be here even after Garreth—

The thought broke off in a hurried reverse. Pack up? He grimaced. *You're a thick mick, you know that Mikaelian? If there's a stake in your future, you deserve it.* He had been looking at the problem with Fowler from the wrong end. The solution was not preventing the writer from seeing the apartment, but keeping Lane's belongings out of his sight.

Relief and resolution washed away his weariness. Dressing, Garreth slipped out into the hall. Voices murmured in Harry and Lien's bedroom. He glided silently past their door and down the stairs to the front door.

Wrench.

Outside, lights still showed in the houses along the street, each behind its narrow strip of grass and hedge. Except for a man walking his dog and an occasional passing car, though, the neighborhood lay quiet. Garreth drew a deep breath, savoring the briny scent of the sea and the muted symphony of city sounds … distant traffic, barking dogs, threads of voices and music from nearby houses. Very different from night in the hills around Baumen, where a cow's bellow or coyote's yodel carried for miles in the stillness and the stars glittered cold and brilliant as ice chips overhead, but no less enjoyable.

Climbing into the passenger side of the ZX, he reached back behind the seat for his thermos. A few swallows finished off the remaining blood. Now the question was, should he refill it and risk storage in Lien's refrigerator, or depend on nightly hunting with *its* attendant hazards?

That question could be answered later, he decided, crawling over the gearshift into the driver's seat. Turning the key enough to free the steering wheel, he slipped the car into neutral and let it roll backward out of the drive, then swung out and pushed it down the street. Harry knew the snarl of the ZX's engine too well for him to risk starting it in front of the house.

"Can't you get it started?"

Garreth spun to find the dog walker eyeing him from the sidewalk. The man's thoughts ran almost visibly across his face: *Man pushing car down the street in the middle of the night. Very suspicious. Possible car thief.* Garreth thought fast. "The damn battery's down. I thought maybe if I got it rolling, that'd be enough to turn the engine over."

He gave the car an extra hard push to make it move, then jumping in, cranked the key. The motor roared to life. With a smile and a wave at the dog walker, Garreth drove away.

Two blocks later he let out his breath, but even then he made himself drive around at random for fifteen minutes, watching the rearview mirror for patrol cars, in case the dog walker had gone ahead and reported him as suspicious activity. Of the several black-and-whites he spotted, though, none showed any interest in him. Finally he headed for Lane's apartment.

11

Cleaning out the apartment went more smoothly than he had dared hope. The neighborhood was even darker and quieter than Harry's had been. Garreth parked at the curb, slipped soundlessly into the house and up the stairs through the apartment door to release the dead bolt from the inside. None of the furniture went, of course, just her personal possessions, as on her flight from Telegraph Hill, and four heavy cartons he found in the bedroom closet held everything. No doubt the very boxes she had used to move everything in. Four soundless trips downstairs had them all stashed in the car, albeit somewhat tightly, then he relocked the dead bolt from the inside and left.

Coasting down the hill before he started the engine, it struck Garreth that of course packing her effects was simple; Lane had planned it that way. She kept only what had personal meaning, like mementos of her past, and things of value that were easy to carry, nothing cumbersome or that could be replaced with a charge card at any department store.

There was the small matter of what to do with everything once he had it out, of course, but he had had the drive over to North Beath to think about it. When he left San Francisco he had stored his own belongings. Lane's things could join them. From the apartment he drove down to Hannes-Katsbulas Storage on the Embarcadero, parked, and slipped through the wire fence around the warehouse.

Less than fifty feet inside, three huge Rottweilers charged around the building, teeth bared.

Garreth stared straight at them. "At ease, fellows."

The dogs slowed, foreheads wrinkling.

"Sit."

They sat.

He patted each on the head in turn. "Good boys. Okay, come on with me. Let's go find the security man." And he trotted on with the three escorting him.

The security guard was having a cup of coffee in his office. Garreth's appearance in the doorway brought him jumping up out of his chair, clawing for his gun. "Who the hell are you? How did you get in here?"

Garreth stared him straight in the eyes. "I have some things to put away. Will you please unlock the front gate for me?"

The gun barrel wavered ... returned to the holster. The guard moved to obey. In ten minutes Lane's cartons joined Garreth's in the compartment assigned to him.

Garreth did not let himself linger. Just seeing the furniture, the boxes of his own books and photographs, and the big pastel an artist in The Cannery had done of Marti, set pain twisting in him. So many memories, sweet and bitter, were entombed here. Would he ever again have an apartment where it could all sit in the open? Did he ever want to? He locked the compartment.

At the gate he patted the dogs and caught the guard's eyes one more time. "Please forget about this visit."

The padlock snapped closed through the gate chain with the guard's eyes staring through Garreth, already having forgotten him.

12

Driving north along the Embarcadero, Garreth sucked in his lower lip. Now what? He still needed information on Irina. Calling on Holle at this time of night was probably not socially acceptable, however, even if the man did keep company with vampires. His thermos also needed refilling. Despite the risk of Lien discovering the contents of the thermos, he decided he preferred to have several days' food supply on hand than to count on being able to slip out hunting every night. But it was rather too early now to skulk around piers after rats. Someone might see him. The traffic remained heavy along here and would be so until the clubs in North Beach closed at two o'clock.

North Beach. Garreth pursed his lips. Lane always found her supper there. Maybe Irina had discovered the same hunting ground. And maybe someone had seen her.

He parked just off the Embarcadero at the foot of Broadway. From there he walked up toward Columbus and within a few blocks had plunged into the show he thought about so often while watching Baumen's Friday and Saturday night cruisers. Baumen must have tempered his memories, though, because he did not remember the sounds, lights, and smells as being this overwhelming ... a bright sea of neon signs, jewel strings of head and tail lights from four lanes of traffic, rumbling motors, honking horns, human voices calling and laughing, the raucous voices of barkers rising above all others as they shouted the virtues of the shows in their particular clubs at the humanity swarming along the sidewalks. The crowds jostled Garreth, people wearing everything from ragged jeans and torn sweatshirts to evening clothes, smelling of sweat, tobacco, alcohol, marijuana, perfume and cologne, and ... blood.

Hunger surged in him, searing his throat. He shoved clenched fists into the pockets of his sport coat. Were the blood scents really so much stronger now than he remembered from that first visit up here after his change, or was it that all blood smelled alike to him then? Experience had taught him the subtle differences between individuals ... and between the clean, salty metallic scent of healthy blood and the sour, bitter, or occasional sickeningly sweet edge warning of pollution by disease and foreign substances.

Good thing you're not *hunting supper here*, he reflected. So many of the men and women pushing past him smelled of tainted blood, more than he had ever noticed in Bellamy or Baumen. It almost killed his appetite. Almost. Some people, it was obvious from appearance alone, had been indulging in drugs and alcohol. With others it was just as obvious that their problem was diease. Some, though, looked outwardly so healthy. In Baumen, where he knew people, he could usually stop to greet someone like that and in the course of a conversation casually remark that the person did not look well and perhaps should see a doctor. Here, as in the theatre in Bellamy, Garreth had to make himself let them go, even the man who passed him arm-in-arm with a healthy-smelling young man.

Watching the couple, Garreth suddenly listened to his own thoughts and grimaced bitterly. He walked up what he had always considered a vital, pulsing artery, where before he had always found excitement in the crowds and color, and what did he think about? Blood.

Setting his jaw, he made himself forget about his thirst and look at faces. Familiar ones began emerging from the crowd, mostly hookers, pimps, pickpockets, and assorted other vermin out from under their rocks for the night. Unlike on previous visits to the area, though, they failed to recognize him in return. Several of the hookers even started to approach him, then veered off with a disgusted expression that told him they had belatedly spotted that indefineable something in his moves and carriage which stamped him *cop*.

Only one portly, well-dressed man failed to notice him; the pickpocket was too intent on prey, a couple at the corner with the flashy look of well-heeled tourists. Garreth watched the dip start forward to "accidentally" bump the man and in the course of it relieve the tourist of his wallet.

Garreth glided close behind. "I wouldn't, Hickham," he murmured. "The tree of evil bears bitter fruit. Crime does not pay. The shadow knows."

Then from the corner of his eye while he pretended to be focused on a display of sexy photographs outside one club, Garreth watched with an inward grin as the pickpocket flung around looking in vain for a known face that had to be the source of the voice.

An instant later, glee died into dismay. Beyond Hickham, pedestrians surged across the street at the light change. Among tham came another familiar face ... Julian Graham Fowler's.

Shit. Garreth spun away and hurriedly joined the crowd crossing to the next block up before the writer could see him. Of all people to meet. Not that it should be unexpected; every tourist visited North Beach sooner or later. What lousy luck Fowler chose tonight.

After half a block Garreth glanced back and to his relief, saw no sign of Fowler. Even without the writer around, though, hunting Irina was a problem with nothing to go on but the description Lane mentioned once in passing.

A mulatto hooker eyed him and brushed on past. He fell into step with her. This might be the place to start. "Don't rush off, honey. Talk to me."

She rolled her eyes. "We got nothing to talk about ... Officer." She shook her head. "I don't know where Vice finds you kids. Don't you have height and weight requirements anymore?"

Fine; let her assume he was SFPD. "I'm Homicide, not Vice. I'm looking for a woman who might have been hanging around the area the past week or so ... small, dark hair, violet eyes. She isn't a professional, but she'll have been up here every night, hitting on a different guy each time."

The hooker snorted. "The amateurs cruise the bars, not the street."

"She has to walk through the street to reach the bars. You sure you haven't seen her?"

She thought a moment. "Violet eyes?"

"And dark hair. A petite woman, pretty. Foreign accent."

The hooker shook her head. "Nope. Sorry." She eyed him more closely, and smiling, moved closer. The scents of her blood and perfume carressed him. "You know, for being a cop and so skinny and all, there's still something kind of ... interesting about you. Did you ever consider that just like you're not always on duty, neither am I?" Her voice went professionally husky. She leaned still closer, the warm, tantalizing scent of her blood setting hunger snarling in Garreth. "Your pistol starts weighting you down, little boy blue, come look me up." Her hand ran down his crotch. "The name's Anita."

If he stayed near her any longer, the hunger was going to take control of him and drag her into the nearest alley. "Anita," he echoed, and hurriedly moved away.

Distance helped push hunger back in its cage. A passing couple helped more. The reek of garlic from what had to be their recent Italian meal snapped around his throat like a noose. Garreth did not collapse or choke enough to attract attention, but he leaned against a light pole for support while he fought for breath. By the time air moved freely through his lungs again, hunger had vanished in the profound pleasure of breathing.

He resumed asking about Irina. Questions to several more hookers and a number of barkers through the area all brought negative replies, however. No one remembered a woman of that description.

A glance at his watch showed fifteen minutes until the bars closed. Smoothing his mustache, he frowned thoughtfully down the street and debated whether to try a few more questions or pack it in for the night and head for the piers.

The debate broke off as he felt eyes on him. Garreth turned to find a tall, lean young man in an Italian-cut suit glaring furiously. In one sweeping glance Garreth took in the carefully blow-dried hair, the silk shirt open halfway down the chest, and the bulging crotch of the tight trousers.

Garreth folded his arms. "What's your problem, cowboy?"

"You, Jack," the hustler snapped. "You're trespassing." His eyes flared red with the reflection of passing car lights.

Shock jolted Garreth. He sucked in his breath. A taste of the incoming air told him no scent of blood came from the other man, either. "You—you're another."

The hustler closed on him. "Right, and this is my territory, Jack. There's plenty of game here for everyone but you find some other block and fucking well stay there." Grabbing the front of Garreth's jacket and shirt, he jerked him almost off the ground. "Or I'll be forced to hurt you."

Any police officer learned to tolerate verbal abuse, but manhandling was another matter entirely. Garreth reacted without even thinking. A knee drove hard into the hustler's groin.

The man dropped into a groaning knot of pain on the sidewalk.

"Don't touch me," Garreth snapped. "Don't you *ever* touch me again, or *you'll* be the one hurt!"

People had stopped and were staring. Barkers for a couple of the clubs started forward.

Garreth whipped out his badge case for a quick flash at them. "Thanks, gentlemen, but I have it under control." He dragged the hustler to his feet and down the sidewalk. "Walk. We have things to talk about."

"We've got nothing to talk about." The hustler pulled loose from him and leaned against a building, grimacing. "I don't care if you are a cop, this is still my territory."

"I'm not after your fucking territory! Look, all I want is information."

"Information?" The hustler blinked, then frowned skeptically. "What kind of information?"

"On a woman ... one of us. Small, dark hair, violet eyes. Eastern European accent. Have you seen or talked to her?"

"I don't think so, but then," —the hustler grimaced wryly—"I don't move in exactly the same circles as some others of the blood around here."

The hair on Garreth's neck prickled. "Others? What circles?"

The hustler snorted. "Jesus. Where've you been living, Jack?" Then his eyes narrowed, a sly light glittering in them. "Say, maybe—"

"Ricky! Hey, Ricky," a female voice called. "Come on. I've got us a three—"

The voice stopped short. Garreth looked around and raised brows at a blond hooker behind him.

She stared back, eyes hard, then focused past him on the hustler, voice going casual. "A friend wants to buy the two of us a drink, Ricky ... if you're interested."

After a hesitant glance at Garreth, the hustler said, "Sure I'm interested." He ducked around Garreth to follow her to a Continental at the curb. A man sat behind the wheel. As he climbed into the car, the hustler called over his shoulder, "I think maybe I can help you, Jack. Meet me back here in two hours and we'll discuss it."

13

Hunting quickly used up the two hours. Once he recaptured the skill he had had to learn to hunt, Garreth slipped like a shadow through the darkness of the covered piers, using his hypnotic power on rats so he could pick them up to break their necks and slit their throats with a switch blade. It took only minutes to decide that he liked hunting around Baumen better. There he had the exhiliration of the run to and from the pastures, often with a curious coyote for escort, and blood from one cow would fill the thermos without harm to the animal, compared to the dozen or more rats that had to die here. The strain of keeping alert for sounds indicating possible discovery added no pleasure to the hunt, either.

Still, it was blood, and with both stomach and thermos filled, he drove up to meet Ricky. The vampire was not there. Garreth waited, sure the hustler would show up sooner or later. The tone of his words made it clear that the discussion he had in mind was to fix a price on his information, and vermin like Ricky never wasted opportunities for making a buck.

After an hour Ricky had still not appeared, however, and Garreth gave up. The three-way trick with the hooker and her john must have proven more profitable than selling information to a cop. Driving back to Harry's house, he slid inside, stowed the thermos in the refrigerator, and slipped upstairs to fall into bed.

14

Pounding on the door and the sound of Lien calling his name dragged him back to consciousness. "Garreth? Garreth, we're leaving for work. Sleep in as long as you like, then help yourself to whatever you want for breakfast. I've left a message for you from *I Ching* on the kitchen table. Be sure to read it. We'll see you later."

So she still consulted the Sage every morning to see what the day held for Harry, and today, for him. "Okay. Thanks," he mumbled.

Sleep in as long as he liked. He would. Sometime he had to see Holle, but afternoon would be soon enough. Late afternoon.

The thought trailed away as he sank back into sleep.

Sleep, not rest. He dreamed of stalking the hustler up Broadway. As he tried to catch the other vampire, however, he felt someone watching him. Lane? The spicy musk of her perfume curled out of the blood scents around him. He swore bitterly. Would her shadow never stop following him? Every time he turned around, he glimpsed her tall, red-haired figure, but when he pursued her, she became a small woman with violet eyes who vanished among the crowd before he could see her face.

Lane's voice remained, though. It called to him from every shadow. *"Garreth. Lover. Come to me. Come to me, Mik-san."*

Mik-san?

In the dream he pounded his fist against a wall. Shit. That had to be a real voice calling him, not Lane's. Cursing wearily, he clawed his way back toward consciousness.

"Mik-san." The doorknob rattled in a futile attempt to open the door. A fist pounded. "It's Harry. Wake up, damn it!"

Maybe Dracula knew what he was doing sleeping in a crypt deep under the castle. From there no doorbell could disturb him, no matter how long and hard friends and salesmen from the daylight world leaned on it. Without opening his eyes, Garreth called through gritted teeth, "I have a loaded gun, Harry. In five seconds I am going to fire it through the door at whoever is stupid enough to be standing there."

"At last. I thought maybe you'd died in there, Mik-san."

The man not only woke him, but had the unmitigated gall to sound *cheerful*! "I'm not kidding, Harry."

"I'm not either, I'm afraid. You have to get up. It's important. Besides, this isn't the middle of the morning; it's three-fifteen in the afternoon."

Three— Garreth pried open his eyes, only to squeeze them shut again in pain. Sunlight flooded around and through the thin window shades. Struggling out of bed, he groped blindly for his sport coat hanging on the closet door and fished his glasses out of the breast pocket. With them on, he stumbled over to unlock and open the door.

In the hall, Harry wore a grimly unhappy expression.

A chill slid down Garreth's spine. "What's wrong?"

Harry grimaced. "You're sure a hard man to wake up. When no one answered the phone, we thought you'd gotten up and gone out. Then the black-and-white spotted your car still here, so they tried knocking on the door. Without any response. So Serruto asked me to drive home and see if you were inside."

The cold in Garreth's spine deepened. "Why, Harry?" And why did he have this sudden vision of violet eyes peering out of the shadows at him?

Harry rubbed at a flaw on the paint of the doorjam. "What do you know about a guy named Richard Maruska?"

Garreth frowned. "I've never heard of him. Who is he?"

Harry sighed. "A male prostitute. Faye and Centrello's new case. Some people they've talked to say they heard a guy threaten him last night up in North Beach, a guy who claimed to be a cop and who fits your description, Mik-san."

Murder,
Murder

1

Harry pushed open the door of the squad room. "Here he is. Now let's get this nonsense cleared up."

Heads swiveled in their direction. Fowler, standing by Faye's desk with his wrists cuffed behind his back and a pick in one hand, broke off in the middle of an apparent handcuff-escape demonstration for Faye, Centrello, and Girimonte, his brows arching expectantly.

From the doorway of his office, Serruto pointed at the glassed-in interview room in the opposite corner, and said, "Not you," to Fowler.

Fowler shrugged and went on working at the lock of the cuffs.

The detectives, the lieutenant, and Garreth filed into the interview room.

Blood scents quickly filled the confined space, washing warm and salty over Garreth, drowning him. He bit the inside of his cheek, but the pain did not provide enough distraction. He remembered how he crouched over the girl at the accident again, rain pouring over him and the taste of her blood sweet liquid fire in his mouth. Longing seared his throat.

Think about something else, man. Think about the hustler. How can he possibly be dead? A vision of a sharp wooden stake flashed in Garreth's mind. He twitched away from it. Harry would surely have mentioned something that bizarre.

"You call this nonsense, Takananda?" Serruto asked.

The blood smells still surged around him. Garreth felt sweat break out under his mustache. He fought the impulse to grab a chair and throw it through a window to flood the room with fresh air. Except that would let in more light, too. The weight of day dragged enough at him already.

Harry frowned from the lieutenant to Faye, Centrello, and Girimonte. "I told you before—he was sound asleep at my place all night."

Serruto sat down on a corner of the table in the middle of the room. "And what do you say, Mikaelian?"

Garreth forced himself to focus on the lieutenant. There was no point in trying to deny he had been in North Beach. Faye and Centrello's witnesses had to be the barkers who saw his scuffle with the hustler; they would make him in a second in a lineup. He had shown them his ID, for God's sake. No, what he had to do was concoct a reasonable excuse for being there.

If he could only think ... but his mind spun uselessly. All he could think about was the blood smells around him and the taste of that girl's blood.

Serruto folded his arms. "Well, Mikaelian?"

Fowler paced the squad room outside, free of the cuffs and obviously eaten by curiosity. Those inside the room stared hard at Garreth. Harry had growing concern creasing his forehead.

Think, man. Think, Garreth snarled at himself. *At least buy yourself some time for it.* "Yes, I decked that hustler." He sent Harry an apologetic smile. "Sorry."

The betrayal in Harry's eyes went through Garreth's gut like a knife. "But—how—"

"How did I happen to be up there?" *Okay, now lie your heart out. Mikaelian.* "I've worked nights for a year and a half, Harry. After a couple of hours I woke up and couldn't go back to sleep. I went downstairs to read but couldn't concentrate on that, either. So I went for a drive and ended up in North Beach." He glanced at Faye and Centrello. "How did just a physical description and a claim of being a cop make you think of me?"

"The guy showed the witnesses a police ID, but the badge was an oval shield, not a star," Centrello said. "How many visiting cops can we have who look and dress like you?" He pointed at Garreth's yellow turtleneck and tan corduroy jacket.

"Tell us about the hustler," Serruto said. Steel edged the words.

That helped him forget about the blood scents. Fast. Garreth made himself shrug while cold crawled through him. "There's nothing much to tell. I was just up there walking around and he grabbed me. I kneed him without thinking. What would you have done?"

They said nothing but agreement flashed in every pair of eyes. None of them would have tolerated manhandling, either.

"After I picked him up it turned out he'd mistaken me for someone else. Then a blond hooker came along and he got into a car with her and another guy—a late-model Continental with California plates. I didn't catch all of the license number. Two-two-something with the last letters UW or VW. Didn't the barkers tell you about that?"

"Yeah," Faye said. "They also said Maruska called something about being able to help you and meeting you in two hours."

"Help you with what, Mikaelian?" Serruto asked.

More steel. He gave the lieutenant a tight smile. "I don't understand why you're so interested in me. He didn't keep the appointment. I never saw him again. How did he die? Did his little three-way with the hooker and her john go bad?"

Serruto repeated evenly, "We'd like to know what he was going to help you with."

The only plausible lie that came to mind was one that Serruto would not like. Garreth used it anyway. "Lane Barber. The hustler thought he might have some information on her."

The lieutenant's mouth set in a grim line. "Mikaelian, I warned you about—"

"I'm not tracking her on my own! I swear. I just stumbled across this possibility while I was talking to the hustler. If it had panned out, I would have told Harry, just like I told him about Holle. So." Garreth made his voice casual. "How and where did the guy die?"

"Not in the middle of the three-way," Centrello said. "The barkers gave us the hooker's name and we've talked to her. She swears Ricky left her and headed back to meet you. His roommate came home this morning and found him in the bathtub. His throat had been slashed and his neck broken. Coroner says he died between three and six."

The nervous system destroyed. Of course. That was the only permanent death. But how did the killer manage it? No human could overpower a vampire at night.

Maybe no human had. Violet eyes floated in the shadows of Garreth's mind.

"Where's the gray turtleneck you wore yesterday?" Serruto asked.

"At the house." Grimy with dust from the piers, but at least not splashed with blood, not even rat blood. He had been very careful about that. The knowledge did not stop the chill of fear biting into him. "Hey, you don't seriously think I had anything to do with it."

They all glanced at each other. Girimonte's eyes narrowed speculatively. Harry looked down. Serruto said, "At the moment, Mikaelian, you're all we've got."

Adrenalin surged through Garreth, icy hot. Could he really mean that? "This is crazy. It's a case with more holes than Swiss cheese and you know it! I was never near the hustler's apartment, wherever it is, and you won't find anyone who's seen me there."

Centrello sighed. "Unfortunately no one we talked to in the building saw *anyone*. At that time of night they were all asleep."

"Then check my prints against the ones the lab—" Schneider rapped on the door. "Harry, phone call for you. A Mr. Leonard Holle. He sounds excited." Harry left to take it. Two minutes later he was back at a run with Fowler right behind him. "Barber's turned up! Holle went to check the apartment this afternoon and it's been cleaned out! He's waiting there for us."

A chorus of indrawn breath rolled around the interview room. Relieved breath, Garreth noted with relief of his own.

Harry smirked. "So we have someone else after all. Barber could have been in North Beach last night and heard Garreth's conversation with Maruska, then killed him to keep him quiet."

"Slitting his throat and breaking his neck are rather her style, aren't they?" Fowler asked. His eyes glittered.

Garreth bit his lip in dismay. Lord, what had he done? Screwed up royally. The department would be wasting its time and manpower hunting the wrong person.

On the other hand, did he really want them finding Irina?

Serruto scowled at Fowler. "It could be Barber." He glanced at Harry. "I expect if it *is* Barber, you're going to want a piece of this hustler case. Faye, Centrello, do you have any objections to giving it all to him?"

The two exchanged glances, then, grinning, shook their heads. Girimonte rolled her eyes and used a short, very unladylike word.

Serruto's mouth twitched at the corner. "Sorry, Girimonte. Okay, Takananda, you have it, but keep a tight leash on your ride-alongs, both of them."

2

Violet eyes. Irina. Garreth chewed his lower lip. If Lane were alive, she would have had an excuse for killing the hustler, but what could Irina's motive be? Why would *she* be so desperate to keep her where-abouts a secret? Could it relate to that mysterious matter mentioned but not discussed in her note to Lane? He frowned at Holle's back on the apartment hall stairs ahead of Harry and Girimonte. The man reeked of cologne today, too. Girimonte and Fowler grimaced at the heavily spiced air sinking back down the stairs around them, but Garreth welcomed its masking of blood scents; it let him concentrate on thinking. He had to talk to Holle. If only he could get the man alone.

"This is a surprise to you?" Harry asked.

"Absolutely, Sergeant," Holle said. "The mailbox hadn't been opened. I took one of those letters addressed to 'occupant' out of it before coming upstairs. Then when I opened the door ..." He unlocked the door and swung it open. "See for yourself."

Garreth let the others go first and watched from the doorway while the others stared around.

"There's still furniture," Fowler said. He sounded disap-pointed.

Harry nodded in satisfaction, however. "But no books or pictures or other personal belongings." He peered into the kitchen. "No dishes or pans, either. It's just the way she decamped from the Telegraph Hill apartment."

Girimonte frowned. "Do you suppose it's worth calling the lab boys to see if she left prints this time?"

Harry snorted. "Fat chance. With our luck with her, all we'd find would be the Bieber woman's prints again."

Shit. Garreth groaned inwardly.

Fowler's brows rose. "Ah, yes ... the mystery woman in the case, even more elusive than your Miss Barber. Have you found any trace of her? I didn't see mention of it in the case file."

Harry grimaced. "None. It's like all that exists of her is fingerprints and that old arrest record."

"Peculiar, isn't it?" With a final twitch of brow at Garreth, Fowler turned away to run a finger along the edge of a bookshelf.

Garreth blinked. What the hell kind of game was the writer playing? He had read the file and seen Mada's name, yet obviously intended to say nothing of what he knew about Madelaine Bieber of Baumen, Kansas. Why? "Mr. Fowler, will you step—"

"I wonder what made Barber bolt," Girimonte said. She looked straight at Garreth. "How could she know that we knew about her new apartment? You didn't happen to mention it to that hustler, did you, Mikaelian?"

He frowned back. "Of course not."

Harry sighed. "Well, I don't see any point in hanging around here any longer. I'm not sure what good having the lab go over the place would be, even if Barber did leave prints. It'd only tell us she's been here. But keep it locked and don't disturb anything please, Mr. Holle. We might change our minds later."

"As you wish, Sergeant."

They locked up and left the house. Holle's car sat parked in a space near the bottom of the block. He left the group to head down for it.

"Excuse me," Garreth said. "I'll be right back." He hurried after Holle. This was his chance at the man. Falling into step with him, Garreth said, "I have one question ... about Irina Rodek."

Holle's start of dismay sent triumph through Garreth. *Gotcha!*

A moment later, however, a mask slammed across the man's face. "I beg your pardon. Who?"

Holle wanted to play games? Garreth hissed inwardly in annoyance and cursed the glare of sunlight that kept him from pulling off his glasses and ending the nonsense by trapping Holle's gaze and using his hypnotic power on the man.

Very well, they would play it out straight. He let himself sigh. "Mr. Holle, you know very well that Irina Rodek wrote the note you left in Lane's apartment."

Holle started. "How could you get in—" He bit off the sentence.

To keep from revealing that he had recognized what Garreth was and that he knew Garreth should not have been able to enter the apartment? Garreth gave him a thin smile. "Get inside to see the note? I'm not barred from this apartment. Is Irina staying with you?"

Holle fought his face back into composure. He arched a brow. "Why should you think that?"

"I can't imagine that you and your housekeeper pour on the perfume because you like it. Isn't it to mask your blood scent for the comfort of guests such as Irina?"

The acid odor of nervous sweat cut through the spicy sweetness of Holle's cologne, but his voice went icy. "Officer—Mikaelian, isn't it?—you are obviously a man with a serious psychological problem. And since you have no authority to be questioning me, this conversation is finished." He spun away.

Garreth walked back up to the others. When he reached them, Harry said, "It looked like you hit a nerve. What did you say to him?"

Garreth shrugged. "Nothing really, just that I hope he isn't hiding anything because cops take it personally when other cops are attacked as Lane attacked me." This evening he would make some excuse to get out of the house and slip over for a look at Holle's while there was a chance Irina or traces of her still might be there.

"It took you a rather long time to say it," Fowler remarked.

Girimonte's eyes narrowed. "Yes, didn't it?"

Harry glanced at his wristwatch. "Lord, look at the time. We'd better get back to the office and do the day's reports. We don't dare be late tonight."

"Oh, yes. The party," Girimonte said, then grimaced. "Damn. I'm sorry, Harry."

Garreth started. "Party?"

Harry sighed. "It was supposed to be a surprise. We've invited most of Homicide and some of your other old friends in the department over for a little buffet tonight in your honor."

"Party. I don't know what to say." Yes he did: *shit*. A cop party. There went his chance to go out for the evening. He would be lucky if it shut down before dawn.

Harry smiled at Fowler. "Why don't you come, too. I promise you'll hear all the war stories you can ever hope for."

Fowler beamed. "That would be lovely, Sergeant. Thank you very much."

"Just lovely," Garreth echoed.

3

As he anticipated, between all the conversations and the liberal intake of liquor, the party's noise level rose steadily toward deafening. Lien nonetheless moved through the crowded dining and family rooms with the smiling serenity of the perfect hostess, a state of mind no doubt helped by the removal of everything remotely breakable from the rooms and a warning posted on the stairs that any intruders upstairs would be summarily shot. Fowler, too, was obviously enjoying himself, all smiles, eyes missing nothing. Garreth could imagine a recorder whirling in the writer's head: making notes on dress and behavior, following Del Roth's drunken efforts to convince Corey Yonning's wife of the therapeutic value of adultery, capturing details of family and department gossip, hearing a debate on the Giants' chances at the pennant and World Series this year, and the war stories Harry had promised.

His own face ached with the effort of smiling. He hated himself for it. All these people had been his good friends. He should be as delighted to see them as they were to see him. Between the relief of darkness and the smells of food, liquor, and tobacco smoke overpowering the guests' blood scents, he felt physically comfortable. Yet he longed for everyone to leave so he could slip away to visit Holle's house.

You know you're widening the gap, don't you? You're throwing matches at the bridge.

The note Lien gave him as they came home burned in his trouser pocket, too.

"You forgot to pick up the message from *I Ching* when you left earlier," she had said, handing him the sheet of memo paper.

One glance at the note knotted his gut. Hexagram forty-four, Coming To Meet. He did not have to look at the text Lien had jotted under the heading. He knew it by heart. Coming To Meet had been the hexagram she threw for him a few days before he first met Lane Barber. *The maiden is powerful. One should not marry such a maiden.* Meaning that he should not underestimate that which looked helpless and innocent. He had, of course. He consistently underestimated Lane. The mistake had destroyed and almost killed him. But there would be no such carelessness with Irina.

"What did you really say to Holle, Mikaelian?" a voice shouted at his elbow.

Garreth looked around at Vanessa Girimonte, who looked more pantherish than ever in a figure-hugging black jumpsuit. He sipped his glass of soda water. "I already told you."

"Bullshit." She pulled one of her long cigars from the jumpsuit's breast pocket and lit it. "Harry will believe anything you say because you're his old partner and a substitute for the son he never had. Everyone else in the squad wants to believe you, too, even Serruto. But you're nothing to me; I don't know you. I'm not sure I even like you. You pick your words like someone on the bomb squad handling a suspicious package."

The memo sheet crackled in his pocket. Garreth gave Girimonte a thin smile. Here was another woman he had better not underestimate. "That's an interesting comparison."

"It's even more interesting that you don't protest it." She puffed her cigar. "I wonder why you're really out here. Not to be in on Barber's capture. If you cared anything about her, you'd show some anger when we talk about her, or at least satisfaction at the leads on her. You're just cat-nerved twitchy, especially around Fowler. I don't suppose you'd care to tell me why."

He met her gaze steadily. "There's nothing to tell."

She smiled. "Maybe we'll see." Her gaze focused past him. "Hello, Mr. Fowler," she called. "Enjoying the party?"

Garreth made himself look around slowly.

The writer grinned. "It's marvelous. Tell me, though, are American parties always so loud?"

Girimonte dragged at her cigar. "Cop parties are."

"Yes, well ... it ought to make good color for the book. Speaking of which," Fowler said to Garreth, "I wonder if I might have a word with you."

Yes, they did need to talk. Garreth glanced at Girimonte, who eyed them speculatively. "Somewhere ... quieter." Somewhere private.

Fowler nodded. "Quite."

Garreth took him upstairs to the living room.

Fowler strolled over to the bay window and stood gazing out. "It's a lovely city. Simply lovely. I wonder how you could bear to leave it." After a few moments he turned. "Interesting coincidence, isn't it, your grandmother in Baumen having the same name as a woman here involved with the murderous Miss Barber?"

Garreth kicked off his shoes and sat down cross-legged on the couch. "Why didn't you mention it to Sergeant Takananda or Inspector Girimonte?"

Fowler came over to take the easy chair at right angles to the couch. "I thought I'd chat with you first. Seeing Mada's name in the case file makes sense of a lot of things that puzzled me before. See if I've got it right. There's only one Madelaine Bieber and she was never your grandmother. That's just a cover story. Somehow you tracked her down to Baumen. Since there's nothing in the case file, I'd say you stumbled across the lead after you resigned." He raised a questioning brow.

Garreth felt every cell of him freeze, waiting. "Go on."

"You settled in as Anna Bieber's great-grandson to wait for Mada, hoping that when she showed up again she would lead you to Barber ... who is what, her *real* grandchild?"

The sentence took a moment to sink in. When it did, it left Garreth weak with relief. Fowler had not stumbled onto the truth about Mada and Lane after all! *Thank you, Lady Luck!* Aloud he said, "A late born daughter, I think. They have to be closely related. The photograph in Mada's arrest record looks so much like Lane."

"Which explains the fingerprints in the apartment. Mada probably helped the girl move out. After all, no one on stakeout was expecting a middle-aged woman. It also explains Mada's disappearance. She wasn't kidnapped; she recognized you at her mother's house, and after she confirmed it talking to you, she bolted."

Garreth took up the lie happily. "Right. But I couldn't tell anyone because then it would come out that Mada was an accessory to murder and the mother of a murderess. I couldn't do that to Anna."

Fowler smiled. "She is rather an old dear." The smile faded into a thoughtful frown. "I wonder if both Mada and the girl are in some blood cult."

"Oh yes, I'm sure of it," Garreth said with a straight face.

The writer's eyes lighted. "You know, if you and I put our heads together, we might crack this case. Wouldn't *that* make an ending for the book?"

A hell of an ending. Garreth said, "I told you, I'm not interested in being in a book." He stood up and started for the door.

Behind him, Fowler said casually, "Blackmail is such an ugly word, but let me remind you, old son, you've withheld evidence in this case. I don't think your Lieutenant Serruto would approve of that."

Garreth spun back. "I can't go hunting Lane on my own. The lieutenant would have my head for that, too."

Fowler crossed his legs and smoothed the fabric of his trousers over the upper knee. "I'll settle for your cooperation then. You know, going over the case file with me, telling me what you felt and thought at various points."

Garreth ran a hand through his hair. Maybe working with the writer would be one way to control what he learned. "All right."

Fowler chuckled. "You don't have to sound like I'm an executioner. It isn't painful, becoming immortal. Really it isn't. I promise."

4

The party ended about three-thirty, after the second, somewhat apologetic, visit by a black-and-white. "Hey, Harry, we don't want to lean on you, but your neighbors are going to bitch about favoritism if we don't look like we're treating you the same as any other loud party. So turn it down, okay?"

Lien smiled at the officers and went into the family room to whisper something in Evelyn Kolb's ear. A few minutes later Kolb and her husband left with loud good-byes, and soon everyone else began drifting out, too. Garreth sighed inwardly in relief.

When the last guest had gone, Lien bolted and chained the front door and leaned against it, shaking her head. "Honorable husband, I think we're getting too old for this. Leave everything. Letty can deal with it when she comes in tomorrow morning. I hope you enjoyed yourself, Garreth."

"It was great fun seeing everyone again." He kissed her cheek. "Thank you both very much."

Upstairs, though, he scrambled into a sweat suit and running shoes and paced impatiently, waiting for Harry and Lien to settle down for the night. It seemed to take an eternity. Once he heard their bedroom door close, he bolted his on the inside and moved through it to glide silently downstairs to the refrigerator for the meal he had not been able to drink during the party. Then he slipped out through the locked front door.

Tonight he did not even consider driving. A man about to commit burglary needed an alibi. His bedroom door and the front door both locked from the inside and his car parked in the drive all night should make it appear that he could not have left.

He regretted having to leave the car, but not much. As his legs stretched and the street streamed backward beneath him, he gave himself over to the exhilaration of running. Forget where he was going and why. Forget burning bridges, the hustler, and violet eyes watching him from cold shadows. For the moment, nothing mattered but the sea-scented air filling his lungs and the power surging through his legs, giving him the heady feeling that he could run forever. He ran soundlessly through the empty residential streets, a shadow, a phantom.

Leaving the Sunset district, he crossed Golden Gate Park, then angled on north and east through Richmond into Pacific Heights. The houses lay dark and the streets deserted except for an occasional civilian car or patrolling black-and-white, which Garreth avoided by moving off the street into shadows by houses or parked cars while the unit passed.

No activity showed in Holle's house, either. Garreth watched it from the shadow of a doorway across the street for five minutes just to be sure. With a look both ways up the street, he strolled across and listened at the front door. Nothing moved inside.

Wrench.

The hall stretched out before him, twilight bright in his night vision, empty but not silent. The house creaked and groaned with the voices of old stone and aged wood. Beneath the lingering traces of cooking odors, Emeraude perfume, and Holle's cologne, it breathed out the scents of its existence, too: varnish, wood, smoke from the fireplace, lemon oil. Garreth glanced around, from the paneling and paintings to the stairs and soaring ceiling. Where did he start looking? Right here?

Still moving silent as a shadow, he walked through the living, dining, and breakfast rooms, and into the kitchen. None of those rooms had heavy drapes. In the kitchen, though, he eyed the refrigerator. The chances of finding anything significant in it were probably slim at best. With a whole city out there to draw on, vampire guests had no need to store up blood for an extra day or two. Obtaining extra from people was not quite like bleeding a cow, either. People noticed the loss of three or four pints at one time. Still ...

He opened the refrigerator.

Holle kept it well stocked for humans. He even kept a selection of chilled wine.

Garreth started to close the refrigerator, then stopped. He pulled the door open again to peer at the wine. Something looked odd about those bottles. After studying them for a minute, he realized why. Four of the eight had no seals. They had obviously been opened and recorked. But the recorked ones all stood in the rear.

Garreth reached back for one. Pulling it out, he blinked. A strip of red tape crossed the commercial label, lettered in black: RAW SEA WATER. DO NOT DRINK! Further examination found that the other three without seals had the same warning.

Odd. Garreth hefted the bottle. He could see someone keeping brine for marinating or cooking seafood, but why would anyone have four bottles of real sea water? There was no telling what pollutants it carried. No one could pay him to drink it! He shook the bottle.

The dark liquid inside moved sluggishly.

Garreth's neck and spine tingled. That was no sea water. He worked the cork free and sniffed at the opening.

The scent from it raised goose bumps all over his body. Human blood!

He stared down at the bottle, hunger searing him. Human blood, ready to drink without having to attack anyone. Hurriedly he returned it to the refrigerator and retreated from the kitchen. No. He could not afford to indulge his appetite.

On the second floor none of the rooms but the library had heavy drapes. At the rear of the house the scents of blood and Holle's cologne wafted around the edges of a locked door along with the sound of a sleeper's breathing. The room must be Holle's. The third floor, all bedrooms, had two occupied rooms at the front, neither locked. The sleepers in both smelled of blood. The next room stood empty. The two rear rooms by the service stairs, though, had been turned into an apartment for the housekeeper. The scent of Emeraude filled them, and the housekeeper herself slept soundly in the bedroom.

He climbed the service stairs to the top floor in the attic. The old servants' quarters there had apparently been turned into more guest rooms. The front ones were unoccupied. Two locked doors closed off storage rooms. Sliding through the doors, he found light from the street shining in the dormer windows to light stacked cardboard boxes and a jumble of old chairs, lamps, and some racks of clothing hanging in zippered plastic bags.

Two rooms at the back remained unchecked. He opened one door. Heavy drapes covered the dormer window. Quickly Garreth examined the bed. Earth filled the plastic mattress cover. The delicious relaxation he felt running his hand over it told him that even before the gritty shifting inside did.

Pay dirt. The room could be meant only to accommodate a vampire.

Only one room remained.

As he opened its door, Garreth froze with his hand on the knob. A spicy muskiness lingered in the air, a perfume he remembered only too well. It had curled around him with such inviting sweetness that Thanksgiving night on the island in Baumen's Pioneer Park.

He fought to breathe. No! Impossible. Lane could not have been here! Could she?

But what did he know ... really? Books with vampire lore could hardly be called authoritative. Beyond that, he had only personal experience and what Lane had told him. How could he trust what she said?

After a few minutes, panic ebbed, and as reason replaced it, it occurred to him that along with everything else Lane had learned from her mentor, Irina, she might also have adopted the other woman's perfume. What he smelled could be traces of Irina, not Lane.

His paralysis dissolved. Swiftly he examined the room. It had the same heavy drapes and earth-filled mattress cover the room next to it did. Both closet and dresser drawers had been cleaned out, but the spicy scent lingering in them, too, told him that they had been used recently. Perhaps as recently as today.

He closed the door and glided downstairs to the next floor, through the door of Holle's room. Sitting on the edge of the bed, Garreth shook the sleeping man's shoulder. "Wake up, Mr. Holle; we have things to talk about."

Holle woke with a start. "What—" He blinked, squinting up at what his dark-blind eyes must see as only a vague shadow beside him. "Who are you? How the hell did you get in—"

"I'm Garreth Mikaelian. So you know how I got in."

Holle sat up. "Then take yourself out the same way."

"Not until I know where to find Irina Rodek." Garreth switched on the bedside light. "Mr. Holle, look at me and tell me you don't know where she is."

Holle squeezed his eyes tightly shut. "I don't know."

"Look at me!"

"Sorry." Holle smiled faintly. "You're obviously young in the life. You don't have the power yet to command by voice alone."

"Someone around here has the power, though," Garreth said grimly. "Great power. Last night that someone killed a man named Richard Maruska. Maruska happened to be one of my kind."

Holle's eyelids flickered but remained closed. "*Killed* him?"

"Broke his neck. At night. How many humans could do that?" Garreth watched Holle lick his lips as the statement sank in, then added, "He was supposed to meet me to tell me how to find Irina."

Sweat beaded Holle's forehead. "Irina couldn't have killed him. She—" He broke off.

"She what?" Garreth prompted. "Tell me about her. And tell me about yourself. How long have you known vampires really exist? Do many humans know?"

But Holle only pressed his lips into a line and turned his head away.

"You're obstructing a murder investigation, Holle."

The man snorted. "Conducted in the middle of the night by an officer without authority who breaks into my house and bedroom? I wonder what Sergeant Takananda would think if he knew about it."

Cold chased down Garreth's spine. He came back, "Who's going to tell him? You? The man with bottles of a very unique and bizarre vintage in his refrigerator and earth mattresses on two of his guest beds? You can't risk close scrutiny any more than I can."

Holle licked his lips again. "Then we have reached an impasse."

"Not really. You say Irina can't be guilty. Fine. Let me talk to her and see for myself."

The stubborn set returned to Holle's jaw. "I told you before, I don't know where she is. She left and didn't say where she was going."

The experience from years of talking to reluctant subjects told Garreth that without more leverage, this was all he would pry out of Holle. He stood, sighing. "Okay. If you *happen* to remember something and care to confide it, in the interests of justice and public safety, you can reach me through Sergeant Takananda. Though it doesn't really matter. With or without your help, I'll find Irina."

The way to start, he decided on his way downstairs, was with a look at the murder scene. Maybe that would give him a lead. Even if he had free access to the case reports—doubtful under the circumstances—they might not help. For all the crime lab's competence, their examination could have overlooked something that had significance only to a vampire.

Holle's phone directory on the hall table listed a Richard Maruska with a Western Addition address. Not the best of addresses, Garreth noted, but there were worse, and it was close. He would have time to reach it and still be back at Harry's before dawn.

Footsteps whispered overhead.

Garreth froze. They came from the guest room. One of the guests heading for the bathroom to take a leak? No, he realized a moment later. The footsteps, so quiet that human hearing would not have detected them, were coming downstairs. The guest must have heard him!

Making sure he moved soundlessly this time, Garreth raced for the front door and slipped out through it with a sharp wrench. On the street he breathed more easily, but he lost no time breaking into a lope and heading south toward the Western Addition.

5

Between siding overdue for repainting and hallway stairs deeply worn in the center, the house had seen better days. The vertical row of mailboxes just inside the street door gave 301 as Richard Maruska's apartment. But it was the other name on the mailbox that startled Garreth: Count Dracula. A chill slid down his spine. How could the hustler be so— Then it hit him—oh, the roommate—and he remembered stories that officers on Vice told about a homosexual hustler who styled himself a vampire, coming out only at night, always dressing in formal evening clothes and an opera cape, affecting a Bela Lugosi accent. Climbing the worn stairs to the third floor, Garreth reflected that Ricky must have found the arrangement very amusing, a real vampire living with a counterfeit one. Did "Dracula" know or suspect the truth?

The door of 301 had a police seal across it. Fingering the broad strip of yellow tape with inner fire licking at him, Garreth swore softly. The whole place was sealed. That meant the roommate had to be staying somewhere else for the time being and could not invite him in.

He turned away. On the other hand, just talking to the room-mate might turn up something, and maybe he could work out some-thing for getting into the apartment. In the meantime, he decided, glancing at his watch, he had better head home.

6

Dragging himself out of bed into the press of daylight after little more than an hour of sleep was pure agony, but Garreth forced himself up. He had to ask Harry about the hustler's roommate before Girimonte was around to question his curiosity.

Harry looked to be in no condition for casual chitchat, though, when Garreth stumbled into the kitchen. He glanced up, winced in obvious pain, and buried his nose in his coffee cup again with a groan.

Lien set a plate of eggs and hash browns on the table. The smells from it curled up around Garreth. Harry groaned even louder.

Shaking her head, Lien slid the plate to her place. "I think honorable husband has quite a head on him this morning." She somehow managed to look as if she had had a full night's sleep. She smiled at Garreth. "What about you? Can you face food?"

"God, no. I'll just make myself some tea." He filled a cup from the kettle on the stove and dropped in a tea bag out of the canister on the cabinet next to it.

"Be sure to eat at noon."

"Yes, ma'am." The water turned straw colored. Garreth discarded the tea bag.

Lien pushed hash browns around the plate with her fork. "I threw a hexagram for you this morning. It was number sixty-four, Before Completion."

His gut tightened. Her tone indicated a less than favorable hexagram. Leaning against the cabinet, he sipped the tea. "Which is?"

"The text says there is success, but if the little fox gets his tail wet before completing a crossing of the river, nothing furthers. Which means that deliberation and caution are necessary for success."

He gave her a thin smile. "A good reminder for a cop. What did *I Ching* say about Harry?"

Her eyes danced. "Number twenty-three, Splitting Apart."

Despite the drag of daylight and the knots in his gut, Garreth had to bite his lip to keep from laughing aloud.

Then Lien went sober. "It does not further one to go anywhere. I wish you'd call in sick, Harry."

Harry sighed. "Half the squad will be feeling as bad or worse than I am this morning."

"Then at least be very careful."

He reached out for her hand and kissed it. "I always am."

Maybe now was the time to slip in a question. Garreth said casually, "Earl Faye is one who'll definitely be worse off than you are." He sipped his tea. "He was reaching a point last night when I didn't know whether to believe him or not. He tried to tell me that Maruska's roommate is Count Dracula."

Lien giggled. "Oh really?"

"Really," Harry said. "That's what the guy calls himself. When Faye and Centrello came back from the murder scene, they said there was even a coffin in his bedroom that he sleeps in."

Maybe living with this dude was a clever move on Ricky's part, Garreth mused. Next to the hamming of the counterfeit vampire, the hustler would have seemed normal. "I wonder if we ought to talk to him again, now that it looks like Lane is connected to the killing. It might give what he has to say a different slant."

Harry started to frown in thought, then abandoned the gesture with another wince of pain. "Maybe."

"Is he still at the apartment?"

"No. There's a temporary address for him in Centrello's notes. We'll look it up when we get to Bryant Street."

7

From the doorway of his office, Serruto eyed his inspectors sardonically. "Ah, the cast from *Dawn of the Dead*, I see. It must have been quite a bash, Takananda. Not without benefits, either. I see our hotshot author hasn't managed to make it in. Let's wish him a long, undisturbed rest while we grab our cups of strong black coffee and go to work." He strolled out to sit down on a desk in the middle of the room and read the list of cases that had come in overnight. In the middle of facts about a cab driver's knifing, he glanced up and broke off with a solicitous, "I'm not keeping you awake, am I, Bennigan?"

The offending detective opened his eyes with a start and dragged himself upright in his chair. "I was just concentrating on what you're saying, sir."

"Good. Then you and Roth can handle this knifing."

After reviewing and assigning the rest of the overnights, Serruto had each team give a brief update on their current cases.

A bright-eyed, rested-looking Girimonte reported for Harry and herself. "No breaks on the liquor store shooting yet, and no ID on the woman in Stow Lake. Which now looks like an accidental drowning. The autopsy found water in her lungs and a high level of alcohol in her blood. The autopsy on our hustler wasn't done until late yesterday afternoon so there's no official report yet, but I stopped by the morgue on my way up this morning and got some preliminary findings from the assistant M.E. who did the post."

Cold shot through Garreth. He had not thought about autopsies on vampires before. What internal differences were there? Any that might generate dangerous curiosity?

He waited tensely while the black woman pulled a notebook from the pocket of her suit jacket and flipped it open. "The victim died of a severed spinal cord. No surprises there. And the reason there wasn't much blood from the slashed throat was because it was cut after death."

"Which fits Barber's MO," Harry said.

Serruto raised a brow. "Not quite. Mossman and Adair died of blood loss, remember? *Both* the broken necks and cutting their throats and wrists came after death."

"Maruska wasn't bled out like the other victims, either," Girimonte said.

"She had a different reason for killing Maruska … self-preservation."

Girimonte sent a glance at Garreth. "We don't know that. There's no evidence definitely linking Barber to the murder."

Harry scowled. "We—"

"This is a briefing, not a debate," Serruto said shortly. "Go on, Inspector."

She glanced back at her notes "There isn't much else. The doc is excited about some internal anomalies, but he says they're unrelated to the cause of death. He found severe pulmonary edema and edema of the throat and nasal passages, which also doesn't appear to be connected to the cause of death but which he can't account for. That's it."

What anomalies? Garreth bit his lip. An unanswerable question at the moment. He had enough to worry about anyway with Girimonte sending suspicious glances at him and Harry frowning at her.

When Serruto dismissed them and returned to his office, Harry turned on Girimonte. "We have evidence that implicates Barber. And if we ask the roommate about red-haired women—"

"Excuse me," a hesitant voice interrupted. "A detective by the door said two of you are the detectives in charge of the case of a woman found in Stow Lake Sunday night?"

They all turned. A young brunette woman in a ski sweater and blue jeans stood twisting the strap of her shoulder bag.

"I'm Sergeant Takananda," Harry said. "This is Inspector Girimonte. Do you know something about the case?"

The young woman drew a deep breath. "I think I know who she is."

Girimonte pulled a chair over by Harry's desk. "Please sit down."

Across the room, the door from the hall opened and Julian Fowler came in. He looked as impeccably dressed and groomed as ever but the writer walked, Garreth noted, like a man carrying a bomb. Or wearing one?

Garreth left Harry and Girimonte with the brunette to meet the writer. "Good morning, Mr. Fowler."

Fowler leaned against a handy desk and closed his eyes. "I think not. Lord. Do American coppers really party like that all the time?"

"Oh, no," Garreth said solemnly. "Sometimes we get wild."

The pale eyes opened to glare at him. "Don't be cheeky. I wonder if your lieutenant would mind if I helped myself to a spot of coffee?"

"He isn't my lieutenant, so go ahead."

Fowler almost dropped the cup, though. Garreth took it away and poured the coffee for him. Harry and Girimonte left the squad room with the brunette, probably taking her to the morgue to identify the body.

They came back a short time later. The brunette had gone pale. Shaking, she sat down again. While Harry fed a report form into his typewriter, Girimonte stalked over to the coffee pot.

"Sometimes I wonder why we bother to protect the public. We ought to just sit back and let natural selection weed the stupidity from the population."

"What happened?" Garreth asked.

She grimaced. "A bunch of grad students from the U of San Francisco were drinking Sunday night. They thought it would be fun to go swimming. No one counted heads before or after, and it took until today, when the professor she works for started bitching because she wasn't there to teach a lab for him and grade some papers, for them to start wondering where she was and remember that there'd been 'something in the paper Monday about a dead woman in a lake.' Christ."

"Yes, but, well, it does clear the case, as you say, doesn't it?"

"Yeah. It clears the case." She carried the coffee back to the brunette.

In another ten minutes the statement was finished and the shaken citizen gone. Harry said, "Let's visit Count Dracula."

Fowler perked up. "I beg your pardon?"

Girimonte smiled thinly. "Our dead hustler's roommate. A weirdo. Perfect for your book."

Harry dug the case folder out of his desk and flipped through the reports in it. "Here's his temporary address: the Bay Vista Hotel."

Girimonte grimaced. "That fleabag."

"I dare say it isn't easy for a vampire to find accommodations," Fowler said.

Snickering, they headed for the door.

They had not been out of the parking lot five minutes, however, when a message came over the radio for Harry to phone Serruto. They stopped at the first public phone.

A grim-faced Harry came back to the car. "Van, forget Count
Dracula and head for Holle's place."

A cold trickle of foreboding moved down Garreths spine.
"What's up, Harry?"

"It's what's gone down." Harry slammed the car door closed.
"Holle's housekeeper just found him dead in bed ... his throat slashed
and his neck broken."

8

From the doorway, Holle appeared to be merely asleep, lying on his
back in bed, the blankets pulled up to his chin. To Garreth, however,
the reek of blood, stagnant and clotting in death, pervaded the room,
and on second glance, peering over Harry's shoulder, the pillow
showed red stains.

Fowler craned his neck to see over Girimonte. "That isn't
much blood for a slashed throat. It ought to be everywhere."

"Not if the killer drained Holle dry first, or used the knife after
the victim was dead," Harry said. He turned toward the housekeeper
hovering tearfully in the hall where she could not see into the bedroom.
"Ms. Edlitza, I can understand you coming up to check on him when he
slept so much later than usual, and going in and realizing he wasn't breathing, but why are you so sure his neck is broken and his throat cut?"

She choked out: "I saw the bloodstain, and—" Her voice broke.
"And I looked under the covers."

Harry exchanged quick glances with Girimonte. "Only one of
us better go in. I'll do it. Ms. Edlitza," he suggested gently, "why don't
you go join the others in the library now?" When she had gone, he
crossed to the bed and lifted one side of the blankets.

"Good god," Fowler whispered.

Garreth swallowed.

Under the blankets, Holle's body lay face down. A wound gaped
in the throat, pulled into a spiral by the near one-eighty twist of the
neck.

"Arguing with you is becoming fatal, Mikaelian," Girimonte
said. "You didn't happen to be restless and out driving after the party
last night, did you?"

Anger flared at the acid edge on her voice. "I was home sleeping it off like everyone." Beneath the anger, however, consternation churned in him. Irina. It had to be Irina doing this, logic said, though why she could be so desperate to cover her tracks he still had no idea. *Lane*, his gut insisted. *She has the motive, Mikaelian.* But how could it possibly be Lane?

His only answer was her laughter echoing in his head.

Harry dropped the blankets back into place. "Van—" he began sharply, only to glance at Fowler and break off. Torn between loyalty to his old partner and the desire to avoid arguing with the new one in front of an outsider?

That, too, Garreth reflected, but something else also showed in the almond eyes, something new that tightened his throat ... uncertainty. In his head, he watched the fires on the bridge blaze higher.

The doorbell rang downstairs. Over the hall railing, Garreth saw one of the uniformed officers from the black-and-white responding to the initial call open the door. The team from the crime lab trooped in with its equipment.

"Up here, Yoshino," Harry called down. "If you need us, send a uniform to the library. Where we'll be listening to what our witnesses have to say before we make accusations, right, partner?" he said to Girimonte, and headed up the hall toward the front of the house.

Today the library looked incongruously cheerful. Someone had opened the drapes and light flooded the room. Three guests waited with the housekeeper: an attractive dark-haired woman and a young couple who looked pasty-pale under their tans and sun-streaked hair.

Garreth moved around the walls to stand by the fireplace, as far from the windows as possible.

Harry slid the doors closed. "Thank you for waiting. I'm Sergeant Takananda. This is Inspector Girimonte, Officer Mikaelian, and Mr. Fowler. Mr. Fowler is a writer riding along with us to do research for a book. Does anyone have objections to talking with him present?"

After a quick glance at each other, the guests and housekeeper shook their heads.

Harry smiled. "Then shall we begin? You are?" He pointed first at the dark-haired woman, then the couple.

"Susan McCaul. That's spelled M-C-C-A-*U*-L."

"Alan and Heather Osner," the man said.

"You're all guests and were sleeping in the house last night?"

They nodded.

"When did you last see Mr. Holle?"

"As everyone was leaving for the ballet," the housekeeper said. She fished a sodden tissue out of her dress pocket and mopped at a new flood of tears.

McCaul bit her lip. "We all got back about one-thirty. He bolted the front door and was headed in the direction of the kitchen when I went upstairs to my room."

Osner nodded. "He said he was going to check the rear door and turn on the security system."

"I heard him coming up the back stairs a little later," Osner's wife said.

"Did anyone see or talk to him after that?" Girimonte asked.

They shook their heads.

Harry said, "What sounds did you hear later on in the night? We need to know all of them, even something you might think is insignificant."

"I didn't hear anything," McCaul said. "I went to bed and d—" She broke off, throat working, then a breath or two later, stumbled on in a strained voice: "I went straight to sleep. The next thing I heard was—was Ms. Edlitza screaming."

"Me, too," Mrs. Osner said.

Her husband nodded. "I slept straight through."

The hair raised on Garreth's neck. "None of you woke up? Not for any reason? No one made a middle-of-the-night trip to the bathroom?"

"No." They shook their heads.

Then unless one of them was lying or walked in his sleep, the footsteps Garreth heard had to belong to the killer. They sounded again in his head, a stealthy whisper on the stairs from the third floor. God. He had fled from them and left Holle alone to die.

"Ms. Edlitza," Girimonte asked the housekeeper, "were all the doors still bolted this morning?"

The housekeeper nodded.

"What about the security system?"

"On and functioning."

"But someone got in past everything." Garreth raised a brow at Harry. "Maybe we ought to find out how."

Girimonte snapped her notebook shut. "I'll check the ground floor."

"And I'll take this one," Harry said. He recorded the home addresses of the three guests, then smiled politely at them and the housekeeper. "Thank you all very much for your cooperation. That should be it for now, except I do ask that you please keep out of the areas our officers and crime lab have marked off until we've finished examining them for evidence."

Garreth caught the housekeeper's eye. "I'll check the upper floors, if Ms. Edlitza will be kind enough to guide me."

Girimonte stopped in midstride heading for the library door and turned, frowning. Harry hesitated visibly, too, but said, "All right."

The housekeeper followed them into the hall. As they reached the stairs, however, Fowler started up after her and Garreth.

Garreth waved him away. *Go with the others*, he mouthed.

Fowler's brows rose, but after a moment, he turned and trotted downstairs after Girimonte.

Garreth and the housekeeper continued on to the attic alone, where he began checking windows, starting with those in the rear bedroom. He pulled aside the heavy drapes. The window was firmly latched.

Outside, the sun no longer shone so brightly, he noted with relief. Clouds had begun rolling in from the west to darken the sky. It would be raining by noon.

He dropped the drapes back in place. "Where did Irina go?"

The housekeeper started. "Who?"

Garreth sighed. "Don't you play that game with me, too. This was her room. It still smells of her perfume." He pulled off his glasses. "When did she leave and where's she gone?"

She hissed and spun away. "Don't you try that with me! The agreement is that your kind will respect the rules of hospitality in this house. You take no advantage and touch no one."

So she, too, recognized him for what he was. "Then talk to me."

She glanced around cautiously, eyes narrow. "What do you want with Miss Rudenko?"

Rudenko! So that was the name Irina used now. He put the glasses back on. "I couldn't very well mention it in front of the other officers but we know she can easily come in and leave without disturbing either the alarms or door bolts."

The housekeeper turned on him scornfully. "That's ridiculous! Mr. Holle and Miss Rudenko are—" Her eyes filled. She groped in her pocket for another tissue and wiped her eyes. "They were friends."

Friends? With a vampire? Knowingly? Garreth wished he had time to pursue the question. "Friends fight and fall out. Irina left very suddenly, didn't she?"

The lady did not shake easily. Give her that. "It had nothing to do with any disagreement." She blew her nose. "Shouldn't you be checking the other windows in case you're wrong about who came in last night?"

Exasperation hissed through Garreth. What hold did Irina have that kept these people so closemouthed? Promises of immortality, like Dracula gave the wretched Renfield? He smiled thinly. "Maybe you should start thinking up explanations to give Sergeant Takananda about why you keep bottles of human blood in your refrigerator and where it comes from." Where *did* it come from?

Not even that rattled her. She just sniffed. "Blackmail? You're wasting the effort. I really don't know where Miss Rudenko is."

Her voice carried a ring of truth. Garreth sighed and headed for the door. "Let's check the other windows."

Those in the bedrooms were all secure with no signs of tampering. As expected.

"There are two storage rooms," the housekeeper said. "Shall I unlock them?"

A quick vision of finding footprints in the dust and having the crime lab identify them as his flashed through Garreth's head. He eyed the dead bolt on each door. "Do they unlock from the inside?"

"No."

"Then I think we can skip those windows. No one could get out into the rest of the house except … someone like me."

Not quite true, but if he mentioned someone would open the doors from the inside by pulling the hinge pins, she might insist on examing the store rooms. He headed down the stairs to the third floor.

The windows on that floor were all locked, too, including those in the housekeeper's rooms. Ms. Edlitza kept a cross above her bed, the Eastern Orthodox type with a double crossbar.

Garreth raised his brows. "Insurance?"

Her mouth thinned. "No, religion. Insurance would be an atomizer full of garlic juice."

Mace, vampire style. Just the thought of the scent left Garreth feeling suffocated.

A whoop went up in the hall. He and the housekeeper raced out to find Fowler at a window by the back stairs. "It's unlocked!"

Harry and Girimonte came pounding up from the second floor.

Fowler used a pen to push open the window and leaned out without touching anything. "There's nothing but wall below, though. You'd need bloody wings to reach it."

Girimonte looked out the window, too. "No, I'd say he let himself down from the roof. Standard technique. Isn't that what you learned in Burglary, Mikaelian?"

If anyone had actually come in the window. Garreth was willing to bet that Irina opened it from the inside to satisfy human investigators with an obvious entry point for an intruder.

Harry said, "We'd better get someone up here to dust for prints."

The housekeeper squeezed past them down the back stairs. "How reassuring to know we're not dealing with someone who walks through bolted doors. I think I'll make myself some tea."

The rest of them headed down the front stairs.

In Holle's room Bill Yoshino nodded at Harry's request for a technician. "Sure thing. Linda," he called to one of the team brushing fingerprint powder on the faucet handles in the adjacent bathroom, "you go when you're finished there. Glad you've come, Harry. I was about to send a uniform for you. We have a couple of things that ought to interest you."

The smells of living blood overlaid that of death, though not enough to mask it completely. The combination sent a small wave of nausea through Garreth.

An assistant M.E., an Hispanic woman, leaned over the body on the bed. She looked around as everyone trooped in. "Good morning, Sergeant Takananda. Gruesome. Is this one tied to that midnight cowboy Mitch Welton posted yesterday? The injuries look alike."

"The two could be related."

"Then maybe this one is a Martian, too. That will—"

Harry started. "Martian?"

The assistant M.E. grinned. "That's Dr. Thurlow's name for people with the certain anomalies. Mitch was all excited about the ones he found in his stiff. He was going to write it up for journal publication. Then Dr. Thurlow said there've been three others like him in the past ten years."

"What anomalies?" Fowler asked.

Head them off at the pass, man. "Harry, look," Garreth said. He touched a vertical cut above Holle's left eye. "Did he do it or did the killer hit him?"

"I'm more curious about the time of death," Girimonte said.

The assistant M.E. shrugged. "He hasn't been dead more than a few hours. The body's still warm and there's no rigor except in his jaw and neck."

"It happened after the party folded, then." Girimonte raised a brow at Garreth.

Harry's forehead furrowed. He turned toward Yoshino. "You wanted to show me something?"

"Yeah." Yoshino pointed at Holle's arms. "Look at his wrists, first off."

A narrow, abraided groove circled each. Garreth bit his lip. At some point Holle had been tied tightly with something thin, like drapery cord, and struggled desperately against his bonds.

"Look at this, too." Yoshino pointed at the hair coming down over Holle's forehead. It lay in clumped points. "It's been wet. The pillow under him is still damp."

Harry felt the pillow. "What else?"

"In the bathroom." Yoshino led the way through the connecting door into a bathroom the size of a small ballroom, lushly carpeted in blue shag that covered even the steps around two sides of the sunken tub. "We've got more water in here ... a soggy rug in front of the washbowl, and marks where splashes on the counter and mirror have dried."

Harry knelt down to feel the carpet. "He didn't do this brushing his teeth."

"Uh-uh. We also collected skin and blood off the edge of the faucet. I'd say that's where your dead man cut his forehead."

"Christ," Fowler whispered down at Garreth. "*Shadow Games.*"

Harry snapped around. "What?"

Fowler grimaced sheepishly. "One of my books. There's a point in it where the protagonist Charlie Quayle needs information from one of the villain's henchmen he's captured. He gets it by filling up the washbowl in his hotel room and dunking the henchman until he's almost drowned."

And that had happened to Holle. Anger flared in Garreth. It was so pointless. Why resort to torture when a little hypnotic persuasion would make Holle answer any question Irina asked? Or did she have to use force because Holle, like the housekeeper, knew how to resist? Garreth felt sick. If he had only thought of using his own hypnotic powers on the person on the stairs this morning and stayed long enough for a confrontation. He would have met Irina instead of a curious guest, of course, and they might have clashed as he had with Lane. Irina being even older and more experienced than Lane, this time he would probably have lost the duel, but ... Holle might still be alive.

"The killer wanted information?" Girimonte asked. She frowned at Harry. "That doesn't fit Barber. Why should she have to torture information out of a man who's been her friend and caretaker? What kind of information could she want anyway?" Her gaze slid toward Garreth. "It doesn't fit *Barber*."

Harry stiffened.

Did she ever let up? Garreth wondered angrily. "Why don't you can it, Girimonte."

Harry sighed. "Both of you can it." He frowned. "The killer tortured Holle and Holle struggled, but the only signs of it are in here. Because he knew, and trusted, the person, and didn't realize his danger until he was in here and it was too late? *That* would fit Barber."

The assistant M.E. appeared in the bathroom doorway. "If you're finished with the body, we'll take it now, Sergeant."

"Fine." Harry watched from the door while they zipped Holle into a body bag and wheeled out the stretcher, then turned away, grimacing. "So much for the fun part. It's time to talk to the neighbors, partner. One of us needs to stay here until Yoshino and his people are finished, though, so how do you want to handle it? Flip a coin?"

She stretched with a cat's grace. "You're the sergeant. You stay. I'll hit the bricks. Want to come along, Mr. Fowler?"

"Too right!" The writer grinned. "Just let's stop at the car first long enough to pick up my mac. The heavens look ready to open any moment."

Harry and Garreth followed the other two out into the hall, where Harry leaned on the railing watching them trot down the staircase and across the hall out the front door. "She's a good cop, Mik-san."

"She certainly has her ideas about who the killer is."

It came out more acid than Garreth intended. Harry straightened abruptly. "You have to admit you've been in some wrong places at the wrong times. She's raised some good points, too. Why *would* Lane torture Holle for information? *What* information?"

The same questions applied to Irina, unfortunately. Could some other vampire be involved, one with other interests here, someone he did not know?

"As computers say, Harry-san: *Insufficient data. Will not compute*. The housekeeper said she was making tea. Shall I see if I can talk her into some for us?"

Harry shook his head. "None for me, but you go ahead. You didn't have breakfast and I expect it's going to be a long time until lunch."

Garreth found the housekeeper at a table in the kitchen with tea, but crying over it, not drinking it. He touched her shoulder. "I'm sorry to bother—"

She started violently. Jumping up, she snapped, "Why don't you people ever walk so someone can hear you!"

He sighed. "I'm sorry. Ms. Edlitza, do you meet many of my kind?"

"What's many? I meet some." She bustled away toward the sink with her teacup. "Mostly they're the same ones over and over, like Miss Rudenko. She's been visiting since I was a child and my parents were part of a full staff here." A fat raindrop hit the window over the sink, followed by another, and another, until it streamed down the window in a sheet.

"Irina and who else?"

Water blasted into the sink. Rain hammered on the window. "Are you trying to involve others in this, too?"

He hissed in exasperation. "What I'm trying to do is find out who killed Mr. Holle!"

Her head bent suddenly. Her shoulders heaved in a soundless sob.

The anger leaked out of Garreth. He sighed. "Ms. Edlitza, I need to meet some of the others, and I don't know how or where."

Her fingers twined together. She studied them as if searching for something there. After a minute she looked up. "I'm sorry, I can't help you. I'm not one of their circle, just a servant."

Instinct told him that she was lying ... but since she appeared to be experienced at resisting vampire powers, what could he do short of using force to get the truth? God knew there had been enough of that in this house already. "All right. Thank you."

He left the kitchen. As the door closed behind him, he heard her move quickly across the kitchen in his direction and he halted. She was not coming after him, however. Her steps stopped on the other side of the door, followed by the sound of a phone receiver lifting.

Garreth plastered himself against the door. Closing his eyes, he strained to hear. There. He could just hear the dial tones, four of one digit, one of another, two of a third. He listened for the voice answering on the other end, but that came through too faintly to make out more than a murmur, though. The voice said something longer than *hello*, and a rising tone indicated a question. *May I help you*, perhaps?

All he could really hear was the housekeeper's end of the conversation, "This is Mr. Holle's housekeeper. I'd like to leave a message for Miss Rudenko. Ask her to call me, please ... Yes ... it's very important. Thank you."

As he heard her hang up, Garreth hurried away from the door. It would not help to have her catch him listening. He headed for the hall extension to try working out the number while the tones remained fresh in his head.

But Holle's guests sat in the living room in full view of the phone. He sighed in regret. Better not play with the phone now. It would arouse their curiosity, and Harry's if he happened to look over the railing. The directory on the shelf under the phone gave him an idea, however. Squatting down in front of the table, he checked the covers on all three sections of the directory. A number the housekeeper could dial without having to look up and expect the person answering to know Holle's name must be noted somewhere.

A sheet of paper taped inside the front cover of the white pages bore a typed list of phone numbers. Garreth scanned them quickly, only to grimace in disappointment. They were only those a visitor might be interested in: numbers for cab companies and airlines; for theatre, ballet, and opera ticket offices; for museums and galleries.

He returned the white pages to the shelf and stood up. Holle must keep his personal numbers somewhere else. The library, maybe. A phone sat on the desk there.

Giving the guests a bland smile as he turned away from the phone table, Garreth trotted up the stairs and along the hall to the library.

The massive old desk looked like two pushed back to back, with a tunnel of a knee hole and drawers on both sides. The five drawers facing into the room contained the standard desk-drawer clutter of paper, pens, and such. But no address book. The drawers on the back side would not open when he pulled on their handles.

Garreth slumped back in the big executive chair, frowning at the locked drawers and listening to the rain hammer the window behind him. Now what? The desk had been carefully built. The space along the top of the drawers looked too narrow for using either the paper knife or rulers from the front drawers to slip the locks. He needed x-ray vision, or the skill of TV's private eye/white knights of justice, who could pick locks like these with a bent paper clip in five seconds.

Harry's voice carried from downstairs, explaining that he wanted to fingerprint the guests and housekeeper as a way of eliminating their prints from those lifted in Holle's room.

Holle's room. Garreth sat up. Maybe breaking into the desk was unnecessary.

Pushing to his feet, he hurried down the hall to the bedroom. Technicians still at work glanced around as he came in. He gave them a nod and smile, then made a quick survey of the room. Keys.

There. On the bureau. Holle's keys lay in a brass tray amid a clutter of loose change, a cigarette lighter, card case, and billfold.

A film of white fingerprint powder smudged the bureau, but Garreth still asked, "Are you finished with those keys?"

A tech nodded without looking up from dusting the bedside table.

Garreth picked up the ring with its brass tag engraved *LEONARD* and strolled casually out of the bedroom.

Straight into Harry.

Harry's brows rose. "Looking for me, Mik-san?"

The evasions racing through Garreth's head choked off as he watched Harry's gaze drop to the keys. Holding them up, he said, "I'm hoping there's a key to the desk in the library. It's locked and I'm looking for Holle's address book. So we can check out his friends just in case Lane didn't do this."

"Address book? Good idea." Harry held out his hand.

No! But the protest remained unvoiced. He, the unofficial cop here, the ride-along, had no grounds for protest. Reluctantly, Garreth handed over the keys. He could only ride along some more, dogging Harry's heels to the library, watching while his ex-partner unlocked the desk and found a slim, leather-bound address book in the center drawer.

Harry picked it up and flipped through. "He certainly has a lot of friends."

Garreth ached with the effort of not snatching the book away. "Any corporate or institutional affiliations?"

Harry shrugged. "I expect. A man like him is bound to be on the board of museums and service organizations. I'll have a close look later."

Garreth could only swear silently, helplessly, as the book disappeared into the pocket of Harry's suitcoat.

9

After the lab finished at the house, Harry and Garreth joined Girimonte and Fowler in the legwork, trudging through the rain to talk to Holle's neighbors around the block and across the street.

"Just like old times," Harry said with a grin.

Not quite, Garreth reflected unhappily. Harry asked all the questions and kept watching Garreth from the corner of his eye.

By the time everyone had been reached, either at home or by phone at their various offices, midday was ancient history. The four of them headed for a Burger King on Fillmore to dry off and compare notes.

Harry frowned at Garreth's ice tea. "Is that all you're having?"

Garreth gave him a rueful smile. "The way I pigged out last night, I met my caloric requirements for an entire week, maybe the month."

Harry chuckled, but Girimonte's eyes narrowed. A moment later something stirred behind them and she sat back, smiling in satisfaction.

Fear washed through Garreth. She had the expression of someone who has finally found the answer to a nagging question. Had she, like Holle and the housekeeper, identified him for what he was?

Harry poured catsup over his french fries. "So what did you learn from the neighbors, Van?"

"Almost zilch." Girimonte put down her hamburger and opened her notebook. "There aren't many people looking out their windows from three to six in the morning. Except one." She flipped through the notebook. "A Mr. Charles Hanneman who lives directly across the street from Holle. He got up around five to check on his year-old son, who's been ill and was crying. He says he happened to glance out the window while he was carrying the boy around trying to sooth him back to sleep and saw someone on the sidewalk outside the Holle house."

Garreth's heart lurched. Carefully, he sipped his tea. "Then we got lucky for a change."

"Not really, sad to say," Fowler sighed.

"He couldn't say the person came out of the house." Girimonte frowned at her notes. "He couldn't give us much of a description, either, not even the sex. The person was either a tall, lean woman or a slender man … shortish hair … wearing a warmup suit."

"Color?" Harry asked.

She grimaced. "Something dark ... green or blue, maybe even red. Hanneman couldn't tell in that light. He didn't really pay much attention. He thought it was just someone out for early exercise, and he's probably right. The person jogged off south, out in the open and making no attempt to hide, according to Hanneman."

Garreth let out his breath.

"We didn't get even that much," Harry said. "There's this, though." He pulled out the address book. "In the interest of completeness, we ought to check Holle's friends."

"In case he includes second story men in his circle?" Girimonte said through a mouthful of hamburger.

"Why does there have to be a burglar?" Fowler asked. He munched a french fry. "Perhaps Holle himself admitted the killer."

Everyone blinked, and Garreth cheered silently. That idea should certainly distract anyone from wondering how a killer could enter a locked door.

"Go on," Harry said.

Fowler took a bite of hamburger. "It's just a theory, mind, but it does explain the apparent lack of forced entry or struggle. What if Barber rang Holle up yesterday afternoon after he left us, pleading innocent to everything and begging him to help her, and also asking that he not tell anyone about her call. Holle arranged to have her come to the house that night. When he ostensibly went to check the rear door and set the alarm, she was waiting outside. He let her in and sent her up the back stairs to one of the rooms on the top floor."

Harry pursed his lips. "Then she came down later, maybe pleading a need to talk to him. He didn't realize how ugly things were going to get until too late."

"Quite." Fowler finished off his french fries. "Of course, you realize the scenario could fit almost anyone Holle considered a friend. I imagine there are a score of excuses for someone to use to warrant a clandestine entrance ... abusive husband, a misunderstanding with creditors, a virago of a wife or girlfriend."

Garreth eyed the address book, mind racing. How could he manage a look through it without appearing to care? Maybe ... Casually, he said, "In the interest of completeness, I wonder if any of the names in that book will also check out as acquaintances of Ricky Maruska, either social or ... professional."

"Now there's a thought," Fowler said. "We could ask his roomate."

Harry traced the initials *LEH* tooled on the cover. "I'd also like to ask Count Dracula about Lane Barber, now that we suspect she's involved in the murder."

Girimonte washed down the last of her hamburger with her soft drink. "So let's go roust the Count out of his coffin."

10

The only vista the Bay Vista Hotel enjoyed was a slantwise glimpse of the Embarcadero, a frontal view of the warehouse across the street and the elevated traffic of I-80 north beyond that. In the lobby, sagging easy chairs held down a threadbare carpet. A blowsy woman behind the desk divided her attention between a paperback romance and the hystrionics of game show contestants on a small TV at one end of the counter.

Harry flipped open his badge case. "What's Count Dracula's room number?"

"Cute," the woman said without looking up. She turned a page. "I suppose you want Frankenstein's room number, too?"

Harry frowned. "There *is* a man registered here who calls himself Count Dracula. Thin, pale, fake Balkan accent. Wears a black cape."

"Oh, sure."

Fowler said, "Do you have a guest named Alucard?"

Of course. *You should have thought of that, Mikaelian.* Especially after taping and watching every vampire movie that showed on the channels Baumen received.

The desk clerk rolled her eyes. "*That* wierdo. Three-oh-six, and if he complains about his room not being made up today, tell him the maid only goes through once and he opens up then or the room don't get done."

With a wink at Harry, Girimonte said in a flat, *Dragnet*-style voice, "Yes, ma'am; we'll tell him."

The narrow stairs creaked a every step. Ribbed rubber glued to the treads flapped loose on several, threatening to trip the unwary climber.

"Fowler," Harry asked back over his shoulder, "where did he come up with the name Alucard, and how did you know about it?"

From behind Garreth the writer said, "Elementary, my dear sergeant, at least to a fan of old horror movies. Alucard—Dracula spelled backward—is an alias used by Lon Chaney's Dracula, so I thought it likely our Count would copy him."

"As he says: elementary, old chap," Girimonte murmured.

They reached the third floor. Harry rapped on the door of 306. "Count, it's the police. Sorry to disturb you but we need to talk to you."

No one came to the door.

After a minute Harry knocked again, harder. "Count?"

No one moved in the room as far as Garreth could tell.

"Count Dracula!" Harry shouted. He pounded the door with a doubled fist. "Open this door!"

"I doubt he'll answer," Fowler said. "Vampires don't move around by daylight, after all."

Girimonte said grimly, "This one will. I'm not coming back at night just to satisfy a fag's idiosyncracies." She hammered on the door hard enough that the numbers shivered. "You! Cupcake! We don't have time to play games. Now open the fucking door!"

Still no response.

"Let me try," Garreth said. He moved up to the door. "Count, it is possible for you to move around in daylight. Dracula does sometimes in Bram Stoker's book, and Louis Jourdan did in the PBS production of *Dracula*. It's a beautiful day out, too … raining. There's no sun shining at all."

Harry and Girimonte leaned on each other, choking with laughter. The corners of Fowler's mouth twitched.

The Count, however, remained silent.

Garreth leaned his forehead against the door. "Count, will you please—"

The plea died abruptly in his throat, strangled by a terrible realization: a hotel room, though just a room, became a dwelling for the person in it, yet he felt nothing touching this door, not a flicker of barrier flames. A distinctive odor seeped through the door, too, the same one which had filled Holle's room. "Shit. Harry, get the pass key."

They gaped at him. "What?"

"The pass key! He's dead in there!"

Still they stared. "Dead? How …"

"I can smell him!"

Girimonte took off for the stairs like a deer.

Garreth slammed the wall with the side of his fist. Another one. He tried to tell himself that this death might have nothing to do with the others. Considering the Bay Vista's usual clientele, he could have been killed by someone ripping off the room.

When Girimonte came pounding back up the stairs with the key a few minutes later to unlock the door, all possibility of that scenario evaporated. The Count lay stretched on his back on the bed as though in state, dressed in a tuxedo, hands folded across his chest ... but blood dried to dirty brown covered the pleated shirt and out of the middle of it protruded a shaft of wood.

"Good lord," Fowler said hoarsely.

The dead man's head twisted grotesquely to the side, but his expression of terror and pain—eyes popping, mouth stretched open in a soundless shriek, hands frozen into claws—testified that his neck had not been broken until after he had suffered the agony of the stake being pounded into his chest. Like Holle, his hair lay clumped in points on his forehead. The crossed wrists bore abraided grooves where he had fought bonds, grooves like those on Holle's wrists. More abrasions from mouth to ears indicated he had been gagged, too.

Dried blood also covered a pillow on the floor, especially around a hole in the middle of the pillow.

Fury boiled up through Garreth. The dead man's final screams had sunk unheard into his gag, but they must have echoed and reechoed endlessly in his head as the killer laid the pillow over the victim's chest to absorb any splattering blood and pounded in the stake through it. Garreth's head rang with those screams. Lane and Irina, blood mother and daughter indeed. They shared the same taste for inflicting wanton pain. This little man had harmed no one with his fantasy. He certainly did not deserve a death like this. *I'm going to find her, Count, just as I found Lane. That I promise you.*

"The stake's been made from a chair rung," Harry said.

He pointed to a wooden desk chair with a rung missing from between its front legs. Curls of wood from sharpening the rung to a point littered the desk top.

Girimonte disappeared into the bathroom. "The washbowl has the plug in and there's a little water still standing in it. Looks like he got the same treatment Holle did."

"But much earlier." Harry sniffed. "Maybe yesterday."

Girimonte eyed Garreth from the bathroom doorway. "Where were you yesterday, Mikaelian?"

Garreth's breath caught.

"You know where he was!" Harry snapped. "I found him at home in bed asleep."

"At three o'clock in the afternoon, yes. What about before then?" She raised her brows. "We have hours unaccounted for between the time you left for work and went home after Mikaelian. Maybe he didn't answer the phone not because he sleeps so soundly, but because he wasn't there."

"Van, don't start that again!"

"Harry, why don't you stop burying your head?" Girimonte ticked off points on her fingers. "He fights with a hustler he claims had information about a killer he has very personal reasons for wanting to find, and the hustler dies. Later that day the hustler's roommate is killed, too, with signs of having been tortured, possibly in an effort to gain information. That afternoon someone else connected to our lady killer has words with him and today *he* turns up dead. Also tortured. And this bloodbath started the day after he arrived in town."

"Oh, come now," Fowler began.

"This is ridiculous," Garreth said. He intended the statement to be calmly firm, but it emerged with the sharp edges of fear and disbelief he felt. How could anyone seriously think he— "I want to collar Lane so desperately that I commit murder myself? Three innocent civilians? Come *on!*"

Girimonte pulled one of her elegant cigars from her breast pocket and lit it. "You come on, Mikaelian. You're dirty. You know a lot more about this case than you're telling anyone. I can smell it."

She was the kind who, believing something, would dig until she got what she was after. He could not afford to have her digging; it would turn up more than she counted on, more than he wanted anyone to know. "Harry, you know me. Straighten her out."

Harry sighed heavily. "A year and a half ago I'd have said I knew you. Now—you've changed, Mik-san. I can't guess what you're thinking or feeling anymore. And I can't help feeling that Van's right about one thing ... killer or not, you do know more than you're telling." The almond eyes slid away from Garreth, dark with unhappiness and profound unease.

Hare and
Hound

1

God he hated daylight! Today even late afternoon dragged on him with as much force as high noon. Garreth splashed water on his face and pushed himself upright.

The mirrors above the washbasins in the men's room at Bryant Street reflected a face thinner and paler than ever, with eyes smudged by weariness. The eyes he saw, though, were violet, dancing amid the flames of a blazing bridge. Since they had come back from the hotel, his former colleagues in Homicide had been watching him sideways with narrowed eyes, and when they spoke to him it was in the flat voice usually reserved for outsiders. Lane's laughter whispered in his ears.

Fowler came out of a stall behind him. "What bloody fools those coppers are!"

Garreth snatched for his glasses. He had almost forgotten about the writer following him to the men's room. "They're just doing their jobs. As luck would have it, I've in been the wrong places at the wrong time."

"I wonder if luck has had much to do with it." Fowler turned on the water in one basin. The heat of it carried his blood scent toward Garreth. Garreth's stomach cramped with hunger. "Have you considered that for purposes of hanging a frame on you, you've been in exactly the right places at the right times?"

Hunger vanished in dismay. "Frame!"

Fowler rinsed his hands and reached for a paper towel. "Of course. I've been thinking about this a good deal and a frame makes sense of everything. I admit I'm no policeman, only a writer, but that's to my favor. I can recognize a plot when I see one. Don't you see? The torture wasn't to gain information at all, only to make it *look* like someone wanted information ... a role your Miss Barber has carefully tailored to you."

"Why? It doesn't gain her anything." Even if Lane were alive.

Fowler smiled thinly. "Except revenge, old son. You've seriously inconvenienced her, after all, haven't you ... making her give up her job and go into hiding, forcing her to move twice, turning friends against her. So now she's returning the favor. It's much nastier than killing you outright. This way she destroys you. Even if you aren't prosecuted or convicted, you'll become a pariah."

But Lane was dead. The same motive fit Irina, though. Since leaving that note at the apartment, she might have found out he killed Lane. He sucked in his breath. "Maybe you're right."

"In which case you'd best find her quickly, before she kills again."

Before another innocent person died. Garreth's mouth thinned. Find her how? The hexagram Lien had thrown for him that morning— only that morning?—ran through his head: if the little fox wets his tail crossing the river, nothing furthers. Thought and caution are necessary for success.

He sighed. "I think I'd be playing into her hands going after her on my own. It's better to lay your theory on Harry and let him check it while I keep low and out of trouble."

"Hang about now!" Fowler snapped. "You're already *in* trouble, up to your bloody eyebrows. And you'll get no help from that lot in the squadroom, either. They're already half convinced by the frame."

"But you're not?" Garreth said sardonically.

Fowler lounged against a washbasin. "No, and I want to help you prove your innocence."

"So you can have a happy ending for the book?"

Fowler jerked upright. *"To hell with the bloody book!"*

A uniformed officer coming in the door stopped short and stared at them.

Taking a deep breath, Fowler lowered his voice to a whisper. "You are a bloody fool! There's a woman out there trying to put you in the dock and she's got to be stopped! That's all that matters at the moment. Look here; I *can* help you. I'm a famous writer. People will talk to me who'd never open their mouths to a copper. And as long as I'm with you, you've got an alibi, haven't you, whatever Barber tries."

Garreth reached up under his glasses to rub his eyes. They burned. But then, everything else in him ached, too. He sighed. "I'll think about it."

"You do that, old son." Fowler headed for the door. "But don't take long or it may be too late."

2

Garreth told Harry Fowler's theory on the drive home.

Harry bit his lower lip. "It's a possibility. I'd like it to be the case; it'd mean your only involvement is as a fall-guy. Van won't go for it, though. Too complicated. She'll have a point, too; most people in Barber's position would just kill *you*. Plots like Fowler's suggesting only happen in books and the movies." He paused. "Mik-san, what is it you know you haven't told me about? It might help if you did."

He wished ... but even if he could feel confident that the resources of the police department would find Irina, not only was there too much risk that they might learn what she was, but Harry could become her next victim. Once before his carelessness had nearly killed Harry. That must not happen again.

In the interest of appearing cooperative, though, maybe he could risk a partial truth.

He shrugged. "It's nothing, just one of Grandma Doyle's Feelings. I'm not even sure how you'd act on it. She warned me to beware of a violet-eyed woman. I ... asked Holle if the woman asking for Lane had violet eyes."

"And?"

"He claimed he never noticed their color. When I asked him if he were sure, he acted like I'd accused him of lying."

"That was the hassle?" Harry shook his head. "Why didn't you say so before?"

"I'm not about to drag my grandmother out in front of your partner and Fowler to be ridiculed or turned into a character in a book."

Did Harry believe that? Garreth could not tell. Harry smiled, but said nothing more, only drove the rest of the way home in silence.

Until they pulled into the drive. Then as they climbed out, he looked at Garreth across the top of the car. "There's no point in upsetting Lien with the ... problems in this case, so—"

"I don't want to distress her with the fact that I'm a suspect, either, Harry," Garreth interrupted.

"Thanks."

Lien met them at the door, shaking her head in mock exasperation.

"I don't know why I bother cooking for you two. Everything is mummified by the time you finally come home. It would make more sense to wait until I see you, then send out for pizza or make a quick run to the Colonel for fried chicken."

Harry kissed her soundly. "Think how dull life would be if you always knew where I'd be and when."

"You might start taking him for granted," Garreth teased.

For a moment the laughter died out of her eyes. She reached out to touch Harry's cheek. "Never."

In the one word Garreth heard her morning ritual with *I Ching* —"Will my husband be safe today?"—and the memory of that terrible wait in the emergency room to learn if Harry would live or die.

A moment later she laughed again. "Come along, honorable husband, honored guest; your tea is waiting."

She served it in the family room as always, but instead of sitting down to enjoy it, they followed her into the dining room and kitchen, joking with each other and her. Garreth pretended to sip from his cup, then set it down and "forgot" it as he helped her set the table. Without actually talking shop, Harry filled dinner with a string of anecdotes about people seen or interviewed during the day, mimicking some like Fowler and the clerk at the Bay Vista Hotel with wicked accuracy.

"It was great being partners with Garreth again, right Mik-san?"

"Right." Garreth wished his tea had no brandy in it so he could drink it. As the kitchen and dining room filled with blood scents, his stomach cramped in a savage hunger that burned all the way up his throat. "Like old times." He gulped down his glass of water. It eased the pangs a little. "How was your day?"

"I had my children's art class this afternoon." She launched into stories about teaching drawing and painting.

As she talked, however, she kept glancing from Harry to him with a searching gaze that dropped his stomach toward his feet. Did she suspect something?

His answer came at the end of dinner. He picked up his plate and started to stand and carry it into the kitchen.

She reached across to catch his arm. "That can wait, Garreth. All right, you two; tell me what's wrong."

Harry regarded her innocently. "Wrong? What do you mean?"

She stared into him. "I mean you've come home running a relentless two-man comedy routine, but you're just picking over your beef stroganoff and Garreth hasn't eaten any at all. Every time you do that, something has happened you don't want me to find out about because you think it will upset me. Once it was a knife wound on your arm. Another time the two of you had fought over whether to release a suspect you felt sure was guilty but didn't have the evidence to hold. What this time?"

"There's nothing—" Harry began.

Garreth interrupted, "Girimonte and I mix like gasoline and matches." He should have remembered. Lien always knew when they dragged home psychological baggage. So give her some to chew over.

Lien eyed them both for a minute, then nodded. "Yes, I can imagine, and my poor Harry is caught in the middle, not sure which to side with, old partner or new partner."

After reaching over to pat Harry's arm, she appeared satisfied and let the subject drop. They washed dishes and adjourned to the TV to watch the news, then to groan and hoot at police procedure as portrayed on the late-night rerun of a cop show.

Garreth slipped out to the refrigerator in the kitchen during the show. He drank straight from the thermos, but even as he gulped down the blood, his appetite continued to snarl in frustration at every maddeningly unsatisfying swallow. The memory of Holle's refrigerator taunted him.

A sound in the dining room warned him that he was about to have company. Blood scent drifting around him told him who. Moving casually, he crossed to the sink and rinsed out the thermos. Hunting time again tonight. "Hi, Lien."

From behind him she said, "You're still using that liquid protein diet you were on when you left San Francisco? Do you ever eat anything else?"

He glanced over his shoulder. "Of course." Water rinsed the last traces of blood down the drain. "I just wasn't hungry tonight."

She leaned against the kitchen door. "Harry's gone up to get ready for bed. I don't suppose you'll tell me what the real problem between the two of you is."

He set the thermos upside down on the drainboard to dry and turned to face her. "I can't."

Her forehead furrowed. "Or what the problem eating you up inside is? Before you left San Francisco, remember, I told you I wished I could help you. I still want to."

"I wish you could, but ... no one can. It's something I have to work out for myself."

"That's what you said last time, but you obviously haven't worked it out yet. *Why* can't you tell me? You let me help when Marti died, and you came here when you ran away from the hospital after that Barber girl tried to kill you." She paused. "I dream about you, Garreth. I reach out to touch you and I can't. You're so far away ... farther and farther each time."

All her dream lacked was the burning bridge. Longing grawed at him to tell her everything.

But he could visualize her reaction ... disbelief first, then concern as she decided he had gone bonkers. He imagined proving himself by showing her how his fangs extended, and how he could move through shut doors. Then disbelief would turn to horror and revulsion, and worst of all, to fear of him. He could not bear that.

He made himself smile. "Don't let a stupid nightmare upset you. I'll be fine."

She ran a hand through her hair. "While I waited for you two to come home tonight, I threw tomorrow's hexagrams. Yours was number Twenty-nine, The Abysmal. If you are sincere, you have success in your heart and whatever you do succeeds."

He eyed her, stomach knotting. "So why aren't you smiling?"

She bit her lip. "A change line in the third place means that every step, forward or backward, leads into danger. There is no escape. You must wait for the way out."

Cold ran down his spine. "No escape? The change line makes a second hexagram. Does it offer a solution?"

She shook her head. "Number Forty-eight, The Well, is a bit esoteric, but in this context, I think it reinforces the first hexagram."

Cold ate deeper. Every step leads into inescapable danger. But he could not afford to wait it out. He had to find Irina before more people died and what remained of his bridge collapsed into ashes.

3

That thought echoed in Garreth's head all night. Even in the exhausting light of morning, sitting on Harry's desk with the squadroom's stew of tobacco smoke, coffee, aftershave, and blood scents washing around him and Centrello droning through an update of his and Faye's cases, urgency drummed at Garreth. Find the violet-eyed vampire.

His gut knotted. Of course, if he did he courted disaster, according to *I Ching* and his grandmother's Feeling. But retreat meant danger, too, and surely it was better to meet danger head-on than in retreat.

The question still remained of how to find her, and no matter how often he asked it, now or last night while slipping out of the house to Golden Gate Park to fill his thermos from a horse in the police stable—a closer source of blood than the rats on the waterfront—one answer came up: the number the housekeeper phoned. A number somewhere in the address book Harry had locked in his desk last night.

The reporting voice became Harry's. "... call from a pawnshop owner last night. He left a message. A watch like the one taken from the liquor store clerk during the robbery has turned up at his shop. Van and I will check it out this morning once she's back from prying the autopsy report on Maruska out of the coroner's office. Holle and Count Dracula—whose name we're still trying to learn—should be posted today or tomorrow. That open window at Holle's isn't going to help us make a case against anyone. The lab found no evidence of forcible entry and the only prints belong to the housekeeper and another woman who cleans part time. It looks like the killer spotted and took advantage of a window someone left open."

"Let's hope he left more in the bedroom then," Serruto said. "Your turn, Kolb."

The front of the top desk drawer felt slick and cool under the sliding exploration of Garreth's fingers. He touched the handle, tried it tentatively. Locked. His hand itched with the desire to wrench the drawer open. A glance around, though, found Fowler eyeing him and he pulled the hand back to shove it in the pocket of his coat.

Kolb finished her report. Serruto nodded. "That's it, then. Carry on, as our esteemed author-in-residence might say." He poured himself a cup of coffee and vanished into his office.

Fowler raised a brow at Garreth. *Have you thought about our discussion?* the expression said.

Harry came over to sit down at his desk. Garreth moved off it.

He had thought about the discussion, yes ... all last night while he filled his thermos and wondered how to find Irina. As much as he appreciated the offer and the support it represented, the idea of a partnership did not appeal to him. How could he effectively hunt Irina when he had to appear to be hunting Lane? On the other hand, Fowler had a point about his fame opening doors, not to mention his presence providing an alibi. All things considered, then ... Garreth dipped his chin. *You're on.*

Fowler smiled.

Occupied with unlocking his desk and taking out the address book, Harry missed the exchange.

Girimonte swept in from the corridor waving a sheaf of papers. "Got it." She dropped the autopsy report on Harry's desk and lighted a cigar. "I gave it a quick read on the way up in the elevator. No surprises."

"You mean he wasn't a Martian after all?" Fowler asked.

Did he have to bring that up? Garreth glanced sidelong at Girimonte, but if she connected the other dead men the assistant M.E. mentioned with whatever she had decided about Garreth, she showed no sign of it.

She shrugged. "I don't know what anomalies Welton was so excited about. So Maruska was obviously healthy and athletic when the total lack of body fat and minimal intestinal contents should indicate severe starvation. There's something about the color of the liver indicating a high iron intake and tarry feces being present without a site for upper G.I. bleeding, but ... all I see that's really different is his teeth."

Garreth's stomach lurched. He peered over Harry's shoulder at the report. "... unusually sharp upper canines, grooved on the posterior side." His tongue traced the grooves down his own fangs. At least the pathologist had missed the fact that the teeth extended and retracted.

"How disappointing," Fowler murmured. "I had hoped for green blood at the very least."

Girimonte blew cigar smoke at him. "Vulcans, not Martians, have green blood."

Garreth smoothed his mustache. Martians. Maybe there was another lead after all. If those bodies *were* vampires, too, then someone they knew must be a link to others of the blood in the city, others who might point the way to Irina.

"This is very interesting, I'm sure, but," —Harry pushed to his feet— "we have a pawnshop owner to talk to, and after we've followed that lead as far as it'll go, we need to look up Holle's friends to talk about possible enemies." He waved the address book. "Shall we hit the bricks?"

Garreth debated hurriedly. Following one lead meant abandoning the other for a while. Which way to try first. *No contest, man. The one without Girimonte.* He smiled at Harry. "While you're working on the liquor store shooting, I think I'll go over the files on the Mossman and Adair murders with Mr. Fowler. We can catch up with you later."

Fowler blinked, then grinned. "Capital."

"Go over the old files." Girimonte's eyes narrowed. She tapped the ash off her cigar.

"Yes of course." Fowler's brows rose. "What do you think, that we'd go haring off on our own?"

"The thought crossed my mind."

"Well, you're wrong ... again," Garreth snapped. "After going over the case files, at most we might visit the Barbary Now and the alley where Lane attacked me, to let Mr. Fowler soak up local color. Nothing more." He focused on her as he said it, though, not looking at Harry.

Harry eyed him and Fowler.

"Cross our hearts and hope to die," the writer said cheerfully. Harry shook his head and started for the door. "Come on, Van. Contact Dispatch for our Twenty when you two want to catch up, Mik-san."

Fowler waited until the door had closed before turning to Garreth. "Right. Now, old son, suppose you tell me what you really have in mind."

4

"The morgue?" Fowler's brows rose as they walked into the reception area of the coroner's office. "Are we interrogating the dead men?"

Garreth gave him a thin smile. "Something like that. This won't take long. Wait for me here." He turned the smile on the receiving clerk. "Morning, Barbara. Where's Dr. Thurlow?"

The clerk stared. "Inspector Mikaelian? I heard you were back. Lord, I hardly recognize you. You got serious about dieting. The old man's in the autopsy room."

The effort needed to walk down the corridor had nothing to do with the drag of daylight. Garreth hated coming here. He always had, even before having to identify Marti's body. Waking up in one of its drawers himself had not endeared it to him, either. The place served the living, but it was a world of death, of tile and stainless steel ... shining, cold, hard.

Pushing through the door of the autopsy room, though, he realized that oddly enough, he disliked this room the least. Perhaps because here corpses ceased to be people. Lying with bellies and chests spread open, scalps pulled inside out down over their faces, they no longer looked quite human.

Down the long line of tables the light shone on a stylish mane of silver hair. Garreth made his way toward it through the flood of smells ... disinfectants, dead blood, diseased blood, putrifying flesh, the acrid stench of intestinal contents, and in sparse, tantalizing whiffs almost lost among the other odors, the warm saltiness of living blood.

The murmur of voices filled the room, pathologists talking to assistants and dictating into microphones dangling from overhead, sentences punctuated by occasional laughter and the sharp whine of a bone saw slicing through a skull. Light gleamed on instruments and clay-gray flesh. Water hissed, running down the tables to carry away the blood. More water swirled rosy in sinks at the end of the tables, where floating organs waited to be sliced open for further examination.

"Dr. Thurlow?"

The chief medical examiner looked up from studying lungs as red as the liver lying on the table beside them. He peered at Garreth over the top of half glasses. "Morning, Mikaelian."

Garreth blinked. "You recognize me?"

"I remember all my patients who recover and go home." Thurlow's knife sliced through the lung in quick, sure strokes, sectioning it like a loaf of bread, then scraped across several of the exposed internal surfaces. "What can I do for you, Mikaelian?"

"I'm interested in your Martians."

Gray eyes peered keenly at him over the half glasses. "You, too? This is the most attention the poor bastards have had in ten years. Mitch Welton has all the autopsy reports in his office."

Where going to ask for them would make the entire staff of the coroner's office aware that he had asked about the Martians? No. "If you know the names offhand, that's all I need." Garreth kept his voice casual.

Thurlow snorted. "After the recent chance to refresh my memory, the facts are graven in my offhand, Inspector." He sliced off several pieces of lung and dropped them in a specimen jar an assistant held out, then picked up the liver. "December 15, 1975, Christopher Parke Stroda, suicide. A jumper. Number whatever from the bridge."

In the middle of grabbing for his notebook, Garreth caught his breath. Suicide! "The fall broke his neck?"

"It broke almost everything," Thurlow replied dryly. His knife sliced expertly through the liver. "Thomas Washington Bodenhausen, October 11, 1979, construction accident. Decapitation."

Garreth stared. "Construction? He had a *day* job?" The words were out before he thought.

He could only curse himself silently as Thurlow's brows went up. "What's so strange about that? But this happened at night, if I remember right. Last Martian: Corinne Lucasta Barlow, July 20, 1981. Traffic fatality. Another broken neck. Multiple fractured vertebrae, in fact. Also fractures of assorted long bones, plus ruptures of liver, spleen, and kidneys. Heart impaled by a broken rib." He paused. "Corinne Lucasta. Unusual name. Old fashioned."

Maybe not when Corinne Lucasta had been born. "Thanks, doc." Garreth headed for the door.

Back in the reception area he found Fowler leaning on the receiving desk flirting with the clerk. The writer abandoned his conquest abruptly as Garreth appeared. "Have a nice chat?"

"We'll see. Come on."

"Ta," Fowler called back to the clerk.

In the breezeway outside, Garreth sucked in a deep breath of relief, and laughed inwardly at himself. Even open daylight was preferrable to the morgue? Hierarchies.

"Where now?" Fowler asked.

"Records."

He picked a clerk there he knew, but she just looked at him across the counter. "Do you have authorization to pull these files?"

Garreth frowned. She was not going to be as accomodating as Thurlow. "Authorization?"

"Of course. We can't hand records over to just anyone."

Cursing inwardly, he put on a mask of indignation. "What? Belflower, that's a crock. You know me."

"I know you don't work here anymore." Then she smiled. "I tell you what, though. You're riding along with Harry Takananda, right? I'll call him or Lieutenant Serruto for the authorization." She reached for the phone on the counter.

Self-control kept him from grabbing her wrist. That would only attract attention. "Belflower." Garreth pushed his glasses up on his head and caught her gaze. "That isn't—" He broke off. Was this a stupid thing to do with Fowler watching?

In the moment of inattention, she broke away from him, but before her hand touched the phone, Fowler finished, "… going to help. The lieutenant doesn't know anything about the lead and Sergeant Takananda is out of the building. I'm sure he would have given us a note or something, but he didn't think there would be this flap." He leaned on the counter and smiled at the clerk. "Look, love, we're just helping out the sergeant, Mikaelian as a favor to an ex-partner, and me tagging along gathering material for my book."

Her eyes widened. *"You're* Graham Fowler!"

He grinned. "Guilty, I'm afraid. Now ... what do you say?"

She frowned. "Well ..."

"I don't need to take the files *out*," Garreth said hastily. "A quick look here will give me everything necessary."

"I'd be most grateful," Fowler said.

Belflower smiled at him. "All right."

She hurried off.

Pulling his glasses back in place, Garreth breathed in relief. "Good show."

Fowler smiled dryly. "Well, we can't have the investigation bogging down in red tape, can we."

Belflower reappeared shortly with three folders. Garreth scanned the reports in each, looking for names, addresses, and telephone numbers of people connected to the victims. It did not surprise him to find very few.

Discovering Bodenhausen was black raised his brows, though on consideration he wondered why it should, any more than finding the names of parents and siblings for Christopher Stroda. The Stroda file also included a transcript of a tape recording left on the Golden Gate bridge with his coat, shoes, and sunglasses. The text whispered its despair in Garreth's head long after he went on to the next file.

"Anything I can do to help?" Fowler asked.

"Thanks, no."

"Do you mind if I have a look anyway?"

Was there more harm in letting him, or in piquing the writer's curiosity by refusing? "Go ahead."

Fowler paged through the folders. "I wonder if I might ask who these people are? They're all old cases, none of them murders. What's their relevance to our murderous Miss Barber?"

The inevitable question. Could he bluff his way out of answering? "Maybe none. It's just a hunch. Don't ask me to explain right now."

Fowler's brows skipped but he did not press the subject.

Garreth grinned inwardly in satisfaction. Moments later, though, satisfaction exploded into a shriek of alarm. The report on Corinne Barlow's accident gave the Philos Foundation as her employer.

Holle drove a car with personalized plates: PHILOS.

The Philos Foundation! The name reverberated in Garreth's head. He could kick himself for not thinking of it when he first saw Holle's tags. The non-profit organization kept a low profile but its storefront blood collection centers dotted the city, and every hospital in the city kept its two numbers handy, 555-LIFE for the bloodbank and 1-800-555-STAT to reach the organ transplant hotline at the central offices in Chicago. He had seen the card numerous times at the receiving desk in San Francisco General's trauma center when he dropped by to visit Marti at work. And 555-LIFE, he confirmed by taking a peek at the telephone on the counter, translated into 555-5433, the same pattern of numbers Holle's housekeeper had called.

"Find something interesting?" Fowler asked.

Garreth thought fast. "I was thinking about transportation. My car's in Harry's driveway. Do you have one?"

Fowler arched a brow. "Yes, of course. One is crippled in America without one. I take it you intend visiting the people on your list there?"

"Give the man a cookie." Garreth shoved the files back across the counter. "Thanks, Belflower. I'm through. I owe you one."

5

Stroda's parents still lived in Marin County. Garreth almost wished they did not, that he had been unable to find them.

The mention of her son brought raw pain to Sarah Stroda's face. "You want to talk about Christopher?"

Only moments before Garreth had been admiring her youthfulness and the humor glinting in her eyes as she handed back Garreth's identification, accepting his story of being temporarily attached to the San Francisco Police through a continuing education program for small town officers. Now the humor had gone, while years etched themselves into her face.

"No." She shook her head. "Let's not talk about him. I've read your books, Mr. Fowler, and except for the way your protagonists treat people as disposable tools, enjoyed them, but I don't want my son in one of your books."

"He won't be," Garreth said. "This doesn't have anything to do with your son himself, just people he might have known."

Mrs. Stroda bit her lip. "Come in, then." She stepped back inside the neo-Spanish house, opening the carved door wide though her expression said she longed to close it in their faces. "I think I'd like fresh air." She led the way through to a deck looking out over the bay, where she stood at the railing with her back to them, fingers white on the wrought iron.

Garreth sat down in a redwood chair. "I'm sorry to be bothering you. I wouldn't if it weren't important."

Without looking at him she said, "It's been ten years. You'd think I'd have gotten over it by now, or at least come to terms with it. Instead—it's like it happened yesterday, and I still don't understand why! He was twenty-four, with everything to live for, and he—" She turned abruptly. "What do you want to know?"

He hated himself for opening old wounds. "I need the names of people he saw regularly before he died."

She groped for a chair and sat down. "I don't know who his friends were. The last two years Christopher became a total stranger."

Protest rose in his throat. She had to know something more, anything, even a single name! He forced his voice to remain soothing and patient. "Think very carefully."

He doubted she heard him. Her fingers twined tightly together. "I wish I could find that woman and ask her what she did to him."

The hair rose on Garreth's neck. From the corner of his eye he watched Fowler's eyes narrow. "What woman?"

She shook her head. "Someone he met in Europe the summer between college graduation and medical school. That's when he changed."

"Do you know her name?"

"No. He never talked about her. We just happened to learn from friends of friends that he'd been in a serious car accident in Italy and would have died except that this woman he was traveling with gave blood for him and saved his life. We asked him about it but he kept saying it was nothing and he didn't want to talk about it." She drew in a shaking breath. "Over the months he had less and less to say to us. He dropped out of medical school, and stopped seeing his friends ... withdrawing, slipping farther away each day, until—" She turned away abruptly.

Garreth fought to keep his face expressionless. Until the widening gulf between Stroda and humanity became unbearable. Going off the bridge was certainly one solution to the pain.

"We thought it was drugs," Mrs. Stroda said, "though he always denied it. I guess it wasn't. The autopsy didn't find any." She turned back. "Who are these people you're looking for? Could they responsible for what happened to him?"

If only he could tell her. Except that could cause far more anguish than it cured. "I can't tell you much about them, but no, they didn't cause your son's death."

She let out her breath. "Good. So I don't have to feel guilty about not being able to help you."

"Perhaps one of your daughters knew something," Fowler suggested.

Mrs. Stroda stiffened. "No! I won't have them hurt again! Allison was only fifteen at the time. How could she know his friends?"

"Mrs. Stroda, it's very important that we find these people," Garreth said.

Fowler nodded. "Lives depend on it ... sons and daughters of other mothers."

Mrs. Stroda flung up her head, catching her breath.

"Fowler!" Garreth snapped.

But Mrs. Stroda shook her head. "No, he's right. I'll give you the girls' addresses and phone numbers." She stood and disappeared into the house.

Garreth turned on Fowler. "That was a cheap shot!"

The writer smiled. "But effective."

"The end justifies the means?" Garreth said acidly.

The smile thinned. "Don't go casting stones, old son. I've noticed you're not above deceit and manipulation when it suits your purposes."

Garreth opened his mouth ... and closed it again. What did he think he was going to say, that he acted for a righteous cause, that he tried not to hurt anyone in the process? Rationalizations. No matter how reasonable, they did not change the fact of deceit.

Mrs. Stroda reappeared with a sheet from a memo pad. She held it out to Garreth. "This time of day Janice will be at work. I've included that address, too."

Fowler glanced over Garreth's shoulder at the sheet. "Your daughter Allison is at the Stanford Medical School. Following in her brother's footsteps?"

"Tracking him might be a better description." Years and grief looked out of Mrs. Stroda's eyes. "Allison is studying to become a psychiatrist. Good day, gentlemen."

6

Good was not quite quite how Garreth could describe the day, not when he opened painful old wounds in three people in vain. Neither Allison Stroda nor Janice Stroda Meers, who worked in a crisis center near the University of San Francisco campus, would tell them any more than their mother had. Maybe the situation would be better with Thomas Bodenhausen. The police report had listed no next of kin for him. Bodenhausen had lived comfortably for a night watchman. The apartment building, a solid Victorian structure, offered its tenants a beautiful view of the Marina and the Palace of Fine Arts. The apartment manager, however, offered little, certainly not help. Frowning at Garreth from the open doorway of his apartment, he said skeptically, "Bodenhausen? Six years ago? Officer, you can't expect me to remember a tenant who left that long ago." He eyed the badge case still in Garreth's hands. "Are police interns paid?"

The question caught Garreth off guard. He had never expected anyone to ask for details of his cover story. His mind raced. "Yes ... living expenses anyway. I think you'll remember this tenant, Mr. Catao. He—"

"Who pays you?"

Impatience stung him. He had no time for this; he had to find Irina! "My department of course. About Mr. Bodenhausen—"

The manager's brows went up. "So the city gets extra officers like you two for free?"

Who *was* this bastard, a member of the budget council? "No. They profit. My department pays a fee to send me here. Now, may we *please* talk about Thomas Bodenhausen!"

Catao spread his hands. "I told you, I don't remember him."

Garreth sighed in exasperation. "He died, Mr. Catao. You must remember that ... a fire and explosion at a construction site? A flying piece of metal decapitated the night watchman?"

"Oh." Recognition bloomed in the manager's face. "*Him.* Yes, I remember that guy ... but I still can't tell you much. I didn't know him. He'd been here since before I took over as manager fifteen years ago and he was a good tenant ... quiet, always paid his rent on time, kept his apartment in good shape. What's this about? I heard that fire and explosion was an accident."

Garreth opened his mouth to reply. Fowler cut in first. "I'm considering making it sabotage for the purpose of my book."

Catao focused on Fowler for the first time, eyes narrowing. "Your book? Aren't you an exchange from Scotland Yard?"

Despite the urgent situation, Garreth had to bite back a grin. Fowler's expression was the epitome of innocent surprise. "Did we give you that impression? I'm terribly sorry. No, I'm a writer. Officer Mikaelian introduced me as Julian Fowler but my full name is Julian *Graham* Fowler. The San Francisco police are very kindly cooperating in some research I'm doing and they lent me Officer Mikaelian to—"

The manager's eyes went wide. "*The* Graham Fowler? Who wrote *Midnight Brigade* and *Winter Gambit*?"

Fowler rubbed his nose. "Well … at the risk of learning you consider them trash, those are two of my efforts, yes."

"Are you kidding?" The manager grinned. "That Dane Winter is great. Have you read the books?" he asked Garreth.

"Not those two." The evasion avoided an admission that he had not read any of Fowler's books.

The manager shook his head. "You ought to. He's this guy who's past fifty and the hotshot kids in British Intelligence keep trying to claim he's over the hill but he can still spy rings around them all. He doesn't go getting himself beat up all the time, either. When you're our age you'll appreciate seeing a hero like that for a change. Hey, why are we standing out here in the hall? Come in, Mr. Fowler." He led the way into his livingroom. It smelled of a sweetly fragrant pipe tobacco.

"It's gratifying to hear my heroes are appreciated." Fowler strolled over to the bay window. "What a magnificent view of the bay. Are you sure you can't help us with Bodenhausen?"

The manager's forehead furrowed. "Damn, I wish I could. But I just never knew him."

"You said he took good care of his apartment," Garreth said. "That sounds like you were in it."

"Yeah, from time to time, when something needed fixing."

"Was anyone else ever there? Or do you know if he was particular friends with any of the other tenants?"

The furrows deepened. "Keith Manziaro, I think. Once when I was up in his apartment he was telling his wife about fighting the Battle of Bull Run against Bodenhausen."

"Bodenhausen was a war games buff?" Fowler asked.

"More than that." Catao grinned. "His spare bedroom where he spread those battlefield maps on the floor looked like a museum. I mean, he had muskets and swords and Civil War rifles all over the walls. He even had some military uniforms from the Revolutionary and Civil Wars, handed down from ancestors who'd worn them, he told me."

Possibly Bodenhausen himself had worn them, Garreth mused.

"And he also had this letter he claimed was signed by George Washington, freeing another ancestor who'd been a slave at Mount Vernon. I don't know if I can believe that, but it makes a good story."

A letter signed by George Washington! Garreth caught his breath. That letter and the other relics would be priceless heirlooms to most families. Who had Bodenhausen's belongings gone to? A friend who could appreciate them, perhaps a fellow vampire? "Mr. Catao, what happened to Bodenhausen's belongings after he died?"

Catao blinked at Garreth. "His executors took it all away, of course."

"Executors? Who were they?"

"Hell, I don't remember." He rolled his eyes as Garreth frowned. "Christ, what do you think, I have a photographic memory? I saw the name once six years ago when this guy shows up with a key to the apartment and papers signed by Bodenhausen making some museum or something his executor."

"Museum?" Garreth frowned. "A local one?"

"I don't know. Probably not. I didn't recognize the name. Hey, I didn't pay much attention, okay? The papers looked legal so I let them have Bodenhausen's things and forgot about it."

A throb started behind Garreth's forehead. "Naturally," he said wearily. Did not know. Did not remember. Had paid no attention. Had forgotten. The same damned roadblocks over and over again. "Isn't there *anything* you remember? What the man looked like maybe? The markings on the moving van?"

"I remember the guy's car."

That was a start. "What about his car?"

Catao grinned. "The name of the museum was on the plates. I remember thinking museum work must pay pretty well for him to be driving a BMW."

The hair rose all over Garreth's body. *Lady Luck, you bitch, I love you!* "This guy, was he in his fifties, average height and weight, graying hair, mustache, glasses?"

"I'm not sure about a mustache and glasses." The manager's forehead creased with the effort of remembering. "But the rest sounds right. How—"

"Thank you very much, Mr. Catao." Garreth hurried for the building door. "Sorry to have bothered you. Have a nice day."

At the car he waited impatiently for Fowler to catch up. The man who came for Bodenhausen's belongings had to be Holle. How many men in San Francisco drove BMW's with personalized plates carrying the name of an organization which might be mistaken for a museum name? The Philos Foundation. This made four people with links to that organization: Irina, Holle, Bodenhausen, and Corinne Barlow ... two of them part of the murder case, three of them vampires. Too many people for pure coincidence. Philos bore looking into.

Fowler unlocked the car. "Hello, hello. Something he said put a piece in the puzzle, did it?"

Sooner or later the writer would have to be given some answers, but ... not yet. "Maybe." Garreth climbed into the car and lay back in the seat, giving up the fight against daylight's drag for a few minutes.

"Maybe?" Fowler said. "You know it bloody *did*. That was Holle you described. Now what's the connection?"

Maybe he needed to confide in Fowler a little at least. "It was Holle. The connection is the Philos Foundation. But since Harry and company will end up there sooner or later, too, on their way through Holle's address book, we can't afford a straightforward visit." Garreth closed his eyes. "Head for Union Street. We'll think up something devious on the way."

7

All that distinguished the yellow-with-brown-trim Foundation headquarters from the other shop-filled Victorian houses around it was drapes instead of some commercial display inside the bay window and a discrete brass plate on the door at the top of steep brick steps. *Philos Foundation*, script engraving read. *Please ring for admittance.*

Fowler pushed the bell.

A minute later the door was opened by a slim young woman whose modish dress and frizzy mane of hair made her look like a fashion model. A spicy scent that smelled equal parts cinnamon and clove wafted out of the house past her. "Good afternoon. May I help—" She broke off, staring past the writer at Garreth.

His gut knotted. She recognized him for what he was! If she said anything in front of Fowler ...

But she said only: "Please come in."

Garreth followed her and Fowler inside, feeling as though he were walking into a mine field.

Judging by the house's interior, the Philos Foundation suffered from no shortage of money despite its non-profit status. Garreth could not help but compare the bargain furnishings and poster-decorated walls at the Bay Mission Crisis Center with this thick carpeting and a front room furnished in chrome-and-leather chairs, modern sculpture, and signed/numbered prints. The spicy odor became more pronounced, drowning the blood scents in the room.

The young woman sat down at a desk made of chrome and glass. An engraved name plate said: *Meresa Ranney*. "What may I do for you, Mr. ...?"

Fowler smiled at her. "Warwick. Richard Warwick. A friend of mine came over here to work for your organization several years ago and as I'm in town for a bit, I thought I'd look her up. Corinne Barlow."

While Fowler occupied the receptionist Garreth strolled around the room, trying to look idle ... peering out the bay window, touching sculpture, eyeing the prints ... all the while studying the house covertly.

"Corinne Barlow?" The receptionist frowned. "I'm sorry but I don't know the name. What does she do?"

The rear wall had a large fireplace with a door to one side. Nothing identified what might be beyond it. Garreth remembered seeing double sliding doors on down the hallway. They probably opened into the same room as this door. Which would be what, an administrative office?

"Corinne works with computers," Fowler said.

The accident report had mentioned that in vital statistics about the victim.

Garreth eyed the doorway to the hall. He could see the bottom of the stairs through it. Nothing indicated what lay up them, however.

The receptionist's frown deepened. She shook her head. "I'm sorry, I'm afraid—oh." Her breath caught. "Now I remember. There was an Englishwoman. I'd completely forgotten her, she was here so short a time."

"She got sacked? Damn." Fowler feigned disappointment beautifully. "I don't suppose you'd know where she went."

"She wasn't fired." The lovely model's face settled into lines of sympathy. "I'm sorry to be the one to tell you. She was killed in a car accident just a couple of weeks after she arrived."

Fowler also acted out shock and grief with the skill of a professional actor. "Damn." His throat worked, then he smiled faintly. "Well, thank you. Sorry to have troubled you." He headed for the hall.

Garreth moved up to the desk ... to the end, so that the receptionist had to look away from hall door to face him.

She regarded Garreth with surprise. "Aren't you with the other gentleman?"

"No, we just met on the steps outside. I'm Alan Osner."

The front door opened and closed. A moment later Fowler slipped past the doorway and down the hall toward the back of the house.

"I've been staying at Leonard Holle's—I'm sorry," he said contritely as her eyes filled. "I didn't mean to upset you." Inwardly, he noted her reaction with satisfaction. They knew Holle here all right ... very well.

"No, that's all right." She groped in a desk drawer. "I'm fine."

"I take it you knew Leonard?"

"He was our chapter president." The groping hand came up with a tissue. She carefully blotted her eyes and inspected the damage with a small mirror from the same drawer. "It's been a terrible—who are you looking for, Mr. Osner?"

Fowler reappeared in the hall and started up the stairs.

"Miss Irina Rudenko. Leonard's housekeeper said I might find her here."

On the bottom step, Fowler started, turning to stare at Garreth for a moment before continuing up the stairs.

"I'm sorry," the receptionist said. "Miss Rudenko isn't here right now. Would you care to leave a message?"

"I'd rather see her personally." He forced his voice to remain casual, to ignore the drumming urgency in him. "Do you have a home phone for her?"

"I can't give out that kind of information, sir."

Garreth casually took off his glasses.

Such improbably blue eyes had to be a product of tinted contacts. The depth and wideness was her own, though, and for an uneasy moment as he caught her gaze, Garreth wondered if a vampire could ever become trapped in his victim's eyes. He forced himself to widen his focus beyond the twin cobalt pools.

A mistake. A pulse pounded visibly in her long neck. The tantalizing warmth of her blood scent carressed him, perceptible despite the spicy odor filling the room. Hunger exploded in him. She stared into his eyes, lips parted as though in anticipation. Anticipation seared him, too ... the feel of her in his arms—pliant, yielding—the throb of that pulse against his lips and searching tongue ... the exquisite salty fire of her blood in his mouth. He started around the desk toward her.

Laughter whispered in his head ... eager, mocking. Lane's laughter.

Garreth caught himself in horror. Jumping back, he jammed on his glasses and shoved his hands in his coat pockets to hide their tremble. He fought to steady his voice. "Do you think Irina might be in later?"

The receptionist blinked up at him with the puzzled expression of a waking sleeper struggling to orient herself. "I ... don't know. Mr. Holle gives—gave her the run of the place since her mother works for the Foundation in Geneva, but since *she* doesn't work for us herself we never know when—" She hesitated a moment, then smiled. "I guess I can tell *you*, though."

The hair on his neck rippled. "Why me in particular?"

She gave him a brilliant smile. "Your aura, of course. People with black ones always seem to get preferential treatment around here. See, I have this gift for seeing auras. Mostly I don't tell people because they laugh or get nervous, like they're afraid I'll read their minds or something. The people here at the Foundation don't mind, though. Mrs. Keith, that's Mr. Holle's secretary, even said it's one of the reasons they hired me. I usually see black just around dying people, but yours isn't the same kind of black. It's ... bright, if that makes any sense, a very intense, fiery black. Very rare. Miss Rudenko has your kind of aura, though, and so does one of the bloodbank techs who works nights. The Englishwoman the other gentleman was looking for had it, too."

Garreth breathed in slowly. This had to be the vampire connection Ricky the hustler and Holle's housekeeper hinted at. He remembered the blood in Holle's refrigerator. How much of the blood Philos collected ended up somewhere besides hospitals and the Red Cross?

"Do you suppose it's genetic?" the receptionist said. "Maybe you're all related somehow."

Hunger still licked at him. He avoided looking at her throat. "We share a common bloodline, yes. You were going to tell me something about Irina?"

"Oh yes. She mostly comes by in the evening, when she's bored with running around town, probably. We're closed then, except for the bloodbank staff, of course," —she pointed at the ceiling— "so when you come back tell them Meresa said for you to."

In the hall, Fowler slipped down the stairs and past the doorway. The front door opened and closed, and a moment later Fowler hurried into the front room. "I beg your pardon, but—"

The receptionist stiffened. "How did you get back in? The door is locked on the outside."

"Really? Perhaps it didn't closed solidly behind me. Be that as it may, I came to inform this gentleman that his car has apparently slipped out of gear and is inching its way along the curb toward freedom. I do think you ought to get *out* there. Immediately."

Garreth caught the emphasis. "Shit!" He raced for the door. "Harry and company?" he muttered at Fowler.

"Quite. I spotted them from the hall window upstairs."

"How far?"

"Half a block."

Garreth's stomach dropped. That close? Step on the sidewalk and they would spot him. Yet where else was there to go? He looked around desperately as the outside door closed behind him.

The space between this and the adjoining building caught his eye.

Fowler followed his gaze in dismay. "You must be joking. Only a shadow will fit through there."

It did look narrow. However ... he could see Harry and Girimonte coming closer every second. Their attention appeared to be on each other and the open notebooks in their hands but the moment they looked up, they would see him.

He vaulted over the side of the steps and dived between the buildings. It was a tight squeeze. It had to be even worse for Fowler. Somehow, though, the bigger man worked his way through the gap after Garreth.

"God bless adrenalin, which lowers every fence, lightens every weight, and widens even the eye of a needle for a desperate man," Fowler panted as they wormed their way free into the alley behind the Foundation building. He brushed at cobwebs clinging to his suitcoat. "I do hope all this is worth something. Am I wasting my breath asking who this Rudenko woman is?"

Garreth blinked. "From your reaction out there in the hall, I thought you knew her."

"Not her." Fowler shook his head. "Mada's stories mentioned a Polish woman named Irina Rodek and I thought at first you were going to say her name." He lifted a questioning brow. "This is the fourth name now you've pulled out of the air."

"Not quite." *Careful, Mikaelian.* They headed down the alley toward the street. "She's the woman who asked Holle about Lane. The housekeeper mentioned the name."

The writer stared at him in disbelief. "I think I'm going mad. There must be a chain of logic tying all of this together, but it totally escapes me."

"No logic, I'm afraid, just the luck of the Irish." Garreth gave him a wry grin. "What did you find out about the rest of the house?"

"That it's quite true you can go anywhere if you appear to know what you're doing. No one questioned my story about checking the photocopiers. Fortunately I do know something about the contraptions from all the time I've spent tinkering with mine to keep it running. I chatted up a secretary in an office at the back of the house downstairs and some medical technologists and a computer operater on the first floor. None of them know the name Lane Barber; neither have they seen a tall, red-haired woman like Barber at the Foundation. What did the receptionist have to say?"

"I just asked her about Rudenko. I can't risk her mentioning to Harry and Girimonte that they're the second people interested in Lane Barber today."

Fowler sighed. "Quite. Well, then, did she tell you where to find Rudenko?"

Garreth shook his head. "I think she knew, but she wouldn't say."

"Wouldn't say!" Fowler stopped short and spun around to scowl at him. "You didn't press her?"

Memory of what had nearly happened when he started to set him shaking again. "No."

"Christ! How the bloody hell do you expect to learn anything! That creature is out there killing people and blaming you and you're walking away from potential sources of information!"

Why was he so angry? "Hey. Easy. You sound like you're the one being framed."

"And you're bloody casual about it all!" Fowler snarled. His eyes narrowed. "Don't you *want* to find her? Don't you *care* she's going to put you in the dock and maybe make you swing?"

"We use lethal gas in this state." A correct hanging that broke his neck would be one way to kill him, though.

Fowler's hands came up as though to grab him by the throat, but before he actually touched Garreth, he stopped short, blinked, and backed away, grimacing sheepishly. "Good lord. I am sorry. I don't know what the devil got into me. Identifying with you, I suppose ... like I do with my characters. Forgive me."

Garreth eyed him. "No problem. The receptionist did tell me Rudenko comes in evenings. I plan to call back then. For now, you must be starved. Let's get something to eat and head back to Bryant Street before Harry puts out an APB on us."

8

Harry and Girimonte dragged into the squadroom after five. Harry headed for the coffee pot. Girimonte flung herself in her chair, propped her feet on her desk, and lit a cigar. Puffing it, she eyed Garreth and Fowler, who sat at Harry's desk with cups of tea and the Mossman and Adair files. "Well, don't you two look comfortable and satisfied with yourselves. Where've you been all day?"

"Retracing my nightmares," Garreth replied. True enough considering the incident with the receptionist.

"You mean visiting the Barbary Now and places like that?"

Garreth sipped his tea. When she and Harry played Bad Cop/ Good Cop she must do one hell of a job in the tough role. Her question smoldered with accusation. "Was someone killed there this afternoon?"

She blew out smoke. "Cagy, Mikaelian, but it doesn't answer the question."

"Oh? Is this an interrogation?"

Fowler slapped the Adair file closed. "What this is, is juvenile! *I'll* answer the bloody question. Yes, we visited that club, *and* the alley, and the Jack Tar, the Fairmont, and half a dozen other sites connected to the case. We also had coffee at Ghirardelli Square and visited a book store so I could buy a couple of little gifts." He picked up three books from a corner of the desk.

Fowler had spotted the Book Circus while they were working their way around the block back to the car and dragged Garreth in. "Call it professional curiosity, or vanity." He grinned at Garreth. "I want to see which of my books they carry."

Looking around as they entered, Garreth wondered if they would be able to tell. The store consisted of three houses joined by doors cut through the common walls. Book shelves covered every available inch of wallspace, floor to ceiling, even along hallways, up staircases, and under windows. Tables of books and revolving racks also filled the center space in bigger rooms. The sheer abundance left Garreth dizzy.

A clerk drifted over while they stood staring around, wondering where to start. "Is there something in particular you were looking for?"

"Books by Graham Fowler," Fowler said.

The clerk had nodded briskly. "Those would be in Mystery and Suspense. That's up the stairs and the last door on your right. Paperbacks are in the same room. If you collect Fowler, you'll also want to see our British editions. His horror novels have never been published in this country. Go through that door on the left, clear through the room and the door on the far side, then up those stairs. The first door."

They visited both rooms. Looking over the British editions, Fowler grimaced. "Good god; they have everything. Doctors bury their mistakes, barristers argue about them, and politicians deny them, but the indiscretions of a writer's youth haunt him on bookshelves forever."

Garreth eyed the titles. Ones like *Shadow Games* and *Winter Gambit* sounded typical of spy thrillers, but others had a ring of horror: *Nightoaths. Wolf Moon. Bare Bones.* "Which are the indiscretions?"

"You don't really think I'm daft enough to say, do you."

Garreth reached for one called *Blood Maze.*

Fowler blocked his hand. "Have you considered there might be sound reasons American publishers don't want my horror? If you want a book let me choose something."

Now Girimonte reached out a long arm to take the books Fowler had picked out. *"The Man Who Traveled In Murder. A Safe Place To Die. A Wilderness Of Thieves.* I've read the last one and some of your others. They aren't bad, though you do have a thing about tall, long-legged women." She pulled out the bookmark the clerk at the cash register had tucked into the book. "The Book Circus, Union Street." She tapped the ash off her cigar. "That's a bit off the path. City Lights is handier when you're running around North Beach."

Harry, Garreth noticed, had said nothing since coming in, had just poured himself coffee and without adding cream or sugar, moved over by a pillar and stood drinking the coffee, listening. Garreth's gut knotted. He could count on the fingers of one hand the times he remembered Harry drinking black coffee.

Garreth looked around at Harry.

Expression inscrutible, Harry said, "A Union Street book store is in the neighborhood of the Philos Foundation, though."

The knots tightened.

"The what foundation?" Fowler said.

"The Philos Foundation, where you went this afternoon using aliases and asking for the daughter of a friend of Holle's and a staff member who died several years ago."

"Did we really?"

Garreth winced. *Shut up, Fowler; you're only making things worse.*

"Come off it!" Girimonte slammed the books down on the desk with a pistol-shot report that brought detectives whirling toward the sound and Serruto tearing to the door of his office. "While we were there a secretary came in to ask the receptionist if the copier serviceman were still in the building. The receptionist knew nothing about any serviceman. So the secretary described him—a tall, good looking Englishman, she said—and the receptionist said, 'I remember *him*, but he wasn't here about copy machines. Where did you see him? After I told him Corinne Barlow was dead he left ... until he came back to tell the skinny little blond guy in the sunglasses that his car was slipping downhill.' Skinny little blond guy in sunglasses running around with a tall Englishman." Girimote stared at Garreth. The scent of her cigar circled him.

"Takananda!" Serruto's voice cracked like a whip. "I want all four of you in my office."

They trailed in under the stares of the entire squadroom. Garreth held his back straight and his chin up.

With the door closed behind them, Serruto motioned them to chairs, sat on the edge of his desk, and looked them each over, eyes narrow. "All right, Takananda, tell me about this."

Harry finished his coffee and set the cup on the desk. In a flat voice he said, "We were going through Holle's address book in a routine check of his acquaintances for quarrels and enemies. The Philos Foundation was one of the entries. It turns out he served as chapter president."

"I heard the part about the secretary and the copier serviceman. Then what?"

"As the situation appeared suspicious, Inspector Girimonte and I proceeded to interview all Philos staff members in the building. According to them, while the 'serviceman' was locating the photocopiers, he made idle conversation, asking the various staff members if they knew a 'friend' of his he thought 'used to work there,' a tall, striking red-haired woman named Barber."

"What was the other man doing?"

"Keeping the receptionist busy talking about this daughter of a Philos VIP in Geneva so she wouldn't realize the Englishman hadn't left the building," Girimonte said. "We figure the Englishman asked the questions because given a choice between those two," —she tipped her head toward Garreth and Fowler— "who would *you* talk to most readily?"

Garreth bit his lip. With luck they would never consider that Fowler had been given the task because questions about Lane did not matter while those concerning Irina did.

Serruto stood and moved around his desk to his chair. Sitting down, he leaned back. "Did you enjoy playing detective, Mr. Fowler?"

Fowler met his gaze coolly. "Suppose I deny being there?"

"We'll just invite the receptionist to have a look at you."

Fowler frowned. "Lieutenant, I fail to see what we've done that's so reprehensible. We just lent assistance to—"

"Lent assistance." Serruto leaned forward in his chair. "When did your status here change from observer to investigator?"

Fowler stiffened.

"And how is it you see nothing wrong in assisting a man who may be involved in three murders with a line of investigation he has conducted without informing official investigaors, an investigation he has conducted with all possible secrecy, in fact?"

Fowler stared at the wall behind Serruto.

The lieutenant sat back again. "So ... I hope you learned everything you needed for your book because ..." —his voice went glacial— "this little stunt has just cost you all your priviledges in this department."

Folwer's mouth thinned. "I doubt you speak for your entire department, lieutenant. We'll see what your superiors have to say about this."

"Fine. Talk to them." Serruto smiled thinly. "Then I'll tell them how you've gone about researching your book and abusing our hospitality."

The anger died out of Fowler's eyes. "No. That ... won't be necessary." Glancing at Garreth, he grimaced. "Sorry. We did have a good go at it, though, didn't we. There are no hard feelings, I hope, Lieutenant." He extended a hand across the desk.

Serruto ignored it. "Goodbye, Mr. Fowler."

Fowler shrugged. "Goodbye, Lieutenant."

When the door had closed behind the writer, Serruto swiveled toward Garreth, mouth set in a grim line.

He already sat board-stiff in his chair. Now Garreth fought to breath. The air had suddenly become suffocatingly thick with the smells of blood and cigar smoke. At least fear kept him from feeling hunger ... fear less of what Serruto might say and do than of having Harry here to see and hear it. Even now his old partner's face did not manage to be quite inscrutible enough to hide the anger and pain behind it. And there was nothing to say in defense. He had broken promises to limit himself to riding along. He had lied this morning about what he intended to do with the day. Had lied by evasion minutes ago about where he and Fowler had been. Worse, he had lied to Harry.

I Ching missed the point today. The danger in floundering ahead was not personal but what his actions did to other people he cared about ... shattering trust, destroying the last vestiges of friendship. Lane chuckled in his head. *That precious bridge of yours may not go down in flames after all, lover. I think you've just dynamited it.*

"I warned you, Mikaelian," Serruto said.

Garreth looked down. "Yes, sir."

"But you wouldn't—take off those damn glasses! I'm sick of looking at my own reflection when I talk to you."

Slowly, Garreth pulled them off. Light slapped at him. He winced. Logic said that exposing his eyes could not increase the pressure of daylight on him, but it felt that way. He gritted his teeth against the drag.

"And look at me. I want to see your eyes."

Garreth focused on a point past the lieutenant's ear. It would not do to inadvertantly hypnotize Serruto to a friendlier attitude in the presence of two witnesses to wonder at the sudden change.

Serruto leaned forward, elbows on the desk. Steel rang in his voice. "Now talk to me, mister. Explain yourself. Tell me why I shouldn't consider you a prime suspect in these murders and arrest you."

The tightness of Garreth's throat made talking difficult, especially maintaining a calm tone. "Because you don't have any hard evidence, no witnesses, no associative evidence that can put me at the scene of any of the murders. More than that, they're clumsy murders. If I can break into Holle's house so slickly, do you see me being careless enough to leave obvious evidence of torture and to kill those men under circumstances that implicate me?"

Not even Girimonte rebutted that.

Serruto pursed his lips. "So … the question becomes, what do we do with you then? This Lone Wolf Mikaelian crap is *over*! Terminated. Finished." He punctuated the words with a stabbing finger. "But I can't just pack you back to Kansas—even if I could be sure you'd go—because if there's no hard evidence, there's also too much circumstantial evidence to ignore."

"I wouldn't go, no. Not until this thing is settled." Garreth folded and unfolded the temples of his glasses.

Girimonte ground out her cigar in the big glass ash tray on the lieutenant's desk. "If you really wanted this case solved you'd be working with us, sharing your information instead of hiding it from us."

How did he answer that without more lies? He put back on the glasses. "There's nothing I can tell you." *Not without giving away too much about myself in the process.*

She snorted. "Nothing you *will* tell us, you mean. Evasions and half-truths are nice strategies … not-quite-lies that still avoid the truth. You use them expertly, but then, you've had lots of practice from using them in the rest of your life, haven't you? Just like my sister."

His chest tightened. "Your sister?"

"She was like you. That's how I recognize what you are. I've seen all the little tricks before, especially the ones for dealing with meals."

The air petrified in Garreth's chest. She *had* figured it out.

"What do you mean, recognize what he is?" Serruto snapped.

There was no way to run, nowhere to run to. *No escape, I Ching* had said. Garreth braced himself.

Girimonte shook her head. "It's personal, nothing to do with the case. But one day soon you and I will talk, Mikaelian. The problem has to be dealt with."

All the relief he felt with the first part of her reply to Serruto vanished beneath a flood of cold. She had spoken of her sister in the past tense. Could Grandma Doyle have mistaken the eye color of the woman deadly to him?

She lit another cigar. "Sorry for the digression, Lieutenant. You were wondering what to do with Mikaelian. Why not call him a material witness?" She drew on the cigar and blew smoke toward Garreth. "That gives us the perfect excuse to keep him under surveillance and on a short leash ... without some lawyer screaming that we're violating his civil rights."

Serruto's brows hopped. "Thinking truely worthy of a future chief." He leaned back, lacing his fingers together behind his head. "All right, you're a material witness, Mikaelian. Any objections?"

"Does it matter if I have?" Garreth said bitterly.

"Of course. If you'd prefer that I find a charge to book you on, I'll accomodate you." When Garreth said nothing to that, he turned toward Harry. "He's already your guest, Takananda. Will you hold the leash? I want it short. I don't want him out of your sight."

Harry sucked in his lower lip. Garreth wondered if he were going to say he would just as soon have nothing more to do with his ex-partner. Right now he must be angrily regretting ever having invited Garreth out from Kansas. After a moment, however, Harry said in a flat voice, "Count on it, sir. Until this is over, it'll be like we're handcuffed together."

9

By unspoken agreement, Garreth and Harry banged into the house tossing one-liners at each other ... despite a ride home in strained silence. The effort was wasted, though. The tightness of Lien's face told Garreth that she already suspected something had gone terribly wrong between them.

She made no attempt at light conversation, either, just gave each a fierce hug and said, "Your tea is in the family room. Don't bother to help me set the table. Sit down and relax."

They sat down and reached for the teacups in silence. Lien must have had a bad day, too, Garreth reflected. She had forgotten to put rum in his tea, though he smelled it in the steam off Harry's tea. Not that he minded. Now he could actually drink the tea. The warm liquid eased the edge on his hunger, if not the knots of misery in his stomach.

True to her word, Lien reappeared in less than five minutes. "Dinner's ready. But, Garreth, dear, I hope you won't mind that I've put yours in the kitchen. I need to talk to my husband alone."

That was fine, except for the scent of shrimp fried rice filling the kitchen, making him simultaneously ache with longing for some and nauseated at the thought of it lying in his stomach. But both longing and nausea vanished abruptly seeing what Lien had set out on the counter for him. Nothing but his thermos and a tall pewter tankard. And a note: *There's no point giving you a regular serving which you'll just leave untouched on the plate. Go ahead and have what you* will *eat.*

He sat down hard on a stool. Lien had written him many notes over the years, but never one that brusque.

He filled the tankard from the thermos and sat sipping the blood, but it tasted sour as dead blood. Lien had tired of him snubbing her cooking. Harry no longer trusted him and along with Serruto thought he had killed Holle, Maruska, and the Count. His bridge had blown up indeed. Nothing remained of it.

There were other bridges, though. The voice on Christopher Stroda's suicide tape played back in his head: "I'm about to jump off the Golden Gate Bridge. If my body is found, please cremate it and scatter the ashes. I want nothing left of me. Mom, Dad, please forgive me for doing this to you. I know it's going to hurt you and spoil Christmas ... but I can't face another family mob scene ... all that gaiety and togetherness ... and food. What I'm doing isn't your fault. It's no one's fault, not even Melina's. All she wanted was to save my life. But it's trapped me on the other side of a chasm from everyone I love, with no way to ever rejoin you, and I can't bear the loneliness. Goodbye."

Garreth swirled the blood in the tankard. Maybe Stroda was right. The price of forever was too high. Even Lane dreaded the loneliness. How many vampires secretly welcomed the stake even as they screamed at the pain? How many, like Stroda, committed suicide? Nothing about Bodenhausen's death suggested anything except an accident, but had Corinne Barlow accidentally swerved into the oncoming traffic, controlled by reflexes schooled to driving on the lefthand side of the road, or was it a deliberate act of self destruction?

Lien banged through the swinging door from the dining room and dumped a load of dishes on the sink. "That man! He's obviously in anguish, but he won't talk to me and he won't hear anything I have to say."

Garreth tensed. Would she ask *him* what was going on?

"No, I won't try to pry out of you what's wrong. That would only aggravate things, I'm sure."

He started, staring at her.

She smiled and reached out to pat his arm. "Don't look so panic stricken. I'm not reading minds, just the expression on your face." She turned back to the sink, reaching for the faucets. "Of course, if you want someone to talk to, I'm always here."

"I know. Thank you." Like Stroda's family, she wanted so much to help, never realizing that the problem lay beyond even her compassionate understanding. He changed the subject. "Did Harry show you the book Fowler gave him?"

"Yes. *That* he would talk about. You have one, too?"

He nodded, then faked a yawn. "I'm bushed. I think I'll go on to bed. Say goodnight to Harry for me."

In his room, he locked the door and stretched out on the bed with Fowler's book. It would pass the time until Harry and Lien went to bed.

It would have, that is, if he had been able to concentrate. He could not. Stroda's tape replayed in his head over and over. No matter how many times he read the print before him, all Garreth saw was a tortured figure arcing off the Golden Gate bridge in a parody of a swan dive. After an hour all he could really say about the book was that Fowler had written a very accurate description of a second-story burglary. The man obviously did his research.

Then a new character appeared, a woman ... tall, red-haired, fascinating. Goosebumps rose on Garreth's neck and arms. Maybe Fowler had another image in mind, but Garreth could only think: *Lane*.

From Lane his thoughts jumped to Irina. Where was she? Planning another murder?

A rap sounded on the door. "Garreth?"

Harry's voice. Slowly, Garreth went over to the door and opened it. His stomach dropped. What was wrong now? He had never seen Harry look so acutely embarrassed before. "What's—" he began, and broke off.

One glance at Harry's hand answered the question. He carried a key. Holding it up, he said, "I—I just wondered if you needed to use the bathroom anymore because—damn it, Garreth, I'm sorry, but I'm going to have to lock you in."

That was how thoroughly trust had been destroyed. Numb, Garreth spoke across the bottomless, bridgeless gulf between them and marveled at how casual he managed to sound. "I understand. Go ahead. See you in the morning."

He closed the door.

The lock clicked.

The sound cut like a knife through his control. Garreth hurled the book across the room and smashed a fist down on the bureau. The wallet/pocketchange caddy on top hopped with the force of the blow. "Irina, you bitch, damn you! *Damn* you!"

If he had had any doubts about what he planned to do tonight, they had vanished. To hell with the warnings from *I Ching* and his grandmother. He had to find Irina, for his own satisfaction as well preventing another murder. Even if it meant dying. Better him than a fourth innocent person, and tonight death seemed less something to be feared than welcomed anyway.

10

Union Street still had enough traffic that Garreth quickly decided using Philos' front door was too risky. Someone might see him. But in the alley behind the Foundation that afternoon, he had noticed a back door opening onto the alley. He found it again now and after pulling on the gloves he had carried with him in the pocket of his warm-up jacket, moved through into the building.

This part of it apparently did not see much traffic. He caught little trace of human scent in the stronger musty odor of basement. File cabinets and open shelving stacked with boxes of office supplies lined the outer wall of the long, narrow room that ended with stairs. An open door in the opposite direction revealed the furnace room.

A second door beyond it was closed ... and locked, as Garreth discovered when he tried the handle. Moving through, he found himself in a darkness so total that not even his vampire vision could see anything. He felt space around him, however, and the air smelled dry and stale. Exploring along the edge of the door, he located a light switch and flipped it on. His brows rose. The large room, occupying nearly half the floor area of the building, was a bomb shelter, equipped with not only a dozen bunks and supplies enough to feed twelve or so people for months but a shortwave radio and refrigeration equipment with a gas motor ... clearly intended to store a massive amount of blood. The unit held several plastic bags of blood even now.

Philos was prepared for the desperate need that would exist if there ever were a nuclear attack, Garreth reflected. Presuming they did not sit on ground zero. But was this just for the future? Eyeing the room, it occurred to him that the shelter would make an ideal place for someone to hide.

A quick examination of the bunks and careful tasting of the air quickly told him no one had done so recently. The stale air carried no trace of sweat or perfume, certainly not the spicy-musky perfume he had smelled in the third floor room of Holle's house.

With a grimace of disappointment, he switched off the light again and moved back through the door.

The basement stairs came out under the stairs in the hallway. After opening the door a crack to make sure no one would see him, he slipped out into the hall and stood pressed against the wall, listening and sniffing. Voices and a laugh floated down the stairs to him. At least two people were upstairs, then, but he smelled no blood scent strong enough to suggest that anyone might be on this floor.

Still, he was careful to move soundlessly as he explored. A large, comfortably appointed office sat behind the reception area. Holle's. Garreth only glanced around it before moving on down the hall. Since Holle never had the chance to come back here after Irina moved out of his house, he could not have a new address for her. At the back of the house lay a kitchen slightly remodeled into an employee lunch room/lounge. A utilitarian office with files and several desks adjoined it and connected in turn to another office next to Holle's, smaller but carpeted and furnished more stylishly. A framed photograph of a woman with two teenage children stood on the tidy desk between a vase of tulips and a Rolodex file and appointment book. Holle's secretary? He hoped so. If Irina had told anyone where she could be reached, it would have been Holle's secretary.

Sitting down, Garreth reached for the Rolodex. This was probably a slim chance. Still … he might get lucky.

He spun the side knob to bring the R's around. RE … RI … RU … RUDENKO. But the card was for a Natalya Rudenko at the Philos Foundation in Geneva, Switzerland. Irina's "mother," no doubt. He eyed the appointment book. Perhaps a local number had been written down there.

He pulled the book over close and turned the page back to Wednesday. Was it only yesterday, well, day before yesterday now, that they had found Holle's body? It seemed an eternity ago.

The page had little writing: a few appointments written in precise, square printing ... crossed out by a shakier hand. But there was one telephone number, scribbled in the margin near the bottom of the page, with a note under it in that same unsteady hand: something heavily crossed out, followed by a legible word *Rieger*.

Garreth stared at it, sucking on his lower lip. Was it what he was looking for? He squinted at the crossed out word but could not decipher it through the scribble over it. He turned the page to study the back side and the preceeding page. And grimaced. Only the impressions of the crossout strokes had come through, not those of the word itself.

Or two words, maybe, he decided, turning to Wednesday again and studying it more. It started with SH, but something looking vaguely like a capital P appeared halfway along the word, and a lower case L shortly after that. Garreth frowned in concentration. Sh ... P.l ...

A click sounded in his head. He grinned. Sheraton-Palace?

The longer he studied the notation, the more logical that seemed. The name fit the space, and the Sheraton-Palace was an old hotel that had survived the 1906 quake. If Irina had been visiting San Francisco for a very long time, it would be one place she remembered from the past. Rieger could be the name she registered under.

He glanced around the office for a phone book. One look at the classified pages should verify if the telephone number was for the hotel.

"I believe directory is locked in lower right drawer," a female voice said behind him.

Garreth whipped around in disbelief and panic, adrenalin flushing icy hot through him. How could anyone sneak up on him? He had not heard or smelled anything!

But now a scent reached him ... sweetly spicy-musky, wafting from a slight figure standing against the still-closed door from the hall.

He stared, breath frozen in his chest. Meeting her anywhere else, he would have taken her for just another sixteen or seventeen-year-old, especially in her designer jeans, ankle-high fashion boots, and and over-sized shirt. Lane had described Irina as exquisite, like a Dresden figurine, but at five-foot-nothing, flat-chested, and dark hair cropped boyishly short above a face with slavic cheekbones, pixyish described her better. Except there was nothing pixyish in her faintly slanting eyes ... nothing childlike, either. Darkness robbed them of color, but not expression; they watched him coldly, appraising, noting his every move.

Nor was there anything remotely pixyish about the Beretta she pointed at him.

"You are Garreth Mikaelian, I think?"

Garreth could not identify her accent. Eastern European originally, perhaps; now very diluted. "And you're Irina Rudenko."

"But of course. I see you're staring at my toy." She hefted the Beretta. It looked gigantic in her small hand. "Do you like it?"

"I'm wondering what you think you're going to do with it." She must know bullets could not hurt him.

"Shoot you perhaps," Irina replied. "Clip has ebony bullets."

Adenalin spurted in him again. Ebony! Little pieces of wooden stake tearing through him propelled by exploding powder! "You'd kill one of your own kind?"

Stupid question, man, an inner voice snarled. *Of course she would. She already has.*

"Why not? *You* do."

The adrenalin turned to ice. She knew about Lane! He covertly eyed the distance between his chair and the far corner of the desk.

The gun waggled fractionally side to side, like a head gesturing *no*. "It would be foolish. I learned to shoot before pistols had bullets or rifling in barrel and I could knock flies from a horse even then."

The matter-of-fact statement drove the ice into his bones. Garreth fought rising panic, fought to think of a defense, or escape.

"But I prefer not to shoot. It's best this seem like an accident and not another murder." She stepped away from the door. "Shall we go?"

His mind raced. Could he jump her as he passed her? No, she had moved well to one side. So he remained seated. "If you want me dead, you'll have to kill me here."

"As you wish," she said calmly. "It just means I must be sure your body is never found." Her finger tightened on the trigger.

Desperation acted where logic had failed. He hurled the appointment book at her, then flung himself after it, grabbing for the gun. But she ducked sideways before he was halfway there. His hands found only empty air.

Movement blurred across his peripheral vision. He had just time to identify it as the gun barrel slicing at him before pain exploded in the side of his head.

The floor smashed up into him.

From a great echoing distance Irina said mockingly, "Thank you."

Dimly, he felt her bend over him. A hand caught the back of his head, another his chin. Terror exploded in Garreth. She intended to break his neck!

He tried to roll, to catch her wrists and break her grip … but his body obeyed weakly, sluggishly. Her foot pinned his left wrist to the floor.

"I've always wondered about Afterlife," Irina said. Her grip tightened. "Usually I have hoped none exists. There are too many souls I would not care to meet again. But for you, I hope there is, so your victims may confront you."

One word penetrated the storm of terror and dizzying pain. Victims? Plural? Who else besides Lane? He struggled to force his tongue into cooperation before she started the fatal jerk. "What … victims?"

"Leonard Holle and that male prostitute, of course."

Confusion thundered through the fog in his head. Relief: she had not learned about Lane after all! Bewilderment: then why had she killed those three men? But she accused *him* of the murders. Except she was one victim short. Because she wanted to confuse him or because … she knew nothing about the Count?

He wrenched at the wrist trapped under the instep of her boot. "I didn't kill either of them, or Count Dracula either!"

The grip on his head tightened still more. "Dracula! What are you talking about?"

Too late he realized how ridiculous the remark must have sounded. He said hastily … through his teeth because of her grip, "The hustler's roommate. We found his body later the same day Holle died. He called himself Count Dracula and acted like a movie vampire. Someone drove a stake through his heart."

Above him, her breath caught. "Holy Mother. And you claim that someone wasn't you?"

"It *wasn't* me."

She released his head, but only to grab him by the shoulders and slam him backward into the desk. "Then why are you here, Garreth?" she asked softly. Glowing ruby red, her eyes stared into his. "Why, if not hunting me to kill, too?"

He squeezed his eyes shut in a chilly rush of fear. He did not dare yield to her. What if she asked about Lane?

She whispered, "Garreth, look at me."

No! he thought.

"You say you didn't kill Leonard and the others, but how can I know that?" Her voice purred. "Look at me, Garreth. Is only one way to be sure. Only one way. You must know that. Look at me."

Her voice pulled at him. Lane had been able to do that, he remembered. While he lay on his driveway with her arrow through his shoulder, her voice alone had almost made him turn where she could take a second, fatal shot at him. Irina had even more of that kind of power, he sensed.

"Look at me."

The whisper slid through the pain and fog in his head.

"Look at me."

It snagged him. Slowly, inexorably, his chin lifted. His eyes opened.

Irina's filled his vision, pulling him in until nothing else existed but their glowing ruby depths. He barely heard her voice, distant and warmly approving. "That's better. Now, did you kill Leonard and the other men?"

"No."

She spun away and paced across the room, hands clasped together at her chin, as though in prayer.

Freed, Garreth slumped back dazed against the desk. "I—I thought you killed them. Only another vampire could have overpowered Maruska that way at night."

Irina looked around. "Go. Leave the city and go home to the prairie where you are safe."

He blinked at her and sat up straighter. The action set his head throbbing. He ignored it. "No way. There's a murderer loose killing people and trying to frame me. I have to find who it is."

Irina's mouth thinned. "What a foolish child you are! You have no idea what you're dealing with. Go home and leave this to those with experience to handle it."

He eyed her. "Could it have anything to do with the reason you wanted to find Lane so urgently?"

She hesitated, and before answering, came back and leaned down to catch his arm. Pulling him to his feet, she said, "Be sensible and go. You are a child of Mada's excesses. Do not become a victim of them also."

A part of him bristled at being shooed away like a bothersome child, especially by someone who looked like a child herself, but the irritation dissipated before a chilling thought. Back at Holle's house he had wondered if another vampire might be involved. What if that were the case? An old, powerful, perhaps crazed one might explain Irina's concern. But only one vampire would explain those last two statements. Lane. He fought to breathe.

"Irina, it is possible—"

Belatedly, he realized he was talking to the air. In the few moments he was lost in thought, Irina had left, moving so silently that not even he heard.

He sat down at the desk again, shaking. Lane. Death waited for him in this city, Grandma Doyle said. Could that mean Lane, not Irina? Could she really be here after all, in spite of everything? But if that were true, if all of his precautions had still not kept Lane in her grave, what was it going to *take* to lay her once and for all?

BLOODLINKS

1

For once it was a relief to be awake and moving around by daylight. The pounding on his door had rescued him from dreams of finding Lane's grave blown open as though by dynamite and Christopher Stroda sitting at the bottom of the gaping hole gestering for Garreth to join him. Lien's *I Ching* reading for the day gave him something else to think about. Number Three, Difficulty At the Beginning.

"It leads to supreme success, which comes through perseverence," Lien said at breakfast. "But no move should be made prematurely and one should not go alone; one should appoint helpers. A change line at the beginning reinforces the need to have helpers, that change line producing hexagram Number Eight, Holding Together. For good fortune we must unite with others who complement and aid one another."

Garreth followed Harry into the Hall of Justice elevator. Helpers. Sure. He grimaced. Who? It would be difficult to team up with Fowler again, even if he wanted to, and telling Harry everything would only make the case against him worse.

Girimonte already sat at her desk when they walked into Homicide. She looked up with a grin. "Good news. We finally ID'd Count Dracula. Clarence Parmley, formerly of Columbia, Missouri. His prints came in from the FBI this morning, on file from an arrest in 1971 for civil disobedience—protesting U.S. involvement in Viet Nam." She puffed her cigar. "I gather that was in the halcyon days of youth, before he became a vampire."

Serruto appeared in the doorway of his office. "Briefing. Let's get to it, troops. Bad news, Harry. Lieutenant Fogelsong in Burglary just called me. There was a break-in at the Philos Foundation last night. A blood bank technician is in the hospital with a concussion and the file cabinets were all jimmied open. Another tech in the building who caught a glimpse of the intruder describes him as a man with light-colored hair and a stocking over his face."

Garreth's stomach dropped in dismay.

"It couldn't have been Garreth," Harry protested. "I had his door locked from the outside."

"Did you have the window barred?" Girimonte asked.

Serruto said, "We ought to know something one way or the other before too long. The tech said she'd come downtown sometime this morning to look at mug shots. You won't mind sticking around here for a lineup instead of going out with Takananda and Girimonte, will you, Mikaelian?"

Harry's mouth tightened.

But Garreth made himself shrug. "Of course not."

He slumped in a chair, closing his eyes. A break-in. It had to have happened after he left. But ... who? Lane? She had passed as a man before. Last night's dream came back to him. Cold ran down his spine. The hair color could be from dye, or a wig.

Had she followed him there? She must have. She must have been watching him all along. It was too much for coincidence that Maruska's killer intercepted him before Garreth arrived and that Holle's killer and the Philos burglar went to work just after Garreth left them.

After the briefing ended, Harry and Girimonte picked up their coats and headed for the door. "Oh, if you need something to do, Mikaelian, you can read the book Fowler gave me," Girimonte called back. "It's in the upper lefthand drawer of my desk."

You know what you can do with your book, honey, Garreth thought.

Fifteen minutes later he found himself reaching for the book anyway. It was the only thing to do. Everyone else remaining in the squadroom avoided him as though he had caught AIDS. Concentration proved as difficult as it had been the night before, though. His mind kept slipping back to the break-in and Lane, a distraction not helped by a tall, charming brunette in the book who reminded Garreth of Lane. He gripped the book, white-knuckled. How could she still be alive? *How*?

Serruto tapped his shoulder. "Let's go. That witness from the Philos Foundation is in Burglary."

Garreth had filled in for several lineups before. Since he had not been the man the technician saw, this should be no different, he told himself. Then while shuffling into the lighted box with four other lean, blondish officers, it occurred to him that the technician might have described not someone she saw at all but someone Lane, using hypnotic powers, told her she saw. He bit his lip. This could be the evidence Lane intended to incriminate him once and for all.

"Face the front," a voice said from the speaker overhead.

Garreth put his back against the height-graduated wall.

"Number three, take off your glasses."

Slowly he complied, and stood squinting into the lights that kept him from seeing who sat on the darkened side of the glass wall facing him.

An eternity dragged by while the hair prickled all over Garreth's body and cold ate into his bones. Smells of blood and aftershave and cigarette smoke pressed around him, strengthed by confinement in the lineup box.

"That's all," said the voice from the speaker.

He put his glasses back on and they all shuffled out.

To Garreth's surprise, only Serruto waited for him. Grinning, the lieutenant slapped his back. "Congratulations; you're too short."

He could not feel much relief. That might lift suspicion from him but a burglar taller than he did not rule out Lane.

2

Being cleared of suspicion in the break-in changed nothing back in Homicide either. The activity in the squadroom continued to flow around him as though he were invisible. He went back to his book and speculation. If Lane broke into the Foundation, why had she bypassed the perfect opportunity to finish the frame? Maybe, he decided hopefully, she was not responsible after all. The burglary did not have to be connected with this case at all. It could have been just some junkie aware of a medical facility there and hoping to find drugs.

In the file cabinets? a thought mocked him.

Questions without answers. Garreth tried to forget them for the time being and concentrate on the book.

He still had trouble enjoying it. Mrs. Stroda's comment on how Fowler's characters treated other people as disposable tools came back to him. The protagonist callously used and discarded several colleagues and supposed friends. Garreth found himself almost regretting that the tall brunette, who proved to be working for the other side, failed in her attempt to kill the hero.

A feeling of danger jerked him up out of the book. Looking around swiftly, he saw nothing new or threatening in the squadroom, only Faye and Centrello marching in with their lunches in carryout boxes.

Lunch! He lurched to his feet. From one of the boxes came the scent of garlic rolls! Panic exploded in him as air turned to concrete in his lungs. Suffocation! Clawing at the turtleneck of his shirt, fighting for breath, he bolted for the door and the untainted air of the corridor. Someone shouted behind him but he kept going.

The odor of garlic hung in the corridor, too, marking the carryout's passage. The movement of air was dispersing it, though. That made the air just syrup instead of concrete. He sagged against the wall, head thrown back, eyes closed, and concentrated on forcing the syrup in and out of his lungs.

Footsteps pounded toward him. He opened his eyes to find Serruto, Faye, and Centrello piling out through Homicide's door and screeching to a halt in the middle of the corridor, staring at him. Other people in the corridor stared, too.

"Mikaelian, what the hell are you doing?" Serruto demanded.

How did he answer without giving himself away? Why not the same excuse he gave Maggie for his tenseness in movie theaters. "Sorry. I get … claustrophobic sometimes."

Serruto raised a skeptical brow. "Claustrophobic? That looked more like a panic attack to me. How long have you had them? Is this what happened in the restaurant the day Harry got shot?"

Faye and Centrello exchanged grimaces. Garreth groaned inwardly. Terrific. Now they thought he was psycho. "No, this is something different," he snapped. "It's a reaction to being a murder suspect."

Serruto scowled. "Don't get cute. Are you over whatever it is now?"

The undertone of genuine concern dissolved Garreth's anger. He sighed and nodded. "I will be if I can stand out here a minute longer."

"Faye, Centrello, stay with him."

Serruto turned and went back into the squadroom.

Mischief glinted in Faye's eyes and tweaked a corner of his mouth. "Panic attack. Partner, I know we're ugly, but this is the first time it's sent someone screaming from the room."

Garreth managed a weak smile. "Not you, your garlic rolls. Garlic has some bad associations for me."

Faye grinned. "It does, huh. Aha! Another vampire."

Only the detective's grin prevented a surge of panic. "*Another* vampire?"

"Sure. You and Clarence 'Count Dracula' Parmley. When we answered that call the other morning, he met us in the hall outside the apartment and wouldn't go back in." Faye's voice went high and mincing. "The place positively reeks. I almost didn't find him because of it. I only went storming in because I was so furious at Ricky for fixing Italian food when he *knows* I can't tolerate garlic.'"

Shock jolted Garreth, followed by a rush of relief. Garlic! Then Lane could not possibly be involved.

Centrello's long face distorted in a grimace and rolling eyes. "I didn't smell anything, but he swore garlic was there, and he refused to stay at the apartment even after the body was removed. He insisted on going to a hotel, only then he started carrying on about how was he going to reach the hotel when it was daylight outside." Centrello shook his head.

Faye chuckled. "Fortunately Fowler knew how to handle him."

Garreth started. "Fowler?"

"Yeah. He was in the squadroom when the call came and asked to ride along. You should have seen him. It was a class act, man. With a perfectly straight face he tells the Count that in Stoker's book Dracula moved around in daylight, so another vampire should be all right, too, as long as he wears a hat to shade him from direct sunlight. Then he takes the Count downstairs and puts him in a cab for the Bay Vista Hotel."

Fowler? Garreth frowned. Later when Harry and Girimonte started talking about visiting the Count, Fowler gave the impression of never—

"Ready to go back inside?" Centrello asked.

With the garlic rolls? Garreth shuddered inwardly, forgetting Fowler. Garlic rolls or not, though, he could not stand out here all day. "Maybe if we leave the hall door open and I sit near it." Where air currents from the corridor would carry the deadly scent away from him.

He eased into a chair by Kevin Chezik's desk, the closest to the door, and took a cautious breath. Yes, this might work. The air tasted mostly clear of garlic. "Centrello, toss my book over, will you?"

Centrello skimmed it across the room like a frisbie, nodding approval when Garreth plucked it from the air.

Instead of opening the book, however, Garreth ran a finger across a puddle of blood pictured on the dust jacket. Garlic in the apartment. If there really were, and he had only the Count's word on it, that ruled out not only Lane as Maruska's killer but any other vampire as well. It also explained how someone other than a vampire could overpower Maruska.

So he needed to confirm or disprove the presence of garlic.

Garlic was insurance against vampires, Holle's housekeeper said, implying all vampires. So it had to be a physiological, not just psychological, reaction. Which meant someone affected must show physical signs. The autopsy on Maruska found severe pulmonary edema. Thinking about it, that was how the garlic reaction felt, like his lungs swelling shut.

Chezik was not at his desk, and aside from an occasional glance toward the desk, no one appeared to be paying much attention to Garreth. He picked up the phone and dialed the coroner's office. "This is Garreth Mikaelian in Homicide. May I speak to any available pathologist?"

A minute later a female voice came on the line. "This is Dr. Alvarez. How may I help you, Inspector?"

"What causes severe pulmonary edema?"

The voice on the other end paused before answering. "There are several possiblities. Cardiac failure is one, also electric shock or allergic reaction—"

"Allergic reaction?" *Bingo*! "Thank you very much, doctor."

He hung up thoughtfully. So chances were good that Maruska's killer was human after all. But ... who? The killer had tailed Garreth around the city night after night. He had seen no one following him, however, not ever. It was understandable, acceptable, that another vampire could do that, but ... a *human*?

Holle's housekeeper talked about keeping an atomizer of garlic juice. Her guilt would also explain why there was no evidence of anyone breaking into the Holle house, but how could she possibly have followed him? The killer had to be someone else, someone who knew Garreth before the first murder, someone athletic and skilled in the art of surveillance.

Fowler's name stared up at him from the cover of the book's dust jacket. Garreth traced the letters with his finger. Strange how the writer had not mentioned riding along with Faye and Centrello on the original call about Maruska's death. More than strange. Suspicious. He had, in fact, acted surprised at the name Maruska's roommate used. Why should he pretend he had never heard it before unless he wanted to hide his previous contact?

Garreth leaned back in his chair. Could Fowler be tied to the other killings? Maybe. The writer had been in North Beach the night of the scuffle with Ricky Maruska. He could have seen it, and heard the remark Maruska tossed back climbing into the john's car. Fowler appreciated the difference between theoretical and applied knowledge and went for the latter when doing research. So he probably knew burglary techniques. Look at his demonstrated wizardry with handcuff locks. So he could have gotten into both the Foundation and Holle's house. Surveillance had to be part of his research, too. Could he actually follow someone, though, and how could he tail a vampire without being seen?

On top of that Fowler lacked one vital qualification for a suspect … motive. What reason could he have for killing three men and torturing two of them?

Did Irina know about the garlic? Garreth wondered. He picked up the phone again. If so, maybe she could be persuaded to tell him what she knew about the killer. If not, she ought to be told, warned that an unfriendly human knew vampires existed.

"I'm sorry, Miss Rudenko isn't here," the Philos receptionist said when Garreth asked for Irina.

He had not really expected her to be. "Will you please see that she gets a message? It's very urgent. This is Garreth Mikaelian. Tell her there was garlic in Ricky Maruska's apartment at the time of his death and we need to talk about it. I should be here in the Homicide section at the Hall of Justice the rest of the day but all evening I can be reached at 555-1099."

"I'll tell her, Officer."

He hung up. Now all he could do was hope she showed up there this evening, and that she bothered to call back.

3

Girimonte showed up again about four o'clock, alone. She dropped into her chair and lit a cigar. "Harry had to make a pit stop. Did you have an exciting day, Mikaelian?"

He gave her a thin smile. "Rewarding. I'm too short to be the Philos burglar."

"Too bad." She dragged at the cigar. "Everyone we talked to says about the same thing about Holle. He was a quiet, friendly man who always had room to put someone up for the night, was always a gracious host and never too busy to lend a hand if someone needed it. He didn't make enemies. And no one has ever heard of a Lane Barber." She blew out smoke. "Face it, Mikaelian; you're still our best suspect.

Why not just save us all trouble by confessing. You can probably beat the rap with an insanity plea. Just say your condition has unbalanced you … vitamin deficiencies due to your diet. The Twinkie defense revisited."

Garreth clenched his fists in his jacket pockets. Her blood scent curled around him with the sweet smell of her cigar. A pulse throbbed visibly in her long mahogany throat. He watched it, malicious hunger licking at him. Perhaps there was a human or two after all he would not mind not drinking from. *Better not wander into any alleys with me, Girimonte.*

The squadroom door, shut now that the smell of garlic had dissipated, opened. Harry came in … not alone. "Look what I stumbled over at the elevator."

Lien followed Harry, but it was the woman behind her who brought Garreth jumping to his feet. "Grandma Doyle! What are you doing here?"

His grandmother gave him a broad smile. "Why else but to visit me own dear grandson?"

Lien said, "I know you want to spend time with Harry, Garreth, but today would you be willing to leave early with Grania and me?"

The name puzzled him for a moment. After a lifetime of calling her just Grandma Doyle, it was hard to remember that she had a regular name: Grania Megan Mary O'Hare Doyle.

Girimonte straightened in her chair, frowning. Garreth caught Harry's eye questioningly.

Harry glanced past in the direction of Serruto's office. Garreth did not turn around to see the lieutenant's reaction, but when Harry's eyes shifted back to Garreth, Harry dipped his chin in assent. As Garreth moved past him toward the door, he warned, "Stay with them. If I hear you've taken off on your own, we'll be after you with a warrant."

Garreth gave him a thin smile. "I don't throw away an alibi, Harry."

Riding down in the elevator he said, "Grandma, do Mom and Dad know you're here?" He had uneasy visions of Phil Mikaelian calling his old buddies and setting every law enforcement agency in the state looking for her.

She sniffed. "Am I a child, that I need permission to go where I wish? I've been looking after meself quite well, thank you, since I was seventeen." She paused. "I left them a note."

Maybe only the San Francisco police would be asked to check on her. "Why did you really come?"

This time she did not smile. "I saw you last night, lying dying and someone laughing like the devil's own above you." Her eyes flashed. "I'll not sit home knitting when me flesh and blood are in mortal danger."

Despite the wash of fear in him, he wanted to hug her. And despite the fear, he could not resist pointing out an error in her Feeling. "Not from a violet-eyed woman."

She gave him the same withering stare she used to in church just before thumping him on the head with a knuckle. "There's a violet-eyed woman involved, isn't there?"

He wilted under the stare as he always had. "Irina Rudenko."

She smiled in satisfaction. "I went to Lien's studio from the bus station. I see why you like her. She's a fine, intelligent woman. We've been discussing you."

His stomach took a sickening plunge. "Grandma—" The elevator opened. Catching her arm, he hurried her out, down the corridor, and into the parking lot. "Grandma, please, you didn't tell her—"

"What you've become?" Lien said from behind him. "She didn't have to; I already knew. After our talk last night, I opened your thermos."

His stomach dropped. He turned slowly. "And from that you figured out the rest." Exactly what he had been afraid of.

She smiled. "After all, I am Chinese, and we understand that reality is not as simple as it appears. Once we made gods out of characters in novels. If fiction can be considered real, then it follows that some of what we consider fiction may be real. It's a relief to finally understand your behavior."

Belatedly he realized she was not shrinking from him, nor regarding him with revulsion. "And ... you don't mind?"

Her chin snapped up. "Of course I mind! Look how unhappy it's made you. I'd like to kill that woman for what she's done to you! But I accept what you are, of course. What else can I do?"

He could hardly believe what he heard. "You ... aren't afraid of me?"

"Afraid of someone I love?" she said indignantly.

He stared at her in wonder. Knowing about him had not changed her feelings toward him? Could it be Irina's "hold" on Holle and the housekeeper was not one of fear after all, that humans and vampires could actually be friends?

"I did wonder where you collected a thermos of blood," Lien went on. "It was ... reassuring to realize that the lip and lid of the thermos smelled of horse." She peered anxiously at him. "Is this change in you responsible for the trouble between you and Harry?"

"Partly." As long as she knew about him, he might as well give her some of the rest. "I thought at first a vampire was responsible for these murders, but since I couldn't tell anyone that, I investigated on my own. Harry suspects I know more about the case than I'll admit. Since he doesn't know why I'm keeping the information to myself, he—" No, he could not tell her about being a suspect! "He assumes I'm shutting him out to grab the glory of the collar for myself."

"You're a terrible liar," Grandma Doyle said. "Why don't you admit he's afraid you're the killer."

Her Feelings were just too damn accurate!

Lien caught her breath. "Oh, god. Poor Harry. Poor Garreth. I wish you'd trusted our friendship enough to confide in us."

Guilt stabbed him. If only he had.

His grandmother poked him. "There's no point feeling guilty about that now. What's done is done."

Lien nodded. "Now we have to clear up this ridiculous mess. Tell us what to do."

Warmth spread through him. What super ladies, both of them. He shook his head. "You do nothing. I don't want you involved. It's dangerous."

"*I Ching* says you must appoint helpers in order to reach success," Lien reminded him.

Grandma Doyle pushed him toward the car. "Tell us everything on the way home."

Now he understood why he had always felt so close to Lien. She and his grandmother were spiritual twins. Caught between them, though, he felt like someone on a runaway train. He sighed. Lack of sleep and the drag of daylight left him too tired to try stopping it. "Yes, ma'am, but, Lien ... head for Pacific Heights while I talk."

4

Holle's housekeeper admitted Garreth with obvious reluctance. "This can't be an official visit, or are these undercover officers?" She eyed the two women.

He gave her a thin smile. "Call it semi-official. Mrs. Doyle and Mrs. Takananda are assisting me with a private line of investigation into Mr. Holle's death. May I see the top floor again?"

The housekeeper frowned. "Why?"

"To check the storerooms for forcible entry. It appears now that a human, not Irina, killed Mr. Holle, and he, or she, had to come in somewhere."

The housekeeper's tight smile said: *I told you Miss Rudenko couldn't have done it.*

She led the way up to the attic. Garreth kept track of Grandma Doyle behind him, but he quickly saw worrying about her was wasted effort. The stairs had Lien and the housekeeper breathing harder than they did his grandmother.

In the attic the housekeeper unlocked the padlocked bolts on the storerooms. Nothing had been disturbed in the first. It lay silent, untouched ... smelling of dust and sea air. The latch handle at one side of the window ran parallel to the sash in the locked position and all of the window's six panes proved to be firmly in place. To Garreth's relief, neither was there enough dust on the floor to show footprints from his previous visit.

From the doorway of the second storeroom, it looked as he remembered, too. Except, he realized a moment later, that in the window the pane by the latch seemed slightly smaller than its companions. Moving over for a closer look, he saw why. Black electrician's tape lapped the edges of the pane on the outside. Using his pen, he pushed on the middle of the glass. It started to give.

The housekeeper's eyes widened.

"It's been cut," Garreth said, "then taped back in place so a casual glance wouldn't spot the damage." A faint circle on the glass showed where a suction device had been attached, first to pull the cut pane loose in one unbroken piece and then to hold it while it was taped back.

"You think Mr. Holle's killer did it?" The housekeeper frowned. "But the door—"

A quick examination of the hinges found what he expected ... scratches at the top where a screwdriver had been worked in to pry up the hinge pin. He pointed them out to the women.

"What do we do now?" the housekeeper asked.

"Pray we find this devil," Grandma Doyle said. She stared at the window, eyes focused on something invisible. "If we don't catch him tomorrow, someone else will die."

5

Lien set him to grating carrots while she and Grandma Doyle worked on the rest of supper. Wrapped the warm scents of food and the women's blood, sipping blood from a pewter tankard while he fed carrots into the food processor, Garreth's mind churned like the blade of the machine. A day to find the killer when he had no case against anyone. Evidence from the storeroom window might help, though. *I Ching* was right; he could not work alone. But he needed fellow professionals. However much they wanted to help, Lien and his grandmother had no experience with murderers and he would be irresponsible to risk their lives. It was time to trust friendship and confide in Harry.

He fed another carrot into the food processor. "Lien, Grandma, I'm telling Harry everything tonight."

Lien stopped stirring to glance around at him. Instead of the smile of relief and approval he expected, she bit her lip.

He eyed her in surprise. "What's the matter?"

She sighed. "You're right; you need to tell him. I ... just wish I could feel more confident that—"

"Feel more confident that what, honorable wife?"

All three of them whirled, startled. Harry stood in the kitchen doorway.

Lien ran to kiss him. "You're home almost on time for a change. What a lovely surprise. Garreth, I guess we can feel confident enough to set the table after all."

Harry held her off at arm's length to eye her skeptically. "That serious tone is about setting the table?"

She raised her brows. "Considering how often the dishes develop cobwebs before you show up—"

"It wasn't about setting the table," Garreth interrupted. "I'm sorry, Lien, but this has to be done." He emptied the tankard and set it in the sink.

"Garreth," his grandmother said in a warning voice.

He ignored her. "Harry, Lien is worried how well you'll take learning why I've been acting the way I have."

"Oh, I think I can handle it. You underestimate me, honorable wife." He gave Lien a hug and shoved her back toward the stove with a slap on the rump. Crossing to the work counter, he took one of the carrots waiting to be fed into the food processor and bit off a chunk. "I already know, in fact. Van told me this afternoon."

Garreth blinked in disbelief. Could Harry, too, really be accepting it so calmly?

Harry chewed the carrot. "I don't know why you didn't say anything before. There's no need to suffer alone, Van says. It's nothing to be ashamed of, though I can see why you might not want your father to know. He'd probably take it personally, as a reflection of some weakness in him."

Grandma Doyle sniffed. "Wouldn't he though."

"Can we leave Dad out of this?" Garreth said irritably.

"He never needs to know," Harry said. "Van told me all about her sister. There's treatment. You can be cured."

Garreth blinked in astonishment. "Cured! Treatment?" In his peripheral vision, he saw the women staring, too. "*What* treatment?"

Harry glanced at each of them with a puzzled frown. "A combination of medical and psychiatric therapy."

In dismay Garreth realized they could not possibly be talking about the same thing. "Harry, exactly what did Girimonte say my problem is?"

The almond eyes narrowed. "Anorexia, of course. What else?"

No wonder Harry reacted so calmly. Garreth sighed. "I'm afraid Girimonte doesn't have it quite right. I'm—"

"Before dinner is no time to be getting so serious," his grandmother interrupted. "It spoils the digestion." She smiled sweetly. "Sergeant, if you'll be good enough to take yourself out from underfoot, I'll bring you the tea your lovely wife tells me you like to have when you come home from work. Garreth, finish grating those carrots if you please. We'll all talk later."

Whatever "later" meant. Not during dinner, Garreth discovered. Between them, Lien and Grandma Doyle kept the conversation firmly on light subjects. Not after dinner, either. Then they insisted on watching television, though Garreth could not believe either had any real interest in *Miami Vice*.

"Grandma. Lien," he said during a commercial. "May I see you a minute?" In the kitchen, out of Harry's hearing, he demanded, "What are you two doing? We're under the gun for time, and we need Harry."

Her forehead furrowed. "Yes, but …" She sighed. "He won't believe you if you just come out and say you're a vampire. He has to be eased into it."

The phone rang.

"I'll get it!" Harry called from the other room.

Garreth ran a hand through his hair. "We don't have *time* to ease him into it. Tomorrow this turkey will kill again, Grandma's Feelings say. Tomorrow! Maybe you underestimate him, Lien. *You* accepted—"

"It's for you, Garreth!" Harry called. "An Irina Rudenko."

Garreth snatched up the kitchen extension. But said nothing to Irina just yet. Harry's breathing came over the line from the family room extension. "I've got it, Harry."

"I'd like to speak to Miss Rudenko, too," Harry said. "Miss Rudenko, I'm Sergeant Takananda of the San Francisco Police. We're trying to find who killed Leonard Holle. I wonder if you can answer a couple of questions."

"About Mr. Holle?" the voice on the far end of the wire said in a tone of disappointment. "Is that purpose of call? What a bummer."

Garreth blinked in astonishment. Only the accent remained Irina's.

The tone went petulant. "Meresa said there was this cute blond guy looking for me. Takananda doesn't sound like a name that belongs to anyone blond."

"I'm the blond one," Garreth said. "Garreth Mikaelian."

"Mikaelian. Mikaelian." She rolled the name around as though tasting it. "Are you guy who kept trying to catch my eye at performance of *Beach Blanket Babylon* last Saturday?"

Harry said patiently, "Miss Rudenko, this is important. How well did you know Mr. Holle?"

She sighed. "Jesus. I didn't know him. I mean, I knew him, but I didn't *know* him, if you know what I mean. He's a friend of my mother. They both work for Philos Foundation. I don't know anything about who killed him. What a horror show. Do we have to talk about it? I'd rather talk to you, blondie. Where do I know you from?"

"You don't," Garreth said, and swore mentally. What a time to have to play games. *Hang up, Harry, please, so I can talk to her.* "A mutual friend suggested I look you up."

"Yeah? Who?"

This version of Let's Pretend could have been fun under other circumstances. Irina played it very well. "Does it matter?"

She giggled. "Nope. Hey, let's get together, say in Japanese Tea Garden, twelve or so, our time? See you then, blondie."

She hung up before either Garreth or Harry could say anything more. But nothing else needed to be said. She wanted to see him and had made an appointment. Garreth grinned in admiration. Harry would interpret it in human terms ... twelve noon. Our time, she said, though. Vampire time. Midnight.

From the other extension, Harry said, "Okay, meet her, but take along a tail, and steer the conversation around to Holle. She might tell you something she wouldn't me."

Garreth smiled grimly. "I certainly will find out what she knows about Holle's death." Until then, he would go along with Lien and his grandmother and not confess to Harry. If Irina did know something, maybe they could clear up this case without official help. Then there would be nearly a week more to break the truth to Harry before his vacation ended.

6

Night robbed the Tea Garden of the color Garreth remembered from walks here with Marti. However, even reduced to the grays of his night vision, and a liming of silver from the setting half moon, the garden retained its elegance and serenity. Scents remained, too, an assault of floral, plant, and water odors filling the night. Slipping along a bamboo-railed path, Garreth realized this was the first time he had visited the garden since Marti died. Perhaps it was just as well he had come by night, when it looked so different from what he remembered.

He shifted the carrying strap on his thermos to the other shoulder, wondering if he should have taken time to fill it on the way here. Except there might still be people around the stables.

The last of the moonlight vanished, leaving only his night vision to see by.

"So," said a voice at his elbow. "There was garlic in male prostitute's apartment. Why is that something we need to discuss?"

Garreth jumped. How did she keep sneaking up on him, especially since he had been watching since he left the house for anyone following him? Her dark slacks and sweater left her invisible to the human eye, but he should have seen or heard her. What if she had been the killer? Irritation at himself sharpened his voice. "Because it means some human, not a vampire, killed your friend Holle and the others."

She reached out to run her fingers across a great stone lantern. "Of course. Such became obvious to me once I knew you weren't guilty."

"How?"

"*Nichevo.* Never Mind." She turned away, moving down the path ahead of him to an arched bridge, where she leaned on the rail and stared down at goldfish moving in gray flashes through the reflecting pool below. "Is not your concern."

He exploded. "The hell it isn't! Look, honey, you may know I didn't kill anyone but there are plenty of other people, some of them cops, who still think I did! And they're going to go on suspecting me until they find someone better. So if you know anything, I'd sure as hell appreciate being told what it is."

She hesitated, then still staring down into the water, sighed and shook her head. "I'm sorry. Is impossible. Is too dangerous."

He frowned. "I've dealt with vicious and dangerous killers before. This one can't be any worse. He's still only human. You point me in his direction. Harry and I will arrest him and the law will take care of him."

Irina turned, frowning, but a moment later, to Garreth's irritation and discomfort, the scowl dissolved into laughter. She swallowed the whoop almost immediately with an appology. "I'm sorry." Was she? Amusement still lingered in her voice and gleamed in her eyes. "Such innocence." She reached up to touch his cheek, then withdrew the hand as he backed away angrily. "Please, I'm sorry. I don't mean to offend. Is just that I never cease being astonished by this age's blind belief in law as an instrument of justice. For of course this matter is one beyond your 'law'."

His gut knotted. Echoes of Lane rang in her words. "No," he said. "There's law or there's only anarchy. Everyone must be responsible for their actions and answerable to other people for them."

The experienced eyes looked up at him from the smooth, adolescent face. "Oh, I agree, but they cannot always answer in a court of law. The danger is not so much to you personally, Garreth, as to both of us. To all of the blood. Even as young as you are in this life, can't you see what we have? This killer knows we exist and stalks us, and our friends. He broke Leonard's neck, not only to prevent him rising again in case he carried the virus, but from hatred of one who would befriend us."

"So he's a vampire hunter," Garreth said. "He's still just a man."

She hissed. "Just? No. Holy Mother, no. In the past year three friends of the blood have been murdered in this same manner in Europe, and all three were intelligent, experienced, alert people who survived times when people actively believed in and hunted us. Dominic escaped the arena in Rome, the Spanish Inquisition, and innumerable witch hunts. Yet this hunter managed to destroy him. *Now* do you see why I want you away from here? You're too ... naive to fight him. And what if you should succeed in capturing him? Punishing him through your legal system will only make public why and what he kills, and you will have helped him destroy us all. Garreth, leave hunter to me."

Cold ran through him and sat in icy lumps in his gut. "I can't. The law you don't believe in won't let me leave. So you might as well use my help. Who knows? My training might even come in handy. Tell me about the killings. Is there clue at all to who's doing them?"

She glanced around. "Let's walk. We've stood in one place too long."

They walked, following the paths winding through the garden. Irina said nothing more for nearly five minutes, then with a sigh: "I talked to people who knew my friends. They could tell me little, but they did say that shortly before each death, my friend had talked to a tall, fair-haired man. One had mentioned to a companion that man asked for a red-haired woman who traveled with Irina Rodek in years just before Second World War. It was obviously Mada, or Lane, as she calls herself here. That is why I came to San Francisco, to warn her, and to warn our friends against talking to anyone asking for Mada."

Garreth felt as though a fist sunk in his stomach. "Was the man an Englishman?"

She whirled to stare up at him. "I don't know. No one I talked to had spoken with him personally." Her eyes narrowed. "There is an Englishman Leonard said is working with your police friends, the one who came with you to Foundation offices yesterday afternoon."

"Julian Fowler." Quickly, he told her everything about the writer. "But ... I don't know that any of it means anything. There's no obvious motive for him killing anyone, and certainly no proof against him."

Irina pursed her lips. "If he were a hunter, hatred of us would be sufficient motive, but this man has a specific quarry."

"Madelaine Bieber," Garreth said. "He's very open about it. Would he be if he wanted her for more than the book he claims to be researching?"

Irina smiled thinly. "If he's clever. Hunter who killed my friends has shown himself very clever." She paused. "I think we need to know something about this Englishman."

Garreth nodded. "The library should have entries on him in books like *Contemporary Authors*."

Irina pursed her lips. "I know better source which will not raise our killer's suspicions if he manages to follow us. Come. My car is parked by Stow Lake."

7

Irina headed her little Honda north.

"Do you have much trouble renting cars and hotel rooms?" Garreth asked.

She snorted. "Of course not. I refuse to suffer inconveniences of being a minor. My papers identify me as twenty-one and when necessary I can make up to look the age or older. I suppose I should be thankful that devil Viktor did not see me at thirteen or fourteen. Ah, here we are." She pulled over to the curb.

Garreth blinked dubiously at the building before them. "How do we find biographical information on Fowler at the Philos Foundation?"

"Is simple. Watch."

Irina swung out of the car, climbed the steps to the porch, and rang the bell.

"May I help you?" a voice asked.

Irina looked up. "I would like to come in."

Now Garreth noticed the small, round eye of a camera winking at them from the roof of the porch.

"Does your mother know you run around at this hour of the night?" the voice asked chidingly.

"Natalya Rudenko knows everything I do. Open door, please."

The door buzzed. Irina pushed it open. Yelling a greeting to a face that appeared at the top of the stairs, she led the way to Holle's office and unlocked the door. "That is to make us look normal. This, too." She switched on the light.

For the first time he saw her in color. She had violet eyes indeed ... deeply, richly purple as pansies. Except when they reflected ruby red.

She switched on the computer to one side of the desk and sat down at it. Her fingers raced across the keyboard ... calling up a communications program, Garreth realized, reading the screen prompts.

He eyed her in surprise. "You know computers?"

Without looking up, Irina replied, "Is a matter of necessity, as is learning to drive an automobile and fly an airplane. Altering electronic records is becoming only way to change identities. Hasn't Mada taught you—" She glanced up then, and sighed. "No, of course not. Is like her to bring you into this life and abandon you without bothering to teach basic survival skills." She turned back to the keyboard and typed rapidly. "Mada avoids use of advanced technology anyway, an attitude which will undo her eventually. One cannot cling to era of one's birth. When this problem of vampire hunter is solved, we must see that you're given proper—ah, there's what I want ... a literary database." She typed some more, then turned away. "Searching out and transmitting data will take a while. Several fresh units of whole blood have been 'discarded' in shelter refrigerator. Shall I go after one?"

He stiffened. "I don't drink human blood."

She eyed him. "So I see." Irina paused, then added, "One can survive on animal blood to a point, but never well. We need human blood. That's why you're always hungry."

"A little hunger is better than treating people like cattle." As the words came out, Garreth winced. God that sounded self-righteous.

Irina regarded him with amusement. "Is that what you believe we do ... that we are all like Mada?" She sobered. "No. Think. How could we have survived all these centuries and faded into mythology if—" She broke off. "*Nichevo.* Never mind. I understand your feelings. Truely. Few of us enter this life by choice. When I realized what I had become I despised Viktor with such passion that I, too, swore I would never treat people as he did and never drink human blood."

"You mentioned him before," Garreth said. "Is he the vampire who—"

"Yes. Prince Viktor." She spat the name. "Some called him Viktor the Wolfeyed. I was sixteen, and much plumper, when he saw me in Prince Yevgeni's household. My mother was a kitchen servant there. She would never say who my father was, but I have always felt he must have been a boyar, quite possibly prince's younger brother Peter. Sometimes I envied his legitimate daughters, but not usually. They had to live confined to *terem* in house and go veiled in street."

Garreth blinked in astonishment. "Russian women lived like that?"

She smiled faintly. "Five hundred years ago, yes." Her eyes focused past him. "My freedom cost me, however, when it gave Viktor chance to see me. He had his men abduct me one day on way to market with my mother. I didn't know *he* was responsible, of course, not until three nights later, three terrible nights of abject terror, waiting for what I knew must appear sooner or later. For years peasant and servant girls had been vanishing, then reappearing days or weeks later as walking dead.

"I was almost relieved when Viktor came out of dark with his fangs bared. I fought him, biting and scratching—my mother's father was a Mongol, after all—and though he still overpowered me and drank, was not before I tasted his blood first. Second night he came, I was hiding behind door. I hit him in face with a stool and escaped." Irina smiled wryly. "Unfortunately was winter. I froze to death before I reached home." The smile faded. "I woke in snow. You can perhaps understand my feelings when I discovered cold no longer bothered me and realized why."

Garreth sucked in his breath. Oh yes, he knew.

Irina focused on him. "Only my hatred of that devil kept me from throwing myself on a stake. I swore to destroy him."

The words reverberated in Garreth. He thought of Lane's grave. "Did you?"

Her teeth bared in a wolfish grin. "I am a Mongol's granddaughter, remember. At home I resume my life, claiming I could not remember where I had been. Pretending to be still human was difficult—agony when I went to church—but thought of vengeance helped me endure pain. At night I spied on Viktor, studying his habits and his house until I knew when he was vulnerable and how to reach him. Then I pretended to recover my memory. I denounced him. Prince Yevgeni gathered a hunting party at Viktor's house. I led them to cellar where he slept by day and persuaded prince to let me drive in stake."

"They didn't suspect you of having become a vampire?"

She smiled grimly. "I had sworn on an icon that I escaped before he fed on me ... most difficult thing I have ever done. Was like putting my hand in fire. That convinced them, but I took no chances anyway. While prince was beheading Viktor and burning body, I helped myself to as much gold and jewels as I could carry from that devil's treasure room and ran away to Moscow."

"Where you gave up your vow of not drinking human blood?"

He winced at the edge on his voice—he had not intended to sound judgmental—but she shrugged. "Where rashness of youthful passion gave way to reality and necessity. Garreth, feeding does not have to be an act of—"

The computer beeped.

Irina spun her chair back toward it. "Finally. Several references, too. Very good." Before Garreth had time to read the list on the screen, she tapped a key.

The printing convulsed and vanished. The drive light flickered for several minutes. When it stopped, the computer beeped again. Irina tapped more keys.

CONNECTION BROKEN, the screen announced.

"Now let's see what we have."

At her tap on another key, the printer spat into life. Paper spewed into the receiving basket. Irina ripped it off and after skimming the readout, handed it on to him. "You will find this interesting."

The database had found and sent them three items: an entry from *Contemporary Authors*, and article on Fowler from the *Writer's Digest* magazine, and an interview that had run in *Playboy* several years before.

According to the biographical data in *Contemporary Authors*, Fowler had been born in London in 1939 to Margaret Graham Fowler, the daughter of stage actor Charles Graham, and Richard "Dickon" Fowler. Fowler's father, who worked for British Intelligence with the French Underground during World War II, died in France late in 1945 of a broken neck sustained in a fall.

A ripple ran across Garreth's neck hair. Fowler said his parents met Lane in France shortly after the war. That could not have been long before the father's death.

He went on reading.

Fowler's mother remarried and Fowler spent the rest of his childhood shuttling between boarding school and his actor grandfather. He enrolled at Oxford, but instead of studying history, began writing horror novels and after selling one two years later, quit college to write full time. A few years later he switched from horror to thrillers. His first American publication came in 1972.

Garreth glanced back at the line about Fowler's father. His skin prickled again. "A broken neck."

Irina glanced up at him through thick, dark lashes. "Interesting, yes? Read farther."

The *Writer's Digest* article talked only about writing discipline and how growing up around his grandfather had provided an atmosphere rich in imagination. Garreth went on to the *Playboy* interview. A few questions into the article one leaped up at him.

"Playboy: In a BBC interview several years ago you stated that you began writing as an act of exorcism. That's an interesting reason to write. Would you care to explain for your American readers?"

"Fowler: Yes, of course. When I was six a savage dog attacked my father. He fell from a cliff trying to escape from the beast and was killed. As a child I could never accept that. How could a mere dog kill my father the spy? It had to be some monster responsible. His death haunted me for years. I'm not sure what made me turn it into a story and write it down, but eventually it became my novel Blood Maze. *In it a boy witnesses a werewolf tearing his father's throat out. No one will believe him so he vows that when he grows up, he will find and destroy the werewolf. As a grown man, he fulfills that vow. In a sense, the same happened to me. By writing about destroying the instrument of my father's death, I laid his ghost. I went on writing horror novels for a while, of course, because I knew I could, but eventually I switched to thrillers. The horror novels were exorcism, the thrillers a kind of memorial. In a sense, each spy hero is my father."*

Garreth felt for his own throat, tracing the scars where Lane's teeth had ripped through the flesh.

"See this question also," Irina said, pointing.

"Playboy: If your characters are symbols for people in your life, who is the tall woman who appears as Chatelaine Barbour in Blood Maze, *Tara Brenneis in* Mind's Eye, *and Magda Eberhardt in* Our Man In Hades, *to name a few of her incarnations? When she appears, she is always the beautiful seductress who turns traitor."*

"Fowler (with a rueful laugh): I'm afraid I'll have to take the Fifth on that one, as you Americans say. I don't fancy being sued for slander. Suffice it to say she was an older woman I fell madly in love with years ago and who spurned me for the callow youth I was. No

doubt it's unsporting to make her the villainess, but ... she keeps popping up when I need one."

"Lane," Garreth said. A beautiful seductress betraying the hero over and over ... as she had turned on Fowler's father? "I could have sworn there was no anger when Fowler talked about his childhood meeting with Lane. I didn't hear any bitterness or resentment, absolutely no hint of hatred. Can someone hide his feelings that well? He'd have to be one hell of an actor." A hell of an actor, too, to come into the squadroom Wednesday morning looking like the most disturbing thing on his mind was a hangover, which had to be a pretense as well.

"He may be mad," Irina said. "Or both."

Fowler would have to be riding the edge of a crackup carrying his obscession around buried that deep all these years.

Irina turned off the computer and stood. "So ... now we must catch this Englishman and deal with him."

Garreth stiffened. "Shoot him, you mean, like you were going to shoot me last night? No." Garreth shook his head. "I won't—" He broke off, but finished the sentence silently: *won't kill again.* The fact that taking Lane's life had, in the end, been a matter of self-defense made no difference in the wrongness of it. *What gives* you *the right to judge* me? Lane had flung at him that Thanksgiving night. He needed no second face haunting his dreams. "There's been enough killing."

The violet eyes reflected red. "How can I convince you how deadly and ruthless vampire hunters are. They are ... driven ... blindly self-righteous, so positive we are evil that they see nothing but their 'cause'. Like berserkers, nothing stops them but death."

"Criminals disregard the law, too, but we punish them through the system. How can you sneer at hunters for being self-righteous if we arbitrarily set ourselves up as *their* judges?"

She sighed. "Ah, your law again. What do you suggest, then?"

It furthers one to appoint helpers, I Ching had said. Garreth took a breath. "First we need proof Fowler is our killer, and since the killer has to be watching me, and now you, we can't be involved or he'll realize we're on to him. We need help, human help, official help ... someone who can find probable cause and enter Fowler's hotel room to search it. We need Harry."

8

Irina said, "You realize you are risking more lives than yours and mine."

Garreth nodded.

The two of them sat at the kitchen counter with pewter tankards of blood, his horse blood from his thermos, hers from a unit of human blood she had brought from the Foundation. He buried his nose in his tankard in an effort to block out the tantalizing scent leaking toward him from hers. Thirst scorched his throat.

He distracted himself by thinking about Fowler. Where was the writer now? Watching the house, they had to assume. To keep Fowler from suspecting he was now the hunted, Garreth had come home from the Foundation on foot, with a stop at the police stables to fill the thermos. Irina had followed later, parking her car several blocks away and approaching the house through the back yards.

An anxious voice said, "Garreth, you shouldn't be out—who is this?"

He looked around at Lien in the kitchen doorway. "Meet Irina Rudenko." Then he noticed Grandma Doyle behind Lien. Introducing her, too, it occurred to him that Irina was also his grandmother of sorts.

A rap sounded upstairs. "Garreth!" Harry's voice called.

Lien glanced up. "I'll say I let you out."

Garreth shook his head. "I have to tell him everything anyway. We need him."

She studied his face for a moment, then sighed and nodded. Moving around the work island, she reached up into a cupboard for a bottle of brandy.

Grandma Doyle stayed near the door fingering the Maltese cross around her neck as she eyed the girl.

Irina smiled. "Mrs. Doyle, you have nothing to fear from me." She held up the tankard. "As you see, I have my breakfast."

Grandma Doyle's expression became accusing. "You're the one responsible for the creature who did this to me grandson."

The smile faded. "To my regret, yes. Even one as experienced as I can be a fool."

Harry came thumping down the stairs and through the doorway from the hall. "Lien, see if you can—Garreth?" He plowed to a stop, staring in open-mouthed, almost comic disbelief. Garreth felt no desire to laugh, however. "Your door is bolted on the inside."

Here it came. Garreth's gut knotted. He took a deep breath. "Yes. I don't have to open doors to go through them."

Irina caught Garreth's wrist. "Gently, *tovarich*. I am Irina Rudenko, Mr. Takananda."

"Rudenko?" Harry's eyes narrowed. "You were going to meet him at noon today."

She smiled. "No. Twelve o'clock our time, I told him. That's midnight."

Harry blinked. "What?" Then he started, staring back at Garreth. "What do you mean you don't have to open doors to go through them?"

That had taken long enough to sink in. "Harry, maybe you'd better sit down. I need to talk."

Tautly, Harry groped for a stool. Garreth smelled an acid tang beneath his old partner's blood scent. Fear Garreth was about to confess to the killings?

Garreth hurried to reassure him. "I didn't kill those men, Harry, I swear."

Harry let his breath out. "I didn't think you could, Mik-san."

"What I have to say is about me ... why I act strange sometimes, how I left the bedroom without unbolting the door."

The almond eyes narrowed. "You went out the window."

Garreth shook his head. "Harry—" *Shit. How do I say this?* Maybe he should take off his glasses and— He discarded the idea in mid-thought. No, this was something Harry had to understand and accept of his own volition.

Good luck, lover, Lane's voice laughed in his head.

He groped desperately for words. "Harry ... if you were watching a movie and the detectives had some murders to solve where the bodies had two punctures in their necks and were all drained of blood, and then one of the detectives was found dead with his throat torn out by the killer only he sat up in the morgue with his throat almost healed, and after that he stopped eating food and preferred night to daylight and he couldn't stand garlic ... what would you say they were dealing with?"

Harry frowned. "I thought we were going to talk seriously."

"Harry, I'm deadly serious."

A pulse jumped in Harry's throat. He stared at Garreth in silence for a long time, then with face smoothed into a bland mask said in a careful, flat voice, "This isn't a movie."

"No," Garreth agreed. "I wish it were. Then we could shut off the TV and go on with normal lives. But everything that happened to me is real. I wake up from sleeping and I'm still a—still changed."

The skin between Harry's brows rippled, as though he started to frown but thought better of it. He said slowly, "You know, Dr. Masethin sees private patients, too."

Garreth's gut twisted. Masethin. The department shrink. Harry thought he had gone bananas. *Well, what else did you expect, man?* He kept his voice even. "Harry, I'm not crazy."

"Of course not," Harry said hastily. "But maybe—you know, the mind plays funny tricks sometimes. Chemical imbalances from starvation might—"

Garreth slapped his hand down on the counter. "I'm not anorectic either! I eat. This." He poured some of the blood from his tankard onto the counter top.

The pulse leaped visibly in Harry's throat again as he stared at the crimson puddle. After a minute he looked up with a friendly smile that sent Garreth's stomach plummeting. "All right. I'm convinced."

Like hell, Garreth reflected in disappointment. That was Harry's let's-humor-the-subject-until-he's-off-guard-and-we-can-jump-him smile.

From the faint shake of Irina's head Garreth saw she read the situation as he did.

Grandma Doyle said, "I'd be thinking of a demonstration, Garreth."

Nothing less was going to convince him, it appeared. Hopping off the stool, Garreth strode over to the hall door and closed it. Then he leaned against it, hands above his head. "Watch, Harry. I don't touch the knob."

Wrench. He stood in the hall. Turning, he pressed against the door again. *Wrench.* Would Harry be glaring in revulsion?

Not quite. Harry stared but with eyes white-rimmed in disbelief, mouth working soundlessly, face drained of blood.

Grandma Doyle eased him backward onto a stool.

Lien wrapped his fingers around a glass of brandy. "There are more things in Heaven and Earth, Horatio, than you or I have dreamed,'" she said gently.

The brandy went down in a single gulp. Garreth doubted Harry even noticed the action, much less tasted the liquor. After Lien refilled the glass and he tossed that off, too, he stared at the glass in astonishment. Then he looked at Garreth and closed his eyes. "Tell me I didn't see that."

"You saw it," Irina said. "Speaking from experience, it is easier if you forget trying to understand what you saw; just accept it."

Lien put an arm around him. "Accept Garreth, too. Basically he's still the same person he always was."

Harry stiffened.

Garreth sucked in his breath.

But it was Lien Harry turned to frown at. "*You* knew about this, and you didn't tell me?"

He seemed almost relieved by the omission, Garreth noticed. Glad to have something comprehensible to think about?

Lien said, "I learned just yesterday. Garreth tried to tell you himself then, but you were too set on believing Vanessa's diagnosis of him." She poured more brandy.

He pushed it away. "I won't be able to drive if I have any more. Or maybe I'll call in sick. I can't handle anything more today." He picked up the glass.

Garreth caught his wrist. "Harry, you have to go in! We think we know who the killer is and we need you to prove it."

"The killer." The expression in Harry's eyes wiped the past five minutes out of existence to leap at Garreth's words. "A killer I can handle. Who is it?"

Garreth told him.

Harry listened with a concentration like a drowning man clinging to a life preserver. At the end of the recitation he jumped up. "Van hasn't been happy about that stair window as an entry point. I'll tell her Garreth mentioned not checking the storerooms because they were locked. She'll jump at checking them. After the lab processes them, we'll bring Fowler in to compare prints and fibers."

"How can you do that without warning him he's a suspect?" Irina asked.

Harry grinned. "Easy. I received an anonymous phone call from a woman saying she'd seen Fowler at Maruska's apartment. I'll say of course it's nonsense, probably some nutcase looking for publicity by accusing a celebrity, but of course we have to check it out to clear him. In the course of it, we'll be checking him against associative evidence from Holle's attic, too." Harry kissed Lien and headed for the door. "I'll call you when I have something."

"Meanwhile," Irina said, draining her tankard, "we must keep our watcher occupied. Show yourself at livingroom window and on patio, then I think we should rest away from daylight."

9

A double thickness of blanket over the bedroom window hardly constituted blackout curtains, but it blocked a good deal of light, making the room at least comfortable. Irina knelt on the floor unrolling an air mattress she had brought in from her car. Dried earth hissed inside as she smoothed it and arranged a sheet and pillow over it.

Watching her from where he sat on the edge of the bed, Garreth felt urgency throb in him. Time was running out. He ought to be doing more than sleeping. Fowler would kill again today if they did not stop him. How, though? He could hardly have Irina hunting Fowler her way.

Irina curled up, pulling the sheet around her, and closed her eyes.

He stretched out on his own pallet on the bed. "You don't approve of bringing in Harry, do you."

Without opening her eyes she replied, "I worry what we will do when he finds proof against Fowler. Arresting the Englishman will make public his motive for murder. Then either sergeant will be ridiculed for believing such a thing and hunter turned loose, or you, I, and all of our kind will be exposed. She opened her eyes and raised up on one elbow. "Destroying hunters is only way to protect ourselves."

"There has to be a way of stopping him without killing him or betraying ourselves."

Irina smiled. The warmth of it enveloped him like a thick, soft blanket. "You are a man of honor, Garreth Mikaelian, kinder toward your enemies than I. Is too bad you could not be with me when I lived near Yasnaya Polyana, Tolstoy's estate at Tula. I think you would have enjoyed listening to Tolstoy philosophize on law and justice."

Garreth started. "*The* Tolstoy? You knew him?"

"I attended many of his parties with a friend who posed as my guardian while waiting out some trouble in St. Petersburg. Talk and debate would last all night. Tolstoy's philosophies inspired nonviolence embraced by Gandhi and your Dr. Martin Luther King, did you know that?" Mischief glinted in the violet eyes. "A Russian influenced them." Then the mischief faded. "Is too bad Mr. Fowler has not been influenced by Tolstoy also." Stretching out, she closed her eyes again. "At which thought I leave you to solve our problem with honor, and within your law, if you can. For myself, I am tired and wish only to sleep."

Garreth turned over. He would have liked to sleep, too; his body ached from exhaustion and daylight. But the clock ticked relentlessly in him, and his mind churned with doubt. Which was more important, law, or finding Fowler? Following procedure took time. Was Irina right? Was he wrong to insist on applying human law to this situation? Would someone else die because of it? He might as well consider that he had killed those other three men. They died because he led the killer to them.

Garreth clenched his fists. *Why* had he not realized he was being followed? Was Fowler really that good, or had Garreth just been so preoccupied with his own interests that he had committed the sin no good cop ever should, failing to pay attention to what was happening around him?

Irina sighed in her sleep.

He eyed her. There lay another problem. After being so insistent that the only way to deal with Fowler was kill him, Irina had given in far too readily to Garreth. Was she just humoring him until they had Fowler? In her place, he might do that, and then, having found the killer of his friends and bloodkind, he would brush aside the young vampire and his precious law to act as he felt necessary to protect himself.

Garreth bit his lip. He had to prevent that. Somehow. Restraining Irina was probably impossible, which meant he had to protect Fowler. He grimaced. As a cop he had often stood between a killer and those demanding vengeance, but never before had he been forced to side with one where the price of doing his job could be the destruction of a whole people ... his own kind.

Grandma Doyle's voice echoed in his head: *I saw you lying dying, and someone laughing like the devil's own above you.* His pulse lurched. It could also mean his own destruction.

He sat up hugging his knees. No, he refused to accept that either Fowler had to die or vampires did. There *must* be some way to protect everyone.

The clock on the nightstand read ten o'clock. Sliding out of bed, Garreth put on his dark glasses, then picked up his boots, slipped over to the bureau, and eased his billfold, gun, and keys off it. Moving just as soundlessly to the door, he passed through without opening it, so no sound of knob or hinges would wake Irina.

His grandmother looked up in surprise from her book as he came into the family room. "Why aren't you sleeping?"

He sat down in a chair to pull on and zip his boots. "I have an errand I have to run." He dared not look up at them for fear they would read the lie in his face. Enough lives were at risk already; he would not involve them further. "Have you heard anything from Harry?"

"He called about an hour and a half ago. They found the storeroom as we described it."

"Good." Standing, Garreth clipped his holster onto his belt.

His grandmother eyed him. "What kind of errand is it you take a gun on?"

He made himself smile at her. "Cops feel naked without a weapon. You know that from Dad, Grandma." He pulled on his corduroy coat. "I won't be using it." He hoped. But neither would he go near Fowler unarmed.

Lien frowned. "Should you go out alone? I mean, Harry knows you're innocent but others like Vanessa Girimonte don't yet and if something happens ..."

They had to stay here, safe. He forced his smile into a confident grin. "What can happen? It's just a short trip. I'll be back before you know it." Blowing them a kiss, he headed for the front door.

10

Being in the ZX again, the wheel in his hands, the engine snarling, felt wonderful. No matter that it was daylight. Despite driving with half his attention on the rearview mirrors, the mere fact of being behind the wheel himself instead of riding along brought a sense of satisfaction and confidence, of finally being in charge again.

The question was where to let Fowler catch up. A public place would be safest, at least until he could make Fowler understand the situation with Irina; then they could find somewhere to hide the writer. The place to meet occurred to him almost immediately, a very public one he could expect to be crowded and one he knew every inch of from playing tag with officers from other black-and-whites at three and four o'clock in the morning on slow watches.

Garreth frowned at his rearview mirror. Unfortunately the writer was not driving a car as conspicuous as the Continental he had had in Baumen. The tan Colt he had rented here looked—deliberately, no doubt—like hundreds of others on the street. A tan subcompact had fallen in behind him a couple of blocks from Harry's house, but he no longer saw it. He had turned onto a busier street, though, and if he were being tailed, Fowler could be tucked out of sight several cars back.

His pulse jumped as tan appeared in his outside mirror. A moment later he let his breath out. The passing vehicle was a station wagon. Checking the traffic directly behind again, he decided there was indeed a tan car back there. Telling any more about it was impossible. The two intervening cars prevented him from seeing the tag and the driver showed as only a silhouette.

The matter shortly became academic because the car turned another direction midway across Golden Gate Park.

With the thickening of traffic on Fulton north of the park more tan cars appeared ... falling in behind, passing, weaving through traffic, turning off. Which made it difficult keeping track of any particular one. That grew still more difficult as Fulton neared the Civic Center and traffic continued increasing. Garreth resisted the impulse to make a series of turns and see which cars stuck with him. He would know soon enough if Fowler were really following him.

To make it easy for any tail, both to follow and hide in traffic, he took a straight route on major thoroughfares ... Fulton to the Civic Center, then north on Van Ness until he could turn east to the Cannery. But anyone following him was on their own finding a parking place. The best Garreth could do after locating one for himself was walk very slowly into the Cannery complex.

That was easy. The bright sunlight weighted and battered him. He felt like he moved through molasses. Oh to be taking refuge in blissful darkness. Barring that luxury, a heavy rainstorm, or better yet, a pea-soup fog, would have made today more pleasant.

Then abruptly the drag of daylight became a minor matter. Glancing over his shoulder he spotted the face he had been looking for. His pulse jumped. Fowler wore a dark wig, mustache, and horn-rimmed glasses, but he was still unmistakably Julian Fowler.

Garreth sucked in a long breath. The chase was on in earnest now.

The red brick complex sprawled out like some vast Florentine palace. He kept moving through its courtyards and arcades and across its bridges, pausing to browse through a shop here and take brief refuge in the shade of a tree there, stopping to chat with an artist doing pastel portraits, then a musician playing her guitar in one of the courtyards. He asked directions to shops so Fowler would see the people pointing.

Covert checks over his shoulder via shop windows found Fowler sticking with him. The writer kept changing his appearance, putting on and removing the glasses, sometimes with, sometimes without a tweed roadster cap.

Garreth took another breath. Time for the fox to catch the hound.

He strode along an arcade and around a corner to a flight of stairs. There he quickly vaulted over the railing to drop down onto a bridge below, startling shoppers and tourists, then raced across the bridge into another arcade.

From the shadow of it he watched Fowler stop short at the top of the stairs, dismay spreading across the writer's face as he realized he had lost his quarry. Inaction lasted only seconds. Face tight with anger, Fowler plunged down the stairs and raced along the arcade, one direction then the other, and finally across the bridge. By that time Garreth had retreated into a shop.

"May I help you?" a clerk asked.

Garreth glanced around at the display of women's sexy undergarments. "Just drooling."

Fowler hurried past the shop door. Garreth waited for several more people to pass before slipping out. He fell in behind two couples, using them to screen him from Fowler.

If Fowler felt frantic, he did not show it. The grim set of his mouth had vanished. Except for turning every few seconds to scan the arcade or pausing to lean out over the balustrade and peer at arcades opposite and courtyards below, he might have been just another shopper.

Garreth waited until a turn in the arcade left a quiet corner, then quickly circled the two couples and closed on Fowler. "What are we going to do with you, Dr. Van Helsing?"

Fowler whipped around. As his face registered recognition, consternation evaporated, giving way to a watchful stillness in the pale eyes. Eyes like ice. "I beg your pardon?"

If Garreth had had any doubts about Fowler before, the question wiped them away. He knew that voice. He had heard it hundreds of times before, in a dozen accents in both sexes, across the table of an interview room and during field arrests, always the same … even, controlled, but not quite able to hide its mocking undertone, its catch-me-if-you-can arrogance. He eyed the writer with angry satisfaction. *You're dirty, Fowler, and now your ass is mine.*

He dropped his voice so only Fowler could hear it above the guitar music coming from the courtyard below. "My pardon is one thing you'll never have. Your appetite for blood is bigger than mine. Those men couldn't tell you where Lane was no matter what you did to them. They didn't know."

The ice-pale eyes focused on his glasses. "Why are you so sure? Because you do?"

Garreth suddenly felt very glad they stood with a crowd moving past them. He savored the eddying currents of perfumes, sweat, food odors, and blood scents. "Yes. You've seen her, too, though you didn't realize it. She was in Baumen, in the cemetery."

That startled him out of his complacency. "The cemetery!"

Garreth grimaced bitterly. "Ironic isn't it. You followed me here and tortured and killed to find her ... for nothing. She's already dead."

Fowler's face hardened. The pale eyes narrowed. "I don't believe you."

"You saw the grave. It had rose bushes on it."

Garreth waited for a sag of defeat as Fowler realized he had wasted those three lives, and his. Instead the writer's eyes narrowed still more. In a low, almost casual voice he said, "You're a bloody liar. You're just trying to protect that ... creature." He jammed his hands into his coat pockets.

You goofed, man, a voice murmured in Garreth's head. Screwed up royally. Fowler looked so rational he had forgotten he was dealing with a looney tune. The man had spent most of his life hunting Lane ... planning revenge, dreaming of it. Of course he refused to accept that it might have been pointless.

Garreth reached for his glasses. This needed more persuasive methods.

At the same time Fowler's hand came out of his coat pocket.

Every alarm in Garreth kicked into action. Weapon! He lunged for the wrist.

The writer held not a gun, however, but a small bottle, the pump type used as a purse-size perfume container. Pushing Fowler's arm up made no difference. Fowler was already depressing the top. Mist caught Garreth full in the face.

Suddenly he could no longer breathe. The air congealed in his lungs. Garlic juice!

Backing against the arcade balustrade he clawed for the turtleneck of his shirt. A part of him recognized the action as useless. It never did help, but he tried anyway, reflexively, in panic, struggling to suck in air.

Several passers-by stopped. One woman started toward him.

Fowler reached him first, catching him under the arm and groping for Garreth's coat pockets. "Christ, Sid; don't tell me you've come away without the bloody atomizer again." He looked around at the woman. "He has these asthma attacks when he's upset. He'll be right in no time once he's had his medication. You shouldn't be so touchy, though, Sid; it was just a joke. Come on. Let's get you back to the car and sorted out."

Fear spurted in Garreth. *No!* Only, he had no breath to say it aloud, and no strength to do anything but struggle to breathe. Maybe he should just collapse.

The grip under his arm held him on his feet, though. Fowler half dragged, half carried him through the Cannery, chattering all the way. "Hang on, Sid; don't panic. We'll be back at the car before you know it. I do wish you'd remember to carry your atomizer all the time. Maybe Heather ought hang the thing around your neck. Where's she got off to, anyway? Come on, come on; do I have to carry you all the way? Try to walk, can't you? Do you know how embarrassing this is? I daresay it looks like I'm abducting you or something. We'll be lucky if some copper doesn't stop us."

Fat chance. Through reddening vision Garreth saw people turn to stare at them, but no one questioned or interfered.

His chest ached from the effort to expand it. His lungs felt as though they were about to burst. Unconsciousness could be only seconds away. It was incredible that he had not passed out already.

"Thank god we're almost there," Fowler rattled on. Garreth could barely hear through the thunder of blood in his ears. "We'll have you set right straightaway. But one more of these attacks of yours, Sid, and I swear you can bloody well count me out of sight-seeing with you and my sister again."

Near the street, Garreth's chest loosened. Air! He wanted to gasp in relief and gulp it in. Instead he forced himself to breathe slowly. If Fowler did not notice he was recovering, he could jump the son of a bitch. He hoped. The hammer of sunlight on top of suffocation left him shaky and wrung-out.

"Hey ho, Sid old son, here we are." Fowler propped Garreth against the car. "Let me just find the key and we're off."

Garreth tensed. Every breath came easier. A few more and he would be breathing normally. Then he would take the bastard.

"And here we are." Fowler held up the key. But he also had the perfume bottle palmed in the same hand, and before Garreth could move, squeezed a second round of garlic mist into Garreth's face.

Anger exploded in Garreth. Not again! Choking, he clawed for his gun.

Fowler caught his wrist and twisted the weapon away. "Naughty, naughty." He released the cylinder, flipped it out, and dumped the bullets in a smooth, one-handed motion. "We won't be needing these." The cylinder back in place, the gun went into Fowler's coat pocket. "Now, shall we get on with it, with no more foolishness?"

Why did the incident give Garreth a feeling of déjà vu? Oh, yes. He had also tried to draw on Lane when she had him pinned in that North Beach alley drinking his blood. With no better results, he remembered bitterly.

Unlocking the car, Fowler shoved him in. Garreth huddled in the seat listening to his lungs creak and his heart slam against them with the strain of fighting to breathe.

Fowler climbed in the other side and started the car. "I'm sure you're uncomfortable. Suffocation is a terrifying sensation. At least in my personal experience it has always been a most effective method of persuading people to share information they might refuse to otherwise. You needn't worry about passing out or dying, however. Your kind doesn't. You only feel as though you're about to. Endlessly." He backed out of the parking space. "We'll finish our chat somewhere quiet. You still haven't told me where Mada is."

The words brought a terror totally apart from the panic caused by not being able to breathe. Déjà vu indeed. Fowler would never appreciate the irony of it, but he was an echo of the woman he wanted to destroy. Another victim of Lane's excesses. And as in the alley with Lane, Garreth was completely in his captor's power. Helpless.

11

Somewhere quiet indeed. Garreth bit his lip. No one would think of checking Lane's apartment when they started looking for Fowler and him.

The lock clicked open. Fowler dropped his lock picks back into the inside pocket of his coat. Picking Garreth up from where he had dropped him by the door, Fowler dragged him inside and deposited him in the wicker basket chair. Then in a quick circuit, Fowler opened the drapes several inches, closed the door, and came back to the wicker chair.

Sunlight streamed across the room in a beam that splashed over Garreth. He noticed it even in the midst of his other pain, and strained away from the slap of it toward the side of the chair still in shadow.

Fowler promptly dragged the chair so the beam fell directly across the middle, where no amount of leaning would avoid it. "We can't have you too comfortable, can we, old son?"

He reached into his coat pocket. Garreth stiffened, expecting the perfume bottle again. Fowler had sprayed him twice more on the drive over and with time between for only a few gulps of air, each renewed loss of breath had felt more terrifying than the last. Instead of the garlic, however, Fowler produced four thin plastic strips of the kind electricians used to secure a group of wires in one neat bundle.

He toyed with them. "Handy little gadgets, these cable ties. One can do all sorts of things with them where one needs a loop or a way to fasten something to something else."

Or tie up someone? The ties looked just the right width to make the marks on Holle's and the Count's wrists.

Fowler wrapped a tie around one of Garreth's wrists, fed the pointed end through the lock loop on the other end and pulled it snug. "I believe your law enforcement agencies use a longer, wider version as handcuffs. It makes sense, really. They're strong and there's no lock to pick." He pulled Garreth's arms behind him and wrapped the other wrist, this time looping the tie through the loop made by the first before closing it. Cable ties went around Garreth's ankles, too. "There now. You won't wander, even if I let you breathe for a while." He smiled. "Or should I say, if you earn the right to breathe."

Garreth tested his wrists. No good. The plastic strip cut in like wire with no feeling of give. At night and breathing normally he might have the strength to break them, but not here, not now.

"The price isn't very high, really. All you have to do is tell me where to find Mada."

The hell. How did Fowler expect him to talk when he could not breathe?

As though reading his mind, Fowler said, "You can whisper if you have a good go at it. I strongly advise you do so, old son."

Why bother when he would not believe the truth?

"Where *is* she!" A hand cracked across Garreth's face,

Through the pain came the thought that if only he could get out of this sunlight he might find a way to fight Fowler. It would halve his handicap anyway.

Fowler slapped him again. The force whipped his neck and rocked the chair. But with the blow came an idea for getting out of the sun. Carefully Garreth mouthed: *fuck you*.

Fowler reacted instantly. Grabbing Garreth by the lapels, Fowler hauled him out of the chair and slung him halfway across the room against the bookshelves beside the fireplace. If Garreth had been breathing, it would have knocked the air out of him. "Tell me!"

Shadow brought no relief, though, no renewal of strength. He sagged to the floor. God if only he could pass out. This was excruciating, swimming on the edge of consciousness ... like the half-death of his transition phase, feeling and hearing everything but unable to roll over to relieve his aches or move to scratch his itches.

Above him Fowler chuckled. Grabbing Garreth by the lapels once more, Fowler jerked him to his feet and slammed him backward again, into the brick of the fireplace itself this time, again and again, once for every word he spoke. Garreth's glasses shook loose and fell off. "You ... will ... tell ... me. You'll tell me or learn just how much pain can be inflicted on one of your sort. It is a great deal, I promise you. I have seen. There's no refuge. You can't even faint. Until the central nervous system is disrupted, you must feel and endure every moment of agony, and you would be surprised how much of the body may be destroyed before damaging the spine or brain."

Garreth fought welling panic. Fowler had to be playing mind games. Not that he doubted what the writer said was true. There had probably been plenty of opportunity for observation of vampires in pain while killing Irina's friends in Europe. No wonder she hated and feared the man. But how much could Fowler do here? Whittle at him with a pocket knife?

Abruptly he wished he had not thought of that. He hated knives. The idea of being cut always bothered him far more than the possibility of being shot.

Fowler hissed through his teeth. "I don't know why you protect the vile creature. She condemned you to this life. One would expect you to hate her, to rejoice in seeing her destroyed." He brushed at dust on Garreth's lapels. "Perhaps what you need is the opportunity to reflect on it. Yes, that's it. I'll hang you up in the bedroom closet with a clove of garlic around your neck. I doubt very much that anyone will discover you there. In a couple of weeks or months, then, I'll come back and resume our discussion. How does that strike your fancy?"

It struck pure terror ... bone-melting, bowel-emptying, paralyzing dread. Visions spun behind Garreth's eyes of weeks or months without food or breath, also without unconsciousness or sleep, unable to die, only to hang there suffering ceaselessly. A living death.

"Or maybe we'll try a stake on you for size. Not kill you, you understand, just give it a little tap so you know what it feels like."

Dumping Garreth back in a chair beside the fireplace, Fowler went out to the kitchen. A cracking noise came back to Garreth, then Fowler returned carrying a chair rung. With his pocket knife he sharpened one end into a long, thin point, carefully cutting so that all the shavings fell in the fireplace. "We don't want to be untidy, do we."

Don't panic, Garreth thought desperately, watching him. That had been one of the first lessons in survival at the academy. Panic kills. He must stay calm and think rationally.

Or get mad, a voice whispered in his head. It sounded a little like Lane, but more like his father and the instructors at the academy. *Think Survival. Fight. Even if your teeth are kicked in and you're shot full of holes, you never stop fighting. Never. Kick, claw, use any weapon you can find but don't let the scum waste you.*

And this bastard in particular. He obviously enjoyed inflicting terror. He had probably hummed and smiled just like this at Count Dracula while preparing that other stake.

Anger boiled up thinking about the savagery of the little man's death. Garreth let it come ... welcomed it. Fowler had had enough fun. It was time to stop him. What was a little suffocation and daylight? Irina had made herself live a human rhythm without any aids like dark glasses, had forced herself even to go to church. He could surely bear some pain in the name of survival.

As anger grew, his mind started working again … planning. The first order had to be freeing himself. By twisting his wrists he could reach around to slip a finger of one hand under the cable tie on the other. He pulled. The plastic bit into his finger and wrist. *Come on man*, he prodded himself. *Work at it. We're talking life and death here.*

Fowler whittled at the stake.

Garreth eyed the knife. That would have him free in a second. He could talk if he made an effort, Fowler had said. He would try, then. Straining, he managed to compress his aching chest, moving a fractional amount of air up his throat. "Fowler." It hardly counted as even a whisper, but it was sound.

Fowler heard. He turned, smiling. "Hello, hello. Do you mean you have something to say to me after all?"

Garreth let the smile and arrogant tone feed his anger. He worked another bit of air out. "Closer."

Fowler came over and leaned down. "Now then, where's Mada?"

Garreth rammed his head into Fowler's nose as hard as he could.

The writer reeled back with a howl, clutching at his face. Knife and stake clattered to the floor.

Garreth threw himself out of the chair on top of them. He could barely feel the knife. His fingers shook weakly as he tried to close them around the handle and the room spun beyond the red haze of his vision. Curses ran through his head. The garlic effect should have been wearing off, unless he was still being affected by some that had soaked into his coat. If only he could breath a little. *Well you can't, damn it*, he yelled at himself, *and you're not going to pass out, either, so forget about it.*

Biting his lip, he locked his fingers around the knife and turned the blade so he could saw at his bonds. It seemed to take forever to find the right position, then a sudden lance of pain in his wrist told him he was also cutting his skin. He kept working anyway. Fowler would not remain blinded by pain forever.

Or even another minute. From the corner of his eye he could see the writer's hands coming down. He sawed desperately with the knife, cursing. How could a stupid damn piece of plastic take so long to cut?

A moment later he swore again. Fowler was stiffening; he had seen what Garreth was doing.

With a snarl, Fowler charged, foot swinging.

The toe connected just behind Garreth's ear. Pain exploded in his head. A little more pain he might have ignored, but the force of the blow loosened his grip and the knife fell out of his fingers. He groped frantically for it.

At the edge of his vision, Fowler's foot swung a second time. Garreth rolled away, cursing. Dodging the kick meant abandoning the knife.

With a snort of triumph Fowler kicked the knife into the fireplace and snatched up the chair rung. He came at Garreth gripping it in both hands.

Garreth rolled again. Not quite fast or far enough. The stake drove into his hip. A spasm of pain wracked him. He kept rolling. Maybe he could jerk the stake out of Fowler's hands, even if it meant landing on top of it and driving it in deeper.

No such luck. The point came free in a flood of wet warmth down Garreth's leg. Through the red fog clouding his vision, Garreth saw Fowler reset his grip on the stake and lunge again. Garreth flung himself sideways one more time and twisted his wrists desperately, straining at the cable ties.

With a sharp jerk, the cut tie broke. His hands came free. Just in time to reach up and deflect the stake. Instead of driving through the middle of his throat, it impaled the muscle where his neck and left shoulder joined.

This time Garreth pulled it out himself. Grabbing the shaft below Fowler's hands, he forced it back up toward the writer. A wordlessly snarling Fowler leaned on the stake to drive it down again. Garreth pushed up, resisting. Even as he held Fowler off, though, he knew he could not do so for long. The writer had gravity and daylight on his side and the strength was seeping out of Garreth's arm along with the warmth of blood spreading across his shoulder.

Garreth abruptly shoved sideways. As his arms went out from under him, Fowler came crashing down on Garreth. Garreth rolled, taking the writer with him. Coming on top, he wrenched away the stake and hurled it across the room.

Fowler caught Garreth's belt and heaved him aside, then scrambling to his feet, dived to retrieve the stake.

Garreth rolled for the fireplace. He had to free his feet! His fingers closed around the knife as Fowler scooped up the stake and turned. Garreth picked up a log from the stack on the hearth and heaved it at the charging Fowler, then reached for the cable ties on his ankle with the knife.

The log struck Fowler's chest. With no effect. To Garreth's dismay, the writer reeled back only a step before recovering and charging on.

Sawing at a cable tie with one hand, Garreth picked up another log with the other.

Fowler deflected it with his arm as casually as though brushing off a fly.

Hunters were like berserkers, Irina had said. They had to be killed to be stopped.

The cable tie parted. Garreth scrambled to his feet. Tried to scramble. His body would not respond. The injured leg collapsed, spilling him back on the floor. The knife popped out of his grip and skittered away across the floor.

Holding the stake two-handed like a dagger, Fowler dropped on him. Garreth caught Fowler's wrists with the point bare inches from his chest. With every ounce of his evaporating strength, he struggled to hold it there ... long enough to lash up with his good leg and sink the toes in Fowler's groin.

Fowler curled up into a squeaking ball of agony and toppled sideways. Garreth rolled one more time to throw an arm around Fowler's throat. The choke hold tightened. Fowler went limp.

Now, tit for tat, quid pro quo. Getting even. Garreth dug through Fowler's pockets. There was his gun. He shoved that back in its holster. And there was the perfume dispenser. He dropped that in his pocket, too. Then here was what he really wanted ... more cable ties. Heaving Fowler over onto his stomach, Garreth secured both wrists and ankles with the ties.

If he could breathe, he would have sighed in relief. Now he could strip off this coat and— But the thought cut off there. He found he could not sit up. His strength had all run out. Maybe his blood, too. It seemed to be everywhere, soaking his trousers, soaking his coat and turtleneck, streaking the hardwood floor.

He closed his eyes. Rest. That was what he needed. At sunset he would feel better. Surely by then the garlic would have dispersed enough for him to start breathing again.

Part of him prodded the rest sharply. *Sunset is hours away, you dumb flatfoot. What do you think Fowler will be doing in the meantime? Waiting politely for you to work up the strength to arrest him?*

No of course not. Garreth forced his eyes open again. He could not lie here. He would only lose the war when he had fought so hard to win the battle. He needed help, though. *It furthers one to appoint helpers.*

Where was the phone? He peered around him, straining to see through red-hazed vision. There ... on a table near the kitchen door.

He never asked himself if he could reach it. *Never stop fighting. Don't let the scum win.* He used his good arm to drag himself on his belly toward toward the phone, praying Lane kept it hooked up while she was away.

Standing was impossible but a pull on the cord brought the phone crashing down from the table to the floor beside him. To his relief, the receiver buzzed at him. Carefully, he punched Lien's number. Calling Harry would also bring Girimonte. Better to have Irina coming with Lien.

"Hello?"

Would he be able to make her hear him? He struggled to breath out just a little more. "Li ... en," he whispered.

He heard her breath catch on the other end, then, quickly, anxiously: "Garreth? What's happened? Where are you?"

"Lane's ... a ... part ... ment," he forced out.

Across the room, Fowler groaned and stirred.

"Hur ... ry."

No time for more. No strength to waste hanging up, either. He left the receiver lying and dragged himself back to where he could keep choking Fowler into unconsciousness until help arrived.

12

It seemed like an eternity before Garreth heard the door downstairs open. From where he lay stretched on the floor with his hand on Fowler's throat, he listened to two sets of footsteps run up the stairs. Three sets. The third were just a whisper of sound. They all echoed as though from a great distance through the thick fog enveloping him.

A rap sounded at the door. "Garreth?" Lien called. The knob rattled. "Damn! It's locked. What are we going to do?"

"Irina ..." his grandmother's voice said.

"Is a difficulty. This is a dwelling and I have never before been invited— *Nichevo.* I will tend to it."

She had discovered the barrier gone. Garreth's pulse jumped. Now she knew Lane was dead. Would she guess how?

"Holy Mother!"

He twisted his head toward the door. Her voice came from this side of it now. She stood just inside. But stood only for a second, then she jerked open the door and ran for the bay window.

"Lien, Grania," she called in a voice turned to a hoarse rasp. "Take him into hall away from this garlic."

Footsteps raced into the room toward him. And halted in two gasps. "Garreth!"

"Mother of god." Grandma Doyle dropped to her knees beside him. "The devil's killed you. I knew it. When you left I felt a wind between me skin and me blood."

Garreth shook his head. He was not dead yet.

Each of them grabbed an arm and began dragging him toward the door.

He pulled against them, shaking his head again. "Coat," he whispered. Being in the hall would not help a bit as long as he wore these clothes.

Irina had the drapes pulled wide and all three windows in the bay open. Coming back to them, she stopped short, too. "Is on him. Quickly; remove his coat and shirt."

They sat him up and stripped him to the waist. Irina removed the two pieces of clothing, carrying them to the kitchen like someone with a bomb, held as far away from her as possible.

Gradually the unbearable pressure in Garreth's chest released. Air trickled in. Nothing had ever felt quite so good before. He leaned back against his grandmother and closed his eyes.

Her arms tightened around him. "He looks like a corpse, Lien."

"I'll call an ambulance." Her footsteps moved in the direction of the telephone.

"No," Irina's voice said firmly. "You cannot."

He opened his eyes to see her holding Lien's wrist with one hand and blocking the dial face with the other.

"But you can see he's seriously hurt. He needs a doctor."

Irina shook her head. "We're strong. We heal quickly. All he needs is blood." She turned to look at him. "Human blood."

Garreth stiffened. "No."

"Yes. This is the point at which animal blood fails us."

Fowler groaned.

Irina crossed swiftly to him. Rolling him over on his back, and removing her glasses, she sat down astride him and stared hard into his opening, dazed eyes. "You are a statue. You cannot move or make a sound, nor can you see or hear anything unless I choose to talk to you again." Fowler went stiff. Irina put her glasses on again. Coming over to Garreth, she squatted beside him and took his face in her hands. "Listen to me, child. This is not a matter of choice but necessity. Only human blood will heal you."

He closed his eyes. "No.

She shook him. "You're being foolish. Taking blood does not have to be an act of rape."

He opened his eyes with a start to stare up at her in disbelief.

She smiled. "That *is* a choice. Ours is by nature a solitary existence, but not one in a vacuum. From humans we come, and we remain bound to them by our needs for food and companionship. Lack of either brings death, of mind if not body."

Like Christopher Stroda, Garreth thought suddenly.

"Does it not make sense, then, to treat people not like cattle but as friends, and ask for what we need rather than just take it?"

"Ask?" There he had her. She was crazy. "Who would say yes?"

"Me," Lien said. While he gaped at her, she unbuttoned the collar of her blouse. "You need blood; please take it."

"Or take mine," Grandma Doyle said. "Your life comes from me already through your mother. Let me give it to you again."

He twisted his head to regard her with wonder. They meant it! But ... how could he sink his fangs into his own grandmother's neck, or Lien's?

Irina murmured, "There are vessels where punctures are less conspicuous than in carotid artery. Brachial at elbow, for example, and popliteal behind knee."

His grandmother stretched her arm out across his shoulder. It brushed his cheek, soft and freckled, smelling of lavender and warm, salty blood. "Take the blood. Don't let that devil destroy you."

Don't let the scum win. Think survival.

With the words reverberating in him, Garreth turned his head and kissed the inside of her elbow. A pulse fluttered against his lips. Blood. He could smell it, could almost taste it. Locating the strongest beat with the tip of his tongue, he sank his fangs into the arm. Blood welled up from the punctures ... warm and sweetly salty as he remembered the auto accident girl's as being, everything he longed to drink, a delicious fire in his throat. He swallowed, again and again. Slowly, strength seeped back into him.

"Enough!" Irina's voice said. "Release her. Let … go."

A grandmotherly knuckle thumped him on the head. Reluctantly, he drew out of her arm. "I haven't had enough," he protested.

"You have taken enough from her."

His grandmother smoothed hair back from his forehead. "I want to help you, but I've no desire to join you. The price of forever's too high."

Lien knelt beside him and held her arm out. "Take the rest from me."

He bent his head to her arm.

This time he drank less greedily, and found himself feeling the rhythm of her blood, watching for signs that he might be taking too much. But hunger ended and he pulled back before she showed any weakening. He eyed her for some evidence of repugnance or regret.

Instead, she smiled. "Now you carry my blood, too. How do you feel?"

"Still shaky." Pain remained in his hip and shoulder. It had lessened noticeably, however, and the bleeding had stopped.

Irina handed him his glasses. "Do you feel strong enough to tell us what honorable, legal solution you have found to our problem?" She gestured toward Fowler.

Garreth bit his lip. If he admitted he had no solution, she might impose her own. Fowler's catatonic state gave him an idea. "We have the power to make people forget us. I think—"

Irina interrupted with a shake of her head. "Our powers are limited. We can edit his memories of today, but not make him forget either us or his hatred of us. That stretches back through his entire life."

"What about making him one of you?" Grandma Doyle said. "To tell anyone about you then would be to betray himself as well."

"I think that would make no difference to him," Irina said. "Would it, Garreth?"

He shook his head. "For a long time I hated what I'd become so much that if I could have brought Lane to justice by announcing to the world what she was, I would have, and not given a damn about the personal consequences. I would have welcomed true death."

"I, too," Irina said. "I planned to confess about myself to Prince Yevgeni as soon as I had my revenge on Viktor. I did not, obviously, but only because by time I could, my instinct for self-preservation had reasserted itself. We wouldn't have time for that with Englishman. He would run into street screaming denunciations of us."

"Let him," Lien said. "There are more people like my husband than me in the world. Who will believe him?"

"Even a few is too many. We cannot afford scrutiny." Irina sighed. "Is a problem with only one solution. Grania, you and Lien take Garreth home. I will see to cleaning up here."

"There has to be an alternative," Garreth protested. He thought desperately. There *had* to be! Clearly people were much harder to convince about vampires than he had been afraid they would be all along. He should be able to use that.

"I am sorry, Garreth."

Lien and Grandma Doyle each slipped an arm under his.

He shook them off. "No. Wait! What if—" What if what? An idea had raced past him just a moment ago. He struggled to find it again in the swirling chaos in his head. There! He snatched at it. Yes. Yes! It might work. "What if the people he denounces *can* bear scrutiny?"

Irina went still. He felt the hidden eyes staring at him. Finally she said, "Explain, please."

He explained.

Irina pursed her lips thoughtfully. "What if he attacks?"

"You and I will be close enough to intervene."

"This will prevent him from killing again?"

"That's the beauty of it. Once he's discredited, he's safe to run through the criminal justice system like any other murderer."

Grandma Doyle grinned. "You're the devil himself, boy. I'll do me best to make it work."

"Me, too," Lien said.

He knew he could count on them. "What super ladies the two of you are." He squeezed their hands. "Let's get cracking."

13

First they had to set Fowler up. While Irina prepared their prisoner to turn from a statue back into a man, Lien closed the windows and drapes. That left the room lighted by only a three-way table lamp beside the fireplace chair where Grandma Doyle sat, a lamp she turned off as soon Lien sat down in the wicker chair they had positioned on the other side of the fireplace. She left her hand on the lamp switch.

The dark felt wonderful. Garreth savored it as he limped to the kitchen.

"Ready, Grania?" Irina asked from beside Fowler.

"Ready."

Curse of the Vampire, Act One. Garreth moved faster.

"Five ... four ..." Irina raced after him. "Three." They pulled back out of sight on each side of the kitchen archway. "Two. *One!*"

In the living room, Fowler opened his eyes right on cue.

"Well now, I think he's rejoining us at last," Grandma Doyle said. "Good evening to you, Mr. Fowler."

Garreth peeked around the edge of the door. Fowler lay blinking in disorientation. After several moments, puzzlement became a frown. His head cocked in a listening attitude, obviously waiting for sounds which might tell him about his surroundings.

"You're uncomfortable, I hope," Grandma Doyle went on.

Fowler craned his head in the direction of her voice. "Who are you?" he demanded.

"Your judge." She switched the lamp on its lowest setting. The shade had been adjusted to cast light across her lap, leaving her face shadowed. "It could be I'm your doom as well."

Lien said in an impatient voice, "Why do you bother talking to him?"

Fowler's head whipped around toward her. She sat beyond the direct light of the lamp. He could not be seeing more than a general form. "Who are *you?*"

She pretended to ignore him. "He's conscious again. He can feel pain." She picked up the stake lying in her lap. Fowler saw that well enough. Garreth watched his eyes widen and heard his breath catch. "Let's kill him and be done."

Grandma Doyle shook her head. "You newcomers to the life are still so full of human impatience. Besides, killing is merciful. After the way he's slaughtered our brothers and sisters, do you really want to be merciful?"

Lien appeared to consider. "No!" She fingered the stake. "I want him to suffer! Let me give him a taste of how this feels."

Fowler spat a curse.

"I'll handle this me own way, thank you. Mr. Fowler."

He craned his neck to look at Grandma Doyle again. Garreth wondered what he could be thinking, lying there with these two half-seen figures talking across him. At least there was no doubt what he felt. Hatred twisted his face. "Who the bloody hell *are* you?"

"Those of the blood call me the Grand Dame ... because I came to this life late in years and I've lived a long time. If there's a quarrel to be settled or a problem to solve, it's me they come to for the settling or solving. You, Mr. Fowler, are a problem in need of settling."

"Go to hell."

She laughed with a note so authentically bitter and savage it sent a shiver down Garreth's spine. "We're already there, Mr. Fowler. Prepare yourself to join us."

Fowler stiffened. "What—"

"Hold him for me, girl ... up on his knees with his head pulled back. You don't have to be gentle."

"You—" Fowler began.

"No!" Lien spat. "I won't have him one of us!"

"Didn't you say you wanted him to suffer? What worse suffering than to be trapped among those he hates, unable to escape because he's one of us."

"I'll escape," Fowler snarled. "I'll see all of you destroyed."

Grandma Doyle laughed. "You think so now, but it's different once you've made the change. Even though you hate us, you'll protect us ... because suddenly you're as terrified of the stake as we are. You'll even protect Mada."

"No!" He writhed wildly, fighting the bonds on his wrists and ankles. "I won't be cheated out of destroying that bloody bitch! No matter what I am, I'll find her and kill her, and then I'll see that the whole world knows you exist! They'll have to believe me with a live specimen in front of them!"

"*Live* specimen?" Lien said with a snicker.

He cursed at her.

Grandma Doyle sighed gustily. "Enough of this yelling. Mr. Fowler, be still."

Fowler froze in response to the command suggestion Irina had given him.

Grandma Doyle and Lien slid out of their chairs to kneel beside the writer. While Fowler's eyes bulged in horror and hatred, Grandma Doyle bent low and closed her teeth on his throat.

Irina's second command took effect. Fowler turned into a statue again.

Garreth limped out of the kitchen. "Great work, girls. Now let's get him out of here."

14

The cars were the big problem. They had three to take home, including the ZX still at the Cannery, but only two people fit to drive. Garreth finally put on his grandmother's coat and cautiously drove her and Fowler in Fowler's car, parking a block away from Harry's house where they waited for Lien to come back from dropping Irina off at the Cannery.

"Are you sure you can manage him?" he asked while helping Lien and his grandmother manhandle the limp Fowler into Lien's car.

His grandmother tossed her head. "Since when did the Irish ever have trouble handling the English?"

"Irina is right behind me," Lien said. "You just watch for the front door lights to go on at the house."

Garreth climbed back into Fowler's car to wait nervously. The ZX passing him a minute later helped only a little. For all his confidence when explaining the plan, he could think of a dozen ways for it to go wrong, all of them disastrous. If it did in the next few minutes, only Irina stood between this wacko and the two women.

To distract himself, he imagined what was happening at the house. They would be tucking Fowler into bed on the earth-filled air mattress, rigging heavy drapes over the kitchen windows, and filling tankards with horse blood.

An hour later yellow flickered in the Takananda door lights, barely visible because of daylight.

It's show time.

Taking a deep breath, Garreth started the car and gunned it down the street. In front of Harry's house he swerved into the curb with brakes squealing. The front wheel ran up over the side of the driveway so that he ended with both right wheels on the grass. Slamming the car door added another loud sound to attract neighborhood attention, then he charged up the front walk, trying not to limp.

"Open up!" he yelled, hammering on the front door. "I know you're bloody well in there. Open up before I break down the bloody door!"

Lien jerked the door open. "Mr. Fowler," she said loudly in a tone of outrage. "What is the meaning of this?"

He pushed at her. She pretended to resist, and fail. As the door slammed behind them, a grin replaced her frown. "We had an audience. I saw drapes move in at least three windows. You'd better hide before Fowler comes down and sees you. Use our room or your grandmother's room."

Garreth shook his head. "I'll be in the living room. It's closer to the kitchen." Though not as close as he preferred to be. "Where's Irina?"

"Out on the patio."

Also farther away than he liked. Too much could happen in the seconds it would take for either of them to arrive. Yet they could not risk being seen at this stage.

Lien rubbed her palms against her slacks. "Do you really think he believes Grania and I are vampires?"

"You know witch hunters; they see their bogeyman everywhere." He smiled wryly. "Fowler's got to be so bent by this obsession with Lane that if the encouragement we've given him hasn't blinded him to rationality already, making him think you're trying to bring him into your bloodsucking brood will keep him too distracted to examine the facts closely."

Grandma Doyle whispered down the steps, "I'm going to wake him now."

Lien nodded. "I'll call the police."

Garreth hurriedly hauled himself upstairs and into the darkened living room.

From there he heard his grandmother go into his room. "Mr. Fowler, I know it isn't sunset, but you've rested long enough. We have things to do."

He imagined Fowler sitting up and staring around, trying to orient himself, feeling the pallet under him. "Where am I?"

"Where we can watch you, of course," Grandma Doyle replied. "We're not finished yet; that is to say, you aren't."

"You've untied my hands and feet." Fowler made it an accusation.

Grandma Doyle chuckled. "Of course. How can you walk downstairs otherwise? But Mr. Fowler, don't be thinking of trying to run away. When the day comes I comes I can't handle a young pup like you, human or otherwise, I'll turn in me cape and fangs. So up with you. Here's your coat. That's it; put it on. Now come along."

Garreth waited tensely in case Fowler resisted, but the writer apparently decided to play along for the time being. Waiting for the chance to escape. From the darkness of the living room Garreth watched Fowler follow Grandma Doyle downstairs.

As soon as the stairs blocked their view of the living room door, he limped quickly to his room. The pallet had to be hidden. Garreth cached it under the conventional mattress.

Lien's voice came up from downstairs. "What would you like to eat?"

"I'm not hungry."

"Really now, Mr. Fowler," Grandma Doyle said. "Do you think we plan to drug you? Nonsense. Your blood's no good to us polluted."

"I'll have a glass of water," Fowler said.

Water ran.

The bedroom looked right. He left and worked his way soundlessly down several steps to where, if he sat down and peered around the edge of the steps, he could see the kitchen door. The opening framed his grandmother sitting on a stool at the work island counter.

"A refill," Fowler said.

Grandma Doyle raised her eyebrows. "Still thirsty? Queer. I've only taken once from you. But here; see if this stops the craving." She pushed the tankard she held down the counter.

Nice move! Garreth grinned. The thirst was not one of the suggestions Irina planted but his grandmother had taken beautiful advantage of—

"No!"

The scream jerked Garreth onto his feet, raising the hair all over his body. It sounded like an animal. Skin crawling, he vaulted the railing. Pain shot through his injured hip and the leg buckled under him, sending him sprawling.

"*No!*"

Grandma Doyle ducked just in time to avoid the tankard flying at her.

"Garreth!" Lien called.

Cursing, he scrambled for the kitchen on his hands and good leg.

"You did it," Fowler screamed. "You've turned me into—into— You bloody bitches! I'll *kill you!*"

Fowler lunged into the frame of the doorway, hands stretched for Grandma Doyle's throat. Garreth hurled himself at Fowler. Grandma Doyle jumped back, pushing a stool into Fowler's path. It hit the writer the same moment Garreth's shoulder caught him at the waist in a flying tackle. Men and furniture went down in a tangle.

Irina came tearing in through the dining room door.

Snarling, Fowler clawed at Garreth's eyes. Garreth caught the writer's wrists before the nails more than scraped his forehead. A knee jerked up toward his groin. He dodged it just in time, but then almost lost his grip in a sudden twist of Fowler's wrists. The man bucked and writhed under him, fighting with animal strength.

Or a madman's, came a thought.

"Irina, get a choke hold on him!"

"I can't reach you down there."

Damn. He abruptly released Fowler's wrists, but only to change his grip to the writer's lapels. Then, heaving sideways with all his strength, he smashed Fowler's head into the cabinet. Fowler went limp.

The doorbell rang. "Mrs. Takananda, it's the police."

Garreth scrambled cursing to his feet, leaving Fowler sitting slumped against the cabinet. Look at this place. A struggling Fowler had been in the script but not a bloody kitchen! Crimson splashed everything: counter, floor, walls, even the ceiling, not to mention every-*one*, too

The bell rang again. "Mrs. Takananda?"

"We will have to use the blood," Irina said.

Garreth thought fast. "We need a source for it, then." His stomach lurched. There was only one logical source. *Shit*. He hated knives. "Lien … throw me a knife." Looking around, he noticed the tankard lying by the dining room door. "Get rid of the tankards!"

"Mrs. Takananda!" The uniformed officers pounded on the door.

Grandma Doyle scooped up both tankards and threw them in the dishwasher.

Catching the kitchen knife Lien tossed him, Garreth set his jaw and before he could chicken out, quickly drew the blade across his forearm. Blood spurted through the slash in his sleeve. He clenched his teeth against the pain. God he hated knives. "Let them in," he gasped. "Irina, you might as well stay out of it."

"Yes."

While Lien ran for the door, he wrapped Fowler's fingers around the knife, then pulled it loose again and tossed it across the room to where the tankard had lain. Irina retreated through the dining room.

Lien jerked the front door open. "Thank god! He's crazy!" She raced back toward the kitchen. "He came storming in here accusing us of hiding that Barber woman and when Garreth tried to make him leave, he snatched up a knife I had on the counter and attacked."

The uniforms stopped short in the doorway. "Christ!"

Garreth looked up from making a tourniquet of his bathrobe belt. "Who'd have thought the old man had so much blood in him.' Hi, Hingle, Rahal."

"Mikaelian?" They glanced at Fowler, then obviously deciding he would keep for a bit, came over to peer at Garreth's arm. "How bad did he get you?"

"It hurts like hell." He rolled up the sleeve for a look. And grimaced. He had not intended to cut quite so deep.

Rahal whistled. "That's going to take a few stitches. Better get a bandage on it."

He had barely finished saying so when Grandma Doyle pressed a folded dishtowel over the wound.

Fowler groaned.

The officers whipped around toward him. They pounced, hand-cuffing his hands behind his back. "Who is this turkey anyway?"

"You won't believe it. Graham Fowler."

Their jaws dropped. "The writer? Why the hell—"

Fowler screamed. It sounded even more animal than the last time. Hingle and Rahal's expressions suddenly became those of men discovering they held a bomb.

"They've killed me! Kill them!" Fowler lunged to his feet and at Grandma Doyle. The officers hung on grimly. "Kill the vampires before they turn you into one, too!"

"Jesus," Rahal muttered. "You should have warned us to bring a butterfly net."

Fowler twisted to stare at him. "You think I'm mad, but I can prove they're vampires. The old looking one bit me last night while Sergeant Takanda's wife helped her. See the mark—"

"Sergeant Takananda's wife is a vampire?" Hingle said in a flat voice. "Right."

"She *is*, you bloody fool. Have a look in the fridge. There has to be some container of blood in there. They were drinking mugs full of it when I came into the kitchen. They tried to make me drink it, too. I threw it back in their faces. That's what all this blood is. Now will you look at the bite mark on my neck?"

Hingle rolled his eyes. "All I see is a hicky."

Fowler hissed. "It's a hematoma, you ass. That's how they hide the bite. There are punctures in the middle of it. There's more, too. I stabbed Mikaelian in the neck and hip with a wooden stake. Check him for marks. Even though it was only last night, he'll be practically healed."

It would not do to let them see his neck. "Why, Mr. Fowler, everyone knows the stake is supposed to go through the heart while the vampire is sleeping in his coffin. Shall we check the bedrooms upstairs for coffins?"

The officers snickered, then shook Fowler's arms. "Let's go."

"No!" He jerked back against them. "Listen to me! They know where Lane Barber is. They're protecting her, though, because she's one of them. You have to make them tell where she is. Then we can destroy her and the rest of them. I'll help. I know how to kill them."

"Like you killed Richard Maruska and his roommate, and Leonard Holle?" Garreth said.

Fowler's mouth thinned. "You know bloody well only Maruska was a vampire. The others were just—"

The front door banged open. "Lien!" Harry came pounding down the hall with Girimonte right behind him. "I heard the call on the radio. What's wrong? Whose car is that on the lawn?" They stopped short in the doorway just as the uniforms had. Harry sucked in a sharp breath. "Good god. Garreth, what happened?"

Holding onto his arm, Garreth shrugged. "It's crazy. Fowler came in here accusing Grandma and Lien of knowing where Lane is but protecting her because they're all vampires."

"You're one, too," Fowler spat. "That's why you don't eat."

Garreth raised a brow at Girimonte. "And you've been accusing me of being anorectic. See how wrong you are?"

She shrugged. A corner of her mouth twitched. "Ignorant me."

"He's also suggested he's responsible for our murder binge."

Her eyes narrowed. "Really. Can you give us enough to make probable cause so we can get a warrant to search his hotel room and check his clothes?"

He nodded.

Fowler shrieked and exploded into struggling violence, flinging himself back and forth, aiming kicks at the uniformed officers. "You bloody stupid damn *fools*! *Listen* to me!"

The officers wrestled him against the counter. Rahal said, "Takananda, will you or Girimonte ride along with us? I'm not having my partner alone in the back seat with this looney tune."

"Van, you go," Harry said. "I'd like to tend to things here."

Girimonte nodded. "Sure."

Hingle and Rahal started Fowler toward the door. Garreth expected him to struggle, but he walked meekly. At the front door he stopped short, however, and looked back. "I'll be back. Don't forget, I have your powers now. I can just walk out of the cell when I please. Mada isn't dead, no matter what you say, Mikaelian. You can't fool me. She killed my father and I won't be deprived of my vengeance. I'll be back; I'll find her; and I ... will ... destroy her. Then it will be your turn."

He marched out of the house between the uniformed officers. Rolling her eyes, Girimonte followed.

Harry waited until the door had closed behind them, then, looking around the kitchen and at Garreth, said, "I think someone better tell me what the hell's been going on."

As briefly as possibly, Garreth told him.

Harry listened with face going steadily grimmer. At the end of the recitation, he let his breath out in a hiss. "I could strangle each and every one of you, even you, honorable wife. Garreth, how could you let Lien and your grandmother—"

"Since when do I let me grandchildren tell me what I can and can't do?" Grandma Doyle snapped.

Harry retreated a step. "It's a wonder someone wasn't hurt. Seriously hurt," he amended, glancing at Garreth. "Christ. I don't want to even think about trying to sort out the case against him. It's either a frame or something we can't use. You are going to clean up that apartment before he talks someone into checking it, aren't you?" He sighed. "Let's hope we find enough physical evidence in his clothes and luggage at the hotel to tie him to Holle's murder."

"You shouldn't have to worry about going to court with a defendant who claims he's hunting the vampire who killed his father," Garreth said.

Harry ran a hand through his hair. "That may be our salvation. If he's judged incompetent, he'll be locked up where he can't hurt anyone, without the risk of a trial and all its publicity."

"This is your humane alternative?" Irina said from the dining room doorway. "Madness?"

Garreth cradled his injured arm more tightly and sighed tiredly. Was there ever a good solution in conflicts between humans and vampires? In the end it always seemed to be a choice between evils. "At least he's alive."

"Unlike Mada."

Garreth sucked in his breath. He felt the violet eyes fixed on him behind her glasses. In accusation? Had she guessed?

"You mean Barber really is dead?" Harry said. "How do you know?"

"We know when our brothers and sisters die," Irina replied. She continued to face Garreth.

She did know! But instead of dismay, relief filled Garreth. Someone else knew. He was not alone with the guilt anymore. He nodded. "I—"

"We can not always tell how or where, of course," Irina interrupted. "Considering Mada's nature, her death was probably justifiable homicide, wouldn't you say, Garreth?"

He stared at her. The implication was clear; she felt sure of what he had done but wanted to dismiss the matter. He said slowly. "Maybe even self-defense." At least she ought to know that he had not just killed in revenge.

Harry glanced from one to the other of them. "I wouldn't be a bit surprised." He put an arm around Garreth's shoulders. "That closes her case then, Mik-san."

Garreth caught his breath. Harry had put it together, too. So had Grandma Doyle and Lien, he saw in a quick glance. They looked back at him, nodding at Harry's words. Those nods, like Harry's arm, told him that they intended to say nothing more about it either.

Warmth flooded him, filling even places which had stood bleakly empty the past two years. Savoring it, he nodded back at them all. "I guess you're right. That's the end of it."

15

He dreamed of life. A bridge stretched before him, massive and solid, its steel girders and cables glowing a pulsating blood red in the darkness. Strange. How had he failed to see before that this was what linked him to humanity, not that fragile wooden one with its combustible floor … ties of need and blood, blood shared and blood shed. Why, too, had he seen himself at one end and humans at the other when in fact they all milled together in the middle? Harry was there, and Lien and his grandmother as well as a mass of relatives and friends from Baumen and San Francisco, all shaking his hand or hugging him.

Irina circulated through the group, too, catching his eye from time to time, and smiling.

Serruto extended a hand. "It's good to have you back. Is it true you're leaving for Baumen soon?"

Garreth nodded. "I have a personal relationship to wrap up. Not everyone can be told what I am. I also need to tell Anna that we uncovered information indicating Mada was killed and her body dumped somewhere in the Rockies. I'll have some of her belongings with me and they can send for the rest. I'll also give Anna the name of Mada's bank and her account numbers, so they'll know where her money is after they're able to declare her dead."

"And after that?"

Garreth shrugged. "I've met a woman who would like me to travel with her. There's an estate outside Moscow she wants to show me, among other places. She says I have a lot to learn and she'd like to teach me."

Serruto's brows hopped. "She sounds like an older woman."

"I think you could call her an older woman, yes. She doesn't look her age, though."

Girimonte slid up beside him, puffing one of her long, elegant cigars. "You heard what we found in Fowler's hotel room, didn't you? Climbing rope, suction cups, and a glass cutter. Fibers from his shirt also match some found on Holle's window, and particles from the soles of his running shoes are like material from the shingles on the roofs of Holle's house and the one next door. His cable ties fit the marks on Holle's and the Count's wrists and ankles as well. Too bad he's so wacko he'll never stand trial."

"Too bad," Garreth lied.

Fowler had come to the party, too. He spotted the writer's tortured face beyond the edge of the crowd. With his wounds healing up, he felt sorry for the man ... another victim of Lane's excesses.

Where was Lane? Surely she had come, too. He searched through the crowd. Yes, there she was, but not among the crowd. She stood alone at the far end of the bridge, calling something.

The sound reached him only faintly through the voices around him. For several minutes he strained to hear, then realized that he really had no interest in anything she said. Garreth turned away, back to the party, and when he looked her direction again a while later, she had disappeared.

MURDER, MYSTERY, AND INTERSTELLAR INTRIGUE

Hellspark by Hugo Award winner
Janet Kagan is back!

Lassti, a newly discovered planet, is the center of political intrigue. Recently, Oloitokitok, physicist for the planet's survey team, was found dead. Was he killed? If so, by who—One of his fellow surveyors? Or by one of the Sprookjes, the birdlike natives of Lassti?

Are the Sprookjes intelligent? If so, then parties that want the planet for development will lose it. Why is the survey team having so much trouble finding out?

Into this situation arrives Tocohl, a Hellspark trader who just wanted to have a vacation on Sheveschke at the St. Veschke festival. After being attacked, rescuing a young woman, and going before a judge, Tocohl has learned all she ever wanted to know about being in the wrong place at the wrong time. Now she is on her way to Lassti to find the answers to the mysteries there.

Janet Kagan, the author of the Star Trek™ novel *Uhura's Song*, has come up with a science fiction adventure in the classic tradition.

She is a multiple winner of the annual *Asimov's* Readers Poll Award for best author.

"Fast-paced, bright and lively entertainment from easily the most popular writer in the known universe."

—Michael Swanwick

Meisha Merlin Publishers, Inc proudly announce the return of Storm Constantine to America!

Herald: an official messenger, a forerunner, or to proclaim the approach of.

Storm Constantine, best known for her Wraeththu series from TOR, is back. We are proud to announce the first of our Storm Constantine short story collections. *Three Heralds of the Storm* contains three short stories by this peerless fabulist. This chapbook marks the first publication anywhere of *Such a Nice Girl*, and the first U. S. appearances of *Last Come Assimilation* and *How Enlightenment Came to the Tower*.

"Storm Constantine is a myth-making Gothic queen, whose lush tales are compulsive reading. Her stories are poetic, involving, delightful, and depraved. I wouldn't swap her for a dozen Anne Rices."
                                                        Neil Gaiman

"Storm Constantine is a literary fantast of outstanding power and originality. Her work is rich, idiosyncratic, and completely engaging. Her themes, constantly explored and re-examined through her novels, have much in common with those of Philip K. Dick—the nature of identity, the nature of reality, the creative power of the human imagination—while her sensibility reminds me of Angela Carter at her most inventive."
                                                        Michael Moorcock

Three Heralds of the Storm by Storm Constantine
64 pages, chapbook, acid-free paper, $5.00

BloodWalk by Lee Killough
456 pages, trade format, acid-free paper, $14.00

Hellspark by Janet Kagan
336 pages, trade format, acid-free paper, $12.00

To order your copies, please fill out the order form below and return it with your payment, check or money order payable in US funds, to Meisha Merlin Publishers, Inc., PO Box 7, Decatur, GA 30031. Please allow 4-6 weeks for delivery.

NAME_____

ADDRESS_____

CITY_____ STATE_____

ZIP_____ COUNTRY_____

HERALDS COPIES _____ X $5.00 = _____
$0.50 per book S&H _____ X $0.50 = _____

BLOODWALK COPIES _____ X $14.00 = _____
$3.00 per book S&H _____ X $3.00 = _____

HELLSPARK COPIES _____ X $12.00 = _____
$2.00 per book S&H _____ X $2.00 = _____

                                  TOTAL _____

Dealer inquiries are welcome.